Where The Light Begins

Book One of the Crown of Nyvenya Series

By

H.C. Vale

ISBN: 979-8-218-69062-5

Cover Design by @saktiawn_ (Instagram)

Published by H.C. Vale Books

Printed in the United States of America

First Edition

Dedication

*T**his book is for those who carry quiet dreams and louder fears. Don't wait for certainty. Leap anyway. The unknown might just hold your magic.*

Prologue One- A Scorned Bargain

The wind howled over the cliffs of Ashwynn Reach, stripping the blackened earth of its ash and salt. Nothing grew here, not truly, which was exactly why Liraeth had been banished to the island. It was a graveyard of scorched soil and jagged rock, brittle remnants of what had once reached for light. Her plan had been uncovered before it reached fruition.

Footsteps sounded behind her on the boat's deck.

A guard approached, muttering a curse as he unshackled her wrists.

"You're lucky he didn't execute you right there you traitorous bitch, remember that he let you live," he spat, shoving her hard toward the ramp.

Liraeth stepped off the ship without a word. Her cloak clung to her form damp from sea spray and salt crystals clung to her lashes like frost. Behind her, snickers rose from the crew as they turned the ship back to sea, leaving her exiled and alone.

How dare they?

She was of higher blood than all of them combined.

And now she'd been cast aside. *Again.*

But her gaze held no grief, only fury. She would make them pay. All of them. Her initial plan may have failed, but this exile would not last. She had always kept contingencies.

Climbing the ridge, her boots crunched over broken glass and shale. One hand rose to cradle her belly as the wind lashed against her.

At the top she stopped.

A man stood alone in the ash below. A sword was planted in the ground before him, like a grave marker. His dark hair whipped in the wind, his posture rigid. His cloak hung in tatters, dusted with ash.

Liraeth recognized him. She had seen him in paintings, in portraits commissioned when the fae courts gathered in splendor.

Lucien Veylas stood before her, brother to the newly married High King of the Fae. The man who had stood behind a throne that would never be his. The man whose brother married the love of his life to unite the realms.

A man broken by fate.

A man she could use.

Surely destiny has provided her with this moment, already a new plan was forming.

A devious smile began to bloom on her lips, but she masked it quickly.

Lucien didn't turn as he spoke. His voice was low, hollowed by bitterness.

"This place is for the broken," he said.

Her lips curled.

"Sometimes the broken are just waiting to be reborn," she replied.

He turned to face her then, the fire in his eyes not yet dimmed.

"You're with child," he said, gaze flicking to the swell she protected.

"Yes, their father was executed just before they banished me."

She let her voice tremble, eyes glistening.

"They believed I was his co-conspirator. But I had no idea what he was planning..."

The tears came effortlessly now.

Practiced. Believable.

Lucien's jaw clenched.

"My brother took everything from me. The throne, the power, the woman I loved!"

He turned away again, the wind screaming between them.

"Perhaps fate has brought us together," she said, stepping forward.

Lucien exhaled like a dying flame. "So, what now?"

"Now," she whispered, "we begin again. You and I. The Gods and the realms think they have chosen their rulers." She stepped closer, her eyes bright with cold fury. "But we'll show them what happens when the forgotten gather their fire."

Together, they stared out across the sea, where the stars blinked above the storm clouds that churned in the sky.

"It will take time," she said. "But we'll build. We'll raise our army, seek allies. And this place, this cursed island, will become our stronghold. And when the moment is right, we will strike and take our revenge on all of them."

Lucien stared into the dark horizon, rage simmering beneath the surface.

He gave a single nod.

The waves roared like the echo of something ancient and wrong.

And on that cursed island, a bargain was struck between the scorned.

Prologue Two - Ashes of A Crown

The throne room reeked of smoke and blood.

He stood at the base of the dais, one hand resting on the hilt of his blade, still slick with royal blood. Moonlight poured through the shattered stained glass, casting fractured colors across the carnage in the room.

He had imagined this moment a million times. Standing here. Staring at the throne that should have been his. In his imaginings he felt nothing. No shame. No sorrow. Only *victory*.

And yet...

The silence in the room, pressed tightly upon him. A hollowness that he felt deep in his soul. He thought of her, his brother's queen. The one that he had loved first. The one who had chosen another. Her eyes had gone wide with betrayal as his fire took her. As if she hadn't known that this would be the cost of hurting him.

A child's scream had echoed behind her.

He forced the memory down.

They had stolen everything from him.

Love. Power. Legacy.

As the eldest, the throne should have been his, but he was found unworthy by the ancient magic bestowed by the Gods.

It had chosen his brother instead.

Just like *she* did.

But now he had taken it all back.

He had his new bride, Liraeth.

A son, not by blood, but one he would raise to be a proper heir.

He bent down over his brother's lifeless body and removed the crown from his head.

This would be his legacy now.

His realm.

His power.

He would now be the High King of the fae, and Liraeth would be High Queen. Soon the world would bend to their will.

The ancient magic would be *his* to command.

The forbidden rites that they had performed had brought him to this point, the high crown would have no choice but to answer to him.

He stepped over his brother's corpse and stalked towards the throne, *his* throne. He raised the crown, splattered with his brother's blood, and placed it on his head.

But no transfer of power occurred, instead the crown withered to dust.

Lucien bellowed with rage.

The dark blue flames that he had let burn everyone and everything around him began to flicker and die out.

A voice whispered from behind a dying flame nearby, almost lost in the crackle.

"The true heir remains."

He turned sharply, dark magic sparking at his fingertips.

"Who speaks?" he roared, voice echoing off the stone walls.

Only silence answered.

He did not see the silver thread that vanished through the cracks in the floor, too small to notice. A thread bound to a girl hidden far from this world.

The true heir still drew breath.

And fate was not done yet.

Chapter One

Darkness.

The kind that presses in on me from all sides, endless. There are no walls, no sky, no ground.

It's like I'm stuck in a void. A cold, shadowy void.

I stand in silence, anxiety clawing up my throat.I force myself to take deep, calming breaths. I have been here before, too many times to count.

I'm having the nightmare again.

I begin to call out for the constant companion that's always in this dark place with me.

"Are you here?" I ask, already knowing the answer.

"Yes... can you hum that song until I find you?" His voice drifts toward me. It was always the same voice, a boy. No... a man now. He has aged with me in this recurring nightmare. I have no idea who he is, or what he looks like, this dark space never lets me see his face. But in this void, *he is the only solid thing.*

I oblige him and hum the melody of the lullaby my mother used to sing to me. Footsteps echo softly across the darkness, though there's no surface here for him to walk on. But I feel him draw near, his warmth brushing against my skin.

"Found you."

I wrap my arms around myself, trying to fight off the chill.

"Did it get darker here?" I ask.

"It always does before it fades, remember?" he murmurs. "But you're not alone. I'm here."

"Do you ever wonder what this is?" I whisper.

My voice sounds small, lost. "Like, why do we always end up here, in this nightmare?"

There's a pause, and then I feel him wrap his arms around me.

"Maybe we are cursed," he says.

I can hear the smile behind his words.

"Do you think this nightmare will ever end?" I ask.

The void around us presses closer with every breath. I swallow, my throat tight. The darkness here unsettles me, it feels like something is watching us.

My heart pounds. Tears rise and blur my vision, even in this sightless space.

"It's going to be ok. Just breathe, I'm here," he says softly, guiding my head to his chest.

His heartbeat is steady and soothing. It always is.

"What if it doesn't ever end?" I ask.

"Then we just keep finding each other in the darkness."

I feel something then, a spark. Low in my chest.

Like a single ember flaring to life in this room of shadow.

"What is your name?" I ask him. I've never asked before. I'm not sure why I'm asking now.

"I..." he starts, then pauses. "I don't know, do you?"

What is my name?

Who am I?

"No," I reply. "I don't know my name either."

Silence falls between us again. Only the sound of his beating heart remains, keeping me grounded.

Keeping me *safe*.

BEEP...BEEP...BEEP.

The sound of my alarm jolts me awake, dragging me out of my dream like claws ripping me from the water. I gasp and open my eyes, fumbling to shut the damn thing off. I slam the button so hard the alarm clock flies off my bedside table.

I fall back onto my pillow and stare up at the old popcorn ceiling. A sliver of light is peeking in from my curtains. My skin feels clammy.

I sit up rubbing my arms.

My room feels...*charged* somehow.

I hear a gust of wind hit against my windows, and I swear the lamp on my nightstand flickers. But when I blink, it's still switched off.

Great.

Lifelong recurring nightmares, and now I'm losing it. Happy

twentieth birthday to me.

I sigh and drag myself out of bed.

I'm sure Mom and Dad have something planned for when I get off work. I shower, then blow-dry my long blonde hair and twist it into a messy bun. I pull on jeans, a long-sleeved floral tee, and my apron for Carlotta's Cafe, it's my standard gear. I have worked there since I turned sixteen. I'm surprised Mom let Dad win that argument.

She usually has the final word, and she's strict. Like *paranoid* level strict.

I wasn't allowed to go to public school with the rest of the kids, Mom didn't trust them.

Was it the kids, or the school itself she didn't trust? Who knows.

So, she homeschooled me. And since we live way in the outskirts of town with absolutely zero neighbors, I never got to make any friends. I had told my dad that I wanted to get a job to save up for college myself. My parents make enough to take care of us, but college is way too expensive. And I wanted to prove that I could do something on my own.

When he finally got mom to agree to let me work part time at Carlotta's, I was *thrilled*. I was finally going to meet people my age and make friends.

And I did. At least briefly.

When I invited them over to hang out, Mom would either scare them off interrogating them with a line of questioning straight out of a spy movie. And if *she* didn't scare them off, I did.

If not with my social awkwardness, then being riddled by uncontrollable panic attacks, as well as having crippling anxiety did the trick. It's not exactly a winning combination for a thriving social life.

I did manage to somehow make one friend though.

Brynn.

She's funny, easy to talk to, and never makes me feel like I have to be anything but myself. Even mom seemed to like her, she told me Brynn reminded her of an old friend she had.

Brynn pulled me out of my shell, and instead of making fun of me, or running away when I had a panic attack, she would help calm me down and talk me through it.

When she left for college two years ago, she promised that she would keep in touch, that we'd arrange visits.

The phone calls and text messages stopped coming about six months after she left for school.

She's probably found new friends and built a whole life out there. I miss her, but I am really happy for her. I hope we'll run into each other again someday.

I slide my cell phone into my pocket and grab my purse before heading downstairs to eat breakfast.

"Well, if it isn't the birthday girl!" Dad calls from the kitchen.

The smell of chocolate chip pancakes and fresh hazelnut coffee greets me before I even reach the bottom step.

I set my purse down and sit at the table.

"You didn't have to make me breakfast Dad," I say, smiling with anticipation anyway.

I'll never admit it, but I look forward to these pancakes every single year.

"Nonsense," he says, bringing a plate of them over to me and giving me a kiss on my temple. "Happy birthday, sweetheart."

"Thanks."

"Oh, the birthday girl is awake and ready before me?" my mother says, gliding into the room. "Happy birthday my little Renna. I love you so much."

She pulls me into a big hug and peppers my cheeks with kisses.

My mother may have been strict my whole life, but I love her dearly. And I know that it has always come from a place of love, and a need to protect me.

From what? Who knows, I don't think I ever will.

"Thanks, Mom," I say with a smile.

"After work, your father and I will pick you up. I made us reservations at Maestro's for a birthday dinner. And afterward, I thought we could all head up to the lakeside cabin for the rest of the weekend. What do you think?"

"You got reservations at Maestro's?" I ask, excitedly.

I *love* that restaurant.

I have only ever been there once. It's a very exclusive place downtown. Brynn got us in somehow. I swear she just talked her way into the place, no reservation necessary.

She was always like that, people always loved Brynn.

We had the best meal I have ever had in my life. I couldn't wait to tell my parents about it when I got home. Mom must have remembered.

"I sure did," Mom says proudly, a huge grin appearing across her face. "So don't fill up on cookies and chocolate croissants at work."

She winks at me.

My parents join me at the table, and we enjoy a nice breakfast together.

"I am absolutely stuffed to the brim with pancakes," I tell my parents, laughing.

They both smile.

"Good," Dad says smiling. "I'm glad you enjoyed them kiddo."

"You guys go ahead off to work, so neither of you are late," Mom says to us, giving my dad a kiss before disappearing into the kitchen with our dirty dishes.

I follow my dad into the garage and get into his car to start my day.

Chapter Two

Morning shifts at Carlotta's are always my favorite.

The cafe smells like cinnamon scones and hazelnut syrup. Light filters in through the slanted windows, and I watch dust motes dance in the golden haze.

I wipe down the counters, humming softly, while my coworker Jeannie helps the last couple of customers that trickle in at the counter. Mornings here are quiet, peaceful, and predictable. All the things I've come to appreciate.

But today, I can't seem to shake that dream from last night. Not completely.

There was always something about him, the man in the dream. He seems so real.

I wish he was.

The thought lingers like smoke in my chest.

"One Caramel Crumble Latte for here please, Renna," Jeannie says.

"Sure thing, coming right up."

I quickly walk around the counter, to start the order. Mindlessly,

I go through the familiar motions of making the latte. I start to brew the espresso, reach for a clean mug to pour it into, and begin steaming the milk.

Then it happens.

Auren...

A voice—no, several voices in unison— slice through the air like a thin blade, soft and distant and yet *unmistakable*.

I freeze, my fingers tightening around the just filled mug. It slips from my hand and crashes to the tile floor, shattering on impact.

"Renna?" Jeannie asks, "Are you ok?"

Auren...

The voices call again. Almost taunting me.

No one calls me that.

What is happening?

I stare at the shards of the mug shattered on the floor, and the latte bleeding from its remnants. My chest tightens.

I haven't heard that name in years, not since I was a child, and even then, only when my mother was upset or emotional. She insisted I only go by Renna, long before I could even understand why. It's just the way it was.

I shake my head trying to snap out of whatever this is, grabbing a towel to clean up the mess.

"Yeah, I'm ok Jeannie. Just clumsy. I'll clean this up and start a new drink right away."

"I'll make the drink, don't worry about it," Jeannie says.

Auren...hide...they're coming!

The whispers hiss.

My blood runs cold. I stand up so quickly I nearly hit my head on the counter. The room suddenly feels too loud. The machine grinding the espresso, the hiss of the milk steaming.

The lights overhead flicker.

"This damn wind is going to knock the power out," Jeannie says.

I grip the edges of the counter. My heart is pounding.

Too fast.

Why am I feeling so much dread? An anxiety attack is on the horizon.

The shadows in the corners of the cafe start to look too dark, too deep. Like the void in my nightmare. They seem to be moving when they shouldn't. And that whisper...is it in my head? Is someone outside messing with me?

They're getting louder now. More urgent.

Auren...Auren! The darkness is coming. Run!

Something inside me snaps.

The world is tilting. I hear the bell above the front door chime like a scream in my ears. Light begins to bleed out the edges of my vision. I stumble back into the counter, gasping and clutching at my chest. My heart pounds, like a caged wild beast trying to escape.

"Renna?" someone says. She reaches for my shoulder, but I flinch away, shaking and becoming dizzy.

Jeannie.

"I...need to go," I whisper. "I can't, I just don't feel right."

"I think you're having one of your attacks, honey. Don't worry about it. Just let me help you to the break room where you can sit down."

I let her guide me to the break room. My chest thuds with every beat of my heart, my breathing becoming more rapid.

"You just sit tight. I'll call your dad and let him know what's going on," she says. "I'll get his number off your emergency contact form."

The whispers continue.

What is happening to me?

Run! Hide! The darkness is coming, Auren!

It's the last thing I hear before I pass out.

***

I wake to two EMT's checking me over.

"Welcome back to the land of the living," a woman says, giving me a reassuring smile.

"Oh, thank God, Renna, are you alright?" I recognize my father's voice.

"Yeah, I'm ok. I had an anxiety attack..."

"We can take you into the hospital to get you checked out if you want," the female EMT says gently.

"No, no. That won't be necessary," I tell her. "I'm used to this. I've been dealing with them my whole life. I just need to go home and relax for a bit."

It's a white lie. I *have* had anxiety attacks as well as panic attacks my whole life, but I have never heard voices during any of them.

Not like today.

I have gone absolutely freaking mental.

What is wrong with me?

Dad helps me out to his car, and I sit in the passenger seat, still pale, my fingers trembling in my lap.

He glances over at me.

"Do you know what triggered this one?" he asks gently.

I can see the worry clouding his warm, familiar face.

"I... I don't know."

I can't bring myself to tell him the truth. That I heard voices. That it wasn't just anxiety building over time. It was fear, real fear, that sent me spiraling. Fear brought on by something unknown. Something that knew my name.

That name.

That name that I hadn't heard aloud since I was small. But today... today it came like it had always belonged to something bigger than me.

Like someone, or *something,* was trying to remind me of who I really am.

I take a deep breath.

"I'm sorry you had to leave work for me."

"Don't be sorry about that," he says laughing. "Now we both have the day off and we can celebrate your birthday properly."

I smile at him, and he takes my hand off my lap and gives it a squeeze.

"Now let's get you home kiddo, there's plenty of time for you to relax with that lavender bubble bath you like, before we go out for dinner tonight if you're still up for it."

"Oh, I'm not saying no to Maestro's," I say, giving him a smile.

And with that he lets go of my hand and drives us home.

Chapter Three

I sit cross-legged on my bed, smoothing out the hem of my favorite dress, midnight blue with silver embroidered stars across the bodice and on the sheer sleeves. My mother laid it out for me while I soaked in the bathtub for what must have been hours. That was the worst anxiety attack I have had in years. And those voices...

A chill runs up my spine.

No, I'm not going to think about it anymore. This is going to be a good weekend. My birthday weekend. A celebration dinner out, and a weekend at the cabin in the mountains by the lake. I should be excited.

My mother stepped into my room holding a pair of silver earrings.

"Your father's finishing up packing. How are you feeling?"

I pause before answering.

"Better. A little weird but... I feel better."

My mother tilts her head, examining me from head to toe in that way that she always does, making sure that I am truly okay. And just like always, she notices the cracks in my facade.

"You don't have to push yourself."

"I want to go," I say. "Really.

She gives me a gentle smile and fastens her earrings with delicate fingers.

"Alright, then let's make it a night to remember."

***

The restaurant is softly lit, and full of murmured conversations. Maestro's looks just as it did when Brynn and I came here a couple years ago. Flickering candlelight, dark wood booths, and the smell of roasted garlic and cream sauce hanging in the air.

Dinner passes in soft waves of small talk, my father cracking the latest dad jokes he's heard, and my mother constantly steering the conversation away from any mention of college or moving away. For once, I don't mind. I just let myself feel normal.

But if I am being honest, the unease of what happened earlier still hasn't completely left me.

My mother sets her fork down, between bites. "How are you really feeling, sweetie? After your attack earlier?"

I look down at my water glass and trace my fingertip in a circle through the condensation. "Something about this attack was.... I don't know... different."

Both of my parents look at me.

"I think... I heard something," I say softly. "Not just in my head. Like whispers. But—"

"Happy birthday to you..."

The waitstaff rounds the corner singing, a small cake in hand, candle lit and flickering as they make their way to our table. My parents both smile and join in on the singing.

The waitress places the cake down in front of me as they finish, then quietly leaves the table. I close my eyes and make a wish, then blow out the candle.

As the flame winks out, I glance down at the cake.

Happy Birthday Auren!

I blink, and my mother shoots to her feet, knocking her napkin to the ground, eyes wide. "No!"

I look at her. *No?* She's staring at the cake, frozen. Does she see it too? I glance down again.

Happy Birthday Renna!

My heart begins to thud. Did I just imagine that? Why does my mother look like she's seen a ghost?

My father glances up at her. "Are you alright?"

I watch as my mother straightens slowly. "I just... I just felt a little dizzy. I'll be right back."

Her voice is too shaky to be convincing. She had to have seen it too.

But how can we both have seen something that was clearly not there?

The waitress comes back with a knife, and cuts the cake, serving us each a slice. Shortly after, my mother returns from the restroom with a smile that doesn't quite reach her eyes.

"Well, I think this weekend getaway will be a good thing for all of us," she says. "Clear air. No distractions. Just good quality time together."

I take a bite of my cake, chocolate with chocolate icing and raspberry filling. It's absolutely decadent. But my appetite is gone. My mother saw what I did. I know it.

***

Before long, we're outside, waiting by the valet. The cool night air brushes against me like a whisper. My father is handed the keys, and we all load into the car and start our route to the cabin.

I stare out the window watching as the dark shadows of the trees blur past the car, and I lean back in my seat. My father is holding my mother's hand tightly while his other grips the steering wheel.

I smile to myself. I hope one day I find a love like theirs. I rest my head against the window of the car and close my eyes.

Auren... Auren... Auren... Auren!

My eyes shoot open. The whispers are back.

They've found you.

Run. Run. Turn back, Run!

The whispers seem to come from right behind my ear. My breathing hitches. My heart begins to hammer in my chest.

"M... Mom!" I stammer. "It's happening again—"

My mother drops my father's hand and unbuckles her seatbelt, and twists in her seat, reaching for me.

"Renna, just breathe. Breathe, okay? Look at me. Are you hearing something again?"

FLASH.

A burst of light, not from the road, not from the sky, but from something unnatural. A shimmering almost invisible wall slams into the front of the car.

Metal shrieks... or is that me screaming... as I watch my mother get thrown forward. She crashes through the windshield in a blur of glass and blood, before I'm slammed back into my seat, my head violently hitting my window. My ears are ringing, as I stare at the windshield in horror.

"Dad... Dad!" I scream, spotting his body slumped against the steering wheel, he isn't moving, and blood is spilling down his face.

"Help! Someone, help us!" I scream, my fingers fumbling to undo my seat belt. I need to get out. I need to get to my mother.

She's hurt. But she has to be okay.

She has to be.

I glance around the car searching for my purse or my phone, with no luck.

I push open the door and fall to the pavement, my ears ringing and body trembling.

And then I see her... just a few feet in front of the vehicle.

She's lying motionless. There is no sign of that shimmering wall that we slammed into.

What *was* that?

Hide Auren, hide.

The darkness has found you.

Hide!

I crawl toward my mother, when I hear a strange crackling sound, it's sharp and unnatural.

I whip my head toward the sound and see a figure step from the shadows.

A man.

If he even could be called that.

Towering.

Clad head to toe in armor of blackened bone, jagged and cruel, shaped like it had been grown from the dead. A long sword rests strapped across his back. A horned helmet sculpted into a skull-like visage, obscures his face. And from within it, two hollow black eyes stare at me.

I hear coughing from the car.

My dad.

He's conscious.

"Renna?" he calls out.

The stranger turns, dragging his gaze from me to the driver's side of the car.

"No, Dad!" I scream. "Run!"

The dark figure rips open the car door, and yanks my father from the seat, his limp body flopping like a rag doll.

"Please. No. No," I cry. "Someone, help us, please!"

The stranger pulls the sword from his back and drives it straight into my father's chest. The sound is sickening, wet and final. I begin to sob and crawl toward my mother.

We are all going to die. This monster is going to kill us all.

I cradle her head in my shaking arms.

"Mom...stay with me...please," I beg.

Her gaze flutters open. Her lips tremble.

That's when I notice something strange.

The blood pooling around her isn't red. It's bright blue. And her ears, visible through her matted golden hair, are pointed.

"Auren," she whispers. "You need to be the light in the darkness."

"What...what does that mean? Stay with me mom, you're going to be okay. You have to be okay..."

Her arm rises shakily. She cups my cheek with blood-sticky fingers.

"I—" she coughs, blood spilling from her lips. "I love you... my sweet girl."

She begins to shake, then goes still in my arms.

I clutch her tightly and sob into her shoulder. Heavy footsteps sound behind me. I turn my head just in time to see the dark figure raise his blade and then slam the hilt into my temple.

Then darkness takes me.

Chapter Four

There is no sky, no ground. No weight here. Like my nightmare, yet something about this place feels different.

You will be alright.

The haunting familiar voices whisper.

I float in nothing, suspended in a place that feels caught between thought and time. My body feels like smoke, scattered and shifting as I pass through this plane. I don't feel the pain that my body had felt moments ago, after the crash. I glance down at my hands and know it was real, my mother's blood drying on my fingertips.

Auren...

The voices are sharp, no longer a whisper. It comes not from outside me, but from within, brushing against my bones like a secret that had been long kept.

I try to speak, but my mouth doesn't work here. No sound comes. Instead, I watch as threads of color begin to spiral past me, holding shape. Not solid, not light, but something older. Something alive.

They drift past me like mist.

This is the veil.

See.

Know.

I'm seeing flashes of memories that aren't my own. My mother. Her golden hair wild in the wind, she's standing in front of a doorway that shimmers with stars, smiling at someone. The memory flashes past me.

Another memory approaches, I see a dark-haired man with haunted eyes, he's standing in a burning throne room, holding a sword soaked in blood.

Another image, this time a large keep, carved from white stone with veins of purple, under a sky full of stars.

The threads keep moving, pulling me with them. It's like they recognize me, and they've been waiting for me.

What are you? I think to myself.

We will guide you.

Help you.

And you will help us, Little Light.

The voices whisper back, the colored threads wrap around me like a promise.

Suddenly, everything goes still. The threads of color are gone, the voices gone with them. I'm in that cold, weightless darkness that I have grown used to in my dreams. I no longer see memories, or the flashes of colored light.

"Where am I?" I ask out loud.

A voice answers, low and warm, one that I have heard so many times in my dreams before. Always in the dark, always unseen.

"You are not lost, you have just not been found yet," *he* says.

I let the words settle inside me like a heartbeat. I reach my hand toward his voice, and for a brief moment, I think I feel fingers brush against mine. But then the threads that pulled me here return, their colors darker, and the air grows an icy chill.

The space begins to shudder.

Cracks of red-light slice through the blackness. Screams echoing from beyond where I can see.

The colored threads from before wrap around me, warming me up.

They whisper.

She's Coming.

You must destroy the darkness.

Be the light Auren.

The red cracks disappear, and the colored threads move past me and into the darkness once more.

Their warmth is gone.

And I begin to fall.

I hit the ground hard. Cold jolts through my bones, knocking the breath from my lungs. Gravel and ash scrape my palms as I try to rise. The air here smells of rot and cinders. I blink my eyes rapidly, looking up to the sky. The light here is wrong—gray and cracked—as if the sky itself had fractured and forgotten how to hold the sun. I'm no longer in my world. But this is not a dream.

I'm here. Wherever *here* is.

A shadow looms to my right. I turn toward it, and the knight in black bone forged armor stands there. Unmoving.

"Where... where am I?" I croak, my throat raw.

He doesn't answer. He simply reaches down, grabbing my arm with his cold iron fingers, dragging me to my feet. I stumble, legs weak, my ears still ringing.

We pass beneath a crumbling stone archway, and then through a gate that looks like the mouth of a dead god. Beyond it, stands a palace.

It wasn't like the shimmering vision I had glimpsed in the place I was before. This place is jagged and twisted. Blackened spires rise from each corner, bone colored stone forming the walls. Vines of crimson thorns creep along the edges. The air is heavy with decay and shadow, nothing living belongs here. And still, somehow, I can feel it pulse with *power*.

The knight pulls me into the main hall, and there at the top of a dais stands a woman. She is beautiful, dressed in black silks threaded with a light silver that shimmers like spiderwebs. Her hair long and dark, skin as pale as the moon. Her eyes are an unsettling red, flecked with gold. Those eyes are staring at me now, conveying something between hunger and delight.

"My Queen," the knight says, his voice almost robotic, before dropping to one knee. "The girl, as ordered."

I stare at the woman, trembling.

"Please... I don't know what's going on. You have to help me."

She laughs, sweet and sharp, full of venom.

"Help you?" she echoes. "Oh, child. You're not here to be helped."

She descends the steps of the dais slowly, each footfall clapping in my chest like thunder.

"You're here because you have something that *I* need."

I stumble back, my limbs sluggish with fear.

"I don't... I don't have anything," I whisper. But the words don't sound convincing, even to me.

"Oh, but you do," the woman purrs. "You have so much power tucked inside that pretty little body of yours. If it hasn't manifested yet, that's fine."

She smiles at me, her teeth like polished blades.

"I'll be more than happy to have that power tortured out of you, and by the time we are done, you will willingly give it all over to me."

Her words send a shiver down my spine. Panic claws at my throat. The air thickens, pressing against my ribs. My heart slams so hard, I think it might burst. I can't catch my breath. I can't breathe.

She's going to hurt me.

"Take her to the dungeons," the Queen commands the knight still on his knee beside me. "Tell the others not to let her see light again until she bleeds it."

The knight rises, his armor groaning, and violently grabs my arm. My body finally reacts, though it's too late. I thrash, scream, kick. Every instinct I have is telling me to break free and run. But there is no escape. No one here wants to help me. No one left alive to come looking for me.

The Queen's laugh chases me as I'm dragged away.

The knight grabs a lantern from the top of a stairway, then pulls me down winding stairs, past locked doors covered in rot, until we reach a pit beneath the palace.

My cell is stone, small and silent, with no windows—no light. Just the chains he shackles me with, darkness, and the scent of old pain.

"Please, help me," I beg as he finishes locking the shackles on my feet, my hands already bound.

He says nothing, instead using his might to throw me into the wall, my head smacks against the stone. I slide down the wall sobbing, pain blooming throughout my body from the impact. He leaves and slams the cell door shut. The lantern light goes with him.

Darkness swallows me. And it's cold, so very cold.

I feel it in my bones. In the stillness here in the dark, this is the place that my nightmares have been trying to warn me about.

Chapter Five

Time has stopped meaning anything.

There is only cold.

Only dark.

Only pain.

I no longer know if I've been down here for days or weeks. This dungeon is a place without seasons.

Without sunrise.

The only constant is the footsteps in the corridor, my chains clinking, and the burn of torn flesh.

No light ever reaches me here, no warmth. I barely sleep. They don't let me. Whenever I slip into unconsciousness, they bring me back. With noise, with agony, with screams. They never use my name.

Perhaps they don't know it.

That's fine.

It's something of mine that I can keep.

"Up hollow one!" a guard yells.

"Still no spark from the empty girl?" the one beside him mocks, his tone sharp and sneering.

"Maybe she's already dead, and no one's told her." The first guard replies.

These monsters wear their cruelty like armor. Whips, fists, blades, something they call firewater in my wounds that makes me feel like I'm burning from the inside out, they've used everything. And somehow, I've endured it.

I think back on what the first guard said. *Am I already dead? Is this some kind of personal hell?* Maybe I died in the car crash, and this is some twisted purgatory.

A blade slices into the meat of my thigh.

Pain.

No, I am alive, I can feel the pain and that means I am alive.

I don't give them the satisfaction of screaming. I bite my tongue until it bleeds, the copper tang of blood swirling in my mouth. I try to disassociate completely.

Fists strike my body, hitting my ribs, my stomach, my face. I feel skin split on my lip and cheek. But I sit there and take it, refusing to give them a sliver of satisfaction.

I'm going to die here. I'm certain of it. It's just a matter of *when*.

This place. This dark cell. The shadowed space from my nightmares, maybe this is where the power these people think I have goes to die.

When the guards are done with delivering their punishments, they leave. Every waking moment is the same. Different guards take turns, cycling in and out of my cell throughout what I assume is a day. They try everything they can to break me, to force whatever it is they're convinced I have out of me.

I endure it.

I accept it.

This is my fate. *I have nothing left.*

But today... if it's even a new day, something has changed.

The rhythm of this place, the one I have grown accustomed to, is off. No guards laughing on their way to my cell. No anticipation in their steps. Those sounds aren't here.

Only footsteps.

Slower.

Confident.

Then light comes—a single lantern. Not the red flickering flames the guards always carry. This one burns blue, it's so bright that it lights up the entire cell. I blink against it, heart racing. Dread blooms in my chest as I shrink into the corner.

A figure steps inside, then shuts the cell door behind him. This isn't a guard.

I know him.

I've seen him before. In one of the visions in the veil. The man in the room that was filled with flames. The man with the sword covered in blood.

He is tall, dressed in black leathers, the gleam of silver buckles glinting in the lantern light. His hair is slicked back, and his dark eyes glitter with satisfaction.

"Well," he says smoothly, "so this is the girl that is to give me what is owed?"

A wicked smile spreads across his lips.

"Oh, I do hope you have enjoyed our hospitality thus far... oh, where are my manners?" he drawls. "I'm Lucien Thorne. Pleasure to meet you."

He mocks a bow.

I make sure I don't move. I don't speak.

He unsheathes a curved dagger, freshly sharpened, and twirls it between his fingers like it's a toy.

"I thought I'd see for myself what all the fuss was about." He crouches in front of me.

"You're not much to look at in this state, but I suppose that's what torture does to a person. It's a pity it hasn't worked."

I force myself to speak. My voice is cracked and horse from disuse. "You have the wrong person; I'm not like you. I'm just human."

Lucien smiles. An ugly, unsettling grin.

"You really don't know do you?"

He stands bringing the lantern closer. "Let's fix that shall we?"

He slashes my arm. Slowly, like he is carving a picture into a wood bench.

I squeeze my eyes shut and grit my teeth. Anxiety rises like bile, but I shove it down. I won't let him see me break.

Another cut. Then another. My body trembles, but I keep my eyes closed. I won't give these monsters the satisfaction of hearing me scream.

"Nothing," he mused. "No power, no spark. Tsk Tsk."

I keep my eyes squeezed tightly shut. I hear the scrape of metal as he wipes off his blade.

"Look at me!" he demands.

I don't. I won't.

"Look at me!" this time sharper, fingers digging into my chin as he jerks my head up.

I force my eyes open.

Lucien leans in, brushing a clump of matted hair from my face.

I flinch, but I don't pull away. Not with his blade so close to my throat. He lifts it until it's level with my eyes.

"Look," he says, low and commanding.

I catch a glimpse of my reflection in his dagger.

My ears are pointed.

My blood is not red.

It's blue.

My breath hitches and my whole body goes cold.

"No..." I whisper. "This isn't possible."

"Oh yes," Lucien says, clearly pleased. "Your mother must have used a glamour to hide it from the humans. Clever."

He tilts his head, voice soft with mockery.

"Hiding what you truly are from the world... seems she hid it from you as well."

He leans closer, so close that I can smell the rot on his breath.

"Surprised?" he asks, voice dripping with delight. "I just love surprises, don't you?"

This can't be.

How?

How could my mother have lied to me my entire life?

This must have been who she was hiding me from.

Why wouldn't she have just told me? I could have prepared somehow.

"I love surprises so much. I have a special one just for you," he says, standing and heading towards the bars of my cell door.

"Bring her in!" he shouts.

Footsteps pound toward my cell.

Two guards appear, dragging something...*someone* behind them.

A body.

A fae woman, limp and bloodied.

Bruises and slashes coat every inch of her exposed skin. Her brown hair has been hacked off, probably with a dagger, it's short and uneven. She's lifeless as they drag her into my cell, closing the door behind them. They throw the woman on the ground in front of me. This woman, her face...

I feel my heart stop in my chest.

"Brynn!" I shout.

I lurch forward, chains biting into my wrists and ankles as I try to reach her.

Lucien's boot slams into my chest with a bone jarring crack. The force knocks every bit of air from my lungs, and my back slams into the wall.

Pain explodes through my ribs, they're cracked, maybe even completely broken.

Panic claws at my throat. I gasp for air but choke instead on the rising tide of my fear. My vision tunnels.

"Ah ah," Lucien says mockingly. "Let's not ruin my surprise."

I look at Brynn. She isn't moving.

Lucien gestures lazily.

"I see you remember your old friend Brynn. How heartwarming that you haven't forgotten about her, after all this time. We sent her to find you, you know. Her mother was... an old friend of your mother's."

"And after we took Brynn's mother in for our special brand of hospitality, your friend here was more than eager to trade your freedom for her mothers."

He crouches beside Brynn, grabbing her chin.

"Of course, when she failed to bring you back...well, surely we had to teach her a lesson."

He smiles, wider this time.

"We slit her mother's throat in front of her. Oh... that noise she made..." He sighs as if it's a fond memory. "Then we started on

Brynn here. Trying to get her to tell us where you were. And she held out. For so, so long too. Touching really. Until she *couldn't* anymore."

He slaps Brynn across the face, hard.

She stirs.

Her eyes flutter open, and she sees me in front of her. A faint broken sound escapes her lips.

"I'm sorry," she croaks.

"Sorry for what, Brynn?" Lucien asks, amused.

I begin to sob. My only friend. My best friend. She's been here enduring what I have, for so much longer.

"It's ok...it's ok Brynn." I say, my voice cracking with tears.

Brynn turns her head towards me, barely able to move.

"Don't...give them...anything," she whispers.

The sickening smile that had been on Lucien's face vanishes. He kicks Brynn with such force that I can hear her bones fracture. An absolutely heart-shattering, agonizing moan comes from her.

His dagger is back out.

"Maybe if I cut her open in front of you, you'll finally glow with that power that you owe me."

"No! Please...please... stop! Just take it! Take whatever you want!" I beg.

"Oh no, you see...what I want can't be taken from you. You have to freely give it to me," he says in a mocking tone, though somehow, I know what he says is the truth.

I extend my hand.

"Then here, you can have whatever it is you want," I tell him.

He walks over to me, glee on his face, and grabs my hand.

I close my eyes and try to communicate with the voices that have been speaking to me.

Whoever you are, please... just give him what he wants.

Do it for Brynn.

No, Little Light! This is not the way!

No!

I feel a quick jolt, and Lucien rips his hand from mine. Whatever just happened seemed to cause him pain. I look down at my hand, and don't see anything different.

"You will give it to me!" he yells, face contorting with rage. "It's mine!"

He stalks toward Brynn with his knife.

"Please, no. Stop!" I beg.

He doesn't.

He carves Brynn slowly, carefully, like he had done to me. She screams, it's raw and broken.

I cry.

I beg him to stop again and again and again. I pull at my chains until my ankles and wrists bleed, trying to awaken something within me... anything.

Nothing comes.

"Oh, don't worry, she can take it. I mean, what has it been now

Brynn?" he asks with a mocking tone. "Nearly two years, correct?"

One of the guards steps back inside and hands Lucien a bucket of fire water, and he begins pouring it all over Brynn's freshly carved wounds.

Then the room fills with more agonizing screams.

Both mine and hers.

I won't forget them as long as I live.

Brynn falls unconscious again, her face pale and smeared with blood.

Lucien stands, brushing himself off like nothing happened, like he hasn't been taking pleasure in hurting the both of us for the past several hours.

"How rude to just exit the party, the fun was just getting started," he says, staring at my friend's limp body on the ground.

He turns to look at me.

"And you are shaping up to be quite the disappointment as well."

He grabs Brynn by the hair and drags her limp body out of the cell, closing the door behind him.

"We'll be back for another visit soon," Lucien calls over his shoulder. "Sleep tight."

The light disappears down the hallway with him.

***

I don't know when I drift off. Maybe minutes after he left, maybe hours. But when I open my eyes again, the darkness feels different.

Familiar.

"You're here again," the voice says.

His voice.

"You haven't been here in a while, I missed you..."

My breath catches. I need his help. Maybe he can somehow find me.

"They're hurting me," I whisper. "I don't... I don't know where I am... but I think I'm dying."

His warm presence moves closer, unseen but *real*.

"You aren't dying," he says. "I can feel you. You're still here."

My voice cracks with desperation. "Please help me, I don't know where I am. But it's bad. It's so bad."

I begin to cry. The physical pain of everything that I've endured crashing into me all at once.

He stands beside me, wrapping me in his arms. Both of us are still cloaked in shadow. I rest my head on his chest, and I can hear his heartbeat.

"They've killed my parents, and they've been torturing my friend for nearly two years. I'm being tortured. It's been weeks, I think." I sob into his chest. "I don't know where I am... I need help."

"Can you remember anything that you've seen and describe it to me?" he asks.

I close my eyes and try to think.

"I'm in a cell. There's no light, no windows. No sound. Only darkness, and cold. Like this place." I shut my eyes and think, really think, about where I am.

"I remember walking through a gate that looked like the open mouth of a dead god, and crimson thorny vines that looked like veins."

My companion stiffens.

"Do you know it?" I ask. But before he can answer, my companion is ripped from this place suddenly.

And I'm left here.

Alone, in the dark.

Chapter Six – Reavian

The dream is already unraveling. Her voice is fading, stretched thin by distance, and something darker. Something clawing her away from me.

"I'm in a cell, there is no light, no windows. No sound. Only darkness, and cold. Like this place," she tells me.

I instinctively hold her tighter.

"I remember walking through a gate that looked like the open mouth of a dead god, and crimson thorny vines that looked like veins."

I stiffen.

I know that place.

I open my mouth to speak but the shadows around her pull taut, and she's ripped from me like a breath stolen by the cold.

"Reav... Reav. Wake up, princess. You're drooling," a voice says, right next to my ear.

I jerk awake to find Kaiel crouched over me, grinning like a demon. I reach up, grab my pillow and smack him in the chest with it.

Kaiel snorts.

"You were talking in your sleep again. Pretty sure I heard the words *mouth*, and *thorns*. Should I be concerned?" he asks.

I sit up slowly, raking a hand through my sweat damp hair. My heart is still pounding.

"Get out of my face Kaiel," I say, irritated that he pulled me from my dream before I could get more information from the girl.

"Nah, I like it here." Kaiel plops down at the foot of my bed. "Sword training. Let's go. Unless you are planning on sleeping your way to combat readiness."

It's been like this for as long as I can remember. After the Rift War, when my stepfather killed High King Veylas, lines were drawn in the fae realms. Kaiel's father, like several others, allied with my mother and Lucien, and quickly became a trusted member of their court. He brought Kaiel with him.

Since we were both the same age, we spent a lot of time together. We are complete opposites. He's all humor and mischief, while I'm quieter and more serious. Broody as he likes to call me. I don't know how he manages to keep his laughter alive in a place like this. Everything here is so heavy.

So wrong.

But we are both trapped. And no matter how often I run through the possibilities in my mind, none of them lead to freedom. Fleeing would brand us traitors. If we're caught, we die. And who would even take us in?

I've thought about escaping for years. I tried once after a particularly brutal punishment from my mother. I was caught, dragged to the dungeons and whipped until she was sure that I learned my lesson. After that, I started making plans with Kaiel. Talking through ideas. Searching for cracks in the wall we might one day slip through. But we came to the conclusion that no one would take us in. Not without risking their realm being overrun by our dark armies.

I swing my legs over the edge of my bed.

"You are absolutely insufferable."

He winks at me.

"That's why you love me," he says with a grin.

***

The training yard becomes a blur of steel and sweat. I move through the motions. Parries, foot work, timing the strike. But my mind remains tethered to my dream. Each time Kaiel lunges at me, I hear her voice whispering beneath the clash of our blades.

The mouth of a dead God.

I shove Kaiel back, and freeze.

This wasn't just a dream. She's in Ashwynn Reach. I'm sure of it.

And the thought that the girl from my dreams, the voice that has guided me through countless shadowed nights over the years, was here somewhere makes my blood run cold.

"You're distracted," Kaiel says, panting as he takes a step back, and lowers his sword. "What's wrong? Trouble with your *dream* girl?"

I've spoken to Kaiel before about the dreams I've had since I was young. I've told him that they felt real. That *she* felt real, he always laughed it off, saying I was crazy.

Only Dreamwalkers can do that, and I am no Dreamwalker. As far as my parentage goes, my mother was a noble woman from a faraway land, she met my father when she traveled here to visit the high courts, hoping to gain favor for her people. She fell in love with my father, a lesser fae. He was a guard for one of the high houses and was executed for trying to assassinate the High Lord of the Realm of Veiled Stars.

The High Lord found out, and banished my mother to Ashwynn Reach, where she met Lucien.

Kaiel raises a brow at me. "It *is* the dream girl, isn't it?"

"I need a favor."

"Uh, oh," Kaiel replies.

"We're sneaking out tonight. Black market," I say quietly.

He narrows his eyes.

"Are you sure about this? I've told you before man, dreams aren't real. She's just something you've created in your mind to distract you from all the crazy shit we've seen."

"We. Are. Sneaking. Out. Tonight," I enunciate each word

slowly.

Kaiel gives me a once over, then shrugs.

"Alright," he says with a grin. "Let's smuggle in some of that high end wine while we're out there."

***

The markets outside the city walls are a winding mix of cloth canopies and flickering torches. The scent of spices and sweat mixes with secrets. Gold passes between hands as information is being sold in the shadows. I came here seeking only one thing. A seer. I had heard that there are a few here, exiled from their realms. They sell information in these markets.

"What exactly are you looking for here?" Kaiel asks as we weave in and out through the crowd of people shopping the market.

"Information," I answer.

"Right, on the imaginary dream girl," he mutters, rolling his eyes.

We make our way down a back alley lined with merchants, and potion hawkers.

"Liquor from the finest of the realms!" one of the merchants shouts.

"Just what I was looking for," Kaiel says laughing as he heads over to the table.

That's when she steps in front of me.

A woman, she's old and blind. Her eyes are silver and empty. And yet somehow, I know she is *seeing* me.

She grabs my arm.

"You dream of her," she rasps.

I freeze.

"How do you know that?" I ask.

Kaiel stalks quickly toward me, his bounty in hand.

"The light in the dark," she says. "The song in the silence. She is beneath you, Prince. In the depths below your home."

"Okay, that's not ominous at all," Kaiel mutters from my side.

I feel the blood drain from my body.

My breath leaves my lungs.

"What...did you say?" I ask the woman.

"She is down in the dark, crying for help. And she will die unless the walker finds her," the woman rasps.

My heart pounds, ready to burst from my chest. I don't wait for more information. I turn without a word and sprint back toward home. I can faintly hear Kaiel calling after me.

But I can't stop.

I need to get to her.

The memory of the girl's voice haunts me.

Please help me. I don't know where I am. But it's bad. So bad.

I need to find her. *Now.*

I reach the palace when a hand grabs my shoulder and pulls me back. I draw my blade and spin, ready to kill whoever stands in my way.

"Woah, man," Kaiel says, stepping back and raising his hand. His other hand still grips the bag of fancy liquor he bought at the market.

"Take it easy, I just wanted to tell you, that you can't run blazing through the front gate like this. You need to sneak back in, the way we snuck out. Otherwise, they're going to stop you before whatever you have planned can even begin to happen."

I blink and lower my sword. He's right. And for the first time in my life, I *didn't* plan how I was going to do something. I reacted purely on emotion.

"I'm...I'm sorry. I wasn't thinking clearly. She needs me. They have her in the dungeons. That's what the woman at the market meant. She's being tortured," I ramble, sliding my sword back into its sheath with shaking hands.

"Yeah, I figured that out when that creepy old bat was talking, and you bolted. Listen, if you really think she's down there... I'll help you get her out. But we have to be smart about this, Reav."

"You're right. We can't afford any mistakes."

I glance at Kaiel, my only friend in this world, he's ready to dive right into danger by my side. He doesn't know her. Hells, he's not sure she even exists. But still, he's willing to risk his life for mine. And I would do the same for him.

"The plan we come up with has to be a good one," I say.

Because her life depends on it.

Because all of ours do.

Chapter Seven - Reavian

I stand at the edge of the outer courtyard wall, my hood pulled low as I wait for Kaiel. Before we sneak back into the palace, we need to secure keys to the dungeon, and two horses for our escape. Unfortunately, being seen this late at night would draw unwanted attention, so Kaiel has to handle it alone. My job? Apparently to stand guard for his prized liquor that he scored at the market.

He had assured me it was *all* part of the plan.

My heart drums like war inside my chest. I can feel her somehow... she's fading.

I spot Kaiel's tall frame in the distance, with two horses saddled and ready. He hasn't bothered to pull up his cloak, his long brown hair whips wildly in the wind. I shake my head as he nears, offering me a mock salute.

"Two horses and some feed saddled and ready to go, Your Majesty," he says, sketching a bow.

I know that he's joking, but I hate it when he jokes about *that*. I'm not royalty. My mother declared herself queen—and Lucien king—but it was never their right. Most of the high houses rebuked this idea as well and Lucien labeled them traitors to the crown.

But no, they are not royalty. *I* am not royalty. The High Queen and High King are chosen by the Gods themselves, and neither Lucien nor my mother have been chosen.

He tosses me a small pouch.

"And the keys off of one *very* intoxicated guard at the local tavern."

"Great work," I say, taking the keys from his hands.

"I even had time to name our horses," he adds with a grin. "This one is Dumb," he says, pointing to the one on the left, "and this one is Dumber," he finishes, gesturing to the one on the right.

He places his hands on his hips, and a proud smile appears on his face.

I raise a brow at him.

"Fitting. You'll be riding Dumber then," I say.

"Can't wait," he replies with a wink.

We lead the horses deep into the scorched forest and tie them up in a small clearing, readying them for our escape. The plan is simple: ride to the docks and steal a trade ship, then sail with the horses and the girl across the sea towards The Realm of Flame and Forest. There, we'll seek asylum with Vaedric Solmere, the High Lord of that realm. After much discussion we decided he may be the most sympathetic to our plight.

I swallow at the thought that even the most sympathetic may

decide to just execute us all, just because of who I am.

They can do whatever they want to me, but not to her—never to her.

"Are you ready Kaiel? You're sure you want to do this with me? There's no turning back."

"Yeah, sure. This place blows. If anything, I feel we waited way too long to plan a high-stakes rescue and escape," he says, with an ear-to-ear grin. "You did a good job watching over my precious items here," he adds, patting me on the back, and swiping the bag of liquor from my hand.

I shake my head at him.

We move around the edge of the outer wall until we reach the sewer grate we snuck out of. When we were kids, we'd found a hidden passage behind some oak barrels in the kitchen. A tunnel that led down to the sewers, and up to this very grate.

The palace was built long before my mother or Lucien decided to take up residence. Someone had intended this to be an escape route.

"After you," Kaiel says, waving me towards the grate.

I begin the descent.

We've agreed to stagger our return to the palace, in case one of us is stopped, the other can distract.

Sneaking back in was easy. No one knew of this path but us. The kitchen staff had already retired to their quarters before we even left for the market, and we both know the guard's rotations by heart.

When I reach the kitchen, I grab two knit bags and fill them with apples, dried meat, and cheese. We need food for the long journey ahead of us.

I move quietly up the stairs and into our wing of the palace, slipping past the massive dark wood doors, and stalking past my mother's room as silently as I can.

Just when I think I'm in the clear, a figure steps out from the shadows ahead of me.

"Where have you been, child of mine? You are not where I left you," my mother drawls, venom clinging to every word.

Where she left me...

Rage churns inside me. She talks to me as if I'm still a child.

She's never wanted me. I knew it. I've known it my whole life. She has always looked at me with hatred, like my very face is abhorrent to her. I was never her son, just a pawn in her grand plan. And when she didn't get whatever it was she wanted from me, I was cast aside like little more than trash.

"Where were you?" she demands, her voice icy.

Footsteps echo behind me, steady and confident.

Lucien.

"What's all the commotion, my dear?" he asks smoothly.

"I'm just wondering where our son has been at this hour," she replies, eyeing the bags in my hands. "Are you planning to go somewhere?" She watches me like I'm prey. Ready to pounce on the first sign of weakness.

He is *not* my father.

Behind me, bottles clink together as someone stumbles into the hall.

"There...yahh...are," Kaiel slurs. "Let's get this party started..."

He raises an open bottle of the liquor, dramatically sloshing some across the floor.

Lucien laughs, wrapping an arm around my mother. She looks at me like she always does, full of disgust and disappointment.

"Come dear, let the boys be boys," he says, guiding her toward their bedchamber.

He glances back over his shoulder at me and Kaiel, who has now stumbled to my side, reeking of liquor and still sloshing the bottle.

"Do *try* to keep it down," Lucien adds, before closing the door behind them.

My relationship with him is...complicated.

Sometimes, it's hard for me to reconcile the monster I know him to be, with the man that raised me like I was his own. Even now, he shows me kindness at times.

Kaiel and I slip into my room, shutting the door behind us.

"How was that for improvisation?" Kaiel grins." You do owe me a bottle of Lightning Wielder, though."

I scramble around my room stuffing a backpack with everything I think I'll need. I grab some of my older clothes that are smaller in size, just in case the girl needs something to change into.

Kaiel and I each take a food bag from the kitchen and tuck it into our packs.

Then we wait until the air of suspicion fades, and make our way through the dark hallways, down winding stairs, until we stand before the dungeon door.

"You ready?" I ask my best friend, my hand on the key.

Then I hear it, a faint sound. The same melody that she hums to me, to help me find her in our dream. It's hauntingly beautiful.

I glance back at Kaiel.

"She's really here," he murmurs, shock flashing across his face. "Let's go get your dream girl."

Without hesitation, I turn the key in the lock and begin my descent into the darkness.

Chapter Eight-Auren

The cold is endless. Not just in my bones, but deep within me, somewhere unreachable. Time has ceased to mean anything.

Pain is my only anchor in this world.

Physical pain from the torment I've endured, stretching across what feels like an eternity. Mental pain from the last moments with my mom and dad.

Watching them die.

Being unable to stop it.

Just like with Brynn.

That monster of a man has brought her in here and tortured her in front of me. Again, and again.

I hear her screams.

I'll always hear her screams. I can't stop them. I can't stop her pain. And when she passes out, he starts in on me again.

I have bruises layered upon bruises, and the steady throb in my ribs tells me something is broken. I curl in on my side, pressing my face to the cold stone floor for relief.

I can't even cry anymore, there are no tears left.

I tremble.

To survive, I have to remember something good.

Something warm.

A lullaby.

My mother's voice—soft and sad.

I don't remember the words anymore, only the tune.

I hum it now, just under my breath, my voice barely audible. It's all I can manage. The faintest breath of a melody, trembling through my cracked lips.

After a while, something shifts in the stillness.

A presence, it's familiar.

Real.

Him.

I widen my eyes in the dark.

Am I dreaming?

"Are you there?" I whisper, like I have a thousand times before. "Please... are you there?"

Footsteps sound nearby, light and cautious.

Then, I hear the creak of my cell door opening. My chains rattle as I try to sit up, but my body doesn't obey. The scrape of metal echoes in the room as they hit the floor.

My heart is in my throat until a voice—soft and breathless—answers.

"It's me."

And I know it is.

Not by sight. But by the sound of his heartbeat as he pulls me to his chest. The steady *thump-thump* grounding me in a way that nothing else ever has. His warmth wraps around me as his hand cradles the back of my head.

Then another presence moves closer. I flinch when I hear hands fumbling at my shackles. I stiffen and take a deep breath.

"It's ok," the voice says gently. "He's my friend."

I barely feel the weight around my ankles fall away.

"Can't see a godsdamned thing in here," the new voice mutters.

"We can't use faelight, they'll know," the familiar voice whispers back.

The shackle around my neck comes off next. I let out a shaky breath as the ones on my wrists fall away.

I'm free.

My arms drop uselessly to my sides.

"I... I can't walk," I rasp.

"I'll carry you," he says, cradling me gently. "My name is Reavian, and the other voice you hear, that's my friend Kaiel."

"You can call me Kai," the other voice whispers. "All my friends do."

"You have literally *never* had me call you Kai," Reavian mutters.

I hear Kaiel let out a soft hushed chuckle.

Reavian lifts me gently, clutching me against his chest like I weigh nothing. Maybe I do now. I feel every cut, every bruise and broken bone scream through my body.

He turns to leave...but we can't. Not yet.

I curl my fingers weakly into his tunic.

"Wait," I breathe. "We have to find Brynn."

"What?" Kaiel asks.

"She's here, please. She's still alive, I know it. We have to get her out too. She's only here because of me. She tried to protect me."

I feel Reavian's hesitation, without a single word being spoken by him.

Then he whispers, "Lead the way Kaiel, I assume you know how to get to the other cells?"

"Yeah," Kaiel replies, his voice low...almost sorrowful.

Reavian carries me through a series of long, empty hallways. The other cells are vacant. It feels intentional, like they wanted us as far apart as possible.

To keep us broken.

"If she's not in this section, she's no longer here," Kaiel murmurs, as he opens the next door.

We find her three cells down. Crumpled on the floor, unmoving. Faint flickering light, almost like moonlight, comes from a single lantern at the end of the hall. It's just enough to see her.

Kaiel drops to his knees beside Brynn and presses two fingers to her neck.

"She's alive," he whispers, "but barely."

He lifts her gently into his arms.

I look up at Reavian. And for the first time, I really see him. The light brushes his face—illuminating a sharp jawline, and tousled black hair. Shadows carve beneath his cheekbones. His eyes meet mine.

And I see it.

The worry.

Flecks of gold and silver shimmer in the dark of his gaze, like stars caught in obsidian.

My fingers lift to his face on instinct. I brush them against his cheek.

"You're real," I whisper.

He smiles at me, but the worry in his gaze stays. His jaw tightens.

The escape is a blur. I drift in and out of consciousness.

We pass through black corridors, down a servant's staircase, then through the kitchens—where the smell of stale bread turns my stomach. That's all that I have been fed here.

Moldy scraps of bread.

Dirty water.

They press on a false panel in the kitchen wall behind some oak barrels. It leads us into a dark tunnel.

The space is damp and narrow. We move through the dark, until we reach the end, where a single rusted ladder waits. Kaiel sets Brynn down gently and climbs quickly, pushing the grate open. He disappears for a moment, then returns lifting her easily into one arm. He climbs again, lifting her above him to position her on the surface before pulling himself up after her.

"Okay, ready?" Reavian asks me.

I cling to him as tightly as I can in response. He lifts me, cradling me close as he begins the climb, one slow painful step at a time. Every part of my body is screaming. But I hold it in.

When we near the top, Kaiel is there, reaching down to help. Reavian only lets go, when he is sure Kaiel has me safely in his grasp. He pulls me to the surface with ease and sets me down next to Brynn. I weakly reach out to her, my trembling fingers brushing across her cheek. Her body is limp and if not for the faint, fragile rise of her chest, I would think she hadn't made it.

"Oh Brynn, we're out. We're out of that awful place. If you can hear me, you have to fight. You have to live," I rasp, tears blurring my vision.

Reavian climbs out and then Kaiel moves the metal grate back over the opening.

His dark eyes find mine, and I see the panic in them. He rushes over to where I have been slumped against a wall, gently lifting me into his arms again.

Moonlight filters through the gnarled canopy of twisted decayed trees, as Reavian carries me further into the night. I blink, willing my eyes to adjust. I have been in the dark for so long that the pale moonlight burns.

My breathing is shallow.

I glance down at myself; bruises bloom across my exposed skin like wilted violets. Cuts, scars, and burns are peppered across every part of my body that I can see. Every inch of me is marked.

My favorite dress, the last thing I have from home, is shredded, every remaining scrap soaked in blood and filth.

I am destroyed. My skin, once sun-kissed and warm, is now as pale as the moon.

How long have I been down there?

I look up at Reavian, and I catch the muscle in his jaw tightening again.

"What have they done to you?" he whispers, voice raw.

"Thank you...for coming to help," I murmur, my voice a whisper of a whisper. Broken and weak, like the rest of me.

It's then that I realize that I haven't given him my name.

I want to give him my true name.

I lift my gaze back to his.

"Auren...my name... is Auren."

The words leave me in a fragile breath, but something inside me clicks into place when they are spoken.

"Auren," he says, holding my gaze. His voice wraps around my name like a vow.

My breathing is growing more and more shallow. Something is wrong. His eyes tell me he knows it too. He pulls me closer, his arm steady around me, his hand protectively cupping the back of my head.

Beside us Kaiel carries Brynn's limp form. His face is sharp with grim determination. The men move quickly, their feet crunching against the blackened earth and brittle red vines. Until we reach a small clearing in the forest where two midnight black horses await us.

"We need a healer," Reavian says, his voice low as he shifts me carefully onto one of the horses. He carefully swings up behind me, then steadies me in front of him.

I cough and feel wetness seep out from my mouth, the coppery taste of blood on my tongue.

"A real one. Not someone with herbs and luck. A real healer, Kaiel," he adds, voice trembling with urgency.

I sway, fighting to stay conscious.

Kaiel adjusts Brynn on his horse and swings up behind her. "There's no one on this cursed island who wouldn't turn us in for favor or coin. You know that."

I hear Reavian curse under his breath. My head lolls to the side. I can't fade. Not yet. Darkness creeps in at the corners of my eyes.

"Stay with me," he whispers to me. "Please."

But I'm not really hearing him. His words are muffled. I barely feel the horse lurch forward, starting its rushed journey toward our destination. I'm hearing something else. Something older. Deeper. It slithers around me like silk, curling beneath my skin, around my thoughts, my bones—whispering like a wind through dying leaves. I feel my eyes grow heavy and begin to close them.

Stay Awake.

Stay Awake.

Stay Awake.

The voices are back; I feel a jolt within me and snap my eyes open.

Stop! You must stop, Little Light.

My lips barely move. "Wait..." I whisper.

"What?" Reavian asks.

"Stop," I rasp, leaning into him, my head falling back onto his chest, my body growing weaker by the minute.

He pulls on the reins. "Kaiel—halt."

Kaiel grunts, clearly annoyed, but obeys. "What now? Why are we stopping?"

I lift my head slowly, barely able to keep my eyes open. The whispers coil again, stronger this time, hissing like snakes inside my mind.

West. Go West.

I turn my head towards Reavian.

"We have to go west," I tell him.

"West?" Kaiel snaps. "There is nothing west. The docks are to the east. You want us to ride into nowhere with two dying girls?"

He's right. Brynn's dying. I'm dying. I can feel myself slowly fading.

West. Go West.

"Trust me. Please," I whisper to Reavian.

He doesn't hesitate. "We go west."

I feel him spur our horse into action.

Kaiel rides ahead of us, he hasn't spoken a word since Reavian made the choice to follow my plea. We ride fast and low, skimming the ridgeline. The trees here are dead are wrong —charred, twisted remnants strangled by crimson thorny vines. The further west we go, the more unnatural the air becomes. It thickens, and hums with something ancient. I can feel it deep within my bones.

Lantern light flickers in the distance. Kaiel draws his horse up short, and we follow suit.

"Wait," he breathes. "That sigil, on the sail. That's from the Realm of Tide and Storm."

Reavian turns sharply. "Are you sure?"

Kaiel's voice drops to a near growl. "Hide. Now."

The men dismount and tie our horses to a nearby tree. I cling to consciousness, my ribs screaming in protest as I'm lifted from the horse and carried to the scorched underbrush nearby. My body wants to give out, to fall into the dark, but the voices won't let me.

Awake.

Stay Awake.

Below us, the dark shale beach is swarming with movement. Knights from Tide and Storm herd people off a ship in neat, silent lines. Wagons wait on the far side of the ridgeline, loaded with people. As each wagon is filled to the brim, its driver spurs the horses forward, before vanishing in the distance. A man in polished black bone armor stands in front of the wagons, waiting for the rest of the people to be brought up by the silver armored soldiers.

Is it *him?*

The man that killed my parents?

"They're being conscripted," Kaiel mutters. "All of them."

I look up at Reavian. His mouth is drawn in a hard line; his eyes shadowed with something like grief. He pulls me closer, gently wrapping his arms around me like he can shield me from the world.

Hundreds of people shuffle past in silence. One by one, wagons swallow them into the night. Four silver armored knights herd them forward. The wagons creak and groan under the weight of bodies, until they vanish into the horizon. The last wagon pauses, until the bone armored knight mounts his steed and disappears with them.

Then, there's stillness.

I sag against Reavian's chest, barely breathing.

About fifteen minutes pass, and then the four silver armored knights turn and make their way back toward the ship.

That's when I see her.

A woman. Small, cloaked and lingering at the edge of the loading ramp.

Save her!

She must be saved!

Save her!

The voices are louder now. Urgent.

Chapter Nine-Reavian

"Auren... Gods no." She's stopped moving, her body going limp in my arms.

I rush onto the ship, heart pounding.

No, she has to be alive. She *has* to. Fresh blood spills from the corners of her mouth, as I lower my head to her chest. And there it is, a heartbeat. She's not gone. Just unconscious.

The woman we just saved appears next to me.

"I'm a healer," she says, her voice still shaking. "I can help her, help *them*."

Hope cracks open in my chest like a sudden sunrise. It's a feeling I'd forgotten exists.

"Down here, the captain's quarters should be below deck."

I follow her down, Kaiel close behind, carrying Brynn. We reach the captains quarters, the room is quiet, lit by a single lantern, a soft bed in the center. I lay Auren down gently on one side and Kaiel places Brynn on the other, before sprinting back up to secure the horses in the ship's hold.

The healer approaches and I take a step back, not wanting to get her way.

Suddenly Auren's eyes snap open, and she grabs my arm.

"Her first. Brynn first," she gasps. Then her hand falls away, she's passed out again.

The woman moves toward Brynn without hesitation, her hands already glowing with a soft pearly white light.

I sit beside Auren and gently brush the blood matted hair from her face, letting my thumb linger just beneath one of the bruises on her cheek.

Rage coils in my chest. I'll make them pay for hurting her, even if it's the last thing I do.

Even now, battered and broken, I see her—truly see her. Not the wounds. Just *her*. Her soul. And it's the most beautiful thing I've ever seen.

I linger for a moment, making sure I see her chest rise and fall with breath, before I rush out to help Kaiel get the ship in motion, to begin our journey to the Realm of Flame and Forest.

***

The sea stretches out like obsidian, glittering beneath the moon. I stand at the helm, my hands resting on the worn wood of the wheel, my eyes scanning the horizon. The wind tugs at my hair, cool and salted, while the sails above me swell with quiet groans. Behind me, Kaiel emerges from the lower deck, yawning and rubbing the back of his neck.

"She's holding steady," I murmur. We've been at sea for a few hours now. No word yet from the healer on how Auren and Brynn are doing.

Kaiel leans against the railing beside me, glancing up at the stars. "Feels strange, doesn't it? Just....drifting away from that place. Almost like we are ghosts now."

I give him a faint, humorless smile.

"Maybe we are."

A long silence passes between us before Kaiel tilts his head. "So, how did she know? Your girl, I mean."

I glance at him.

"Auren, her name is Auren."

Speaking her name settles something restless within me.

Kaiel nods toward the dark water.

"Auren," he says. "How did she know? The healer. The boat with plenty of rations for our journey. All of it. How the hell did *she know* to go west?"

I exhale slowly. I've wondered the same.

"I don't know. But when she told me...I just couldn't ignore it," I say.

Kaiel's brow furrows. "It's more than that. You knew to listen. Like you were always meant to. You've been seeing her in your dreams, man. Honestly, I just thought you were just a little bit crazy."

My fingers tighten on the wheel.

"Maybe it was just desperation," I murmur. "Or survival instinct."

Kaiel shrugs, but his voice is quieter now. "I don't believe it's just coincidence. We found a boat—nowhere near the docks. We found a healer, when that's exactly what we needed to save them. That's not just a bunch of coincidences, Reav. That's *something else*."

I don't respond. Instead, I turn toward the stairs leading below deck, where Auren lies being healed in the captain's quarters. I feel a silent thread tugging me toward her, soft and invisible, but somehow also unrelenting. I didn't feel this tug when we met in dreams, when I held her in my arms there. But I did feel like I was always searching for her. Always meant to find her. Like we were destined to meet in the darkness and carry one another out of it.

I turn back to Kaiel, but before I can speak, soft footsteps creak against the stairs behind me. The healer appears, her long cloak fluttering behind her like a ripple on water. She looks like the sea itself, calm on the surface, but something churns just beneath.

"They're stable," she says quietly, sinking onto a barrel beside the mast, clearly exhausted. "The healing process will take time. Some of their bones were shattered in places I couldn't even *feel* at first."

"Thank you," I say, the heavy weight of worry slowly lifting from my chest. "Truly."

She nods, her breaths shallow from the effort. "I'm Iska."

Kaiel steps forward, offering his hand. "I'm—"

"I know who you are," she cuts him off sharply.

I still, and she turns her gaze to me.

"I know who *both* of you are."

Silence falls between us all.

Her voice trembles, but not with fear. No... this is *fury*.

"How could you? How could you *let this happen* to my people?" Her eyes snap to Kaiel. "To *your* people!"

Kaiel takes a step back, visibly stricken. His throat bobs, but no words come out. He was just a boy when his father, aligned himself with my mother and Lucien. He was the commanding General of the Storm Knights, and he brought most of the army with him, leaving the realm essentially defenseless.

My chest aches for my friend as well as for Iska and her people.

"We didn't choose any of it," I say, desperate for her to understand.

"Didn't you?" she asks.

"We are victims of their evils too," I say quietly. "Just in different ways. We were born into a life we didn't ask for. Prisoners of those meant to love and protect us. Instead, surrounded by cruelty. We have always tried to find a way out. We *are* trying. But it's like a curse, Iska. One we never wanted."

She stares at me for a long moment—then slowly her shoulders drop. The anger on her face softens.

"Thank you for helping Auren, and Brynn," I add sincerely.

"Of course," Iska says. "And thank you...both of you...for helping me."

I nod once solemnly. "We are sailing to the Realm of Flame and Forest. To seek asylum with High Lord Vaedric Solmere. It will take us several weeks, but you are more than welcome to join us. Or...if there is somewhere else—"

"I can't go home," she interrupts. "You know why."

I meet her gaze. She doesn't have to explain. The emptiness in her voice says it all. She'd been chosen, offered up by the High Lady. Going back after escaping that fate would mean execution for treason.

"My family is gone," she continues. "Conscripted before me. There's nothing left to return to. *Nobody* to return to."

She turns to face the wind, thinking for a long moment.

Then, finally, she whispers, "I'll come with you."

Chapter Ten-Reavian

The days blur together. I spend my daylight hours below deck in the dim captain's quarters, where the only sounds I can focus on are the steady rise and fall of Auren's breaths, and the soft creak of the ship. A chair now sits permanently at her bedside. I never leave for long, and I haven't slept much either. Even when Kaiel offered to stay with her and Brynn while I rest in one of the other actual beds on the ship, I refused. I'm drawn to be at her side. That thread between us is pulling me closer, making it almost painful to be away.

There are moments when she stirs, her eyes fluttering open. Beautiful, deep blue eyes that are rimmed in gold. Her voice is raspy and uncertain. During those moments, we speak.

She had cried. Silent tears streamed down her cheeks as she told me about the night she was taken. She spoke of the shimmering barrier, and the crash. Her mother's bright blue blood...fae blood. Seeing her mother's pointed ears. The knight in bone armor that took her father from her. Before ripping her from the only life and world she'd ever known.

"I didn't know," she had said. "I didn't know I was fae."

"I'm sorry," I said to her, brushing her freshly rinsed, damp hair back to comfort her, until she fell back asleep.

Another afternoon those eyes fluttered open again.

"Do you believe in fate?" she whispered.

I hesitated for a moment.

"I didn't use to."

"I heard them," she murmured. "Voices. I think it's fate whispering to me. I heard them before the crash. They're the ones who told me to go West. Told me to save Iska. I thought I was losing my mind...*am I* losing my mind?"

"You're not," I told her. "When you told us to go west, something in me told me to trust you. To believe you. So, I did."

Today, I walk down from the upper deck and head to my spot next to her bed and she's sitting up on her own, she's waiting for me. My heart flutters in my chest. She looks much stronger today.

"You're awake," I say, voice rising with excitement, as I rush to her bedside and sit in the chair I've called home for weeks now.

"Yes. But Brynn still isn't," she says, looking sadly at her friend. "Iska told me that she's keeping her asleep for now. She needs deep rest to recover fully."

"Yes, she told me that as well. Try not to worry, she's strong. She must be, to have endured what she did," I tell her.

She opens up and begins telling me exactly what happened to them in the dungeons for the first time. She tells me of the things she endured from the guards, before telling me how Lucien took over the torture himself. She speaks about how Brynn was sent to find her in the human realm, and how she was punished when she failed to return with Auren.

A year and a half.

Brynn endured daily torture for A year and a half, to try and protect her friend.

"He made me watch," she whispers, her voice cracking and tears streaming down her cheeks. "He *made me watch*."

"I'm so sorry," I tell her, my voice breaking.

I know what goes on in those dungeons. The horrors they inflict on people there to get what they want. I have even been in them myself. I look at Auren, and I know that I won't let anyone touch her *ever* again.

I think of all the ways I'll make Lucien—and every guard who touched her, or her friend pay. I clench my fists at my sides discreetly and try to remain calm. *For her.*

"I don't have them. These powers they think that I have... they wouldn't come. They thought that I would manifest them, to maybe save myself. But they never came, because I don't *have* any power. If I did, when he started to hurt Brynn in front of me, I would have given him every ounce of it. To make her pain stop, to make *my* pain stop. Every last drop of it."

She sobs and I grab her hand in mine, rubbing it softly to comfort her.

And then she asks the question I have been dreading since the first time we spoke. Because once she knows who I am, she'll never look at me the same again. I won't be the boy from our shared dream, who held her in the darkness. She'll see me for what I truly am.

"How did you get to me inside that place?" she asks.

The silence after the question feels heavy. I take a deep breath, preparing myself to tell her the truth. She deserves it. Even if she hates me for it afterward.

"I told you my name was Reavian. My full name is Reavian Nyvaris. The woman who had you sent to the dungeons was my mother, Liraeth Nyvaris Veylas. The man that did unspeakable things to you, is her husband— Lucien Veylas," I say, my voice cracking. My eyes begin to sting with tears threatening to surface.

I look at this beautiful woman my own family tried to destroy. They tried to break her. And if I hadn't found her, they would've killed her.

"I live there. *Lived* there, I mean. That's how I was able to get to you."

I can't hold them back anymore, the tears of my shame now staining my cheeks. The sensation is strange, I don't cry. I never have. But in this moment, with *her*, it feels safe to be vulnerable.

Auren doesn't flinch. Instead, she reaches out with her other hand and covers mine, squeezing it gently.

"It's okay," she says softly. "It wasn't you. You saved me. Even in my darkest dreams, you were always the one who reached for me."

***

Nights on the sea were mine to command now. I grip the wheel and feel the sea breeze against my skin. Heavy footsteps sound from the stairs behind me, and I recognize them as Kaiel's.

"You should be resting," I say to him.

"Meh," Kaiel says. "She's healing well, both of them are."

I nod, smiling briefly. She has been getting stronger; she's doing so well. How anyone could be this strong after enduring what she has baffles me. The realization that she is going to be alright calms me. For the first time in my life, I feel at peace.

She brings me peace.

I guess, in a way, she always has. I would look for her every time I ended up in that shadowed dream, and when I found her, my soul would settle.

Kaiel looks at me sideways.

"You're in deep, huh?" he asks, that shit eating grin of his, plastered across his face.

I give my friend a faint, crooked smile.

"I don't know how to explain it. I don't know her yet. Not *really*. But it's like...I've known her forever. My chest aches when I leave her side. And when she's awake, when she speaks, it's like...the rest of the world just disappears."

Kaiel is quiet for a moment. Then he says, "Maybe you two are fated."

I turn toward him, and he shrugs.

"The priestesses in the Storm Temple used to speak of it. It happens. Not often. But when it does...they say the bond is ancient. Souls linked by fate itself. They find each other over and over, in every life. It's destiny."

I swallow. "That's what this feels like. Like she is mine, and I am hers. I would die for her without a second thought."

Kaiel smiles, though I note that it seems tinged with a little sadness. He claps his hand on my shoulder.

"Well, don't die brother, you have only just found each other again."

"Don't say anything about this to her, please Kaiel," I say. "I don't want to scare her, she's been through enough."

My friend nods and pats me on the back.

"Alright, I'm going to sleep. Don't wreck us before I wake up," he chuckles as he disappears below deck.

***

Before I know it, a couple weeks have passed.

I wake to Kaiel calling me and swing myself out of bed. I have been sleeping on a cot just outside the girls' door for a few days now. It's as far away as I will allow myself to be from her. I run above deck to see what he needs.

"What is it?" I ask. "Is something wrong?"

"Look," Kaiel says, pointing ahead of us.

In the hazy distance, I see the Pyrethorn Divide. A scarlet mountain range that protects Solmere Hold, in the Realm of Flame and Forest.

"We've made it," I say to my friend with a smile tugging at my lips.

I hear footsteps behind me and turn to see Auren slowly making her way up the steps, Iska and Brynn just behind her.

The girls have begun to walk on their own again, slowly and stiffly.

Brynn has been quiet. Hollow-eyed. She flinches at loud sounds and won't meet anyone's gaze. Not even Auren's. She hasn't spoken a word to anyone. Kaiel has been visiting her and Auren, telling them stories and jokes—anything he can to try to cheer them up.

I watch as Auren and Iska help sit Brynn down on one of the barrels on deck, before she begins to walk over to me.

"Can you keep an eye on things here for a second?" Kaiel asks me.

I notice his gaze on Brynn and nod. I watch as he walks over to strike up a conversation with Iska, but his gaze remains on Brynn.

Auren approaches and leans against the rail near me, watching the horizon. I don't say anything, I just watch as the golden light of the day dances across her now rosy skin and glitters in her long golden hair. She closes her eyes, and tilts her head up, feeling the warmth of the sun on her face. Taking in deep breaths of the salt kissed air. She's perfect. Every part of her is perfect.

She opens her eyes and turns to me.

"Is that it? The place you told me about?"

"Yes," I answer her. "We should be at the shore in a few hours."

"Do you think he will help us? Hide us away from those that want to hurt us?" she asks.

"I don't know, not for sure," I answer her honestly.

She nods.

"I'm glad it was you... you know," she says, her voice soft. "When I was alone in my dreams, and that night alone in the dungeon. I wasn't sure if I had imagined you..."

I lock the wheel in position moving next to her, taking her hand.

"You don't have to be alone ever again if you don't want to be. I'll be there whenever you need me," I say to her, and I mean it. I know how ridiculous it sounds. She's been through so much. We have only just met. But if she'll let me stand by her side, I *know* I will remain there for the rest of my days.

Realizing I might be coming on a little strong, I panic a bit and take a small step back.

But she doesn't seem frightened.

Instead, she embraces me like she used to in our shadowed dreams, resting her head on my chest. And in that moment, with the fire-kissed mountains in the distance, I know my life is no longer my own.

It belongs to her.

Chapter Eleven—Auren

After being at sea for weeks, I'm ecstatic to see solid land in front of me. Kaiel and Reavian have dropped anchor at the shoreline and are now getting the horses saddled and ready to descend the ramp onto the shore of the Realm of Flame and Forest.

I cannot wait to get off this boat.

"I don't know about you, but I am so glad to see dry land," I say to Brynn, who's sitting silently next to me.

She doesn't reply. She never does. It's strange seeing her this way. She has such a bold personality. She's strong, brave, and the life of the party, the total opposite of me. I brush away a strand of hair that the wind has blown into her eyes. Iska found a pair of scissors on the ship and evened Brynn's hair into a short bob. It looks better now, but it still feels like a loss. Her hair used to be so long and beautiful before they hacked it to pieces.

"It's a beautiful day, isn't it?" I ask her.

The sun is shining, blanketing us in its warmth.

Over the last couple of weeks, our skin has gone from pallid, to being rosy and a tad sun kissed. That part of us is getting back to normal. Iska's healing abilities have rid us of all the physical reminders of what happened to us. The bruises and the cuts have all healed. The scars have disappeared, as if they were never there at all. But the mental scars…I believe they will always be a part of us.

No magic will be able to erase those.

Kaiel and Reavian are walking hurriedly up and down the ramp, bringing bags of supplies down for the horses to carry. Reavian told me it may take a couple days of land travel to get to Solmere. Apparently, it's surrounded by those giant scarlet mountains, protecting the keep and the city from anything outside of it. Only one guarded entrance.

"What do you think about them, our companions?" I ask Brynn, not really expecting a response. "Iska is nice, though she *is* quite stern and serious."

I suppose that fits with her being a healer. I watch her as she discusses something with Reavian. Power in a petite package. Her presence is more intimidating than even Kaiel.

"Kaiel is kind and funny…which is ironic because he looks absolutely terrifying," I say, shaking my head.

He is so tall, must be nearly seven feet, almost a foot taller than Reavian. Wild long brown hair and built like what my dad would have called a *brick shit house*.

Dad.

A wave of sadness washes over me.

I force a smile, trying to remain positive in front of my friend.

"And that one," I say pointing at Reavian. I watch his tall, lean muscled frame carry a final bag down the ramp, his tousled black hair blowing into his eyes. "Somehow, I feel like we have known each other forever. Remember when I told you about my nightmares? And you told me that sometimes dreams are a link to other possibilities?"

I squeeze my friend's hand. No reply reaches her lips. She's still staring down at the ground.

"Well…I believe you were right. Turns out the guy from them is real. And never in a million years would I have thought that somehow, I would be fae—*or* that fae were real for that matter, and not just part of some fairytale that children read about. I wish you would have told me, I wish Mom told me…"

I sigh.

The memories of my mother and father the night of the crash flash through my mind. I fight back the tears that are trying to force their way out of my eyes.

"I'm sorry, Brynn. I'm sorry for what happened to you because of me… and that I couldn't make it stop. I'm sorry that I couldn't manifest whatever power they thought I had."

The tears begin to flow down my face freely now, my efforts to hold them back in vain.

Brynn squeezes my hand. It's faint, *but noticeable.*

"If I could have given them what they wanted to make them stop hurting you, I would have. I hope you know that. My dad was human, so I have to be half human. I must not have gotten whatever power they think that I have," I say.

Another faint squeeze on my hand.

"Thank you, for trying to protect me."

Iska is approaching us now, her footsteps quick.

"How are you feeling?" she asks.

"I'm alright, stronger every day. I feel way more surefooted now," I tell her, wiping away remnants of my tears.

She nods in response.

"Good, then help me get Brynn down the ramp, it's been decided that the men will be walking, and we will be riding the horses," Iska says.

***

The heat is rising with every step we take. We have been traveling through the outer edges of the Realm of Flame and Forest for hours now. The Pyrethorn Divide is looming ever larger ahead, a deep crimson, jagged against a now hazy ember-streaked sky. Around us, towering giant trees with blackened trunks and canopies of glowing red and orange leaves that flicker in the wind like tongues of fire. It's as if the entire forest burns eternally, without ever being fully consumed.

I can't stop looking.

I turn my head slowly, trying to take it all in. Hearing the way the leaves rustle like whispers, and how the branches bend slightly toward me as we pass, almost like the trees are waving a greeting.

No one else seems to notice.

Overhead, sleek birds with flickering wings soar between the trees, trailing embers behind them like comet tails. Their cries are melodic and haunting.

"How is any of this real?" I whisper to Brynn, who is behind me on the horse, her grip on me strong.

"It's beautiful, isn't it?" Kaiel asks from my left. He's walked alongside Brynn and I this whole time. Reavian has been walking ahead of us, scouting for any signs of danger.

"Breathtaking," I reply.

I glance toward him and smile.

"Thank you...for what you did. For helping save me, for saving Brynn."

Kai gives me a small but genuine smile.

"Nah, I was being selfish. If we hadn't saved you guys, we wouldn't be able to have our very much overdue vacation now," he jokes.

I laugh.

"Seriously though, thank you."

He nods.

I note the sword strapped to his back. My mind flashes to that night on the road with my parents. I was helpless. I *felt* helpless. If I'm being honest, I've felt that way my whole life. Constant anxiety about what could happen. I let fear cripple me. I don't want to feel...to *be* helpless like that anymore.

"Do you think you could teach me how to use one of those?" I ask, nodding toward the sword on his back.

"Sure. If they don't roast us at the gates of Solmere, I can train you there. I'll make sure you become a menace with a sword like me, and I *guess* Reavian too. But don't tell him I said that. Gotta keep him humble and all," he laughs.

I smile.

"It's a deal then," I say, then remember the first part of what he said. "Wait, you don't think they'll actually roast us at the gates, do you?"

He shrugs.

"Anything is possible, but it doesn't seem like it would be Vaedric's style, at least from what I have heard about him."

"He would not. Not only because he is a good, fair man. But also, because of his curious nature. He will wonder why certain members of this party have come here, and will no doubt want to know what they want," Iska interjects from her horse just ahead of us.

When we were on the ship, Reavian had told me about who he was, who his mother was. And that Lucien was his mother's husband. He told me of the atrocities that Liraeth and Lucien had committed against the High King as well as the other realms. Declaring themselves king and queen of Ashwynn Reach, when no such title even existed. There are High Lords and High Ladies. But there has not been a High King or a High Queen since Lucien stormed the castle and murdered them, as well as their child.

His own flesh and blood.

His brother.

They are monsters. Not people. Not fae. Only beasts, with no care for anyone other than themselves and what they feel is owed to them.

One night when Kaiel came in to talk to Brynn and I, he told me of the beatings that Liraeth would give Reavian for not being like she expected him to be. She sensed the kindness in him and called it weakness. Lucien apparently took an interest in Reavian and Kaiel, forcing them to train for his private army. Sending them on missions to do awful things.

The memory of what he told us that night makes me eye the sword on his back again.

They need to pay for what they have done to the innocent people here, for what they did to my parents, to Brynn, and to me. I need to get stronger, so I can defend myself and those that I care about if I need to.

"Hold!" I hear Reavian call.

We all stop, and he strides toward us.

"Let's take a break, rest, and get something to eat," he says.

"Let me help you," I hear from my left as Kaiel helps lift Brynn off the horse. I watch him as he leads her over to a tree and has her sit down. I slide off the horse myself and then rifle through one of the saddlebags for a waterskin and three apples. I walk over to Brynn and hand her the waterskin first.

"Here, I know I'm thirsty, so you must be too."

Without a word, she takes it and drinks a few sips. She notices the apples in my hand shortly after.

"I bet you're hungry too," I say, handing her an apple and smiling when she bites into it.

I toss an apple to Kaiel, which he catches expertly, and I take a swig from the waterskin before tossing that to him as well. I take a bite of my apple. My mouth explodes with the flavor of it. The food here has so much more flavor than what I was used to at home. The sweetness of the apple seems to dance on my tongue.

"She's getting stronger," Kaiel says, nodding towards Brynn. "She's not a hundred percent, but her steps are getting steadier."

I smile. "She is."

"Well..." Kaiel says, approaching me after I discard the core of my apple into the forest. "Now that we're done eating, how about a lesson?"

I blink.

"A lesson?"

"You said you wanted to learn, and it seems that I've found myself with some time." He removes the sword from his back and gestures for me to follow him a few feet away, to a small break in the trees.

"I'll be right over there, Brynn. If you need anything, just come and get me ok?" She doesn't respond, but stares toward the clearing where Kaiel stands waiting for me.

"I thought you said you would show me *after* we got to Solmere," I say.

"Eh, I guess I changed my mind," he says, extending the sword toward me hilt first.

I smile and take it, the weight of it nearly yanking my arm toward the ground.

"This is heavier than I thought," I tell him, trying and failing to adjust my grip on it.

Kaiel circles behind me and gently adjusts it for me.

"Loosen up your fingers a bit and rest the hilt here, along your palm. You don't want to fight the sword, you want it to move with you, like an extension of you."

I do as he says and adjust my grip. It's still heavy, but markedly easier to hold this way.

"Do I look cool yet?" I ask him, still struggling against the weight of the sword.

"You look like you may drop it and stab yourself in the foot any moment now," he teases, moving his hand down to guide my elbow up. "But hey, I'll give you some points for effort."

I laugh. It's light and breathy, a rare moment of levity in the shadows of all that has happened. I try to take a swing...wobble...and then stumble back with a surprised yelp.

"Okay," Kaiel says quickly, taking the sword back from me. "I think that's enough for the day."

I spin toward him, frowning a bit. "What? It's only been a couple of minutes..."

I trail off, noting the subtle glance Kaiel throws over my shoulder.

I turn, seeing Reavian standing off to the side of Brynn, mid-conversation with Iska. His arms are folded, and he has a brow lifted in amusement, or is that *judgement*?

I turn back to Kaiel, who reads the question right off my face. He smirks.

"He gets like that if I steal attention away from him. I try not to enjoy it. *Too* much."

We both share a laugh, and I shake my head. But I feel a little flutter in my chest at the same time.

I look back toward Reavian. Iska is saying something, her expression serious. He responds to her with a nod. His shoulders seem tense.

"Soon," he tells her, the word quick and his voice low. Not at all like the caring male that I had become accustomed to on the ship.

"What's wrong with him?" I ask Kaiel, noting again how closed off Reavian seems. "Is he upset about something? I haven't seen him like this before."

Kaiel shrugs, and his expression softens. "He's always that way. Quiet, broody... in his head."

"But he hasn't been that way with me," I say. It comes out more a question than a statement.

Kaiel smiles.

"Yeah. That's the strange thing. I've known him most of my life—we're basically brothers. But it took years for him to really let me in. He doesn't *ever* let people in. Where we were raised, showing emotion is weakness. We are trained from a young age not to have emotion, or emotional attachments. It's a vulnerability we are told we cannot afford."

I look down and grip my fingers tightly on the hem of my tunic.

"I had memories of my mother to keep me grounded. Reav didn't really have anyone, it took me a long time to break through the wall he keeps up. Even after all this time, I think I've only made a small hole in it," Kaiel says.

I glance back over at Reavian and as if feeling my gaze, his eyes meet mine. His face relaxes and a soft smile forms on his lips.

"That right there," Kaiel says, his voice low. "I have never seen *that* happen. Don't let him pull away from that."

And with that Kaiel walks away.

Chapter Twelve–Auren

Another few hours have passed. The sun that once shone brightly above us, is now beginning to set. The trees thin just slightly, and the dark earthy ground gives way to stone, our horses' hooves skitter across slick patches of obsidian. The tree line breaks, and we come to an open clearing of stone, dense forest picking up again on the other side.

"Dismount," Reavian calls out from ahead of us, "We should walk through here."

It's then that I see fissures cutting through the ground like open wounds, glowing faintly orange from within. The wind hisses. It's hot, dry, and smells of smoke.

We get off our horses, Kaiel lending his left arm to Brynn, to help her keep steady as we navigate the terrain. I grab the reins for my horse, guiding it gently forward. After a few dozen steps, a low groan rumbles beneath our feet.

Iska's horse startles, rearing up.

"I can't hold on to him if he keeps this up much longer!" she cries out.

Reavian, who is still ahead scouting, spins and runs back to help her.

Another groan sounds beneath our feet. This one is louder, and way more ominous. My horse rears, pulling against the reins, and jolting me off balance. I lose my grip and stumble backwards. My heart races as I watch the horse bolt, vanishing into the forest we just came from. Half of our supplies disappear with it.

"Shit!" Kaiel shouts, seeing my horse disappear.

"I'm sorry," I say. "I couldn't hold on."

Another rumble, deeper and more violent. I slip on the rocks beneath my feet and land hard on a large piece of warm obsidian.

I stand up quickly.

Then, the earth around me splits wide.

I scream as the stone beneath my feet gives way. Without thinking, I leap to a narrow outcropping just a few feet ahead. The stone trembles but holds.

Suddenly, steam bursts upward behind me, cutting me off from the others with a network of widening cracks and hissing vents.

"Auren!" I hear Reavian shout, his voice booming like thunder. I watch him drop the reins, our final horse fleeing into the safety of the forest, then he surges toward me.

Before anyone can stop him, another geyser explodes behind the group, this one dangerously close to Brynn. I watch in horror as she cries out, slipping on loose stone.

Kaiel reacts instantly, throwing himself between her and the blast, yanking her back by the waist and shielding her with his body just as steam erupts behind them.

The blast scorches his left arm, searing away his sleeve in an instant. Angry blisters rise across reddening skin.

Somehow, he doesn't cry out, he just grits his teeth and mutters, "That's going to hurt later."

As he stumbles back with Brynn in his arms, I see Reavian already moving toward me again, panic etched into every line of his face.

"No, stop!" I shout, throwing up my hand. "Don't move!"

Geysers begin to erupt all around me at different intervals. The ground beneath us is breaking apart, alive and breathing with instability. The air pulses with heat and danger, and the earth groans like it's going to split me from them forever.

Reavian doesn't listen, I watch as he steps forward anyway, his jaw clenched with desperation.

Iska grabs his arm just in time, yanking him back as a geyser of scalding steam explodes just inches from where he'd been standing.

"I'd *really* rather not have to heal both you and Kaiel today," she snaps.

Reavian stills, breathing hard, his eyes locked on mine like I might vanish at any second.

"I'll figure it out," I say, forcing my voice to stay steady. Forcing myself to stay calm. I take a deep breath, shoving down the fear and rising anxiety. *I can't let it overtake me.*

"Just...give me a minute," I tell him.

The ground pulses beneath my feet, pressure building and releasing in waves.

I close my eyes.

I can feel something beneath my skin, and beneath the stone.

A rhythm, a breath.

And then... the voices come.

Yes, Little Light. Feel.

Listen. Trust.

Step Now.

I open my eyes and take a step forward, somehow timed perfectly with a pause in the geysers.

"Auren, wait... stop I'll be right there, Reavian calls.

"No, it's ok. Just wait, please..." I tell him.

Another step. Then two.

I turn back toward the others.

"There's a pattern. I can feel it...I can hear it!"

Reavian looks at me stunned, but nods.

I close my eyes and reach for those inner voices again.

Yes, Little Light.

We will help you.

Trust. Listen.

I open my eyes and feel that I can fully trust the voices within me. I begin moving, calling out the rhythm I've found to everyone.

When to step, when to wait. I map the pulses and guide them across.

Iska helps Kaiel, supporting his injured side while he carefully helps Brynn over the fissures.

Reavian crosses last. Not moving an inch, watching every step I take until I reach the other side safely.

When everyone makes it across, it feels like we all exhale as one.

Kaiel collapses to the ground, clutching his arm. "Worst vacation ever," he murmurs.

Iska kneels beside him, already summoning soft, glowing light to her palm. "Hold still," she commands.

Brynn walks to Kaiel and sits down beside him. She grabs his hand and holds it. Their eyes meet, but no words pass between them.

Reavian steps close to me and brushes my face with the back of his hand.

"You...you could have died," he says quietly.

"But I didn't," I whisper back, my voice steady. For the first time, I didn't let the anxiety overtake me.

He quietly checks over me, making sure I'm not injured. When he's satisfied, he sits down beside me and pulls me into his arms. And for a little while, he just holds me.

After Iska finishes tending to Kaiel's arm, and we all catch our breath, we walk to the edge of the rocky terrain, and into the forest on the other side. We put enough distance between us and the geysers that we feel comfortable resting for the night. I lean up against a tree near Brynn and close my eyes.

Letting sleep take me.

Chapter Thirteen - Auren

I wake below flame colored canopies. Birdsong laces the morning air, it's haunting and melodic, unlike anything I've ever heard at home. When I sit up, the trees around us sway in the breeze, their towering trunks are an almost charred looking black. Sunlight filters through the branches in golden shafts, casting flickering patterns on the forest floor.

I stand slowly, brushing debris from my shirt and pants. Around me the others begin to stir. Kaiel stretches with a groan. Reavian rises slowly at the tree across from me, where he slept all night. Iska walks over to Kaiel, grabbing his arm to check her work, her golden eyes narrowed in focus.

I stretch and look up at the trees again, and I notice some of the branches bending toward me, ever so slightly. Not shifting with the wind, but with *intent*. It feels like the forest is greeting me.

I reach and gently touch a branch, whispering, "I see you too."

We set out on foot through the forest, heading toward our destination. A slow and deliberate pace is set. Brynn is getting stronger every day, but she still has to walk slowly. I notice that

Kaiel's arm is pink now, but all of the horrible blisters are gone. Thank goodness for Iska, because that had looked incredibly painful.

I look up and see those birds again, gliding silently above the trees, their wings trailing faint sparks almost like comet trails.

"What are those called?" I ask no one in particular, watching them while walking forward with the rest of the group.

Suddenly, my foot catches on a twisted root, sending me stumbling forward. A hand catches me around my waist before I hit the ground.

Reavian's hand.

He steadies me easily.

"Sparksingers," he answers, giving me a soft smile.

I straighten myself, my cheeks warm with embarrassment.

"Try not to faceplant in the sacred forest. The trees may take offense," Kaiel jokes.

"I don't know, I think the trees seem to like me," I retort.

"They aren't the only ones," Reavian says to me softly, before stepping ahead again.

My cheeks flush at his words.

We haven't gone too far before the trees part into a narrow glade, where the sun pours through, reflecting off a small pond filled with glowing red water.

Firewater.

I stop dead in my tracks. Remembering the excruciating pain

of that substance being poured into my open wounds. Of seeing Lucien pour it into Brynn's wounds. I start to breathe heavily, my heartbeat pounding out of my chest. I can't get enough air. I feel the pain again. I can smell and feel the burning of my flesh. I can't breathe. I can't... My hands start to tingle, and my vision darkens at the edges.

"Auren?" Reavian asks. "Are you alright?"

I'm not. I'm not alright.

I hear footsteps approaching me, but I can't take my eyes off the water. Someone grabs my hand and squeezes it gently. I look up and see Brynn looking at me.

"It's ok," she says softly, her voice cracking. The first words I have heard her say since we escaped that place. I slowly start to catch my breath. My heartbeats begin to slow. Brynn doesn't let go of my hand.

"I have missed your voice so much," I say, gently squeezing her hand back.

A half smile appears across her face, and we both turn back toward the pond. We escaped that place, and we are *never* going back.

We continue walking hand in hand, providing each other with strength. The others just a little ahead of us.

A small herd of strange, elegant creatures emerge from our left, nearing the pond. They are deer-like, with branch woven antlers that match the trees above. Their skin looks like bark, and their movements are fluid, almost dreamlike.

"Cradlehorns," Iska says, her voice softer than usual.

The creatures stop in the center of the glade and watch us, before gliding away back into the forest.

I turn my head slightly to study Iska. She's striking, a little older than the rest of us, with tawny skin, and silver hair braided down her back. Her bright golden eyes shimmer in the sunlight. She looks like she is built for battle, but something behind her eyes tells me she carries quiet pain.

"I haven't been here since I was a little girl," she says after a moment. "My parents and I used to visit a family friend in the city here."

"Where are you from?" I ask her.

"I'm from the Realm of Tide and Storm, like Kaiel. I was born along the coast. Storms were like lullabies where I grew up...but this place always stayed with me."

She looks around with a flicker of nostalgia.

"What else lives in these forests?" I ask her.

"Emberbeasts," she says with a faint smile.

"That sounds...ominous," I reply.

"Quite the opposite actually," she says, explaining "They are large, cat-like creatures. Made of the ash wood, shaped by magic. Glowing red hearts of Eternal Flame beat in their chests. They are guardians of this realm. Wise, fierce, and beautiful."

"I want to see one," I declare.

"Count me in *if* it's in a good mood," Kaiel chuckles.

I walk in thoughtful silence for a while. This world is incredible. I'm awestruck every time I see something new.

"Can I ask you all, something personal?"

"Sure," Reavian says.

"Do you all have magic, like special powers? When I was...well you know. They wanted me to manifest power that I clearly don't have...I was wondering if you guys had powers."

A beat or two passes.

"Well, you have seen mine. I was blessed with mending magic," Iska says. "Which has been very useful as of late."

I hear Kaiel snort.

"Behold," he lifts his hand and summons a tiny ball of glowing light no bigger than an apple. It hovers lazily between his fingers. "And... that's about it."

I stare.

"I mean that's still pretty cool to me, you know. I lived in a world where magic is something you only read about in books," I tell him.

"My father can command storms, and my mother could control the tides. Me? I'm basically a glorified lantern. Pretty sure I'm a disappointment to dear old Dad," Kaiel says.

I don't miss the hurt in his voice.

I offer him a small sympathetic smile. "Maybe it just hasn't been awakened yet."

"Maybe," he says with a shrug. "But most likely, I'm just defective."

Brynn lets go of my hand and walks a little faster, placing herself beside Kaiel. He gives her a soft smile. She doesn't say anything as she walks beside him, she doesn't seem to need to.

"I can summon shadows," Reavian says, his voice grim.

"You've never told me that," Kaiel says, his brow furrowed.

"I've only done it a couple of times," Reavian says, the words sounding like something he'd rather forget. "But it's not something I let myself explore. I push it down."

"Why not?" I ask him.

He doesn't look back at me. "Because the power comes from my mother's bloodline. Everything from her is tainted, and I'm not interested in becoming like her."

There is no humor in his voice, only steel.

I can somehow *feel* his inner turmoil and his pain. It's sharp and deep. His hands are clenched at his sides. I walk faster to catch up with him.

He notices and slows his pace slightly to match mine.

"I'm sorry, I didn't mean to..." I murmur, my voice hushed.

"Don't be sorry," he says quickly. "It's alright."

I reach out and take his hand on instinct, and feel that turmoil fall away from him, his posture softens.

As the day stretches on, I find myself talking more. I tell them about my parents, my world, and the differences between where I came from and this place. The others listen with a quiet awe—except for Brynn. She lived there with me once, even if only for a little while.

"I miss a lot of things," I tell them laughing. "Like Captain Crunch Cereal— the one with the crunchy berries. Or folding laundry while my mom hummed her favorite songs in the kitchen, and Dad's pancakes…"

Kaiel grins. "What is Captain Crunch Cereal?"

"A magical thing from my world, that I will figure out how to recreate if we survive all this."

Even Reavian cracks a faint smile.

Iska looks at me, her golden eyes full of something soft. "You were lucky," she says.

"I was," I agree. "And I didn't even realize it."

***

As the sun sinks lower, and the shadows lengthen, I notice the forest beginning to change. The trees grow sparse. The red and orange leaves give way to ashen branches. Brittle and silent. These trees do not greet me as the others did. The air grows thick with the scent of burnt earth. The birds have vanished; the only sound we hear now is the crunch of our boots through the ashen soil.

This scarred expanse of forest not only looks but *feels* dead. The trees are split and charred. No signs of life anywhere.

I can feel a wrongness deep in my bones.

"Something feels *off* here," I murmur. "Do you guys see any fissures? Geysers? Like before?

A chill skims down my spine. Just the memory of what happened last time is enough to twist dread deep in my gut.

Reavian scans the path ahead of us.

"Nothing yet," he says, his voice low. "But stay close." He tightens his grip on my hand and gently draws me closer, like he's already preparing for what we might find.

With every step we take, the peaks of the Pyrethorn Divide seem to grow taller. It shouldn't be much farther now.

Iska stops abruptly. "I need a break, and if any of you argue, I'll wait 'til you're asleep and set your boots on fire. We've been walking nonstop for hours."

Kaiel raises both hands in defeat. "Alright, alright –you win."

"I don't like the look of this place, I'm not sure it's the best spot to rest," Reavian says.

He's right. This place feels strange.

"We. Are. Resting. Right. Now," Iska snaps, plopping down onto the ground dramatically.

I sit down in between Brynn and Reavian. He puts his arm around me, pulling me close and I rest my head on his shoulder.

"Just stay close. Something's not right," he murmurs.

We act like we have been together forever. It's odd, especially after physically knowing one another for such a short time. But it feels right...*natural*. Like our souls have been searching for each other forever and are content to have finally been reunited.

The forest is still.

But I can almost feel eyes in the stillness, watching from the dark.

And for the first time since arriving in this realm it doesn't feel welcoming.

It feels like a warning.

Chapter
Fourteen—Auren

Night has fully swallowed the land, and the decayed forest around us remains silent and heavy. Even the wind doesn't seem to move here. Where the trees had once seemed to be whispering silent greetings to me, leaning close with curiosity, now they stand still. Burnt and broken, hollowed by something far more ancient and cruel than just fire alone.

I sit cross-legged, my arms wrapped tightly around me. I can feel it, the emptiness. This place has no hum like I felt in the other parts of the forest, that thrumming I had felt in the marrow of my bones is now gone. There is just silence.

Wrong and aching silence.

Kaiel tries to break the tension. He stands and stretches out with a dramatic groan.

"Well," he says, summoning a sphere of soft bluish light with a flick of his fingers, "I suppose this is one of the only times my little party trick comes in handy."

The orb he summoned hovers above us, casting its gentle glow across our dirt-streaked faces.

It's actually quite beautiful. Soothing, even. But it doesn't chase away the wrongness pressing in on me from our surroundings.

I notice Reavian watching me from where he sits beside me, his eyes catching the fae light, the silver and gold flecks in them glimmering like stars.

"What is it?' he asks me softly, sensing my tension.

"I can't feel it. The forest, I felt it before. It felt full of life, almost happy to see us. This place... I don't feel that anymore, it's gone."

I look around, the dark withered branches looming over our heads look like skeletal arms. "Everywhere else, it seemed to whisper to me. But here...it's silent. Dead."

Reavian's brows furrow, and for a moment he says nothing. Then he quickly rises to his feet, his expression turning to stone.

"We move. Now. We are not far from Solmere," he says in a tone that brooks no argument.

Even Iska grumbles her agreement and stands brushing off her thighs. "Fine. But if any of Vaedric's men try to stop me from getting my sore legs into a hot bath, be prepared for battle."

Kaiel chuckles. "Gods above, I believe she means that."

"I'm *always* serious about hot baths," Iska mutters.

We press on, walking through the graveyard of blackened trees and brittle ash. The forest floor crunches beneath our feet like bone dust.

I stay close to Reavian, and my thoughts drift back to my old life, the one I've lost. The darkness around us now seems to creep inside me, feeding on the sadness I carry.

Reavian breaks the silence.

"If you could go back," he asks, his voice low, earnest. "To your world...would you?"

I think on it for a long moment, my eyes fixed ahead.

"There's nothing left for me there. My parents are gone," I say, holding back tears. The ache of it pulses in my chest, cracking my heart in two.

"And Brynn...she's here. She is the only friend I've ever had. So, no... I don't think I would go back."

Reavian glances at me, his strides one with mine.

"I know this situation we are in isn't ideal. But I would like it if you stayed," he tells me, his voice soft, tender. "I would like to know you, Auren."

My heart flutters. Something about the way he says my name makes me feel anchored, even here in this creepy forest. It's strange how comfortable he makes me feel, like I've known him forever. But I guess, in a way I have. He was always there in my dreams. Always providing me comfort, distracting me with stories. Sometimes even making me laugh. With what I know about his life now, I hope that I provided him with some comfort too.

Kaiel's voice chimes in behind us. "Well, I would like to be someone that you would consider a friend, Auren. In my own, how do you describe me, Reav... insufferable way?"

Reavian groans and Kaiel laughs.

"Yes, that's it. I would like to be an insufferable and yet also still charming friend to you," Kaiel says.

"I would like that, Kaiel," I say with a giggle.

I turn my gaze toward Reavian, and speak to him softly. "I would like to know —"

Before I can finish, I can feel something change. My breath catches.

The air itself has shifted.

I freeze.

Then I hear them.

Run.

Run now.

They are coming.

They hunt.

"What's wrong?" Reavian asks me, stopping dead in his tracks. The others follow suit.

"We need to run," I say sharply. "Right now."

Kaiel blinks, "What?"

Run.

Run now.

They hunt. They hunt.

Run.

The voices seem more urgent this time.

"We need to run," I say, my voice raised. "Now!"

A sound crackles through the night, a low and heavy snap of a branch.

We all turn toward it.

Dark shapes move in the shadows in the distance, illuminated by the moonlight. Twisted and crawling low with malformed limbs.

Iska's voice comes out like a hiss. "Emberbeasts... no it can't be, their hearts," she squints. "They're supposed to glow red with Eternal Flame. That glow, it's blue. They're corrupted!"

Reavian steps in front of me. "They've found us," he says to Kaiel.

Kaiel nods, his expression grim.

They both draw their blades in unison, the steel catching in the pale fae light.

"*Run!*" Reavian shouts.

I quickly grab Brynn's hand and take off. Kaiel's light guides the path ahead of us as the beasts begin to give chase. They seem to move like liquid shadow, fast and snarling as they charge through the dead forest. We need to go faster. *Run* faster. But Brynn can't move that quickly. I'm practically dragging her behind me. I tighten my grip on her hand.

I spot something ahead. A glowing light.

No, another part of the forest, *alive*.

The trees seem to burn with living fire, their leaves glowing a golden crimson in the night, trunks shimmering with emberlike veins, pulsing gently.

A breeze kisses my cheek, beckoning. The trees seem to wave me over, their canopies flickering like torches.

"This way!" I cry out.

Brynn stumbles behind me and we both fall. Kaiel scoops her up effortlessly, while Reavian helps me to my feet. All of us flee towards the trees in the distance, another warm breeze grazes my skin and seemingly tells me to hurry.

We reach the flaming forest, and run further in. I can feel it again, the life here. This part feels different, sacred. The sounds of the beasts have disappeared. Did they stop pursuing us?

They hunt.

They hunt.

The moment the beasts step into the sacred wood, the land *cries out*. I can hear it screaming, it's in pain. I feel it too.

A bloodcurdling scream comes out of me that rivals the ones that I hear within me.

Reavian startles and turns to check on me.

I scream again, feeling the pain, the agony, the death of the land.

Every step the beasts take poisons the ground, turning vibrant flame to ashen rot. The trees wither and blacken. Their embers snuff out.

I catch Iska drawing a dagger from a sheath hidden at her thigh, her expression grim.

Reavian and Kaiel stand shoulder to shoulder, swords raised and waiting.

I clutch my head screaming and fall to my knees. I can hear it, it's agony. I can feel what it feels as it dies. I double over.

"Renna?"

I hear a soft voice, Brynn's.

She drops to the ground and wraps me in her arms, hugging me tightly. I try to focus on that.

Two of the four beasts lunge.

Steel meets claws in a clash of power. Reavian dances expertly around each lunge and swipe of claw. Kaiel brings down his sword with mighty blows. But their blades draw no blood.

The creatures won't fall.

Iska rushes behind Brynn and I, crouching at our backs with her dagger drawn.

"The other two approach us from behind," she says.

Reavian and Kaiel fall back, giving up ground between us and the beasts. Nothing they do can take them down. They box us in, leaving us with nowhere left to run.

And then... they stop.

To everyone's surprise, all four creatures sit, as if following a silent command. Suddenly all their heads tilt.

They're *waiting for something*.

The voices within me surge to the surface of my mind again.

The darkness is here.

You must be the light in the darkness

A light in the darkness. The last words my mother said to me.

A pained scream tears through the night.

It's Kaiel. His body seizes, eyes rolling back for a breath—then he snaps forward.

Smiling.

But it isn't the smile I have grown accustomed to.

It's wrong.

All wrong.

His posture changes, his steps too precise as he moves toward me.

The way he moves... flashes of memory from the night of the crash flood my mind.

The knight in bone armor, it was...

Him.

"It was *you*," I whisper, my heart shattering. Reavian moves closer to me, his sword raised at his friend. I can see the confusion on his face.

The heartbreak.

"What?" Reavian whispers softly, taking a single step toward Kaiel. Like he's still hoping...praying, that it isn't true.

Kaiel opens his mouth to speak, but the voice that comes from his mouth is not his.

It's hers.

Liraeth.

"Did you really think that I wouldn't find you?" she asks, her voice skittering under my skin like thousands of spiders.

"It was you, you killed my parents," I say, my voice loud this time, anger rising in my chest.

The voice in Kaiel laughs.

"No, no...it wasn't *my* hand that took them from you. It was Kaiel's. Though, I did have to activate him and give him the command."

"Activate him?" Reavian asks.

Kaiel's... *Liraeth's* gaze moves to Reavian.

"Ah, my son," her voice hisses, slippery like a thousand snakes. "Perhaps if you weren't always such a weak disappointment, I could have shown you how to make anyone bend to your will."

"What did you do to him?" Reavian demands, his voice sharp, and body tense.

"I did what was necessary to keep him in line. What I should have done to you as well, but your father insisted that you would come to heel," she says, shaking Kaiel's head and arms like he's a puppet on strings.

Reavian flinches, just barely, but I see it, the way his hand tightens around his sword. Pain twists across his face.

"He is *not* my father!" Reavian shouts.

"Why? Why are you doing this?" I ask, pulling her attention away from him.

Another sickening laugh escapes from Kaiel's lips.

"I already told you, you have something that I want," she says, clearly annoyed to be repeating herself.

I stand, summoning every ounce of strength within me, and bring my eyes to hers— to Kaiel's.

"If I go with you, will you leave everyone else here alone?"

"No..." Reavian breathes, a plea laced in his voice.

"Yes," she hisses. "For now."

Kaiel's arm reaches out toward me, and I close my eyes ready to accept my fate.

"No!" Reavian yells, and I open my eyes in time to see him slam into Kaiel so hard he staggers backward.

"I tire of this. Kill them all, and bring the girl to me," Liraeth says.

Kaiel's eyes flutter, as if she's gone. But he's still not himself.

Reavian and Kaiel clash. Steel on steel, sparks flying.

Kaiel moves too fast. His strikes are sharp, brutal, and come without hesitation. He fights with precision meant to kill. Reavian blocks a blow, but barely. He stumbles back as Kaiel presses forward, blade arcing like it's being guided by something far darker than instinct.

"Kaiel, stop!" Reavian shouts. "It's me!"

But Kaiel doesn't flinch. His eyes are glassy and vacant. His face remains expressionless, like this fight means nothing to him.

Reavian ducks another blow meant to split him open. Another slash comes from a strange angle, it's unnatural, like Kaiel's joints are bending just a little too far. A puppet strung up and pulled by invisible hands.

"Run!" Reavian yells, desperately to us.

The Emberbeasts rise now, ready to join the attack.

"Auren, run...please," Reavian begs, his voice pained.

I can't leave him. I *won't.*

"No," I tell him, tears welling in my eyes. "I can't."

The beasts are stalking Reavian now, lunging at him as he fights Kaiel.

Two of them approach where Iska, Brynn and I are standing.

Reavian cries out in pain as one of the beasts claws his back, while he's still locked in battle with Kaiel.

"Reavian!" I cry out.

He looks at me for a beat, sadness in his eyes. Like he knows he's going to die here, like he's willing to.

"Run. Please," he begs.

Blood spills from the wound on his back.

I shut my eyes. Desperate to find whatever it is inside me that Liraeth wants.

Yes, Little Light.

Deeper.

Deeper.

Be the light in the darkness.

I grit my teeth and look within myself. If I don't do something he will die, we all will.

And there it is, inside me. A well. Brimming with something

locked away, desperately clawing to break free.

I open my eyes.

Kaiel kicks Reavian down to the ground, and the beasts circle him.

Iska cries out in pain behind me.

"No!" I scream, a war cry ripping from my throat.

She will not harm any of them anymore. I won't let her.

Suddenly ...

Bright white-gold flame spills from my hands. I *will* it to spare those I care about.

The beasts cry out, disintegrating into ash in an instant, as I move the flames carefully around my friends. Reavian is back on his feet, clashing with Kaiel.

That's it Little Light.

Now the land.

Heal the land.

I will the flames to rise again, to come and engulf the area.

Kaiel turns at the sight of a rolling wave of white-gold fire sweeping in from behind us, giving Reavian the opening he needs to knock Kaiel unconscious with the hilt of his sword.

The wave of flame moves quickly over us, but it doesn't burn us. It heals each patch of corrupted earth it touches, reforming the trees that had been brutally taken from the forests here moments ago. Golden light from the fire spreads through the ash like roots made of hope. I will it to heal all of it. Every bit of corrupted land,

and dead forest we came in contact with.

I pour everything into it, every drop of power I can find. Until I feel that where we are is no longer touched by any darkness.

The land and I are whole again.

I drop to my knees, weak with exhaustion. Staring at my hands, the glow of the power I just used begins to fade.

"What the hell was that?" I hear Iska ask.

Reavian staggers toward me, collapsing at my side, he reaches his hand into mine. Blood stains his back, the shredded fabric of his shirt fluttering in the breeze.

Iska rushes to him, magic already at her fingertips to heal the wound.

Brynn kneels beside Kaiel, silent tears slipping down her cheeks.

I look up at the healed forest, to the trees swaying. The flame topped branches flickering like torches again, waving their thanks to me in a breeze I can barely feel.

It's beautiful.

A breath shudders out of me.

I did it.

I feel hollow. Maybe I gave too much. But they're safe. The land is safe. I feel peace.

"It's you—the one the forests foretold of coming," a stranger's voice says behind us.

And then I let go.

Chapter Fifteen - Auren

Warm light presses against my closed eyelids.

I blink awake, breath catching in my throat as the haze of slumber lifts. The bed beneath me is impossibly soft, wrapped in deep red and gold silk sheets. A gentle breeze teases long ivory curtains that drift like ghosts from open terrace doors. The air carries the scent of something warm; it smells of smoke kissed flowers and sunlit earth.

My heart begins to pound as my senses catch up to me.

I'm not in the forest anymore.

I sit up slowly. The room around me is nothing like I have ever seen. It's regal and elegant, glowing with amber morning light. Ornately carved dark wood columns frame the walls, inlaid with dark stone that's peppered with glowing orange crystals that seem to pulse as if they are alive. A mural stretches across the domed ceiling, painted in rich tones of crimson and copper, depicting Sparksingers soaring over forests of flame, and rivers of firewater.

I glance to my right. A silk ivory robe lies folded neatly over the back of an intricately carved chair. I glance down at myself, and notice I'm dressed in a sleeping gown of deep red silk that clings to my skin like water. My skin feels soft and clean, and smells faintly of sugar and chestnuts.

Someone has cared for me.

I rise quietly and slip the robe over my shoulders, tying it at my waist. I move toward the open terrace, the breeze kissing my cheeks as I step out into a world beyond anything I could have ever imagined.

This must be Solmere.

It stretches out before me like something out of a dream. Towers of dark basalt and obsidian rise in elegant spirals, laced with golden veins that shimmer. Crystalline bridges arch across canyons filled with glowing rivers of firewater, their surfaces catching the rising sun like liquid light.

Below, the city bustles with morning activity—market stalls shaded by red and gold canopies, carts pulled by antlered beasts, children darting through the cobblestone streets. At the city's heart, a giant obsidian tower burns with an almost blinding red flame.

Perhaps the Eternal Flame Iska spoke of.

And all of it safely nestled in the arms of the Pyrethorn Divide, its crimson peaks watching over the realm like ancient gods.

Beyond the city, the sacred flame trees spread out in lush groves, their magical flaming canopies dancing in the wind. Fields of green roll between them, dotted with glowing flowers and stone paths.

And above it all, the sun rises in all its glory. Fiery and gold, filling the realm with warmth and wonder.

I place a hand on the railing, my chest tightening.

It is...breathtaking.

Otherworldly.

How long have I been asleep? My thoughts scramble, panic rising. Where is *Reavian? Brynn? Iska?*

My breath catches in my throat.

Kaiel.

Flashes of what happened play in my mind. Kaiel's eyes no longer his own. His voice twisting into hers. The way he moved. The way he...

Killed my father.

I flinch and shake my head, as if that could banish the memory. I need to find everyone.

I turn and cross the room toward the large carved wooden door.

I open it, and Reavian falls backwards into my room with a startled yelp.

He scrambles to his feet, brushing himself off with an exaggerated dignity. "I... I was just—"

"Were you sleeping outside my door?" I ask, lifting a brow.

He rubs the back of his neck, the faintest blush rising on his pale cheeks. "I... *may* have been. I didn't want to leave you unguarded, not in a strange place."

I peek around him into the hall, where two guards in leather armor stand silent and still.

"It seems I was already guarded."

"Doesn't matter," he says simply. "I needed to be close by."

My heart squeezes, I step back and gesture him inside.

"Come in," I say.

He crosses the threshold, and I notice how he looks. Washed and dressed in clean black pants with dark leather boots. A fitted black shirt clings to his lean muscled frame, embroidered at the cuffs and collar with silver thread shaped into curling flames.

He looks like something out of a fairytale. The handsome misunderstood dark prince.

My eyes dart to his back, remembering the hit he took from one of the corrupted Emberbeasts. My hand reaches out and I brush it gently with my fingertips.

"Your injury, are you alright?"

He nods. "Iska and the healers here took care of me."

"And Brynn? Iska? Are they alright too?"

"They're alright. Iska insisted she be the one to tend to you. She cleaned you up, changed your clothes."

His lips twitch.

"Brynn's ok too. Talking a little more now. She's mostly been spending time in the infirmary here waiting for news...," he trails off.

I hesitate for a moment, then whisper.

"How is Kaiel?"

Reavian's jaw tightens.

"Vaedric's best..." he pauses for a moment, his lips forming a thin line. "They're called Emberwrights. They are gifted healers. Their magic is tied to the Eternal Flame. They can burn away curses and unravel spells."

He exhales. "They've kept him in an unconscious state since we arrived, restrained in the infirmary. They're trying to sever whatever leash my mother has on him. But... they haven't seen anything like this before."

I take it all in, my chest tightening. A strange combination of emotions stir inside me. Grief, relief, anger, guilt, and sorrow. All tangled together.

"I'm sorry," I tell him. And I mean it. Though it may take me some time to heal from what Kaiel did... I know that it wasn't him. Not really.

It was Liraeth.

"When did we arrive?" I ask him. "How long have I been asleep?"

"Two Days," Reavian replies.

I gasp.

"I've been asleep for two days?"

He nods solemnly. "What you did Auren... that kind of power, it could have killed you."

I walk to the bed and sit on its edge stunned.

Two Days.

"You should have run... you shouldn't have done that. Put yourself at risk like that... It was dangerous...," he says, and I hear the worry in his voice.

The fear.

"I did what I had to," I whisper. "What the voices asked me to do. I saved us, and I healed the forest...the land."

Reavian tilts his head. "The voices?"

I nod.

"They speak inside me...they warn me, guide me. It's how I got us through the geysers erupting in the forest. They warned me of the beasts hunting us..." I trail off.

He sits on the bed beside me, listening quietly.

"They told me that I needed to be the light in the darkness. I looked deep within myself and felt it there. The flame. It felt like it had been hidden away... waiting. And it was bursting with joy to finally be let free."

I glance at him.

"You said you only used your power a couple of times. What did it feel like to you?"

He exhales slowly.

"Like something uncoiling inside me," he hesitates. "I feel it. It's there, *waiting*. Pushing. Urging me to let it out."

"Do you ever feel like it's...desperate? Like it needs to be free?"

I ask because that's how the power in me felt.

I watch as Reavian's eyes darken.

"Always."

I close my eyes and reach inward. The power inside me is still there, but it's much calmer now. Not frantic.

A knock sounds, sharp and sudden. I open my eyes.

Reavian rises and crosses to the door.

When he opens it, a tall imposing man stands in the hallway.

His presence fills the room without him needing to step inside. He's regal, broad-shouldered and striking. Long black locs peppered with gray, half tied back in a high knot. His skin is a rich russet brown, sun-kissed and glowing. His eyes are unusual, one a bright shade of verdant green, the other an ember-red-orange, flickering faintly with an inner flame.

"My men informed me that you were awake," he says, his voice smooth and warm. "I'm Vaedric Solmere."

"Hi," I say carefully. "My name is Auren Whitlow. It's... nice to meet you."

"We would have come to you ourselves, when she was ready," Reavian says, his voice edged in that steely tone he seems to reserve for everyone but me.

Vaedric smiles. Amused, not offended. "I'm sure you would have."

He looks past Reavian to me.

"Your private bathing chamber is beyond that door on the far wall. The wardrobe has been stocked with various clothing in your size from my court. Choose what is most comfortable for you. And when you are *ready...,* "he says pausing to glance at Reavian, giving him a slight smile. "Then I would like it if you could *both*, please join me in my study. There is...much to discuss. I have a guard wait for you in the hallway. They'll show you the way."

With that he turns and disappears down the hall.

"I'll wait outside," Reavian says quietly.

I shake my head.

"There's no need. You can sit on the terrace, or here," I say while pointing to the elegant chair next to my bed. "I feel safer when you're near."

His throat bobs, and he nods, moving toward the terrace.

I open the wardrobe, it's packed with beautiful gowns and dresses in every shade of red, gold, cream, and brown I can think of. Silks, velvets, cottons, and fine leather. Garments of the Realm of Flame and Forest.

I chose a simpler outfit. Gray fitted pants embroidered with red and orange blossoms at the thigh, a long-sleeved cream blouse with flowing cuffs, and a brown leather corset that's stitched with matching flame touched flowers. I find knee high brown leather boots and set them aside.

In the bathing chamber, I wash quickly. Then I tie my hair into a relaxed bun, letting layered strands fall to frame my face. I feel clearer.

Lighter.

When I step out again, I notice Reavian is still on the terrace, observing the city. I slide on the boots I set aside and join him.

"I've never seen anything more beautiful," I whisper, staring at the view.

Reavian's voice is soft. "It is lovely here."

"It really is," I say, turning towards him. My breath catches, when I see he's not staring at the city.

He's looking at me.

"What?" I ask.

He brings his gaze from my lips to my eyes; it lingers there for a moment. My heart flutters, and heat blooms across my cheeks. There is something there between us, like a thread pulled taut. The space we share almost hums. I wonder if he feels it too.

Then he straightens suddenly without a word, turning his gaze back to the city below.

"We should get going if you're ready," he says. "He's probably pacing in his study already."

Chapter Sixteen - Auren

The hallway leading to Vaedric's study is dimly lit, lined with walls of black stone veined with molten gold. Torches flicker in ornate sconces carved into the walls.

The guard posted to guide us stops in front of a set of tall double doors, their surfaces carved with flame-touched trees, and a large bird rising from a ring of fire.

He knocks once and then pushes the doors open.

The study is magnificent.

The walls curve inward, like a cathedral, lit by slanted beams of sunlight pouring through tall arched windows. Books line the walls, their spines embossed in copper and crimson, and in the center of the room stands a massive desk carved from charred wood, glowing faintly with internal embers, like the trees from the sacred forest.

Vaedric stands behind the desk, his presence commanding, and yet calm. His dual-colored eyes fix on me the moment Reavian and I step into the room.

"How are you feeling?" he asks, his voice warm but seemingly tempered by something deeper.

"I'm alright," I reply softly, standing straighter beneath his gaze. "I feel rested."

He nods. "Please, sit."

Reavian and I take the chairs across from him. As soon as we sit, a steward brings us a plate filled with assorted pastries, then places a steaming carafe of spiced tea on the desk, before leaving without a word.

"I thought you might be hungry. Please help yourselves," Vaedric says.

"Thank you," I reply, pouring myself some tea before grabbing one of the pastries. I am absolutely starving. The smell reminds me of Carlotta's, and I relax a bit, feeling more comfortable in my surroundings.

Vaedric leans forward, folding his hands. "I've been waiting to speak with you. There's much to discuss, and much that I believe... you deserve to know."

I nod slowly. "That night in the forest. It was you right? You said... the forest foretold my coming."

"It was, and yes I did," he replies.

Reavian remains quiet and pours himself some of the spiced tea.

Vaedric studies me for a long moment. "But before I speak of the past, and what was foretold. I'd like to hear your story, in your words."

So, I tell him.

Everything.

From my quiet life with my parents in the human world, to the events in the cafe, to the crash and my parent's deaths. My abduction into this world, the torture that I endured. What Brynn had suffered. Our escape. The whispers that guide me, the dangers we faced in the forests here, trying to reach Solmere. I told him about Kaiel, what Liraeth had done to him, how she spoke through him.

"One of the last things my mother said to me was to be the light in the darkness," I say.

Vaedric's expression shifts, it's grief...raw grief.

"She had been protecting me my whole life, and I had no idea. I just complained because..." I trail off, emotion rising up my throat. Tears begin to stream down my face. "I feel like...like I have had no time to process anything that has happened. No time to grieve."

Vaedric stands abruptly walking to the window as if he couldn't sit still a moment longer. "Your mother...," his voice catches. "Calyra...I knew her. She grew up here, in this realm. Right here in Solmere."

My heart skips. " Calyra..."

My mother had gone by Callie, I guess this...her *true* name, is just another truth in all the lies she told to protect me. I know I shouldn't be upset. But I didn't even know my own mother's *real* name. Why didn't she just tell me about all of this? Maybe things could have been different. Maybe her and Dad would still be here.

Maybe I could have helped defend them. But there is no point in wondering what if. It's already done. The worst has already happened.

"You knew her?" I ask.

"She was fire and light, and... defiance," he says quietly. "She was beautiful."

He looks out over the city, his expression unreadable.

"She grew up here in Solmere, and I..." he hesitates, then continues. "I loved her, but she only ever saw me as a friend. Her heart belonged to another."

My breath hitches.

"To my father? Is that why she went to the human realm? Did she meet him somehow... and flee with him?" I ask, wondering if there could have been a way she found our world. A portal maybe? Somehow throwing my father into this world or my mother into his.

"No," he says quietly. "Her heart belonged to High King Alarion Veylas."

Reavian audibly gasps, looking between me and Vaedric.

"They loved one another deeply," Vaedric continues, "but their union was forbidden. Alarion's mother had arranged a political match for him, one blessed by the Gods. She felt they needed a powerful ally to secure peace between all the realms. He tried to fight it; he didn't care that your mother wasn't high fae. But in the end, he was forced to comply."

"His last name... I've heard it somewhere before," I say.

"Lucien was his brother," Reavian says grimly.

Vaedric turns from the window to face me, pain flickering in his eyes.

"Your mother disappeared shortly after the wedding. Everyone believed she moved to the edges of the realm, somewhere remote, to live in solitude out of heartbreak."

He pauses.

"*Others* thought the grief was too much for her, and she ended her life."

He exhales slowly, gaze steady.

"But I see now... it was not just grief that drove her away. I believe that Alarion knew about the pregnancy. About *you*. He knew that his brother was coming for him. Only someone like Alarion, someone as powerful as he was, could have opened a portal to the human world. At that time, the veil wasn't weakened like it is now."

His voice softens.

"He sent her away...to save you both. *You* are the daughter of King Alarion Veylas. You are the heir to the High Crown."

I sit frozen. Reavian doesn't move either. I try to process the weight of what I've just been told, but the words won't settle.

"But my father, I knew my father, he's always been there, I don't understand ..."

Vaedric walks over to me.

"Your father will always be your father, he's the man who raised you. Who helped make you who you are today. Nothing can take that away from you."

I begin to sob. So much has happened. *Too much* has happened. That man, that awful man who tortured me.

He's... my uncle?

How can this be?

Reavian reaches for my hand, covering it with his own, his thumb moving in small, soothing circles across my palm.

The memory of what those colorful threads showed me in that place they called the veil flashes in my mind. Lucien, standing in a room with a bloodied sword. My father's blood was on that sword.

"My mother and Lucien built an army," Reavian says quietly. "Lucien stormed the castle with it. He murdered the High King, the High Queen, and their child, hoping to claim the throne and the power for himself. But the power didn't come to *him*..."

"Because it went to *you*," Vaedric finishes for him. "You healed the corrupted land here with fire that cleansed, but didn't destroy," he continues. "You heard the trees when the rest of your party only heard wind. The land chose you. The magic has chosen you. The Gods have chosen *you*."

Vaedric rises and walks around his desk, lowering himself into the chair. He leans forward; eyes fixed on mine.

"Lucien didn't just take the castle," he says, voice low. "He started what is known as the Rift War. The moment he spilled royal blood, the realms fractured. Alliances collapsed. Magic itself has begun to falter. It tore the land apart and it hasn't healed since, corruption and darkness spreads into all of the realms to this day."

The weight of it all presses against my chest. The Rift War, my father, the broken magic, the corruption. It's too much. Too fast. My breath stutters, and though I'm still sitting in this chair, I feel like I'm falling.

Reavian releases my hand and shifts his chair closer, his palm finding the small of my back. His touch is steady, grounding.

"It's alright," he murmurs, his voice low, meant only for me. "I'm here."

The pressure in my chest eases just enough to breathe again. I wonder if he can feel it... me unraveling. The fear. The weight of something too big for me to carry alone.

"Now that you are here, the true heir...the chosen...you can do what none of us can. Even the High Lords and Ladies of Nyvenya cannot do what you've done. You can restore what has been broken. You can be the flame that purges all the darkness this world has been plagued with. You can help us end Liraeth and Lucien's reign of terror, for good."

"No." Reavian's voice is cold steel.

Vaedric blinks.

Reavian rises to his feet. "She just told you she hasn't even had time to properly grieve the death of her parents. She is not some weapon for you to point at our enemies. She's not a tool, or your savior. And I won't let you, or anyone else use her like she's something to be godsdamned sacrificed!"

Vaedric stands as well, his face calm, but his eyes fierce. "I would *never* force her. Not now, not ever. But you underestimate her if you think she needs protecting from what is her destiny."

"I don't underestimate her," Reavian snaps. "I *respect* her. She should be given a choice, not to just be told this is what you have to do. Fuck destiny, she owes us nothing."

Something cracks open inside me as I watch Reavian, standing tall, unyielding and furious on my behalf. He's fighting for me. But I can't let him carry this burden for me. Not when I feel, in my bones, that I was brought here for a reason. That I'm meant to help these people. Maybe this is my purpose, perhaps it always has been. I have to try. Even if it terrifies me.

"Reavian, it's alright." My voice comes out steadier than I expect. "I want to help. I believe that I *need* to. But I am not ready. That night...the power, I don't know how to control it. It just poured out of me in waves. I struggled with all my might to try and command it...I think I came very close to not surviving it."

The two men fall silent.

"If we are to do this, I will need help. I will need *time.* If I'm meant to fight to save this world, then I want to do it right. I want to learn how to properly wield my magic. But I do not want to have to rely on that alone. I want to be trained for combat as well."

Vaedric nods slowly. "I can train you myself, if you'll have me. I have held the flame within me for a long time, and though it's not quite as strong as yours, I can show you how to wield it. As for the combat training, I can have one of my best soldiers—"

Reavian cuts him off. "I'll train you for combat."

"Alright," I reply, looking between both men. "I'll learn from you both then."

Vaedric looks between us, then gives a single nod.

"So, it shall be," he says, voice firm.

Chapter Seventeen - Auren

The hallway is quiet as Reavian and I leave the study, our footsteps muffled against the black stone floor. The air holds the weight of everything that Vaedric revealed. The history, the pain, the truths that I hadn't been ready to hear. My mind buzzes, too full and too empty all at once.

Reavian walks beside me, his hands curled into fists at his sides, shoulders held with tension. *Is he upset about my decision to help?* I notice that we're not heading in the direction we came from on our way to meet Vaedric.

Finally, I ask, "Where are we going?"

"To find Brynn and Iska," he says. His voice is rough and wrought with emotion. A tone he has never taken with me.

Guess he *is* upset then.

"And Kaiel," he continues.

I nod, and my stomach tightens.

The corridors are dimly lit by flickering sconces, their globes of flame casting long shadows on the walls.

The warmth they cast would usually be comforting, but unease coils in my chest with every step.

As we round the final curve toward the infirmary, I see them. Brynn and Iska, sitting on a stone bench just outside a pair of tall, iron-branded doors. Brynn is hunched forward, her hands covering her face, her shoulders trembling violently with each sob. Iska is beside her, one hand on her back, murmuring something too low for me to hear.

Then a sound tears the air wide open.

Raw.

Gut wrenching.

Male.

"Please—just kill me—please!"

Kaiel.

I stop short, my breath catching. The sound isn't just pain, it's torment. Bone deep and soul breaking torment.

Beside me, Reavian goes rigid. He doesn't speak, and for a moment he doesn't move. Then he strides forward, toward the bench, with me trailing close behind.

Iska looks up as we approach. Her silver hair is disheveled, and deep shadows cling to her golden eyes.

"What's happening?" Reavian demands. "Why is he... what are they doing to him?"

Iska exhales through her nose, weary. "They're removing the tether."

I blink. "The tether?"

Iska nods grimly. "The one Liraeth planted within him. Her influence. Her control. It's rooted deep. We hoped we could remove it while he remained unconscious, to spare him this, but her magic resists passivity. It's dark, ancient magic and it's pain bound. It's designed to break the will. To make what's necessary feel impossible."

Reavian swallows. "So most would choose death instead of breaking it."

Iska nods. "It's painful, not only physically. But he's...reliving everything that he has done while under her control. Each part they burn out... unlocks a memory, it seems."

Another scream rips through the air, followed by a crashing sound from inside. Brynn lets out a choked cry, and buries her face in her hands again.

Iska rubs her back. "The Emberwrights are trying, Brynn. They know what they're doing. He'll survive."

Brynn shakes her head, tears pouring down her cheeks. She looks at me with wide, wet eyes and whispers, "His pain... I can feel it."

My heart stutters. "What?"

"I can feel it," Brynn says, her voice cracked. "Like it's mine."

I drop beside Brynn, wrapping my arms around her, confusion swirling in my chest. What does she mean? Is it bringing back what happened to her? Her trauma? This isn't the time to ask. I hold Brynn tightly as Kaiel screams again, louder this time, his voice hoarse and cracking.

"I'll go watch over him," Iska says, going back inside.

And then. We Wait.

And wait.

The hours blur.

Kaiel's cries become fewer, but more ragged. There are long silences, punctuated by pained gasps or soft murmurs within the infirmary. Reavian paces the corridor like a caged animal, fists clenching and unclenching. I sit with Brynn the entire time, my legs numb and my thoughts tangled.

Can I forgive him?

Finally, the door creaks open.

Iska steps out, looking drained. Her tunic is soaked in sweat. She wipes her brow and meets our eyes.

"It's done," she says.

Brynn gasps. "He's...?"

"He's alive," Iska confirms. "But he will need time to recover. The tether... It fought us all every step of the way."

I stand slowly, not sure if my legs will hold. Reavian is already moving, pushing past Iska and into the infirmary. Brynn and I follow. Every step I take is hesitant.

The infirmary glows with a dull orange light, warmth humming through the walls. Shelves are lined with various vials and glass jars along one side, and the air smells of medicinal herbs and smoke. Several Emberwrights are standing in the corner, murmuring amongst themselves.

Kaiel lies in a small side chamber, his body sprawled across a stone bed. His tan skin now pale beneath a sheen of sweat. His chest rises and falls as if he has just barely survived a battle, and perhaps, he has. His shirt has been stripped away, revealing what appear to be burns along his arms and chest, glowing faintly with what must be a healing salve.

Reavian rushes to his side. "You're going to be okay," he says softly. "Just rest now, we've got you."

Kaiel groans faintly in response, his head lolling to one side.

I hesitate outside the doorway into the chamber, my pulse roaring in my ears. I don't move. I can't.

He was the one.

The one who killed my parents.

The one who took me here.

Even if he hadn't meant to. Even if he hadn't known.

I grip the door frame so tightly my knuckles turn white.

Kaiel's eyes flutter open and find me.

"Auren," he croaks. "I'm sorry." His voice is cracked, raw and trembling. "I'm so sorry, I didn't know, I swear I didn't know."

I don't respond. My throat is thick, my thoughts are fractured. I feel like the walls in the building are closing in on me. Part of me wants to scream, part of me wants to run, and part of me wants to stay and make sure that he's ok. I choose none of those options and just stand here, my eyes locked on his, saying nothing. I didn't even notice that Brynn had not yet entered the room.

She scoots past me holding a damp cloth, her hands trembling. She crosses the room silently and sits beside Kaiel.

"It's ok," she whispers, her voice soothing as she dabs at his forehead and neck.

Kaiel's eyes meet hers and soften. He looks at her like she is the only thing holding him to this world.

"Thank you," he whispers weakly, his voice barely audible. Then his eyes roll back and he passes out.

I'm still standing motionless in the doorway, watching as Brynn continues to gently wipe the sweat from his brow. His chest is rising and falling in shallow, labored breaths. He is alive. Free. I know that I should feel relief. Gratitude even. But all I can feel is the knot that is twisting inside of me.

I know it wasn't him.

Not his will. Not his mind.

But it is his body I had seen in those final moments.

His voice that had barked commands to me.

His arms that dragged me into the darkness.

It hadn't been Kaiel.

And yet—it *was*.

The lines of what happened blur, and no matter how many times I try to remind myself of the truth, that night on that desolate mountain road, lives inside me like a wound that will not scab. Every scream I made in that dungeon, every breath my parents will never again get to take—it all wears his skin.

I press my palm into the doorframe, grounding myself, jaw clenched against the tide rising in my throat.

He didn't know.

But neither do I.

I don't know what to do with the rage, the sorrow, the fragile ache that trembles somewhere between forgiveness and fear.

I turn and leave the room, nearly running. I need to get back to my room. I need to get away. I need to think. It's all so much.

Before me the torchlight flickers.

Behind me, Kaiel recovers.

And I remain in the space between.

Chapter
Eighteen-Reavian

I stand at my friend's bedside and watch the slow rise and fall of his chest. Brynn is dabbing his brow with a quiet sort of devotion. Kaiel's body is covered in horrific looking burns across his arms and chest. He's permanently scarred where the Emberwrights removed the vile tether my mother held on him. I can't help but feel responsible for this, for all of this. I'm so thankful that we made it here, and that the Emberwrights and Iska have saved him. He's alive. I should feel relieved.

Instead, I feel the weight of everything pressing in on me from all sides. Kaiel's pain, Auren's silence when he spoke to her, the inevitable war looming over the horizon. The war *she* wants to fight in. My jaw clenches. I will not let them take advantage of her, if she wants to fight, I will fight by her side. But I will not let anyone sacrifice her for the so-called greater good. I have to make sure she is prepared, that she knows what she will be up against.

I turn to say something to Auren—only to find that the space

152

she had occupied just moments ago is empty. My heart stutters. *It was too much, this was too much for her.*

"I'll be back to check on him later," I say to Brynn.

I walk to the doorway and scan the hall quickly. There's no sign of her. No sound of retreating footsteps.

I move quickly down the corridor and check every corner for her, each branching hallway. I make my way back to the bedroom Vaedric had assigned to her upon our arrival. It is empty. Silent. Panic pricks at the edge of my chest as I search all of Solmere Keep in order to find her. And then, after rounding a shadowed corridor, I see her.

She's sitting on the floor back against the cold stone wall, arms wrapped around her knees. Her hair is falling out of the bun she placed it in earlier and cascading across her face. Her breathing is shallow, her fingers trembling.

"Auren," I drop to my knees beside her, reaching out. "Are you hurt? What's wrong?"

She flinches slightly but doesn't move away. She speaks softly, her voice trembling. "I... I got lost."

Relief tangles with worry in my chest. I gently touch her arm. "It's alright, I'm here."

She turns her face toward me, her bright blue eyes shimmering with unshed tears.

"I don't know where I am, or what I'm supposed to do." Her voice cracks. "I can feel that you are upset with me Reav, for choosing to help. But Vaedric was looking at me like I am the answer. I don't want anyone else to be hurt. I feel like I am *meant* to help. But I'm afraid, because right now I don't even know how to ask the right questions."

"I'm not upset with you—"

"You are." Her words come out fast, panicked. "I can see it in your body language, and you've barely spoken a word to me since our meeting with Vaedric. I can *feel* it," she says, her voice cracking.

"And Kaiel. *I know* he wasn't himself. I *know* he was being controlled. But when I look at him, all I see is that night. My mom...My dad..."

Her voice breaks entirely, and the tears finally come. My heart shatters into a million pieces. I don't speak at first, I simply turn and lean back onto the wall to sit beside her, shoulder to shoulder, to let her cry.

When she quiets down just enough to breathe again, I speak, taking care that my voice comes out low and steady.

"I'm not mad at you, Auren. I'm worried. And frustrated, but not with you. It's this place. This impending war, this path that we are all on. You didn't ask for any of it, and I'm angry that you are being asked to clean up our mess," I say.

She swallows hard, her chin quivering.

"And Kaiel..." I let out a long breath. I can't help but feel like this, all of this that's happening is my fault. "You are allowed to feel conflicted. But the monster that did those things, was not him.

It was my mother. I've known Kaiel since we were children. He was the only one who ever stood up for me. He's taken blame and punishment for things I had done. Whenever my mother would look at me with hatred, he would find some way to make me laugh. I wouldn't have survived the hell we grew up in without him."

I look at her, searching her eyes. "He *is* good, Auren. My mother must have seen that in him and set out to destroy it. And with time, however much time you need, I think you'll see his true heart too."

She nods, tears still slipping silently down her cheeks. I stand and offer her my hand.

"Come on, let's get you back to your room."

She hesitates for only a moment before slipping her hand into mine.

We wind our way down the halls and find our way back to her room. I pull the covers back on the freshly made bed , while she goes to the wardrobe grabbing a nightdress then disappears into the bathing chamber. When she emerges, she has let her long golden hair down, and the red silken sleeping gown she chose clings perfectly to every curve of her body. *Gods*, this woman is perfect. She is the most beautiful creature I have ever seen. I clear my throat. "Here, I've gotten it ready for you, climb in."

As she walks over to the bed, a breeze blows in from the terrace, carrying the sugared scent of the soap she used to me. I breathe it in. She climbs into bed, and I tuck her in gently.

"Alright, get some sleep. I'll see you in the morning," I say.

I walk to the door, knowing that I am going to go wash up and then spend my night sleeping outside of it again.

"Stay," her soft voice calls to me.

She sits up.

I hesitate for a breath before I cross the room, and sit on the edge of her bed, my shadowed gaze searching hers.

"Are you sure?" I ask her.

She nods at me, peeking up through the golden hair tangled around her face. "Yes," she whispers. "Please...stay."

Something in my chest splits wide open. I nod once in reply and reach down to take off my boots, setting them aside. She shifts to the other side of the bed, to make space, still facing me. I slide in next to her, close but not touching, and I turn to face her. We lay here, in the moonlight peeking in from the terrace. The silence in the room stretches.

She reaches her hand out, her fingertips brushing the line of my jaw. Her thumb lingers on the corner of my mouth, tracing the faint scar I have had there since I was a boy. Her soft touch sends sparks through my entire being. My breath catches.

"I don't want to be alone," she murmurs. "Part of me has felt alone my whole life."

"You're not," I tell her, tracing my palm along the side of her face.

Our eyes meet, and something passes between us—it feels weightless and inevitable.

I lean in slowly, giving her the chance to pull away. She doesn't.

Our lips meet in a kiss that is soft at first, tentative. But it deepens with the ache of two souls who have been searching for one another far too long. Her hand curls into my shirt, and my fingers lift to cradle her face, something delicate and rare—something I feel that I have waited lifetimes to touch.

When we finally part, both breathless, I press my forehead to hers, eyes closed. "You don't have to be everything right now, Auren," I whisper. "Just be here. That's enough."

She nods against me, her eyes much clearer now. She calms me in a way that no one has. I feel at peace with her. The feeling is foreign to me, but I welcome it.

"Will you stay here with me?" she asks, softly.

I shift slightly and pull her toward me. She tucks her head beneath my chin and rests her hand over my heart. Her breathing begins to slow, steadying, and within minutes, she is asleep.

I watch her for a bit, my arm curled around her. Thoughts begin to spin in my head like distant storm clouds.

I think of the horrors we've already escaped.

The enemies we've yet to face.

The truth of her blood, her power, and her birthright.

And what it would mean when the rest of the world realized who she was.

But here, in this moment, all that matters to me is that she is safe. And as long as I draw breath, I will keep her that way.

Her body is soft and warm against mine. Her breaths deep now, relaxed. Those small, steady exhalations sing to something inside me that I had never known was waiting.

I close my eyes.

For the first time in years, I relax and drift off into a deep peaceful sleep.

Chapter Nineteen - Auren

I wake with the soft warmth of Reavian's arms wrapped around me, his heartbeat steady against my back. For a moment, I don't move. The early light filtering through the curtains casts a golden glow upon the room. I let the peace of it settle into my bones.

I turn slightly in his hold, careful not to wake him, and study his face. His short, dark tousled hair has fallen over one eye, soft and unruly. He looks so peaceful, so unguarded, as if all the weight he carries has momentarily lifted. I reach up and brush the strands back from his brow with delicate fingers.

My thoughts drift back to the kiss we shared last night—gentle, warm, and filled with emotion. I had fallen asleep with my heart fluttering and have now awoken to find it still beating with that same quiet intensity.

Reavian stirs beneath my touch, his eyes blinking open, slow and sleepy, those gold and silver flecks within them almost twinkling. When he sees me, he smiles. A rare, real smile that softens the sharpness of all of his features.

"Morning," he murmurs, his voice low and rough.

Before I can reply, he leans in, pressing a kiss to my forehead, lingering there for a moment.

Three crisp knocks sound against my door.

We both startle slightly, pulling apart as the door swings open, and a pair of stewards step into the room. Each carries a silver tray piled with food. Steaming eggs, crisped sausage, golden toast with sweet preserves, fresh fruit, a pot of spiced tea, and a carafe of chilled juice.

We both sit up.

"Oh," I say, my voice still drowsy with sleep.

One of the stewards bows.

"Your breakfast, my lady. My lord."

They move quickly and efficiently, setting the trays on a low table near the bed before retreating.

Another steward enters, this one holding folded leathers over one arm. "These were prepared for you, my lady," she says, offering them to me. "The High Lord thought them more appropriate for your training today."

I stand and accept them, laying them on the foot of the bed. The stewards retreat quickly, and I stare curiously at the table they set breakfast on. Each tray has an envelope on it; one labeled with my name and the other Reavian's. I sit at the table, and I pick up the one with my name.

Auren-

A guard will be posted outside your door in one hour's time. He will take you to meet me, and we will begin your training.

-Vaedric

I glance up and notice Reavian is watching me with interest.

I pass the note to him, and he reads it with a small nod, though I catch a flicker of hesitation in his eyes.

"Everything alright?" I ask him, as I take a bite of the fluffiest scrambled eggs I have ever eaten.

He nods again, and says, "Just...wish I could go with you." I smile at him, touched by his concern.

"What does your note say?"

He opens the note, and his expression falls into one of annoyance. He shakes his head, and hands me the note.

Reavian-

I would have had this delivered to your room, but I figured you're probably sleeping outside her door again. Do you have an aversion to comfortable beds? Or perhaps is there something else that keeps you there...I wonder...

-Vaedric

I laugh after I read it. Reavian's expression is stony.

"Don't be upset, he's only teasing. And besides, you didn't exactly sleep *outside* my door last night, did you?"

A faint blush creeps onto his pale cheeks, and he smiles.

"No, I suppose I did not," he says.

We eat breakfast together, quietly enjoying one another's company.

When we finish, Reavian stands and stretches.

"I should probably go clean myself up and check on Kaiel and the others," he says.

I follow him to the door, and before he leaves, he turns to me. I can still sense worry in him, a hesitation. It's almost as if I can feel him thinking that when I go to train today, all of this will become *real*, and there will be no turning back.

"Don't worry, I'll be fine," I tell him, standing on my tip toes. I press a kiss to his cheek.

His eyes soften, in the way they do only for me. "I'll find you tonight, and you can tell me all about your training."

"I'd like that," I reply.

I watch as he exits and close the door behind him. I move to the bed to examine the leathers the steward brought to me. They are unlike anything I've ever worn. Sleek black with embroidered flames in an even darker thread, subtle and striking. I wash up and then quickly put them on. The material moves like a second skin but feels reinforced, like it can withstand both blade, and flame. I then tie my hair into a braid.

When I step out into the hall, the guard that Vaedric promised stands waiting.

"I'll take you to the High Lord," he says, turning on his heel.

I fall into step beside him.

We pass through the winding halls of the keep, and out into the city, which is buzzing with activity. Crimson leafed trees bow in the wind, as if greeting me. Sparksingers fly above, and children are playing in fields of orange and red glowing blossoms. All the buildings are carved from dark stone, etched with glowing lines that pulse vaguely with magic.

We walk to the edge of the city, through the gate, and into the sacred forest beyond. The deeper we go, the quieter everything becomes, until only the sound of rustling leaves remains. We finally reach a break in the trees, a clearing where Vaedric stands, tall and regal, his dark red cloak fluttering behind him.

"Welcome to your first day of training," he says with a smile. "Come, sit."

Vaedric sits down on the grass, legs crossed. I sit across from him, my heart pounding ever so slightly.

"Magic here is not commanded," he begins, "but gifted. I was chosen by the magic in this realm to protect it and its people. In return, it gave me the gifts of flame and of forest. My flame differs from others gifted the flame in this realm. My flame comes from the Eternal Flame itself, the only others that have received this gift are the Emberwrights, though their gift differs from mine in the way that theirs can only be used for healing. Mine can be used to heal *and* be used in battle. The gift of the forest allows me to communicate with the land here, the trees, the grass, the earth, all of it. It speaks to me. I can *feel* its intentions. It is alive, Auren."

I take in all the information he gives me and know it to be true. The power I have—my fire can destroy and heal as well—in a way. And I've noticed the trees trying to communicate with me.

"I... think somehow, it has been speaking to me too. The forest I mean," I start, "The trees...when we arrived here...they moved as if greeting me. I felt them."

He nods. "It did. They did. And they will continue to do so. You are the heir to more than just a crown. But your fire differs from even mine, your fire healed the corruption. It purged the darkness. I believe you will come to have gifts from all of the realms in this world, because you have been chosen."

My breath catches.

"I hear these inner voices, and they seem to... guide me along. Other than the fire, I don't seem to have any other powers."

He pauses, thinking for a moment.

"The land does not speak to me with voices. But I can feel its intent, much like you did when you entered this realm. Perhaps...maybe, the voices you hear within you may be something different. Threads of fate maybe? Guiding you. Shaping you. Whispering you towards your purpose."

What he says strikes a chord within me. It's beautiful, terrifying, and... just a bit overwhelming.

He gestures toward the earth. "Place your hands in the grass, dig your fingers in. Feel the ground, the soil. Close your eyes and allow yourself to feel everything."

I obey and feel the blades of grass dance against my palms. Then I gently dig my fingers into the ground feeling the earth beneath them.

"Now, in your mind, go deeper, feel what's around you," he urges. "Past the roots, reach for the magic in the land itself."

I inhale deeply, then slowly exhale and search.

I feel it. A pulsing of power beneath my hands.

A breeze brushes against my cheek and seems to be somehow saying thank you.

I can *feel* it.

I open my eyes, and look at the trees swaying gently above us, a smile spreads across my lips. Joy ripples through my chest.

"It's happy, and thankful," I say, my lips twitching upward.

Vaedric smiles.

Movement sounds from the trees behind Vaedric, and four massive cat-like creatures emerge. I instantly recognize what they are. Carved from ash wood, and glowing from within. Their hearts pulse with flame, the same flame as what's in the tower at the center of Solmere. The Eternal Flame. They seem to be greeting me. *Emberbeasts*. They're beautiful, and not at all terrifying like the corrupted versions we were greeted with when we arrived.

"Emberbeasts," Vaedric says, "The forest's guardians. They were created by this very land to protect it. And they came to welcome you."

"They came... for me?" I ask.

His eyes are bright.

"You feel their intent, do you not? It's because the land knows you. It wishes to protect you, so they will also," he says.

I watch as the Emberbeasts vanish into the trees, awestruck.

"Can you tell me about the Eternal Flame?" I ask curiously.

He nods.

"Of course. It burns brightly, the living heart of the power in this realm. It never extinguishes, burning strongly through all weather. It gives life to the Emberbeasts, and is the source of power for our realm."

"So... the Eternal Flame *is* the source of the magic here, and it gifts those it deems worthy with its power?"

"Precisely," Vaedric replies.

"The fire I used that night, in the forest....it doesn't look like the fire from the Eternal Flame, it's unlike the one that is in the heart of the Emberbeasts..."

"Your power is different in a way. I can't know how for sure, but your father, the High King, had the same flame. You told me before that you poured your will into the flame. You wanted it to heal the land, destroy the threats, and keep you and your companions safe. My power is similar, so I can help you with what I know."

I take in what he has said and find myself somewhat disbelieving.

"Alright. Show me how to use it," I say.

"Look within yourself. Search for the flame. It will be there."

"Look deep," Vaedric says calmly. "Feel."

I take in a deep breath and close my eyes. I look deep within, feeling around for the flame.

There it is. An ember, flickering red, pulsing like a heartbeat.

"I see it," I whisper.

"Good, very good. Now will it forward. Just a small piece of it. Let it come to your palm. Picture it. Shape it. *Control it.*"

I keep my eyes closed focusing within me on that burning ember and raise my palm up. I concentrate on it and will it to hover above my palm in the shape of a tiny golden flaming orb.

Suddenly, I feel heat hovering above my hand, and I snap my eyes open.

"I did it," I gasp, watching a perfect sphere of fire hover above my palm.

"Yes, you did," Vaedric says, pride in his voice. "You can choose how you shape it, whether it be orb, wave, or even to wreath your blade."

I laugh. The thrill of this buzzing through me.

"Now what?" I ask.

"Now...put it away. Extinguish it."

I blink.

"Put it away?"

"Just will it back to where you found it," he says, like it's something that should be easy to do.

I close my eyes and try but snap them open quickly when I feel my palm getting very hot. I look at the sphere of flame above my hand and it wobbles, then shoots downward.

I watch in horror as it scorches the earth with a hiss, setting the grass aflame.

Vaedric reacts instantly, dousing it with water from his waterskin. A puff of steam rises.

"I'm so sorry," I say, absolutely mortified. "I didn't mean to, I'm just sometimes a bit... chaotic."

"This is why we are training," Vaedric replies, unfazed.

I look down and watch as the charred blades of grass begin to shimmer, then turn green again. Brighter than before.

"How?"

"Flame is a part of this land, what burns here often returns stronger," he replies.

I frown. "But what Liraeth corrupted, it didn't heal. It was dead. I felt it."

"We believe she is using dark magic. Its source remains unknown to us. But *you* can combat it." He looks at me with a quiet reverence. "Your fire ripped through her corruption like it was nothing. No one else has been able to do that."

I swallow hard. Thinking of the other realms.

What are they suffering through right now?

"That's why you must train, so you can learn to control it. So that you can help us," Vaedric says, his voice tinged with sadness but also hope.

I nod.

My heart feels heavy and fierce all at once. I need to do this. It's my destiny. I will help these people.

"Good. Let's try again," Vaedric says.

We train for hours. Summoning flame. Extinguishing it. Failing. Trying again. Laughing when I nearly set my hair on fire. Fumbling. Succeeding. Nearly setting *his* hair on fire. Doubting myself. Improving.

I hear the voices within me again.

You can do this Little Light.

And this time, I believe them.

Chapter Twenty-Auren

The door to my chambers clicks softly shut behind me as I step inside. My limbs feel a bit like melted wax, my thoughts hum with exhaustion—but beneath it all, pulses something fierce and steady.

Pride.

I didn't burn down the forest.

In fact, I think I've nearly mastered the fire within me.

I peel off my leathers and let them fall to the floor padding toward the carved stone tub in my bathing chamber. I start the water, and as steam begins to curl from the surface, I choose a bottle bath oil labeled lavender and ash blossom and add it to the water, the fragrance instantly fills the room. I sink in with a hiss, the warm water and oils soothing my aching muscles. I'm surprised that using magic strained them. I tip my head back against the edge of the tub.

And not only the forest, but the land, *speaks* to me.

Not in words, but in song and sensation. I had felt the stirring of its roots. I can feel the hum beneath my feet in the same way the flames dance along my skin without burning me. I called to it, and it answered. For the first time since I was taken away from my home, I don't feel like a prisoner of fate, but a piece of something larger.

Chosen.

"I didn't burn the forest down," I murmur to the ceiling, a small smirk clinging to my lips. *Though I did nearly set my hair on fire...* I laugh softly.

I stay in the tub until the water cools and then rise and dry myself off. I slip into the deep green sleeping gown I chose, my fingers brushing over the soft silk. It clings to me in all the right places, the delicate straps nearly leaving my shoulders bare, the hem just whispering at my thighs. I grab a matching short, satin robe and tie the sash loosely around my waist, when a knock sounds at the door.

My heart skips a beat. I don't have to ask who it is.

I open the door.

Reavian stands there, a loose dark shirt unbuttoned at the top, revealing a sliver of his chest. His eyes—dark and steady, sweep over my body before flicking away.

For a moment, I just stare. He looks like something out of a dream—pale skin like moonlight, sharp jaw, dark hair falling in tousled waves that brush his cheekbones. His loose shirt clings to his frame, just tight enough to hint at the strength beneath. And those eyes, dark and flecked with something brighter, sweep over me like a slow drawn blade.

Standing here in the low light, he looks devastating.

And he's looking at *me,* like he's barely holding himself together.

"Hi," I say, leaning against the doorframe. "Here to find out if the rumors are true, and Vaedric barely made it out of training alive?"

One corner of his mouth twitches. "That bad, huh?"

"No, it went pretty well actually. But I *did* almost set his hair on fire, as well as mine."

He laughs, low and warm. "Gods, I'll have to stay out of range then."

I step aside and let him in, catching the way his gaze lingers on me.

"You're doing ok?" he asks.

"I'm exhausted," I admit. "But... I'm proud of myself. I'm learning to control the flame. But speaking to the forest and the land, that just feels natural."

He nods.

A second knock interrupts the moment. Two stewards enter, bowing slightly before laying out a lavish meal on the table. Plates of roasted venison glazed with spiced berries, golden root vegetables, a warm loaf of a cranberry honey bread, wine, and two delicate chocolate tarts each topped with what one of the stewards tells me is a firefruit glaze are placed on the table. The other steward lights two candles and places them in the center, casting the area in an amber light before they both excuse themselves, and leave the room.

I blink. "What's all this?"

Reavian shrugs casually. "I stopped by the kitchens earlier. I figured you would be hungry when you returned... I just thought we could eat together."

He *planned* this for us. My heart flutters. Truth is I was riding such a high from training that I completely forgot about eating all together.

I smile and sit in the chair across from him. "You are full of surprises aren't you, Reavian Nyvaris?"

"Don't say that like it's a bad thing," he says, grinning.

I love when he smiles like this. A true, real smile. I wish he did it more often.

We eat slowly, laughter bubbling between bites as I recount the near-miss with a fireball that *may* have grazed Vaedric's hair. Reavian nearly chokes on his wine.

"I swear, the man didn't even flinch," I say, wide-eyed. "He just raised an eyebrow, like it was just a wayward spark."

When the laughter between us fades, I ask him about his day.

"I spent most of it with Kaiel, he's healing well," Reavian says, setting down his wine. "It'll probably still be a few weeks before he's back to his old self again though. Brynn's talking more now, mostly to him, but it's more than she's spoken since I've met her."

"I should visit with her tomorrow," I say. "I want to tell her all about my training so far."

He nods, then leans back slightly in his chair.

"Iska's been spending her time in the infirmary, working with the Emberwrights. She met one of the Flame Wardens today—Tharen Durn. He came in with a minor injury, I guess. She said she talked with him about the state of the realms," his voice lowers. "It's worse than we thought—Liraeth and Lucien... their reach is spreading. Much faster than anyone expected."

A heavy silence settles between us. I reach for my wine glass, the candlelight dancing softly across its surface.

Reavian watches me for a moment, then smiles faintly. "Let's forget about all that for tonight. For now, let's just enjoy spending some time together."

And we do just that, small talking between bites, our words trailing into soft silences and stolen glances. Our chairs have edged closer without us realizing, and when his knee brushes mine beneath the table, neither of us move.

After some time, the stewards return to clear the plates, and I murmur a quiet thank you as they leave.

"You didn't have to plan all this for us tonight, thank you," I say.

"I wanted to," he replies.

I glance at him, and catch the way his eyes soften, how his fingers brush the edge of his glass like he needs something to do with his hands. The room warms from the way his eyes linger on me. Maybe it's the invisible thread that always seems to hum between us.

I draw in a breath.

"Do you...feel it too?" I ask. "The pull between us, like there is something there?"

His eyes meet mine, and for a long heartbeat, he doesn't answer.

Then he looks away.

"Auren..."

I wait for him to continue. But instead, he says almost too gently, "It's been a long day for you. I should go. I'll come by and take you for weapons training tomorrow."

He stands, and I rise with him.

"Reavian, what's wrong?" I ask, my voice soft.

Did I say something wrong? Do something wrong?

"Nothing," he says, moving toward the door.

"You're lying to me."

He reaches for the door handle but doesn't open it, clearly battling with himself over whether or not to tell me what is bothering him.

I step in front of him and reach up and touch his face, my fingers brushing his jaw, coaxing him to look at me.

He does. Slowly.

Our eyes lock.

Something cracks open between us.

His hands grip my waist in a flash of motion, and then his mouth is on mine, it's hot and demanding. I barely have time to gasp before I'm lifted off the ground. My back presses into the door with a thud that rattles into the hall. I wrap my legs around his waist on instinct, the satin of my robe slipping against his shirt, my fingers diving into his hair as he kisses me like I'm fire, and he needs to burn.

I moan into him, my whole body feeling alive and *wanting*. His lips move against mine with purpose, not gentle— ravenous. His hand grips my thigh, sliding up, tracing the edge of my sleeping gown, as if he needs to touch every inch of me to make sure that I'm real. I clumsily remove my robe, letting it fall to the floor beneath us.

My name escapes him between kisses, fragile and hoarse, like a secret meant only for the dark.

"Auren..."

My breath hitches, and I roll my hips toward his without thought. I kiss him back, harder, devouring him—my hands trailing down his back and gripping the hem of his shirt. I curl my fingers into the warmth of his skin.

Every touch sets me on fire, it's rising and roaring.

His mouth moves to my jaw, then my throat. He kisses a place beneath my ear, that makes my body go taut. One of his hands cups the back of my head as the other slides under my gown, his fingers grazing the bare skin of my inner thigh, then slowly moving higher. I gasp, my head falling back against the door, his palm still cradling it.

"Gods," he breathes against my skin. "You're...everything."

I let my hands roam across the hard lines of his chest, sliding under his shirt. He shudders when I lightly rake my nails down his stomach. My lips find his again. We kiss like we can't breathe without it, like the very fabric of the world would fall apart if we stopped.

His hips press into mine, and the friction steals the air from my lungs. My pulse pounds in my ears, in every inch of me. I feel like the fire within me has somehow escaped, and I burn wherever he touches me.

He grips my ass with both of his hands and pulls me harder against him, and I make a sound that I don't quite recognize—a needy, aching cry that lights something deeper within him. His response is a low growl, and he finds my mouth again, this time more desperate.

It's messy.

Real.

I don't know where I end, and he begins.

And then—he stills.

His hands freeze on my body. His breath is hard and ragged on my cheek.

Slowly, he pulls back.

My legs loosen around his waist as he gently sets me on the ground, his touch lingering like he doesn't want to let me go, but he does.

I stand trembling before him, my lips swollen and my chest

heaving. The silk of my sleeping gown clings to my skin and my fingers are still tangled in his shirt.

Why did he stop? I want *more*.

"I don't understand," I whisper. "Did I do something wrong?"

Reavian looks wrecked, like it's taking everything in him not to reach for me again.

"No," he says, his voice rough. "You're perfect."

He leans in, kissing my forehead with an aching softness.

Then, he walks out the door.

It closes behind him, leaving only the echo of my name on his lips and the heat of his body still tangled with mine.

I curl into bed, dazed and aching. The flame inside me is still burning, unfulfilled. I pull the blankets up, but sleep doesn't come.

Not with my heart pounding.

Not with the ghost of his hands still on my skin.

Not when I was left wondering what he'd meant by *perfect*, and why it suddenly feels like I am anything but.

Chapter Twenty One-Reavian

I haven't slept.

I sit in silence, planted in the high-backed chair near the window in my room, my arms braced in the armrests like I'm trying to anchor myself to something solid. But nothing feels solid. Not when every breath I take still carries her scent. Not when my lips still burn from the heat of her kiss.

The fire in the hearth that lit my room has long since died, the coals dark and cold.

But still, I burn.

I stand abruptly and begin to pace again. The boards beneath my boots creak faintly, a rhythm now worn into the very floor from my restless path. I've walked a line between resolve and regret for hours, my mind spinning through every second of what happened between us.

Her body pressed to mine. Her legs around my waist. Her lips—gods, her lips on mine, on my neck. That silk gown. Her voice whispered my name like it was something holy.

"Do you... feel it too?" she had asked me, just before I tried to leave her room.

Of course, I feel it—that pull, that thread. I felt it the moment I saw her. I felt it when I had that conversation with Kaiel on the ship, the one where he told me we were fated. But I hadn't let myself believe that she felt it too. Not truly. Not until she had said it aloud and shattered every invisible wall that I built to protect her from the truth.

I wanted this to be real. I want her to choose me because she made that choice, not because of some ancient magic deciding her future for her. I want her love because it is hers to give.

Not because she is forced to give it to me.

Not because the stars had written it.

Not because of some thread she couldn't see but still felt pulling her in my direction.

What if it isn't me she wants? What if it's just the bond?

I wanted her when I couldn't even see who she was, when I would dream of her, both of us shrouded in darkness.

But did she feel that way too?

I lean heavily against the fireplace mantle, gripping the cold stone until my knuckles begin to ache. I glimpse my reflection in the dark glass above it. I look broken, my eyes shadowed and hollow.

I look like a monster.

You're perfect, I had told her.

Because she is.

Because I am not.

I am the son of Liraeth. Born from blood, shadow, and cruelty. The child of the very monster who had stolen Auren's family from her, the woman who had destroyed her world. My veins carry the same darkness. The same hunger. I have spent my entire life trying to bury it, but it's still there.

She should hate me. The thought echoes in my mind sharply. And yet, she looks at me like I am the only thing keeping her steady. Like I am something... *good.*

It terrifies me.

Because she deserves more. She deserves light, peace, and safety—and all I have to offer her is a sword, shadow and a name soaked in blood.

I will give her space. Be the version of myself that she can walk away from easily.

Even if it kills me.

***

I stand outside her door, my cool mask already in place.

The dark prince. The soldier.

Controlled.

Composed.

I knock once, and when she opens the door, my chest thuds at the sight of her. Dressed in her training leathers, her golden hair tied into a crown braid. The soft green sleeping gown she wore last night is lying on the floor.

"Ready?" I ask, my voice flat and professional, making sure I don't let my eyes linger.

She studies me for a moment, her brows pinching slightly, but she nods.

We walk in silence to the training circle. I keep just ahead of her, giving her space.

Distance.

The sun beats down over the stone, casting long shadows across the space. Auren stands across from me, sword in hand, her expression focused, but uncertain.

I don't let myself smile at the way she grips the hilt too tightly, or the fire flickering just beneath the surface of her eyes. I don't tease her. I won't let the softness that I've only ever given her slip through.

We train.

Hard.

I stand a few paces away; the dark sleeves of my shirt rolled at my forearms. I adjust my stance and make my face unreadable and distant.

"Feet shoulder-width apart," I say cooly. "Wider. You're off balance the way you're standing."

She adjusts, and I circle her, giving a slight nod of approval. I step closer, close enough to feel the heat radiating from her skin. I move my hand to her waist, briefly and impassively, correcting the angle of her hips.

"Lower your center of gravity. You're not a tree swaying in the wind. You're a blade. *Rooted*. Controlled."

The contact between us is gone in an instant, but it lingers on my skin like a brand.

I move back in front of her, and draw my blade, positioning it with a fluid ease.

"Now, swing," I tell her.

She strikes, and I parry without effort, my blade flashing as it meets hers.

"Again."

The word comes out harsher than I intend.

I want to tell her she's improving. That her grip is getting steadier, her strikes are getting more confident. But I don't. I can't. If I let myself be kind, I won't be able to keep the distance that she needs.

I continue to give her commands, short and clipped. No softness, no encouragement. Just cold instruction, and the occasional correction when her grip falters or her foot lands too far forward.

Inside... I'm unraveling at the seams.

She smells like lavender and something that I don't think I will ever be able to name. And every time she looks up at me with hurt in her eyes—confused and searching—I feel my resolve crack a little more.

You're too close.

She's too close.

I step away again, trying to put distance where none really exists. "You're swinging too high," I bark. "You leave your ribs exposed. That's where they'll strike, and you'll die."

She flinches, not from my words themselves, but from the bite that I give them.

My stomach twists. I hadn't meant to sound so harsh.

But maybe I *had*.

Because if I soften, even for a moment, I don't know if I would be able to stop myself from touching her again. From kissing her. From falling headfirst into a fate I'm not sure she really wants.

Auren resets her stance, her eyes flashing with frustration now. She moves through the form again—this time smoother, stronger. Her shoulders roll back with confidence. Fire blooms in her expression.

God's help me, she looks beautiful when she fights. Fierce and alive.

I want to tell her. I want to drop my sword and step closer and tell her she is *everything*. That I have been hers since we met in our dreams back when we were young, before she ever ended up directly in my arms. Before I could even see who she was.

But I don't.

Instead, I step forward and disarm her with a quick twist of my blade and catch her sword before it hits the ground.

"You're getting sloppy," I say flatly.

Her chest rises and falls with heavy breaths. She doesn't reach for the sword, her eyes now fiery and tinged with tears.

"You clearly don't want to be here, so I won't keep you any longer!" she snaps.

My heart stumbles in my chest.

I watch as she shakes her head slowly, eyes narrowing.

"You've barely looked at me. You've barely spoken to me. It's obvious that you feel what happened between us was a mistake."

My lungs refuse to work.

Every word she says is a blade, sinking in deep, twisting.

No. Never a mistake. You are the only thing in this world that feels right.

But I don't say that. I can't. She deserves much better than me.

I let the silence speak for me.

She scoffs softly, hurt flashing across her features before she masks it.

"I'll ask Vaedric to find someone else to train me," she says. Her voice is steady, but her eyes are not. "Someone who actually wants to."

And then she turns and walks away.

I watch her go, my hands limp at my sides. Only when she

vanishes back into the keep do I allow myself to breathe, and that breath comes out ragged and hollow.

She's not a mistake.

She is the only source of light in the night of my soul.

But still... I let her go.

I remain in the center of the training circle long after she's gone. The silence left in her wake feels louder than any sword clash. My grip on her training blade tightens, knuckles turning white. I have let her believe that she was a mistake. That I regretted touching her. Kissing her. That everything that happened between us has been nothing more than some fleeting moments of weakness.

And I hate myself for it.

I drop the sword with a hollow clang and turn away, my shoulders rigid as I head back toward the keep. But the moment I pass through the shadowed arch of the corridor, I press both hands to the stone wall and let my head fall forward.

My breath shakes, and my throat burns like I've swallowed fire. I feel something inside me crack a little more. She is the only light I have ever known, and I just sent her walking into the dark.

Chapter Twenty Two–Auren

The stone corridors of Solmere Keep send a chill across my skin. A breeze is drifting through the high, carved archways, barely stirring the heavy feeling pressing into my chest. I keep walking.

I don't know where to go.

The conversation with Reavian during training—if you can even call it that—has left me hollowed out. My heart aches from the weight of his silence. How have we gone from a kiss last night that shook my world to today, where he didn't even want to look at me?

You clearly don't want to be here, I had said.

His silence, his only reply, has ripped me to shreds inside.

My steps carry me toward the infirmary, almost of their own accord. I know exactly who I'll find there.

Brynn.

I move quietly through the threshold, my boots muted on the

smooth stone floor. The space is still, bathed in soft light from some high arched windows. A few Emberwrights work quietly, but my eyes go straight to the back of the infirmary, to Kaiel's room.

Brynn sits by his bedside, her body curled slightly toward him, and one of her arms draped protectively across the edge of the mattress. Kaiel looks pale, but better than when I last saw him.

I approach the doorway, slow and uncertain. Brynn tilts her head.

"I—" I hesitate. "Can you come talk to me for a minute? I really just need a friend to listen."

Brynn studies me for a moment.

"Sure," she says, standing and following me to a bench outside Kaiel's room.

She sits beside me, and I let the words pour out. I tell her everything—about our first kiss, how he held me through the night. How last night he came to my room and planned a private dinner, just for us. How it felt like something powerful was building between us... only for him to pull away like it meant nothing.

I tell her that when we kiss, it feels like our souls are reaching for each other.

And then I tell her about this morning—his coldness, the distance. The sharp commands like he was trying to burn away every trace of what we had shared.

"Maybe I imagined it. Maybe I'm the only one who felt that way," I whisper.

There is a long pause before Brynn says quietly, "He's pushing you away."

My eyes lift to hers.

"He looks at you like you're the only thing holding him together. I've seen it." Her voice is calm, measured. "He's at war... with himself."

I blink.

Her words catch me off guard, I'm not sure what to make of them.

"I don't know, Brynn. You didn't see him today," I say, my voice low. "He was so distant, cruel even. He's never been like that with me."

"I've seen how he looks at you, this isn't about you. It's something he's fighting in himself," she says, certainty coating each word.

I sit with that, the silence stretching between us for a moment. I take in a shaky breath, not wanting to fall back into the ache of my splintered heart.

I clear my throat.

"So, where are you really from?" I ask her. "In this world I mean, since I know it's not Chicago, like you told me before."

I give her a crooked smile.

Brynn blinks, the question and my change of subject clearly

catching her off guard.

"The Realm of Tide and Storm," she says, her gaze drifting toward one of the arched windows. "My family had a little house built into the cliffs on the outskirts far outside the borders of the city. You could hear the waves crashing below at night—like thunder, but wilder."

I close my eyes and imagine it.

"That sounds... beautiful."

"It was," she says softly, her voice growing distant. "Before everything changed."

Before I can ask more, a quiet presence shifts the air around us. Vaedric.

He stands a few feet away, his arrival silent. I sit up straighter. How much of our conversation did he overhear?

He offers a calm nod. "Shall we meet again tomorrow for more training?"

"Yes," I reply quickly. "I'd like that."

He regards me for a moment, then inclines his head. "I'll send someone for you in the morning."

"I also need to keep training with weapons. I want to be ready," I tell him. " Reavian will no longer be able to train me, I was wondering if there is someone else here who might have the time?"

"Kessa Valryn is one of my best Wardens. Precise, principled, and skilled in all forms of blade. I'll assign her to you," Vaedric replies smoothly. "You shall train three days with me, three with

Kessa, alternating between us. One day of rest."

"Alright. I'll be ready," I reply. "Thank you."

He gives me a respectful incline of his head, before he disappears down the corridor.

I let out a breath. At least I'll be keeping busy, and there will be less time to dwell on whatever is happening with Reavian and I.

Brynn reaches over and takes my hand, her grip firm but gentle. "You will follow the right path, you both will. You always do," she says, her voice low and sure.

I look at her sharply. "What?"

But Brynn is already standing. "I need to check on Kaiel."

I start to go in with her but pause as a memory flashes behind my eyes.

My body flinches instinctively before I catch myself.

"How is he?" I force out, keeping my voice quiet and steady.

Brynn glances back. "He's getting stronger. He... asked to see you today."

My heart tightens. "I'm not ready."

"I know." Brynn squeezes my hand once more before she slips back into his quiet room.

I turn to leave and spot a familiar figure as I step out of the infirmary, leaning up against the wall.

Iska.

Her silver hair gleams in the light and her expression is grim.

"Hey... is everything alright?" I ask, approaching her.

"No," Iska replies.

"Reavian told me last night that the state of the realms is much worse than we thought."

Iska nods slowly. "It is."

"How bad is it?" I ask her earnestly.

Iska's voice turns grave. "The Realm of Veiled Stars is nearly sixty percent corrupted. Tharen, one of the wardens I have met here, says that they estimate we only have around six months before that entire realm falls."

My breath catches. "Six months?"

"Yes." Iska confirms. "And if we lose The Realm of Veiled Stars, Tharen believes that we will likely lose the war that looms over us entirely."

I clench my fists at my sides, rage building in me for what the people there must be going through, for what the land there must be feeling. "Then I will stop that corruption from spreading. I don't care what it takes—I *will* stop it."

Iska studies me for a moment and nods, seemingly accepting my resolve to see this through. "Good."

***

I strip off my leathers and step into a steaming bath. I sink beneath the surface, absorbing the warmth into every inch of me. My limbs ache and my soul feels bruised.

The flame within me feels stronger. It hasn't dimmed even after everything that happened with Reavian today. If anything, it's grown. Fierce and steady.

Perhaps Brynn was right, and Reavian's battle is with himself. Either way, I need to focus on my training, so that we may all survive.

When I emerge from my bath, I wrap myself in a soft robe and walk out to the terrace, and stare into the night. The stars shimmer above.

Help us, they seem to call. For beyond them somewhere, in The Realm of Veiled Stars, corruption spreads like rot. I press my hand to my chest; my fingers splayed over the place where my power pulses within me like a second heartbeat.

My blood feels alive with a purpose. I will *not* let the darkness take over this world.

I whisper to the stars above, barely audible to even myself. "I'll train until I can no longer stand. I'll fight until I bleed. I will burn brighter than anything that tries to snuff me out. I will save you, and the people here in this world. I promise."

They shimmer in response to my words.

I slip into my bed and lay in the dark.

The power within is growing. It flickers behind my ribs, and curls at my spine, it whispers in my every breath.

It's rising in me.

And tomorrow, I will rise with it.

Chapter Twenty Three—Auren

The first breath I take in smells like smoke and dew. The air over the stone circle is cool, but the ground beneath my feet feels warm, ancient heat threading its way up through my boots.

I can feel the power and magic here.

I stand at the center of the circle, a fine layer of nerves buzzing through my arms.

Vaedric stands across from me, his dark cloak pulled back, his expression unreadable.

"Today we will begin," he says. "With wielding your fire for combat."

I nod, exhaling slowly. I remember his words from our previous lesson.

Let it burn, but do not let it consume you.

We start with orbs. Small, concentrated spheres of flame, summoned to my palm.

"Control it, but do not force it," he says. "The flame responds to you, but if you push it too hard, it *will* bite back."

The first orb I summon fizzles out halfway to formation. The second one nearly singes my eyebrow. But by the fifth, I have it hovering, a pulsing golden sphere alive in my palm.

I practice launching them at stone targets—concentric circles carved into heavy slabs that line the far edge of the ring. My first few miss by a large margin, but gradually they begin to find their mark. The formation of the spheres themselves is starting to feel like second nature now.

Then we move on to streams of flame. I pull ribbon like fire from my hands and shape them into long flowing arcs. Vaedric teaches me to guide the streams of flame into the targets.

I then start doing some combos.

Stream. Orb. Stream.

The air smells like ash and ozone. Sweat slips down my spine. But the flame answers to me now, doing what I want it to.

Orb. Stream. Orb.

Each one hits its mark. I keep sending the fire forward at the targets. My heart keeps in time with each strike, the flame becoming an extension of myself. Burn. Breathe. Burn again.

By midday, my leathers are stuck to my skin with sweat, loose strands of my hair sticking to my cheeks. Vaedric hands me a skin of cool water.

"You're doing well," he says, his tone softer now. "You're a natural at channeling it. But for close combat, you will need to learn how to make it serve your blade."

I wipe my brow and tilt my head curiously towards him. "How do I do that?"

Vaedric steps forward and draws his own sword. With a flick of his wrist, flame blooms along the steel, encasing it in a steady wreath of heat and light. It moves with the blade, dancing but controlled, like a loyal shadow.

My breath catches.

"This is fire-forging," he says. "Not true forging, like a blacksmith would. You are essentially weaving your flame onto your blade's edge. Call upon your fire and will it to purge the darkness, and the corrupted it strikes will wither to ash."

He steps forward, and hands me a sword, lighter than the one I used while training with Reavian. It appears to be custom made; it's fitted to my hand perfectly.

The blade is unlike anything I have ever seen. Forged from black steel marbled with gold, it looks like light and shadow have been folded into the metal itself. The corded grip matches seamlessly. The hilt is gold, inlaid with onyx. I brush my thumb over the vines carved along the guard—sweeping delicate patterns etched with care.

But it's the pommel that takes my breath away.

A crimson jewel sits embedded in the base, and within it a flicker of flame burns inside. Magic hums beneath my skin, almost as if answering it.

"I had it made for you," Vaedric says quietly. "Forged with your flame in mind, the fire in the jewel is from the Eternal Flame. It's yours now, to claim it all you need to do is name it, it's tradition here."

I run my fingers along the hilt, tracing the contrast of dark and light. The shadow-like curve of black obsidian, the sunlit glint of gold. It feels balanced, and familiar.

"Virethyn," I whisper. "That's its name."

I'm not sure where the name comes from, but it feels right. Like this is what it was meant to be named.

Vaedric tilts his head, studying me. "What does the name mean to you?"

"It's light and shadow—opposites woven into something whole. Something that endures, even in the dark."

He gives me a smile, small but true. "Then, it's a worthy name."

Silence lingers for a moment.

I hold out the sword.

"How do I ...?"

"Call the flame to the hilt," he says, stepping behind me. "Let it wrap your grip. Then guide it, slowly. Give it a reason to want to cling to the steel."

My hands tremble as I try. At first, the fire sputters along the blade and vanishes. The second time I try, it sparks only at the tip.

But the third time...

I focus on the weight of it in my hand. *You need to be the light in the darkness.* The memory of my mother's voice rings through my head, and the fire roars to life. It clings to my blade, dancing along it like a flickering golden second skin.

I laugh, stunned that I pulled it off. "I did it."

"You did," Vaedric says. "Now show me how you'll use it."

The rest of the afternoon passes in blur and blaze.

I slash and spin, flame trailing my movements in vivid arcs. The sword sings with every strike, the heat from the flame within me dancing along my spine. He pushes me to vary my attacks—cutting waves of fire that flare outward, and spiraling strikes that send ripples of the flame across the circle.

My muscles burn, and my arms ache. But I won't stop.

Each swing is a release.

Of pain and worry.

Of longing.

By the time the sun hovers low, casting a crimson light over us, I finally drop to one knee. My chest heaving.

Vaedric approaches me quietly. "You didn't have to push yourself so hard."

I don't look up. "I wanted to."

Silence hangs between us for a moment before he asks gently, "Do you want to talk about it?"

I shake my head. "No."

He crouches beside me, resting his forearms on his knees. "Your mother...she was like that too," he says. "Always pushing forward, even when she was fighting battles inside."

I turn to face him, sweat beading down my cheeks. "Before... you said you loved her?"

He gives me a soft chuckle. "Everyone did, in some way. But she was not mine to keep."

He pauses, then smiles. "Would you like to hear about the time she got us banned from an entire tavern district?"

I blink.

"What?" I ask, I can't even imagine it.

"When we were young, she stole a warden's horse," he says with a fond shake of his head. "Claimed she had to do it, because he insulted her hair. She proceeded to ride it straight through a wedding procession and dumped it off in a fountain."

I burst into laughter, wiping my face with the back of my arm. "That sounds nothing like her... are you sure we are talking about the same person."

He smiles. "Oh, I'm sure. What was she like... raising you?"

The smile on my face softens. "Super strict, fiery. Full of love," I say, remembering her smile. "She never wanted me to feel afraid... even when I know now that she must have been terrified every day."

Vaedric's expression shifts—grief and pride warring in his features. "She would be so proud of you."

"Did she have power, like me?" I ask him earnestly.

"She had a minor magic, her ability to glamour. Your flame

comes from King Veylas's bloodline, but she had her own type of fire. Everyone could see it," Vaedric says, losing himself in the memory of her for a moment.

I lower my gaze. I wish I'd had more time with her. Not just the version who raised me, but the one who lived here. The one who stole horses. I wish I could ask her about her life here.

Footsteps begin to echo behind us, light and rhythmic. I turn to see a woman approaching. She's slim, tan skinned and clad in leather armor. Her curly black hair is pulled up in a high ponytail. I notice two swords sheathed at her back, and her grin is instant.

"Well, *someone's* been setting this circle on fire," the woman says. "You must be, Auren."

Vaedric stands. "Auren, this is Kessa Valryn. She will be doing your combat training with you, starting tomorrow."

Kessa drops into a low bow, then pops back up with a wink. "You can call me Kess. I specialize in dodging, dual-wielding, and getting into just a *little* bit of trouble."

I laugh. "It's nice to meet you, Kess."

Vaedric clears his throat, trying not to smile. "She's one of the best warriors in the realm."

Kessa nods in agreement. "I'm also the most fun. I can't wait to train with you. Ya know, it *could* be the three mugs of sunroot tea and two honey cakes I had before coming here, but I think we are gonna be fast friends."

I laugh, the exhaustion falling away from me just a little.

Kessa gives me a two-fingered salute. "See you at dawn, I'll bring extra tea."

And just like that she turns to leave.

I turn to Vaedric. "She seems fun," I laugh. "And she only gets into a *little* bit of trouble, huh?"

"Yes," Vaedric says with a smile. "She grew on me, Like a rash or... wildfire."

I chuckle and then say softly, "Thank you for today."

"You've earned your rest," Vaedric says, his gaze warm. "Go. Eat. Hydrate. You'll need your strength to deal with her in the morning," he says.

He winks at me, then claps his hand on the back of my shoulder, before walking into the keep.

***

I walk the halls of Solmere Keep, Virethyn strapped across my back, my hair still damp from washing the day of training away. My steps take me past the guest wing. I pause, hand hovering near a door that isn't mine. I found out from Iska earlier, which room was his.

I knock.

No answer. Reavian isn't here.

I tell myself that I'm not disappointed. That I just wanted to tell him about my day of training. About my new sword. About the story Vaedric told me about my mother.

After I stand awkwardly outside his door for a while, waiting to see if he'll appear, I leave and head toward the dining hall. It's quieter than I would have expected—only a few scattered fae at tables, lost in their own conversations. I grab a plate and fill it with roasted vegetables, soft bread, and some sort of spiced meat—and decide to just bring it up to my room.

I carry it out to the terrace and eat it in silence.

Alone.

The stars in the sky twinkle their hellos to me, and I give them a nod and a soft smile back.

I did well today. I'm getting stronger.

When I'm done, I walk back inside and collapse into bed, ready for sleep.

As I close my eyes, I wonder what Reavian's fighting.

Where he is, and if he's okay.

Maybe I'll see him tomorrow.

Chapter Twenty Four-Reavian

The scent of bitter herbs clings to the walls here like ghosts. The infirmary is quiet, but not empty. It never really is. Somewhere behind me, one of the healers hums as she crushes something with a pestle. On the other side of the room, someone coughs behind a partition. My footsteps are soft as I approach Kaiel's room. He stands near the center of it, for the first time since that night in the forest.

He's bracing himself on a walking staff, his weight uneven. He moves slowly across the space, skin pale, his arm and chest healing in jagged red patches. But he's up, and he isn't alone.

Brynn sits by the far wall, perched on the end of his cot. She's watching him. Carefully. As if the thread that keeps her steady now is wound around him.

I pause in the doorway, unseen for a moment.

"You're going to have to stop hovering like a nursemaid eventually," Kaiel says to her with a crooked smile.

Brynn smiles back at him. A real smile, soft.

I feel a strange twist in my chest.

Jealousy?

No, perhaps just wonder.

Are they fated too?

I'm not sure, but there is something in the glance Kaiel gives her as she stands, and the way she lingers in the doorway for a moment before slipping out. She gives me a smile as she walks past.

When I step into view, Kaiel gives me a smirk. "Well, look who crawled out of his brooding cave."

I step inside, my boots silent on the stone. "I didn't want to interrupt your dramatic recovery montage. Besides… it's only been a day."

Kaiel laughs, slowly walking over to his cot and sitting down on the edge of it.

"You're up and moving around, that's great," I tell him.

"The healers say that I should be able to start training again soon, I'll be able to get back to my old self." He lets out a slow breath. "How is Auren?"

I don't answer right away.

"Reav?" Kaiel blinks.

I turn my gaze away, my jaw tight. "Something happened between Auren and I."

My friend straightens.

"She said she felt it, Kaiel. She said she felt something between us. And I..." I let out a sharp breath. "I walked away. Or I *tried* to. As soon as she asked, I wanted to run. Because if she's only drawn to me because of some fated mate bond, then none of it has been real."

Kaiel remains silent, listening.

"But as I tried to leave... I looked at her, and I couldn't leave her. Instead, I kissed her." My voice dips low and rough. "We had kissed before, but this wasn't like before. It was desperate, like we'd both been starving. It felt like kissing her was the only thing that could bring me back to life."

I run a hand through my hair, my fingers clenching tight at the nape of my neck. I can still remember the scent of her hair. Lavender and ash blossom, with something else, something sweet.

"And even then, I pulled away. Because it's not *me* she wants. It's the bond, it's that pull that she feels. Maybe she thinks it's her choice but we both know that it isn't."

Kaiel shakes his head. "You really believe that? Is that all that draws *you* to her? Just the bond?"

I don't answer. But I know it's not.

"So, what then? You're just going to pretend that you haven't been in love with her since that first night you dreamed of her?" Kaiel asks, his voice softened.

"I'm trying to give her space. Time. The chance to choose something other than me if she wants to. I'd rather break my own heart, than trap her with fate."

Kaiel studies me for a moment, then slides back onto his cot, swinging his legs up and leaning his back against the wall.

"She's begun training," I say finally.

Kaiel nods, his expression turning a bit more serious. "I heard, she's got everyone here whispering about her already."

"She's strong, I've been watching her," I admit.

Kaiel raises an eyebrow at me. "You do realize how deeply creepy that sounds, right?"

A breath escapes me, almost a laugh.

Almost.

"I can't stay away," I admit. "But I can't stay near her either."

"Why?" Kaiel asks.

"I already told you, I want to give her a choice," I reply, looking down at my hands.

"If I tell her about the bond, if I say that out loud—then what? How do you tell someone they are *destined* to love you, and then ask them to decide for themselves? I'm a monster, Kaiel. She deserves better than to be saddled with someone like me. We both know it."

Kaiel sits there for a moment, something shifting in his expression.

"You think you're protecting her by stepping back," he says quietly. "But you're not protecting her. You are hiding from what you feel."

I don't answer him, and silence lingers between us for a

moment.

Kaiel's voice drops, steadier now. "You want her to choose you freely? Then stop running from her. Stop pretending that this is about her, when it's really about you. *You* don't think that you deserve her. But you do, Reav. You aren't your mother, you never have been. You're good."

I flinch slightly, his words hitting their mark.

Kaiel leans forward a bit, the edge of pain still visible in his posture. "I didn't get a choice Reav. Not in the woods that night, not when I was sent to kill Auren's parents and drag her here, not when I did the hundreds of other terrible things Liraeth sent me to do. I got to see all of it when the Emberwrights burned her control out of me. If I had had the choice—things would be very different. By not telling her, you are *not* giving her a choice, you are deciding for her."

And if she does choose me? What then? How can I even believe that it's real?

"I'm afraid that if I tell her, it will cage her," I reply, my voice barely more than a whisper.

"And what if, by not telling her, you're leaving her thinking that you don't care at all?"

His words linger within me, casting doubt on my decision to stay away.

I sit and visit with him for a while longer, before Brynn comes back in with something for him to eat. I say my goodbyes to them both, and head to my room to think.

I lie in my bed staring at the ceiling for hours.

Do I tell her?

Yes.

Kaiel was right. I'm going to tell her and then give *her* the choice to decide.

The decision settles in me like a stone that's been dropped into still water. I rise, heart pounding. Every step I take is a confirmation that this is the right thing to do. She deserves to know the truth.

Her room is tucked into one of the quieter wings of the keep. I know the path by heart. I stop in front of her door, the lantern beside it casting a soft glow of light across the stone floor.

I stare at it.

I raise my hand to knock, but then I stop.

Do you...feel it too?

The question she had asked me, strikes me like a blade. I remain standing at her door, my fingers grazing the wood. I think of how well she has been doing in training, how strong she looks.

Without me.

She's better off without me.

Even if I wish she wasn't.

I pull my hand back from the door, clenching it into a fist, and walk away.

Chapter Twenty Five-Auren

The morning sun slants across the sparring yard in golden streaks, warming the stone beneath my boots. I tighten my grip on my sword, breaths coming out fast from the drills we ran earlier.

Kessa does *not* believe in easing into things.

We have been at it for well over an hour now—footwork, blade angles, and defensive positioning. Again, and again and again. My arms are trembling, sweat sliding down my spine, and still, she circles me like a wolf just waiting for the right moment to strike.

"You're going to have to stop stabbing the air, and start stabbing *me*, princess," Kessa calls, spinning her blade in one hand like it weighs nothing.

"I'd love to. Stop moving so damn much," I pant.

She grins. "Poor thing. Is this big bad training session too much for the chosen one?"

I roll my eyes at her and lunge. She deflects the blow with a sharp clang and pivots into a low sweep. I barely jump back in time.

"Sloppy," she says, but not unkindly. "You drop your back shoulder every time you go for a high strike. Do it again, and I *will* smack you with the flat of my blade."

"Noted," I say, gritting my teeth.

We clash again. Steel against steel, sparks of our effort flying between us. This time I duck low, and feint left before twisting into a spin that has Kessa backpedaling. She raises a brow, impressed.

"Now that's more like it," she says. "Who taught you that?"

"No one," I smirk, my chest heaving. "Made it up."

"Well damn, maybe you *are* learning something."

We break apart and circle each other. My arms now heavy from the ache. My legs are burning, but something about the rhythm of it all keeps me moving. Kessa comes at me harder this time—prodding me and pushing me past my limits. I block one strike, then another. Her blade kisses the edge of my tunic, and I twist out of the way, breathless and laughing.

That makes her pause.

"What?" I ask between gulps of air.

"You laughed,"she says.

"So..." I reply.

"What's funny?" she asks me, and I catch a slight hint of confusion on her face.

"Nothing," I shrug. "I'm just having fun."

Kessa blinks. "Gods help us all."

We go again, our blades singing across the training yard, our boots scraping against the stone. The world narrows for me to only movement and breath, to sweat and steel and the challenge in Kessa's eyes. I am faster now, sharper. Each block comes with more precision, each attack with more intention.

Then, I hesitate.

Just for a breath.

A sudden tingling traces down my spine, and I glance over my shoulder toward the high stone wall, and my gaze lands at one of the tall pillars there at the far end of the yard. No one stands there—just the shadows beneath the arched doorway. But something about the air has shifted. Like someone had been there a moment before. Watching me. It isn't the first time I've felt this.

My heart skips.

And in that instant of distraction, Kessa sweeps my legs out from under me.

I hit the ground hard, landing with a thud and a gasp, the sky spinning overhead.

"Damn it," I groan.

Kessa leans over me, smirking. "Let's talk basics, princess. If you lose focus, you lose your footing."

I stare up at the clouds for a beat before sighing. "Got it."

But even as she helps me to my feet, I glance toward the shadows once more. The feeling has vanished, but something inside me whispers that it had been real.

I take the cloth Kessa tosses me and wipe the sweat from my brow.

"I didn't completely suck today, did I?" I ask.

"Nope. I think it's because you have yourself a damn good teacher," she replies.

And I have to admit, she's right.

I smile, my breath still coming in shallow bursts. "How did you learn all this?"

Kessa's expression shifts, just a flicker, but enough for me to see it wasn't always this way for her.

"I joined the Wardens when I was fifteen," she says looking towards the wall of targets. "Didn't have a fancy reason. Just saw too many people who couldn't defend themselves. Too many villages left to rot. Someone needed to stand between them and the monsters. Figured that someone might as well be me."

The quiet steel in her voice hits something inside me.

"I used to feel helpless all the time," I admit, surprising even myself. "Afraid of everything. I used to give my parents shit for keeping me sheltered, shielded from everyone and everything. But deep down... I think I liked being sheltered and protected. I felt small and breakable then, but now..." I look down at my hands. "Now I can feel myself getting stronger. And I want to use that strength to protect people."

Kessa gives me a long look, then nods once. "Well, it looks like you're learning the right things."

We stand in silence for a moment, feeling the breeze dancing across our skin.

Then she claps me on the shoulder. "Come on, we've earned a good meal."

The dining hall buzzes with low conversation and the clatter of cutlery as we enter. Kessa and I grab plates of spiced rice and roasted vegetables, before making our way to a long table where Iska and Brynn are already seated.

Brynn looks brighter today, her eyes clearer. The tension that normally sits in her shoulders has softened. Iska gives me a small nod as I sit down, her golden eyes then flicking toward the entrance.

A few minutes later a tall warden strides toward us—broad shouldered, sandy-haired, with bronze skin and the easy air of someone used to being noticed. He spots our group and makes his way over with a practiced confidence.

"Tharen," Iska greets, sounding entirely unimpressed.

"Iska," he replies with a mock bow, "still pretending that you aren't pleased to see me?"

Iska rolls her eyes, but I catch the faint blush that creeps into her cheeks.

Kessa leans toward me and says, "He's been trying to flirt with her. She just keeps pretending it's a game that she hasn't agreed to play."

"Do you ever shut up?" Tharen asks her, setting down his tray.

"Only when unconscious," Kessa replies sweetly.

Their banter warms something in my chest.

We start eating, and for a while it's just quiet conversation and the scraping of forks. Then Brynn glances around the table.

"Kaiel is doing much better... he's back on his feet," she says. "He's supposed to still be using a walking staff, but of course he ditched it the second no one was watching."

"That idiot," Iska mutters with a fond smile. "He'll fall and hurt himself or rip something open and then land himself right back in the infirmary."

"He's out of the infirmary now?" Tharen asks.

"Yes, he was given a room here today. Across from where Reavian's room is," Brynn replies, sending a quick glance my way.

Iska looks at Brynn with narrow eyes. "So... what's going on between you two anyways?"

Brynn flushes, her eyes darting down to her plate. She doesn't answer. When she looks up, it isn't Iska she looks at, it's me.

I hold her gaze and give her a small smile.

"Whatever it is... I'm grateful for it. Because it's brought you back to me," I tell her.

Brynn's mouth trembles slightly, and she gives me a slow, grateful nod.

The conversation between us eases again, shifting into small talk. Tharen brags about outshooting another warden during drills, Kessa loudly doubts his story, Iska pretends not to be impressed.

Tharen smirks. "I'm beginning to think that Kessa is just jealous."

"Oh, yes," Kessa says dryly. "I stay awake at night wishing I were a mediocre archer with zero fashion sense."

"Hey!" he protests. "This tunic is perfectly respectable."

"It's half buttoned and covered in your soup stains," Kessa replies.

"And still, I wear it better than half the court," he says with a wink in Iska's direction.

Iska doesn't smile; I do notice that another blush quickly sweeps across her cheeks though.

As the laughter fades into the clinking of dishes, I look toward Tharen. "Can I ask you something?"

He tilts his head. "Sure."

"What exactly is the current situation in the Realm of Veiled Stars?"

The energy at the table shifts instantly. Iska's hands still, Brynn looks down, and even Kessa falls silent.

Tharen's expression sobers. "The corruption is spreading. Fast. It's like rot, black and red vines choking out the trees turning them brittle, and the stars are dimming out in the skies over the border. My unit has been selected to scout again in a few weeks, near the northern edge. But last time Vaedric sent a scouting party..." he swallows. "Not everyone came back."

The silence at the table is heavy. The air is thick with worry, and grief.

I straighten my shoulders. "Then we will have to make sure it doesn't reach this realm again. And we will help the people, and the land in the Realm of Veiled Stars, we have to."

My voice is firm, sure.

Kessa looks at me with a steady intensity.

And Tharen, after a moment, gives me a slow nod. "We'll hold the line."

The others murmur in quiet agreement.

I sit back, the weight of the situation pressing into my chest. I don't let it crush me though, I let it become something I can stand on.

Chapter Twenty
Six-Auren

Weeks have passed in a blur of rhythm and flame. Some mornings were spent trading blows with Kessa, until sweat slicked my back and laughter burst unbridled from my chest. Others wreathed in flame, learning from Vaedric how to command and not just summon the magic that lies beneath my skin.

Today, I have felt a shift.

The fire bends to *my* will now.

It curls through the air as if it recognizes me, it welcomes me. I extend a hand, fingers steady, and a perfect circle scorches into the sand at my feet. No flickering, no stutter of doubt.

Just heat, precision and control.

"Again," Vaedric commands.

I obey. I stretch my arm outward, focus my breath, and conjure a spiral of flame this time—narrow and fast. It slices clean through the air and extinguishes with a sharp snap of my fingers.

I gather the flame within me again, this time shaping it into a wide wave that rolls across the training grounds with ease, before I extinguish that as well. I control the magic within me, it doesn't control me.

Vaedric's eyes narrow on me, watching the way that I wield it now. I no longer wield with fear or hesitation, but with *understanding*.

"You've stopped trying to tame it," he says. "Choosing to partner with it instead."

I nod, panting. "It speaks to me, I hear it now. Not with words exactly. But I *know* when it wants to rise, and when it is waiting."

He watches in silence for a beat longer, then offers a nod of pride. "You are—"

Before he can complete his sentence, a sharp whistle cuts across the training circle. I turn just in time to see Tharen storming towards us, three wardens at his side. They're all filthy and pale, blood crusting the edges of their armor. One of the wardens limps heavily, supported between the other two.

Vaedric's posture shifts instantly. "Get the healers," he commands a nearby guard, then he turns to me. "That's enough for the day, report here to Kessa in the morning."

"Alright," I reply, already moving away.

"What happened?" I hear Vaedric ask as I head toward the door into the keep.

What did happen?

Needing to know for myself, I quickly tuck behind the pillar near the far stone wall just before the door. The same place *he* watches me from. I can see the tense set of Tharen's shoulders.

"We were scouting the edge of Veiled Stars as ordered, near their southern border," Tharen says. "We were attacked by conscripted."

There is a pause then Vaedric's voice, low and thunderous. "How many did we lose?"

"We are the only four remaining of the ten that you dispatched," Tharen replies, his tone hardening. "The corruption is almost at the river's bend. If it crosses that, Starfall Keep will fall. And Vaelisar, he will..." Tharen trails off. "He needs help, reinforcements, he needs *Auren*. We should send help at once High Lord, he needs us."

There's a pause and then Vaedric's voice reappears, low and thunderous.

"*No.*"

I freeze.

"What do you mean no?" Tharen asks, his voice spiking with disbelief.

"I mean that Vaelisar made his choice. He turned us away, when the tide first shifted. I will not risk this realm to protect one that refused us aid when we needed it."

"He didn't *refuse*—"

"He did!" Vaedric snaps. "And now he must deal with the consequences. My duty is to *this* land. To *these* people."

"And Auren?" Tharen asks, "This world's chosen? You will just keep her hidden behind your gates, while the world burns outside them?"

The silence that follows his question is sharper than any shout.

I quickly back away before I can hear Vaedric's answer. My heart thunders as I slip through the corridors.

I know what I need to do.

I need maps. I need information. Anything that can help me understand this world better, its terrain, its people, its dangers.

I need to go to the keep's library.

The scent of parchment and wood greets me as I arrive. A pair of scholars look up as I enter. I offer them a polite nod and head in, looking for where the map archives would be.

"Are you looking for something specific?" the elder of the two scholars asks.

"Not really," I reply, calmly keeping my voice level. "I guess I'm just wanting to understand this world better. The geography, the history."

He eyes me for a moment before gesturing to a wide wooden cabinet. "Here is the central cartography collection. Realm boundaries, trade routes and the like can be found there. If you don't understand any symbols or glyphs, don't hesitate to ask."

I thank him and begin pulling maps out of the cabinet, before wandering over to the shelves and pulling out a book that seems to have information on the four realms of this world.

Four.

I have only heard anyone speak of three, the book seems to explain the ancient divisions of the courts, I add it to everything else I've gathered.

"Can I bring these to my room to read, or do I have to view them here?" I ask sweetly.

The elder scholar watches me, while the younger one replies. "No, you can bring them to your quarters but do be careful and bring them back when you are done."

"Thank you," I say with a polite smile.

I carry everything to my room.

Hours pass.

The desk in my room is a sprawl of paper—ink-stained sketches, curling corners of parchment, and a new sheet at the center of it all, where I've started to draw my own map of the realms.

I sketch Ashwynn Reach high in the northwestern part of the map, surrounded by sea. In the southwestern corner, I sketch the expanse of the Realm of Tide and Storm. In the center of everything, connecting to everything *but* Ashwynn Reach, a place called Soltharyn. The drawings on the original map indicate that this place is a scar across the land.

In the southeastern corner of the map, The Realm of Flame and Forest sits, the Pyrethorn Divide circling Solmere. And above that, just north of Flame and Forest, a large land mass in the northeast—the Realm of Veiled Stars.

I trace the path I'll need to take with my fingertip. I have to exit Solmere through the gate we came in, and ride around the eastern side of the Divide, then head north through the sacred forest until I reach the border of Veiled Stars.

I rise and walk out to the terrace.

The stars burn through the night sky, soft and silver.

"Guide me," I whisper to them. "No one else will come, I need you to tell me if I should."

A breeze stirs around me. The stars blink their reply.

Yes.

I step back from the terrace, my heart pounding. I grab a fresh piece of parchment and begin to write.

Reavian,

I know you'll notice I am not at training. The people of Veiled Stars are dying, Tharen told Vaedric today, and he refused to help them. I cannot sit behind these walls pretending that I am not a part of this. I'm the only one that can help them. Please try not to worry, I'm ready.

-Auren

I fold the note and leave it on the small table beside my bed. Then I pack quickly. Spare clothes, dried fruit, a flint, flask of water, the books I took from the library, and my map.

I find a horse at the stables in the city, and saddle and mount it, suddenly super grateful for the horseback riding lessons Mom and I took when I was younger. I ride toward the gates. When I reach them, the two guards standing there stiffen.

"Where are you going?" one of them asks me gruffly. "Vaedric is not with you."

"Surely, I'm not a prisoner here. I just want to ride my horse out in the sacred forest for a bit. Just to clear my head. It calms me," I say coolly. "Vaedric has already given me his permission. You don't want me to ride all the way back and drag him out of his bed to tell you himself, right?"

They both hesitate for a moment before opening the gates.

"Thank you, I'll be back soon," I tell them.

I hear the gates close behind me and trot the horse out into the sacred forest. As soon as I am out of view, I kick my horse into a full gallop.

I do not look back.

The stars above me seem to shimmer brighter in response.

Chapter Twenty
Seven - Reavian

The morning feels off.

There is no other way to describe it. The air too still, the corridors too quiet as I stride through them. Auren's laughter is usually echoing through the halls by now, sharp and bright, like a match struck in the dark. It's become part of my morning routine, listening to her laughter as I walk toward the training grounds—before hiding like the coward that I am to watch her train.

The silence is following me today like a shadow I can't shake.

I round a corner nearing my destination, when Vaedric steps out from a side passage and nearly collides with me.

"Reavian," he says, brow lifted.

"I was just going to—" I start.

"Hide in the shadows and watch her train again," Vaedric replies, his voice filled with a bit of amusement.

"I... yes," I say.

There's no point in denying it. He clearly knows exactly how I have spent every morning these past several weeks.

"She didn't show this morning," Vaedric replies. "Kessa is assuming she overslept. I however am wondering if there is something else afoot. Did you finally tell her?"

"Tell her what?" I ask, my throat going tight.

"That you are fated."

My pulse stutters. "How do you…?"

"I'm not blind Reavian," he says softly. "Did you finally tell her?"

"No."

Vaedric watches me for a moment, almost like he sees every thought passing behind my eyes.

"Well, perhaps she overslept then. She's been working hard. She deserves the rest if she needs it," Vaedric says, starting to walk past me a bit.

Then he stops, his back still facing me.

"You should tell her, don't wait too long. I regret not telling her mother how I felt, don't repeat the same mistake."

And with that, he silently walks away.

I pause in the halls for a moment, thinking about what he said. A feeling of dread overcomes me. He never got to tell Auren's mother how he felt.

And with everything going on, all the dangers we face…

I can't waste another breath.

I turn and sprint down the corridor, rounding corners too

sharply, nearly slamming into startled guards and wardens as I race toward the guest wing. My boots thunder over the stone, my heart slamming against my ribs. I reach for her door and knock hard.

No answer.

"Auren?"

I knock again.

"Please, can we talk?" my voice softens, and cracks a bit. "I'm sorry... I've been a fool."

Nothing.

I begin to panic.

I don't feel her near, that thread between us seems weaker, like it's far away.

Something is wrong.

I open the door slowly, it creaks wide.

She isn't here. No cloak draped on the chair. There is parchment and maps all over her desk. The doors to the terrace are open, a breeze tugs at the curtains.

But she is not outside.

"Auren?" I ask, walking hurriedly to her bathing chamber, its door is ajar, and there is no sign of her in there either.

Where is she?

And then I see it.

A note with my name scrawled across it, on the little table next to her bed. My hands shake as I reach for it.

Reavian,

I know you'll notice I am not at training. The people of Veiled Stars are dying, Tharen told Vaedric today, and he refused to help them. I cannot sit behind these walls pretending that I am not a part of this. I'm the only one that can help them. Please try not to worry, I'm ready.

-Auren

The words blur.

I blink hard, the paper crumpling in my fist as I bolt from the room. I don't think, I just run. I run to Kaiel's room as fast as my feet will take me.

He's fitting his sword into the sheath on his back when I burst in. He looks up, startled.

"She's gone," I gasp. "She went to the Realm of Veiled Stars. Alone." I hold out the note, and Kaiel grasps it out of my hand to read it.

He doesn't waste a second.

"What the hells are you standing here for? I'll get the others, and we will be right behind you. Go!" Kaiel says, snapping me out of my shock. "Be careful!"

We were both moving before his sentence was even finished. I grab a bag and hastily fill it with some spare clothing and provisions from my room. He runs by my side as we barrel through the keep. He turns off towards the dining hall where everyone else must be, and I don't stop running until I reach the stables. I grab an already saddled horse and ignore the stablemaster shouting behind me.

The morning sun blinds me for a moment, but I don't pause. I race for the gates.

When I arrive, two guards are sitting there, arguing about something.

"I need to get out," I tell them, my voice stony.

"Oh no, we aren't letting anyone else out. We are already going to be in deep shit when Vaedric finds out the last person we let out, didn't come back."

Auren.

Rage fills me. My heart beats so quickly it might burst from my chest.

"Let me out *now*, or I will fucking kill you both!" I shout.

The two guards exchange a look and immediately open the gates.

I kick my horse, it responds to my command instantly, increasing its speed.

The hammer in my chest doesn't ease.

Gods help me...I can't lose her.

Chapter Twenty Eight-Auren

The border of the Realm of Veiled stars shimmers like the edge of a dream. I cross its threshold, my breath catching in my throat. Before me, tall and willowy trees—their bark a smooth metallic silver, threaded with glowing veins of blue light. Their leaves flutter in silence, casting a pale violet-blue luminescence across the moss-covered floor.

Everything here shimmers.

Lantern-like bugs drift lazily between the trees, their wings glowing soft blue like fallen stars. Some blink in quiet pulsing patterns, like constellations shifting across the forest. One flutters past my cheek, and I catch the gleam of golden filaments in its delicate wings, like stained glass kissed by moonlight.

The ground beneath me is blanketed in soft moss that glows brighter with every step my horse takes. The air here is different. Cool and comforting, and it isn't silence that hits my ears, but stillness.

The sky above doesn't look like any sky I have ever known. Light ripples in it like water, beautiful waves of teal and purple and blue. Stars glittering everywhere, welcoming me.

I feel at peace here, in this place where time itself seems to slow, it's like I'm riding into a dream.

My eyes sting with tears because I feel it deep in my soul. This land, this magical beautiful place *accepts* me. It embraces me. Like I belong here in a way that I never have anywhere else.

Just like I felt with Reavian.

I ride for hours, my fingers grazing the trees, my eyes tracing the delicate flickers of light in their canopies above. Eventually, I pause to rest near a still pool of silver water. I tie up my horse, take a drink from my flask, then eat some dried fruit from my pack, letting the realm just breathe around me. For the first time since my journey began, I allow myself to just be for a while.

Welcome, we've been waiting for you, the stars in the sky seem to whisper in greeting.

I sit here for several hours, enjoying the calmness of my surroundings.

Then, I get myself up off the mossy rise and get back on my horse. The farther we go, the more the beauty begins to fade.

At first, it's subtle. A tree with drooping leaves that glisten with dark sap. Moss that no longer glows. A faint stench, like a damp rot, clinging to the wind.

Then it worsens.

I dismount my horse and walk beside it, leading it through the thickening gloom. The trees grow twisted, bark split open like gaping wounds. The ground pulses beneath my feet with black and crimson vines that writhe with sickness. Mushrooms bloom in grotesque clusters, their caps slick and dark. The stillness breaks and is replaced by a feeling of being watched.

Help us. Heal us.

The whispers stir in my mind, they're soft and pleading, and urging me forward.

So, I do what I can.

I drop to one knee and press my palm to the soil. I look within me and call forth my flame, willing it to purge this corruption. A burst of heat radiates from me in a circle, rippling outward in a cleansing tide of flame. The rot shrivels and dies. The trees straighten. The moss begins to glow faintly again.

It worked.

I healed the land in this area. And it feels *right*.

I press onward.

And do it again.

I heal the land with controlled pulses of purifying fire, watching as the rot and darkness retreats. But with every act of healing, my strength drains further.

Suddenly—I hear a sound in the distance to my left.

A shriek.

Piercing and inhuman.

I whirl towards it, grabbing Virethyn from its sheath at my back, my heart thudding in my chest.

A pale, naked creature skitters through the brush in the distance on all fours, it's gaunt with twisted limbs, and hollow eye sockets that are fixed on me. Its mouth is an almost unhinged open gaping maw of jagged teeth. It screams again and then charges toward me.

More shrieks answer it. All around me.

Run, Little Light.

The voices urge me.

There are too many.

I turn and sprint. Twisted roots claw at my boots, dead branches tearing at my clothes. Behind me, I hear the slamming of limbs against earth.

Getting faster...*closer*.

One of them dives toward me from my left, I catch it in my peripheral vision and spin toward it mid stride launching a ball of purifying flame at it from my palm. It strikes center mass, incinerating the creature in a burst of gold and white.

But it doesn't matter.

I'm surrounded.

I plant my feet and summon fire to my blade.

One of the creatures leaps for my throat, its maw gaping and snapping. I dodge and slice in a downward motion, it's engulfed in my flame and turns to ash before hitting the ground. Skittering comes from behind me, and I throw up a wall of fire to protect my back. But the flame is flickering, it's faltering.

My magic.

I've used too much.

It's fading.

Another creature drops from a mangled tree above. I drop low and plunge my sword up into its belly. It shrieks as fire erupts from within.

I kick off what remains of its body.

The flame on my blade is gone, so is the wall of fire that shielded my back.

I've depleted my magic.

The creatures surround me making strange clicking noises, low guttural sounds from deep within their throats.

There are three left.

Gaping mouths, their teeth sharp and dripping with saliva.

They have fae ears.

I raise my sword with shaking arms. I am outnumbered.

They all lunge at me at once.

And then—**shadow**.

A wall of pure darkness surges up between me and the creatures. They slam into it with screeches of rage, claws skidding off its surface.

I know who it is, even before I see him.

"Reavian," I breathe.

He steps from the trees like night given flesh, cloaked in a flickering shadow. His eyes glow faintly, his power lashing out from his fingertips.

With a flick of his hand, the shadows in the wall he raised begin to coil like ropes, lifting the creatures off the ground. They flail as the darkness tightens. A sickening crack echoes through the trees as the shadows twist and snap their necks.

Their bodies drop, twitching, but they aren't dead.

I look deep within and beg for just a little more power. It answers wreathing my blade in a weak, flickering flame. I quickly drive it into the fallen, one by one, and they turn to ash. The flame sputters out.

More shrieks echo in the distance.

"They're coming," Reavian says tightly. "We have to run."

I hesitate. "Our horses—"

"They're already gone, come on," he says, reaching for my hand.

I take it.

"You came for me," I say, my voice cracking a bit.

He looks at me, fierce and gentle all at once.

"I always will."

We run.

Branches tear at us, and the creatures scream in the dead forest behind us. Reavian's shadows surge at our heels, cloaking us from their sight.

A cave looms ahead in the ridgeline. We dive inside, hearts pounding.

Reavian leads us deeper, his shadows flaring to search the dark, his hand still wrapped around mine.

"It's empty," he says. "Just us."

I make it about two more steps before collapsing to my knees. My magic is depleted, I need rest to recover it.

He crouches beside me.

"What the hell were you thinking?" he demands.

Is he fucking kidding me?

I stand, my anger rising with me.

"What was I thinking? Where the hell have *you* been? It's been *weeks*, Reavian. You made it very clear that you wanted distance, so I gave it to you!"

He flinches.

"But that's not what you really wanted, is it? You have been watching me train. But you haven't tried to speak to me. Why?" I demand. "Why have you been punishing me? Why have you been keeping me at a distance?" I cry out, my frustration lacing every single word.

"Because I love you!" he snaps, voice breaking.

The cave falls silent.

He takes a step back from me, guilt shadowing his features.

"Because I thought it was the right thing to do," he says, softer now. "Because you deserve more than me. Because the only reason you feel drawn to me, or want me, is because of a stupid fated bond."

I still.

"What... what are you talking about?" I ask.

"That pull that you mentioned that night? That connection? That's the bond. I didn't want to trap you into something that you didn't choose for yourself," he says, his voice is low now.

I pause, absorbing the weight of his words.

"Is that the only reason that you wanted me?" I ask, my voice soft, uncertain if I truly want to know the answer.

"No," he says, his eyes raw with emotion. "I wanted you before I felt the bond. When we met in dreams. When you were the only thing that made the darkness bearable."

I step toward him and press my hand to his cheek.

"What makes you think that I didn't feel the same?" I whisper. "You were always my safe place. My protector in the dark."

He shudders. "You saw what I just did. What my power is. I *am* darkness. I'm just like *her*."

I meet his eyes with mine. "You used it to save me. That's the difference. You're *not* her Reavian."

I brush his tousled black hair away from his face.

And then he kisses me—hard.

Our mouths meet in a clash of fire and shadow, hunger and heat. Reavian backs me into the cave wall, hands already working to unfasten my leather corset, then my tunic. When my chest is bare, he pauses to cup my breasts, brushing his thumbs over my nipples, and I gasp. Then his mouth descends, kissing one of them gently, then sucking and teasing it with his tongue. When he grazes it with his teeth, my back arches and a soft moan escapes my lips.

I pull at the fastenings of his shirt, and tug it off, revealing the hard lines of his chest, the tight cords of his muscle beneath skin streaked with old scars. My hands roam freely, reverent and hungry, committing every inch of him to memory. I brush my hand over his lower abdomen, moving it down and then cup him with my palm. He is thick, long, and hard. Reavian hisses slightly at the contact, his jaw tightening.

He kisses his way down my body slowly, before pausing to remove my pants.

Then he kneels.

I am bare before him.

I cry out as his tongue finds me, my hands tangling in his hair. He holds me open for him, licking and sucking in gentle circles. My hips roll against his mouth, and my thighs begin to tremble.

"Reavian," I moan, breathless.

He works me with devastating control, stroking and circling my clit with his tongue, slowly... skillfully. He seems to savor the sounds I make as my hips buck against him, groaning into me with satisfaction. I'm shaking, the tension inside me stretched tight like a drawn bowstring. Then he slips two fingers inside of me, while his tongue continues its slow, skillful torment, my back arches and my knees go weak.

"Reavian..." I gasp.

I shatter.

The orgasm crashes through me in waves, my breath catching as he holds me steady, licking me through every shudder. I sink back against the wall, dazed and trembling. My body pulsing with aftershocks. Then he stands and rises above me, his mouth slick with my release, his eyes burning.

"That's not enough," he rasps. "Not even close."

He kisses me deeply, letting me taste myself on his tongue, letting me feel how undone he is. I reach between us, and unfasten his pants, freeing him.

My eyes widen at the sheer size of him.

He lines himself up against me, wrapping my legs around his waist. One hand braces my back, the other cradles my face.

He pauses going completely still.

His eyes search mine.

"Do you want this... want me?" he asks, his voice low and rough.

I cup his cheek.

"Yes," I say softly, still breathless. "I want you, I've always wanted you."

Something breaks in him, just a little. His thumb brushes my bottom lip, and he exhales like he's been holding a breath for days.

"Then I am yours, and you are mine," he tells me, his voice tender.

With a groan, he pushes in—*slowly*.

I gasp, stretching around him, my fingers gripping into his

shoulders, arching my back as he fills me inch by inch.

"Gods, Auren..." he gasps. "You feel like home."

He pauses when he is fully seated, letting me adjust. My eyes flutter as my body molds to him, perfectly.

And then he moves.

Slowly at first. Deep.

My back slams gently into the cave wall with every thrust.

I moan, clutching at him.

He kisses me deeply, his tongue delving my mouth in time with each of his thrusts.

"Gods...you're perfect," he rasps into my neck.

He slides his hand between us and finds my clit—circling it with his thumb as he thrusts into me. Deeper, harder, the rhythm growing more desperate. I gasp his name, my head falling back, the pressure in my core mounting again, *quickly*.

"You're mine," he whispers, kissing my throat.

"Yes," I moan, already close again. "I'm yours."

My second orgasm tears through me, more powerful than the first. My body clenches around him, and with a broken moan of my name, he follows—pulsing deep inside me as he groans into my neck, every part of him lost in me. We hold each other, trembling, panting, our hearts thudding in time. Reavian slowly slides to the mossy cave floor, pulling me into his lap, still wrapped in each other.

After several long, quiet moments, I trace the lines of his chest with my fingertips.

"I love you too," I whisper.

I think deep down, I've loved him since the day he first found me in our shared dream. When the darkness closed in and my breathing would falter, he was always there. Calming me. Steadying me. Talking me through the storm until I could find myself again. He's been my grounding force, long before we ever met in the waking world.

He's always been the one.

He leans down and kisses me with an aching softness. "I'm sorry I pushed you away."

"No more," I tell him. "From this point on, we're together. No more distance. Never apart again."

"Never again," he swears, kissing my forehead gently.

A few moments pass before we dress, reluctantly. The shrieks of creatures echo faintly through the woods beyond the cave. Reavian lays back, pulling me to his chest once more.

"Sleep," he whispers. "I'll watch over you."

My fingers curl into his shirt, holding him close to me.

"I always will," he tells me, rubbing the small of my back.

Outside, the night screams.

But inside this cave, shadow and flame curl together. Two halves of a future not yet spoken, but already begun, as destiny begins to unfold quietly in the dark.

Chapter Twenty
Nine-Auren

I walk through a field of glowing flowers, the earth soft and warm beneath my bare feet. The blooms rise tall around my knees. Red, blue, and violet petals unfold like secrets. In the heart of each flower pulses a tiny flicker of starlight, as if the heavens had scattered their embers across the land and let them take root.

The field glows in waves, as though it is breathing with me. A breeze stirs the blossoms, carrying the scent of warmth and something sweet.

I don't know where I am, but I feel safe.

I keep walking.

The sky above shimmers with gold and pearl, a dreamy twilight untouched by time. The wind whispers through the grass, and though it carries no words, I understand the meaning beneath it.

Keep going.

So, I do.

But slowly—too slowly—the light begins to fade. The stars in the flowers blink out one by one. The sky dims into ash and the warmth drains from the wind.

Then the earth falls away from my feet.

I stumble forward with a cry, catching myself on a rough stone. The lush field is gone—replaced by a mountain path, steep and treacherous. Coiled red thorns pulse along its edges, their glow dim and angry.

The air has turned sharp.

Wrong.

The silence breaks with shrieking. More of those creatures, their twisted limbs and mouths hidden in the darkness.

I run.

Barefoot and bleeding, and I don't dare look back. The cries follow me, echoing all around.

The ground disappears beneath me, and I tumble into a void before slamming into solid earth again.

I now stand before a river of silver water, roaring rapids slapping against stone. Crossing it would be dangerous, but there is no darkness here, no corruption. Shrieking sounds behind me, and I tumble again into darkness.

I land and I'm back in the field of flowers. I walk forward through them, the light in each of them winking out with every step I take.

Then comes the choice.

The path now splits ahead.

To my right, a fog draped mountain pass. To my left, a violent silver river, rapids crashing like distant thunder. Neither path offers complete safety. Between them, nestled in a crack inside a boulder, blooms a single flower.

Pale blue.

Its petals curl protectively around a single point of light, a lone star still burning. My heart tells me the flower matters.

That the choice matters.

You must choose.

But I can't.

I step toward the flower.

And the ground shatters beneath me.

I fall into a void of darkness, tumbling toward my end.

I wake up gasping. My heart pounds as I blink into dimly lit stone. It takes a moment for the cave to come into focus, lit only by the glowing blue moss scattered throughout. Reavian's warmth cradles me. His steady presence grounds me instantly.

I turn my head up to look at him.

His eyes are already on me. He hasn't slept.

"How long was I asleep?" I ask him.

"Most of the night," he says softly. "You needed to rest, I kept watch."

Time must be different here. It's still as dark as when I went to sleep.

I sit up slowly, rubbing at the ache in my arms. "I had a

nightmare," I murmur. "But I think it was trying to tell me something."

Reavian's brows draw together, sharp and thoughtful.

"What did you see?"

But before I can answer his body shifts. He goes completely still. Listening.

His hand closes around the hilt of his sword, his focus narrowing to the mouth of the cave. A quiet tension pulses from him, not fear but instinct. Shadow begins to curl unconsciously around his boots, flickering like smoke.

"What is it?" I whisper, my heart jumping. Reaching for my own sword.

"Something is coming," he says. "Stay behind me."

I do as he asks.

He steps towards the cave entrance with a practiced grace. He doesn't speak, doesn't even breathe too loudly. A soldier at the edge of battle.

A clatter of rock echoes ahead of us.

A soft curse.

And...

"Don't stab me sunshine," Kaiel's voice rings out. "Seriously, this face is the only thing I've got going for me."

Reavian exhales sharply and lowers his blade.

A moment later Kaiel steps into view, followed closely by Iska, Brynn, Tharen, and Kessa. All of them dust covered and seemingly exhausted.

Relief swells in my chest so fast it might crush me. It's not more of those creatures. It's just our friends.

My gaze meets Kaiel's, and I flinch.

It was an instinct—just a flicker of hesitation—but Reavian sees it. He reaches back, his fingers lacing with mine, a quiet anchor.

But Kaiel sees it too. And I hate myself for it.

His playful smirk falters for just a breath, but he turns his attention to Iska like it didn't happen.

Brynn moves to his side and places a gentle hand on his arm. Kaiel doesn't look at her, but he also doesn't pull away.

Kessa scans the cave, her eyes narrowed. "Love what you did with the place," she says, nodding her head toward the cave entrance. "Too bad that the corruption just kept swallowing it up as fast as we could ride through it."

"Everything I healed is corrupted again?" I ask, disbelief lacing my voice.

Tharen steps forward, his expression serious. "We heard shrieking deeper in the woods. Conscripted."

Conscripted.

There's that word again. Kaiel used it when we stole the ship that had carried the fae from Tide and Storm. Then I remember.

I saw fae ears on one of them.

My blood goes cold.

"I saw them. Fought them last night. We both did," I say. "I saw they had... fae ears. What are they?"

"They *were* fae," Reavian confirms. "My mother uses a ritual to strip their magic, transferring it to herself, and then she twists them into those creatures. An army at her disposal. I don't know exactly how she does it. It's not a magic that anyone knows of. I think it's old... ancient magic."

My stomach drops, and I don't speak the thoughts that bloom inside me. They were people. And I just destroyed them with my magic. But what if they could be healed?

Could I heal them with my flame somehow like I do the land?

"Well, that was depressing...who wants soup?" Kessa says, breaking the silence after Reavian's words. She pulls a tin of dehydrated stew out of her pack.

"No one wants to eat right now but you, Kessa," Tharen says.

"Speak for yourself, I'm starving," Kaiel replies with a laugh. "I'll start a small fire to heat it up with.

We all stay in the cave for the day, taking turns at keeping watch so everyone can rest. At dawn, if you can call it that, we ready the horses they managed to guide through the pass.

"How did you guys find us?" I ask Brynn.

"At first, we followed the land you healed. When the land became corrupted, the stars themselves seemed to guide us to you. Blinking in a line that led us to the cave," she replies.

Brynn rides with Kaiel, her arms loosely wrapped around his middle, her face turned toward the horizon.

I will ride with Reavian.

He helps me into the saddle and climbs up behind me, his arms hold me steady as the horse shifts beneath us. I lean back into his chest, and he presses a hand to my side—not possessive, but protective. A reminder that he's there.

We ride west for a bit, and then begin to ride north, towards where I have Starfall Keep on my map.

Days pass in hazy twilight giving way to star scattered skies. The sky never brightens. The Realm of Veiled stars blurs the line between time and memory. I have tried healing various parts of the land, but the corruption here is different. It swallows what I restore within hours. I make the decision to conserve my strength, at least until I can understand what makes the corruption here so persistent.

On the fourth day, the trees thin.

The wind grows colder.

An open field stretches before us, completely overrun. Red vines choking out the blossoms that once bloomed here. I get the sense I've seen this place before.

Ahead, two paths emerge.

One climbs up into a jagged mountain pass, draped in curling mists. The other slopes down toward a river of silver rapids—roaring, wild, and treacherous.

And there between them, a large boulder, and in its crack grows a single flower.

Pale blue.

Its petals curl protectively around a flicker of starlight.

My breath catches.

The others are already discussing the climb.

"We should take the mountain path," Tharen says. "It's harder terrain, but we should be able to keep the horses."

Kaiel nods. "That river would drag us under. There's no crossing *that* safely."

You must make a choice, Little Light.

The voices whisper to me.

My heart skips in my chest as I look toward both paths. Neither is showing any signs of corruption yet, but I remember the twisted red vines in my dream curling around the mountain path.

"We can't go through the mountain path," I say, my voice resolute.

They all turn to me.

"There's danger there. I saw it in my dream. I know it doesn't make any sense, but... we must cross the river somehow. Please, trust me."

Tharen frowns. "We'd have to leave the horses behind, and without a bridge to help us cross..."

"We'll figure something out," Reavian says. "We cross at the river."

Tharen's jaw flexes, but he nods.

"Don't be such a baby, Tharen," Kessa jokes.

Iska lets out a soft laugh.

"Shut up Kessa, I actually have a great idea," Tharen says.

We approach the river, and Tharen reaches into his pack. He pulls out a coil of rope and ties one end around an arrow shaft. With a practiced precision he notches it, aims high and shoots it across the river, striking a silver tree trunk and embedding itself in it. He gives the rope a hard tug to test its strength before securing the other end to a corrupted tree branch behind us.

"We will have to move quickly," Tharen warns. "Hold the rope and lean in. Don't let the current take you."

Let them go first.

The whispers sound certain.

"Ladies first," Kaiel says.

Brynn moves to go first.

"Be careful, don't let go of that rope. If anything happens, I can pull you back in with it," Kaiel tells Brynn.

She nods and makes her way across the river. Then Iska, followed by Kessa.

Send them first, Little Light.

Send them all first.

"I need to go last," I say. "You guys have to cross first."

"No—" Revian begins.

I shake my head, certain I need to trust the voices that speak to me.

"Please, just—" Reavian starts.

"You have to," I say.

"Absolutely not," Reavian replies.

"The voices...something is telling me this is how it has to be. Please, trust me and cross," I tell him.

Kaiel looks to Reavian and then to me.

"Alright, guess I'll go first," Kaiel says.

He crosses quickly. Tharen follows him soon after.

Reavian turns back to me, his eyes filled with fear and fury. "Please, let me stay until you're across safely."

I reach for the collar of his shirt and pull him down, kissing him quick and soft.

"Go. I'll be right behind you," I tell him.

He hesitates for a moment, then nods and crosses, glancing back at me with every step he takes. When he reaches the other side, I take a breath and grab the rope.

That's when it starts.

Shrieking. High and feral, coming from the mountain pass.

I turn. The ground is quickly being swallowed by more corruption, red twisted thorned vines strangling the edges of the mountain. One by one the stars in the sky above it blink out. At least twenty conscripted begin to barrel down the slope, eyes wild, limbs twisting unnaturally as they charge straight toward me.

The creatures reach the riverbank.

One steps forward, and shrieks as its skin sizzles in the water.

They can't cross.

Another lunges for the rope and begins hauling itself toward me.

Now I understand why I had to go last.

I summon flame to my fingertips and send it racing down the rope behind me, killing the conscripted, and severing its tether to the tree behind me. I cling to what remains, and with a breathless lurch, plunge into the rapids.

The current yanks me under. Cold, silver water swallows me. I cling to the rope still in my grip, choking, spinning, gasping for any air. I slam into jagged rocks, and they cut into my flesh.

Hold on, Little Light.

The sound of the rapids is deafening.

"Auren!" Reavian's voice tears through the noise.

Hands grab the rope from the other side.

Reavian. Kaiel. Tharen. Kessa.

They pull.

My head breaks the surface. I cough and choke, spitting water, my vision swimming.

The others hiss and pace at the edge, but none step in.

The moment I am close enough, Reavian hauls me the rest of the way up and wraps his arms around me.

"You're okay. You're okay," he murmurs, his hands trembling as he checks over me. "You're safe."

I cough, still spitting out water.

Iska crouches beside us and begins to heal my cuts with her

magic. "How did you know they were there?" she asks.

I swallow, my chest heaving. "I saw it. In a dream. The flower in the boulder. The mountain. The river. I saw it all before it happened."

They all stare at me for a moment, no one saying a word.

"We need to keep moving," Brynn says, breaking the silence.

Reavian stands, then helps me up.

"The river, they can't cross it. The water burns them," I say looking at the creatures still pacing along its edge.

"It must be the only reason they haven't breached the city and reached the keep," Tharen says.

"We shouldn't be far now, maybe another few hours," Kessa replies.

"Then let's go," I say, assuring Reavian silently that I'm alright.

He nods, and grips my hand tightly, not letting go.

Chapter Thirty-Auren

The river roars in the distance behind us, and I can't stop shivering. Even with Reavian's cloak wrapped around me tightly, the soaked fabric clings to my skin like ice. The farther we walk from the crossing, the colder the wind becomes. It slices through me like teeth, sharper on this side of the river, as if the land itself is warning us that we've stepped somewhere sacred and protected.

My teeth chatter. I don't say anything, but Reavian notices.

"We're stopping," he says firmly, already pulling me toward a clearing in the brush.

Tharen turns. "We should try to go for at least a few more—"

"She's freezing," Reavian snaps. "I'll be taking no argument. We're stopping now."

Kaiel raises his hands with a grin. "Hey, we can take a break. You could just ask nicely, Reav. You catch more flies with honey, you know."

Reavian doesn't laugh. His attention is locked on me; brow furrowed in that quietly intense way he has. I try to protest, but my voice comes out brittle.

He guides me down to the mossy ground and slides in behind me, pulling my back against his chest. His arms wrap around me tightly, cocooning me in his warmth. I feel the tremble of his breath, and the way his jaw tenses at my temple.

"I've got you," he murmurs. "Just breathe."

Kaiel and Tharen begin setting up a fire, gathering discarded tree limbs and branches from around us.

"Shit, I can't get it to catch." Kaiel says after a few moments have passed, trying to get his firestarter to spark onto the timber.

"I can use my flame..." I stutter out, and try to stand, but my body convulses with the cold, and I topple back over.

"Everyone move, now. Back by Reavian and Auren," Brynn says standing.

Everyone freezes, a little stunned by Brynn's tone, and then moves toward Reavian and I.

She steps forward, her face unreadable, and lifts one hand toward the sky.

The wind shifts.

Lightning splits the sky with a crack like a war drum and strikes the center of the makeshift fire pit. The strike is controlled, not moving a single piece of wood or timber.

Flames erupt instantly, dancing across the wood, with a life of their own.

I stare at her, eyes wide.

"Brynn…"

She doesn't look at me, she just sits down near the newly lit fire, wrapping her arms around her knees.

"What? I told you before I was from Tide and Storm… it's just a little lightning," she says. "I only just started feeling it again."

"Yes… you did," I murmur. "I just… you didn't mention that you could do any of that."

She shrugs. Silence falls between us. Until she speaks again.

"My village was one of the first taken. Conscripted to Liraeth's army, you know."

The revelation haunts me.

She's been through so much.

"I'm sorry," Kaiel says softly, sitting beside her.

Brynn stares into the fire. "The only reason my mother and I weren't turned into those things, is because my mother knew yours Auren. They were friends," she says, finally looking at me. "My father and my brother were taken right away, but my mother convinced her to spare me, in order to help them find you. She told her we were close in age, that it would be easier for me to find you, befriend you, and bring you back here. They needed me to lead you to them. They kept my mother alive, to keep me motivated. And to provide them with any information she had on your mother."

My breath catches and Reavian holds me a little tighter.

"But how did they even know where I was? I was in a whole other world."

Brynn shakes her head. "I don't know all of it. But Lucien knew your father had loved your mother. When he found out there was an heir, outside of the one he killed that day, he knew it had to be your mom. He set out to find her, and when he couldn't he knew the High King had sent her away. He knew the Alarion must've opened a rift between worlds to get her out, sacrificing any happiness he might've had by seeing her again, in order to ensure you were both safe."

"How did they know there was a human world at all?" I ask.

"Our ancestors lived alongside humans, until there was a war. Our magic became considered a disease, one the humans decided they had to eradicate. Some of the most powerful fae used their gifts to create Nyvena, which is this world. They opened a rift to aid all the fae in traveling here. The humans eventually forgot us. And the rest is history. The realms were created, borders made, and no more contact with humans..." Tharen says, trailing off.

"Do you know how they opened a rift for Kaiel?" Reavian asks Brynn.

I flinch, the memory still too sharp. Kaiel stepping out of the darkness, the wet final sounds my father made.

Reavian kisses my temple.

Brynn looks up. "Lucien had the gift to open rifts, the world walking gift, like the King did. But I think Liraeth took it from him somehow. I think *she* uses it now."

I turn toward Kaiel, hesitant. "But it wasn't her body walking through the rift, it was his."

The statement comes out colder than I mean it to.

Kaiel goes still.

Brynn reaches out, gripping his hand.

"It wasn't him—she was controlling him. She used him as a vessel somehow. Maybe it has to do with that awful tether she had on him. I don't know exactly how...but it *wasn't* him," she says.

The slight snap in her voice surprises me. She looks at Kaiel, a soft smile forming as she tries to offer him comfort.

"It's alright," he says quietly, rising to his feet. "You guys get some rest, we can head out again in a few hours. I'll take first watch."

Brynn stands and silently follows him into the trees.

"Tag me in for round two?" Kessa says, rubbing her hands together with a spark of energy.

My chest aches.

"I didn't mean it," I say softly to Reavian, eyes on the ground. "I know it wasn't really him. But I can't help it, I still see what happened when I look at him."

Reavian leans in closer. "He feels it too. He hides it but... I've seen the guilt. We've talked about it, he's devastated by what happened, by what he did. He knows he's destroyed everything you held dear. Even though it really wasn't his fault. He holds all of that inside, every day."

I nod, remaining quiet.

I need to talk with Kaiel.

To set things right for both of our sakes.

But I need a little bit of time.

Across the fire, Iska and Tharen are speaking in low tones, Tharen offers her something from his pouch while she rolls her eyes. Kessa sits against a tree, chomping loudly on a strip of dried meat, muttering something about *Gods damned dramatic lightning*.

Reavian lets out a soft breath. "We should get some rest."

He lays down behind me, drawing me close. His warmth presses against me like a shield against the cold, as he wraps his arms around me. I curl into him, resting my cheek over his heartbeat.

"Don't let go," I whisper.

"Never," he murmurs back.

"I love you," I tell him softly.

He presses a kiss to the top of my head. "I love you too."

I shut my eyes, and drift to sleep wrapped in his warmth.

***

We're awakened by Kessa's voice.

"Uhhh... guys?"

All of us open our eyes and slowly focus on what's going on around us.

The landscape shimmers.

We shoot to our feet.

Silver trees twist, folding in on themselves. Roots surge upward, tangling themselves into walls. Branches grow impossibly fast, forming hedges thick with glowing blooms.

In moments, the forest becomes a maze of hedges.

Everyone scrambles, trying to stay together.

Reavian yanks onto my hand pulling me to him, just before a hedge rises between us and the others.

"Don't let go," he says. "No matter what."

"We have to find the center of it. There is always a center. We'll regroup there!" Tharen shouts.

We step into the maze.

The path winds left, then right, then left again—each turn bordered by towering hedges that rise higher than Reavian's head. The leaves shimmer, their edges silver tipped. As we walk the hedges seem to breathe, their shapes subtly shifting when we aren't looking.

It's quiet. Too quiet. Even the sound of our footsteps is muffled by the moss-covered ground beneath our feet.

No wind, no breeze, no sky.

My fingers stay tightly laced with Reavian's, my heart thudding louder than it should in this silence. It feels like the maze is *watching* us.

Around us, the light grows dimmer.

The starlit blooms on the hedges flicker, then blink out one by one, as if they are being extinguished by unseen hands.

Then the mist comes.

At first, it's barely more than a fog curling around our ankles. But within moments, it thickens, rising in slow waves to our knees, then our hips, until the world around us disappears into a haze of pearl and gray.

The air is damp and cold.

Heavy.

Reavian slows beside me.

"Something is wrong," he tells me.

"*Auren...*" a whisper says around us.

I shiver.

"Did you hear that?" I murmur to Reavian.

There's a long pause.

"*Auren....*"

The voice comes from somewhere in the mist.

My breath catches, it's my mother.

Faint and trembling, it echoes through the hedges like it's trapped in the mist itself. The sound turns my legs to jelly.

"*Please...Auren...*"

"Mom?" I call out.

A different voice comes, closer this time.

"Auren!"

This one is filled with panic and desperation.

It's Reavian. Shouting from the fog ahead of me.

I yank my hand free before I can think and turn toward the sound.

Reavian catches my wrist. "Don't. It's not me."

"But it—"

"It's not me."

He steps in front of me—his silhouette barely visible through the haze—then places my hand on his chest, over his heartbeat.

"This is me, I'm right here."

I'm instantly grounded.

The fog pulses.

More voices surround us—my father, then Brynn. Kaiel. Screaming, laughing, weeping. Their words twisting in on themselves, distorting their very meaning.

I press my hands over my ears.

"I can't..."

Reavian cups my face. "Close your eyes, I'll move behind you. I'll guide you."

I nod, shutting my eyes.

His hands slide from my cheeks but remain in contact with my body as he quickly moves behind me.

He wraps his arms around my shoulders and bends down putting his lips near my ear.

"One step forward," he says.

We move.

"Left, just a little."

The mist thickens, pressing against my skin like a second body.

"Now take a step up, there's a root. Be careful."

I lift my foot as instructed and keep moving.

I let him guide me, until the voices around us begin to fade.

I open my eyes, and see the mist dissipating slowly, revealing the maze once more. It's dimmer, the path now tighter than before, the hedges pressing closer with every step.

The silence around us feels heavier somehow.

I exhale, my shoulders trembling. "Thank you."

Reavian brushes a hand down my arms, then steps back to my side, lacing his fingers with mine again.

"We aren't done yet," he says.

We walk for a while, deeper into the maze. The air changes again, it's drier now. The scent of ozone curls into our noses, and the path under our feet shifts from moss to something harder. A smooth stone, etched with shallow grooves.

We turn a corner and freeze.

Before us is a hedge wall that shimmers with what I can only describe as liquid metal. A mirror... but not glass. Silver undulating leaves show us distorted versions of ourselves.

I step closer, my heart thumping.

My reflection radiates light—too much of it. It pours from my skin in searing waves, blinding and wild. My eyes glow white-hot, and everything my reflection touches, flowers, stone and even Reavian blacken and crumble beneath my fingertips.

Reavian's reflection is cloaked in shadow. His eyes black voids, darkness dripping from his fingertips like ink. He stands tall and godlike, and there's something broken about the set of his jaw. In his hand he holds a sword of obsidian, it's cracked down the center and bleeding red.

"That's not us," I whisper.

"Maybe, what we could become?" Reavian asks quietly.

The mirror solidifies and then cracks.

With a shriek that splits the stillness, the reflections escape their mirror prison and lunge at us.

I duck and roll, coming to my feet beside a line of starlit vines that recoil from my twin's heat.

Across from me, Reavian is barely holding his twin off. Every blow comes with a pulse of shadow that chips away at the hedge walls.

I don't hesitate.

I reach over my shoulder, fingers closing around Virethyn's hilt. The blade slides free with a whisper.

My reflection is waiting for me. She's twisted and wild, her features contorted with rage. Her hair is ablaze, and her skin glows with what looks like a corrupted light. She raises a blade that looks just like mine.

But it's *not* mine.

I charge and we clash.

The sound rings through the maze, like thunder. Each strike

drives into me like I'm hitting my own bones. Her movements mirror mine perfectly.

"You'll never save them," she sneers. "You're still afraid of what you are."

"I'm not afraid," I breathe, teeth gritted. "Not anymore."

She lunges and I spin.

We clash again; I swing my blade at her with such force that she staggers back.

I look down at my hands.

They are glowing.

I don't think, I just act.

I plant my feet and reach inward. Into my well of flame, and let it go.

A pulse of fire erupts from me, not searing, but *pure*.

The reflections of us scream their forms cracking. They shatter like smoke breaking apart in the wind, shards of glass falling onto the stone beneath our feet, before they turn back to liquid and seem to get absorbed by the land again.

The maze falls still.

Reavian drops to a knee, breathing hard.

I run to him.

"Are you alright?" I ask, checking him for any sign of injury.

"I'm ok, are you?" he asks, quickly checking me over as well.

"I'm fine," I assure him.

I take his hand, and we walk on in silence. After several twists and turns, the hedge line ahead of us begins to shimmer. It unfolds into a silver arch. A locked gate, covered in thick wooded vines. The bark pulses with ancient symbols. I recognize them somehow, but I can't read them.

Something stirs in my chest as I step forward. Words etch themselves into the air before my eyes.

Speak what you fear most.

I hesitate for a moment, but then remember the others are still lost in the maze, and only Reavian can hear me.

My voice trembles. "I'm afraid I won't be able to control what's inside of me. That I'm going to mess all of this up, and that instead of saving everything, I'll destroy it."

The gate doesn't open.

Not yet.

The symbols pulse again.

Demanding more.

"I'm afraid that even if I survive this, if we win..." I glance at Reavian, my voice cracking. "I fear that the people I love won't all make it with me."

The vines around the gate tremble and begin to unfurl.

Before I can step forward, Reavian reaches out and stops me. The vines have only partially uncovered the gate.

"I need to say mine too," he says.

I turn to him.

"I'm afraid of losing Auren," he says. "Above all else, above losing this war, even my own life. I fear losing her the most."

The vines curl open fully, revealing a path beyond.

He reaches for my hand.

"Let's get to the center," he says.

Together we step through the gate. A wide clearing stretches out before us beyond it. A circular grove of silver blossomed hedges with smooth pale stone underfoot. At the center stands an old pedestal wrapped in vines. Above it floats a soft orb of violet light, pulsing like a heartbeat. The sky above us is still hidden, the air thick with magic, but the pressure that had been suffocating me in the rest of the maze has lifted.

I exhale.

"This is it," Reavian murmurs. "We made it."

He doesn't let go of my hand.

The silence is heavy, but peaceful, until the hedges opposite us rustle.

Tharen bursts through, hand clasped tightly around Iska's. Both look out of breath, scratched up and wild eyed—but alive.

Then Brynn and Kaiel emerge from another path. Kaiel has a gash along one temple, and Brynn's cloak is torn at the shoulder, their hands are linked too, knuckles white.

They pause just inside the clearing, taking in the sight of all of us, relief flashes in Brynn's eyes.

"You made it," she says to me.

I smile.

Then a sound shatters the stillness.

A crack.

Sharp and violent.

Like glass breaking.

Everyone turns toward it at once.

A high-pitched whistling fills the air, and then a shape is hurled through one of the hedge walls in a burst of shattered glass.

It's Kessa.

Her body slams into the ground in the center of the circle, limp and broken.

Shards of silver glass protrude from her arms, her ribs, and her throat. Her wide unblinking eyes stare up at the skyless dome above us. Blood pools beneath her, soaking into the stone in silent ripples.

No one moves.

For one terrible second, it's as if the whole world holds its breath.

Then Brynn screams.

Kaiel staggers back in horror, his mouth open, but no sound coming out.

Tharen rushes toward Kessa, then curses and drops to his knees.

My hands fly to my mouth, and my heart shatters.

I stagger towards her, and my legs give out.

Reavian's arm shoots out, instinctively catching me before I can collapse.

"No," Iska whispers, her voice trembling. "No... she was right behind us. She was just—she was just there. Let me see if there is anything to be done," she says, reaching towards her lifeless body.

Reavian kneels beside Kessa first, gently sliding her eyes closed. "She's gone," he says.

Brynn drops down next to me sobbing. Kaiel crouches beside her, wrapping both his arms around her shoulders, his own eyes brimming with tears.

The orb in the center of the clearing blinks.

I stare at Kessa's face.

A moment ago, I believed we would all make it through.

And now.

"Why?" I ask softly. "Why her?"

No one has an answer.

Broken sobs echo around me, then comes silence.

Thick and suffocating.

No one speaks.

Then I feel something.

A gentle pressure—like a pulse at the base of my skull. A quiet whisper rising beneath my ribs, not a voice I can name, but something ancient and steady, woven into the land here itself.

The orb pulses again.

I step forward, drawn to it.

Reavian reaches for me, but I swat his hand away gently, unable to resist the pull.

I move slowly across the stone floor, every step echoing too loudly. The magic in the air hums louder the closer I come to the pedestal. The orb hovers above it like a suspended star, glowing with soft violet and silver light, threads of energy dancing around its edges like spider silk.

I didn't have to question what to do.

I *know*.

I raise my hand and reach toward it.

The moment my palm touches the orb everything changes.

A sound like rushing wind roars in my ears—though there is no wind here. The hedges begin to unravel in silence, curling in on themselves like they had never existed. The walls of the maze dissolving into motes of starlight that scatter and vanish, revealing the world beyond.

A new sky stretches above us, deep twilight and stars that burn brighter than any I have ever seen.

Dark stone walls and silver towers carve into the cliffside, aglow with silver-blue veins that pulse through the rock like a heartbeat. Beyond it, I can faintly see a building carved from white moonstone.

Starfall Keep.

Wards shimmer over its gates like gossamer, and the land around it seems to sigh, ancient and strange and... watching me.

But the stone beneath our feet remains.

I whirl around feeling a bit of hope.

It's quickly shattered when I see that Kessa's body remains lifeless. Her blood still stains the ground.

I fall to my knees.

"I thought...maybe I could undo it," I whisper.

Reavian walks over and kneels beside me.

"This isn't your fault," he says, his voice gentle.

"I couldn't save her," I say, my voice cracking.

No one else speaks.

A low growl rumbles across the clearing, and from the shadows figures begin to emerge.

Wolves.

Large, silent and black as night. Their fur shimmers with faint silver edges, like the stars themselves have dusted them with their light. Their eyes glow a brilliant blue, seemingly lit from within. There is at least a dozen of them, moving with an eerie grace, as they form a perfect circle around our group.

Weapons are drawn instantly.

Kaiel steps out in front of Brynn.

Tharen stands protectively in front of Iska.

Reavian reaches across my chest shielding me with his body.

But I don't feel fear. I don't even flinch. They remind me of the Emberbeasts.

"I know you," I say, stepping out from behind Reavian. "I mean we are only just meeting... but I know you all in here." I touch my chest, placing my hand above my heart. "Do you know me too?"

These wolves are not predators, they are *guardians*.

"Are you seeing what I'm seeing?" Kaiel asks, his blade still raised.

"They're not here to hurt us," I say gently. "Look."

The largest wolf steps forward, lowering its head respectfully. Then, tail swishing in a smooth majestic arc, it sits. One by one the other's follow.

Reavian slowly lowers his sword but stays directly by my side.

"I think they're waiting…. for *you*," he whispers to me.

"Can you help us get through those wards and to the keep?" I ask them softly, pointing toward the far horizon where Starfall Keep rests.

The wolves throw their heads back and howl, not a warning, but an acknowledgment. They will help us get beyond the protective ward, so we can reach the keep.

"Thank you," I tell them softly.

I walk towards Kessa's body; everyone follows even the wolves.

"Can you… can you help her?" I ask the wolves.

The largest replies with a soft whimper.

No.

I kneel down next to Kessa.

"This is my fault, she came here… to help me. I need to bury her," I say to no one in particular.

Tharen says softly. "You didn't force her to come. She was happy to be part of something real, to help in this war in any way she could."

I feel cold. Numb.

"Help me carry her, she deserves a proper burial," I say to Reavian.

"We have nothing to dig, we will come back for her, I promise," Reavian says gently.

The largest wolf approaches my side and gently licks my cheek. He whines softly and looks towards Kessa.

Without warning, the rock below us shifts, turning into earth. Then the soil opens, soft, slow and reverent. It folds around Kessa as if cradling her gently into the land, without sound, without force. Her blood vanishes, and the field blooms into the one of beauty I saw in my dream. Starlit flowers surround us. And from the place where Kessa had fallen, pale blue flowers begin to grow. Star shaped, and soft-petaled.

No one moves.

Even the wolves watch in silence.

"She's part of the magic here now," I whisper. My eyes are burning, and yet the tears still don't come. "The land has taken her home."

Reavian helps me to my feet. And together, surrounded by wolves and starlight, we all turn toward the path that leads us to the keep. The light from it glowing faintly in the distance.

But behind us the cost still lingers, etched in silence, soil, and memory.

Chapter Thirty One—Reavian

It's quiet. The kind of silence that comes after something sacred has been broken. All of our steps fall in rhythm as we press toward the edge of the magical ward protecting Starfall City. My mind isn't on the road ahead, though.

Auren hasn't said a word since we left Kessa in her final resting place. She walks ahead of me, her hair curling around her face. My eyes never leave her. She is holding herself together with sheer will—her spine straight, and her hand resting lightly on the flank of the wolf that walks beside her. The same wolf that had agreed to lead us to safety.

She hasn't cried.

That more than anything terrifies me. They had become so close.

Auren's fingers twitch occasionally, like she wants to go back and fix it, change it. I wish I could take all her hurt and pain away.

I let my thoughts drift to what she has accomplished so far. She defended herself against several conscripted before I found her the other night, and had chosen the river path for us, before the danger of the mountain path had been revealed to anyone. She fought the mirror version of herself expertly. And now, she has just spoken to the wolves, and they *listened*.

She is more than brave. More than powerful. She is a queen in every sense of the word.

And I love her.

Gods, I love her so much it hurts. So much that it scares me. Because if anything happens to her—if I were to lose her—there would be nothing left for me in this world.

Just ahead of us now, a shimmer pulses in the air.

The massive ward protects the city beyond it, woven with magic to keep my mother's corruption at bay.

Auren steps forward, the wolf beside her doing the same.

I watch as she kneels, placing a hand gently on its fur.

"Can you help us get inside?" she asks it softly, her voice barely above a whisper.

The wolf understands and turns to its packmates letting out a single yip. They all step forward in unison, forming a wide arch before the invisible wall. Then they begin to glow.

Starlight shimmers from within their bodies, pale and silver-blue, casting a luminous beam into the air between them. The ward hums, it's unraveling like thread being pulled from fabric.

The barrier opens, a path now exists, just wide enough for us to pass.

No one moves at first. All of us are staring, awe wrapping around our lungs like vines.

Auren stands, her eyes shining, and walks through the gap, with the rest of us following behind her. Once we are all inside, she turns toward the wolves.

"Thank you," she says. "Truly."

The largest wolf pads forward, he lowers his head nudging her hand. She pets him gently, smiling through the weight of her exhaustion and sorrow. He licks her fingers once, then turns to the second largest of the pack and gives it a low yip. It trots forward and walks through the barrier, stopping beside Auren.

She looks between the two wolves.

"He's...coming with me?" she asks.

The big wolf gives her what can only be described as a nod.

Her brows furrow. "Well, what about the rest of you guys?" She glances at them all. "There is much darkness, and danger coming. I can feel it, I know you can too."

The large wolf steps closer to her, pressing his head into her hand. Around us, the others howl, a chorus of something ancient and wild, it's heartbreakingly beautiful.

"What the hell is happening?" Kaiel whispers, low enough for only me and him to hear.

I shrug my shoulders in response.

Auren nods slowly. "I will protect him too, I promise," she tells the large wolf.

Then she pauses, hesitating.

"I don't know how your magic works," she says to the large wolf. "I expect we'll be making several journeys...can you leave your natural habitats?"

The large wolf nods once.

"Then he will always stay by my side. I hope we meet again someday," she tells the wolves.

With that, the pack turns and disappears into the night becoming shadows swallowed in darkness. The gap in the wards is closing.

The one left behind sits at her side now, proud and calm, tail sweeping the ground. I feel as if I am witnessing something sacred.

I step toward her. "How are you...communicating with them?" I ask.

"I can just...feel what they want to say. Like their thoughts are already inside me," she says softly.

She turns back to the wolf and kneels. "My name is Auren," she whispers. "It's nice to meet you... *Noctis*."

The wolf gives her a quiet chuff and then presses its face into her hand.

We walk to the gates of Starfall City, beneath a sky veined with stars.

The guards at the gate stand frozen. One bows in front of

Auren, and the other turns toward the courtyard beyond.

"Commander Valeaon," he calls out.

From the shadows near what must be some sort of guard barracks, a man emerges in dark armor edged in silver. No cloak, no helmet. Just authority that I can already recognize has sharpened into cruelty.

He walks toward us like the ground owes him a debt.

"Well, what's this?" he drawls. "A party of vagrants and beasts at the city gates? Hawkins, stand up this instant, why on earth are you bowing to these lowborns?"

The younger guard stands, hesitant. "Sir, the wolves opened the barrier for her. She asked them and they obliged. That one there," he says, pointing at Noctis. "he's stayed as her guardian, they only do that to the true heir...she must be—"

Valeaon scoffs. "Fairy Tales, Lucien wiped out the true heir many years ago."

He turns toward Auren, his expression dripping with disdain.

"You'll all be coming with me, the High Lord will want to see to this nonsense himself."

Then to Auren directly he says, "The wolf leaves the city."

Her jaw tightens.

"No, I'm afraid that will not be possible. He stays with me," she replies firmly.

Noctis growls low, a sound that vibrates the very stone we are standing on.

Valeaon laughs. "He leaves or I kill him, up to you."

I step forward.

"He stays with us," I say, my tone is flat and lethal. "Or I will kill *you*."

Kaiel and Tharen move to my side, without hesitation. I reach for my sword.

Valeaon's smile curves like a blade. "Oh, I've been itching for a fight. It'll be my pleasure—"

"Enough, Halrex!" a voice booms.

A tall figure approaches, robes deep blue and embroidered with constellations in silver thread. His long silver hair catches in the moonlight.

This must be High Lord Vaelisar Thorneveil.

"Commander Valeaon," he says. "That is not how we receive guests, especially those able to breach our wards with the aid of the guardians themselves."

Valeaon straightens, his face stiff. "High Lord I—"

"*You* are dismissed. We'll speak of your conduct later," Thornevail replies, shutting him down.

There is steel in his words. Valeaon clenches his jaw, bows stiffly, and turns without another word.

"Nice to meet you, *princess*!" Kaiel shouts after him, his tone dripping with sarcasm.

I can't help myself and smirk.

Vaelisar's gaze sweeps across our group—Iska, Brynn, Tharen,

Kaiel, Me, until it finally lands on Auren.

"You must be Auren," he says, lifting her hand to his lips.

How does he know her name?

I immediately shift forward, subtly stepping between them.

The High Lord doesn't miss it, his gaze flicks to mine and something ancient and aching passes through his expression.

"I know who you are," Vaelisar says to me quietly.

I blink.

"Then you should know I'm not here as an enemy. I stand against my family. I stand with her," I say, glancing at Auren.

Vaelisar nods once. "I know."

He then returns his attention back to Auren, his voice quieter now.

"I dreamed you would come," he says. "Long before you ever set foot in this world, I saw your face. I heard your name."

I watch as Auren stares at Vaelisar, her lips parting slightly. She says nothing, one of her hands slides into Noctis's thick fur, the other into mine.

I squeeze it in silent support.

Vaelisar's gaze softens. "You've come a long way," he says. "And there is much to be done. Please, follow me."

"Are you alright?" I whisper quietly to Auren as we follow Vaelisar through the city and into Starfall keep.

"Don't let go of my hand, please," she whispers back.

The sadness in her eyes shatters my heart.

The keep is quiet, grand and dreamlike, with walls carved of pale moonstone veined with violet, and glass domes showing the starlight above. Orbs of blue light sit in sconces on the wall. Magic feels *alive* here.

Kaiel speaks first. "How did you know that we were coming?"

"I saw it," Vaelisar says. "In a dream. I often see fragments of what is to come. Sometimes full visions. But I rely on the Dreamkeepers to interpret the deeper meaning."

Brynn looks up. "Dreamkeepers?"

Vaelisar nods. "They have the ability to read prophecies from dreams. They weave through the memories of a dream, separating the truth from the fantasy. I saw you *all* coming. I just didn't know when. I saw you Auren, as a child with a boy cloaked in shadow. Then a girl with a wolf. None of us knew when you would come, only that you would."

I look toward Auren. "Like the dream that you had, you knew what path for us to choose."

Vaelisar's expression sharpens. "So, you have the gift of premonition like me. That means you must be—"

"The lost heir of High King Veylas," Auren replies grimly.

Vaelisar stiffens.

"You already know." He looks at her accepting what she says, like he knows it's true. "I believe you, but the council here will want more proof."

We enter a throne room, its clear glass-domed ceiling casting the light of all the constellations in the sky to a dark stone circle inlayed in the center of the moonstone floor. Vaelisar calls for a few stewards and then tells them to show us to our rooms.

"Reavian and I will share a room," Auren says.

I look at her, a small smile forming on my face.

"Are you sure?" I ask.

She nods.

"We are not to be separated," she tells Vaelisar.

"Very well," he replies, his gaze sweeping from her to me briefly. "You all get some rest, I'm sure your journey was long. There will be food sent up for you shortly."

"Thank you," I say, speaking for all of us.

"I would like to speak with you both in the morning. I'll stop by your room, we can have breakfast together," Vaelisar adds.

I note a flicker in his eyes, and slight tension in his jaw. His gaze lingers on me *just* a second too long.

Like I'm a threat that he hasn't yet figured out how to deal with?

I can't place it.

But instinct tells me he is hiding something.

And I am going to find out what.

Chapter Thirty Two-Auren

The halls of Starfall Keep whisper with echoes—soft footfalls on polished stone, the rustle of silken banners in the breeze, and the distant hum of starlight filtering through the domed ceilings above.

I walk in silence beside Reavian, my hand resting gently in his. Noctis pads beside me, ever watchful, never straying more than a step from my side. I barely register the beauty of the keep around me. Everything is heavy. Dim. Like the sun dipped beneath the horizon and never rose again.

Kessa isn't coming back.

I couldn't help her.

I couldn't *save* her.

We are shown through a corridor filled with violet glass sconces, orbs of light reflecting off carved moons and stars etched into the stone. At last, the steward bows, and gestures towards a dark wood door trimmed with silver.

"This is yours," he says. "Prepared for you on High Lord Vaelisar's order, it's been waiting for you."

The door creaks open.

I stop at the threshold, my breath catching in my throat.

This bedchamber is...*otherworldly*.

Soft violet light bathes the room, spilling down from the massive domed ceiling above the bed, where the constellations gleam in brilliant clarity, it's as if they are shining just for us. The walls are draped in gauzy silver fabrics; floors laid with deep indigo and midnight blue rugs woven in curling star patterns. A large hearth is near the door, fire already crackling within. In the center of the room stands a vast bed, draped in black silken sheets and a black velvet comforter stitched with threads of silver that shimmer. Beyond the bed, down a short set of steps, is a sunken bathing pool. It's large enough for at least six people, carved from a polished dark stone that's veined with deep purple and gold.

I smile and thank the steward, my grief still wearing a mask.

He pulls the door closed for us, and I hear his footsteps travel down the hallway, away from our room. My shoulders fall the moment the steward is completely out of ear shot. I walk to the bed, letting my fingers graze its silver frame. Noctis lies down in front of the door.

"I never should have left," I whisper.

"What?" Reavian asks, turning to me.

My voice cracks. "If I hadn't left... if I hadn't gone alone, none of you would have had to come to find me. She wouldn't have..." my breath stutters. "Kessa would still be alive."

I drop to my knees. My head falling into my hands.

"I'm so sorry," I whisper.

Soft steps approach, then Reavian kneels beside me, his hand rests gently on my back.

I pull my hands from my face, look at him, and the dam breaks. Tears spill down my cheeks, fast and hot. I bury myself in his chest.

"It's all my fault," I sob. "And I... I thought the orb...when I was guided to interact with it, I thought it would reset everything. I thought it would save her. But it didn't. She's gone. She's gone forever, and it's all my fault."

Reavian holds me tightly, kissing the tears from my cheeks one by one.

"No," he murmurs. "No, it wasn't your fault. You could have told us, and we could have all traveled together, and we might have still had the same outcome. She would have come either way, you know that. Even if we tried to tie her to a tree to stop her. She would have cut herself loose, called you a pain in the ass, and marched right into danger anyway."

I let out a watery laugh, my face now tucked under his jaw.

"She would've," I say.

He smiles faintly, brushing my hair from my face.

"You're not screwing everything up, Auren. You're doing your best. And that's enough," he says.

I blink up at him, my whole body trembling.

"If you want," he says quietly, "I'll run with you. Right now. Just say the word, I'll find a way to tear a portal to another world—one just for us. And we can live a long peaceful life together."

The lump in my throat cracks again, but this time not from sadness. This time it's from *love*.

I lean up to kiss him softly.

After a long moment, Reavian pulls away and whispers, "Let's get you out of these river-soaked clothes, and into a nice hot bath."

He moves to the bathing pool, twisting a set of obsidian knobs embedded in the stone. Warm water rushes in, steam curling upward as he reaches for a silver vial on an embedded shelf and pours its contents into the water. The scent of flowers from the meadows here fills the air.

"I'll give you some privacy," he says walking to a chair near the bed and turning it so that when he sits in it his back faces me.

I strip off my clothing, kicking everything into a pile. I look at Reavian, and even though he's just on the other side of the room, he's too far away.

"I don't want privacy," I tell him.

He stills for a moment, then stands. I turn to face the tub, slowly walking down into it, and I glance over my shoulder.

"Join me?" I whisper.

He doesn't hesitate.

He undresses quickly, and steps into the tub behind me. The warm water laps at my calves, then my hips, until it swallows me whole. Reavian has paused to watch me get in, his eyes meet mine and darken a bit.

Every inch of his body makes something inside me tighten. His form is lean and powerful, he's beautiful in a way that makes my chest ache.

He steps in fully and sinks into the water beside me, sitting on the built-in bench. For a long moment, we simply exist there. Staring, breathing, letting the silence hold the weight of everything unspoken.

Then he reaches for me.

Not with hunger or urgency.

But with *care*.

His fingers thread through my hair, lifting the strands gently into the water. I watch as he pours a crystal vial of soap into his palm, then massages it slowly into my scalp. His touch is tender.

My eyes flutter shut when his thumbs trace circles behind my ears. His fingers comb through my tangles with patience. He touches me like each rinse, each caress, etches me deeper into his soul.

"You're beautiful," he murmurs, his voice hoarse.

I open my eyes. He is closer now. His hand drifts down to cup my jaw, thumb brushing my cheek.

"You're looking at me like I'm something precious," I whisper.

"Because you are," he replies.

I take the vial from him, scoop water into my hands and stand leaning forward.

I smooth the water over his thick, dark hair, then lather the soap gently between my fingers and work it in.

He closes his eyes, he's relaxed.

Something that the thread between us tells me he hasn't felt before. He exhales when my hands move to his shoulders, my thumbs kneading into tight muscle. He always carries so much tension. So much weight. I want to lift it, if only for a moment.

I reach for the cloth beside me and run it over his chest, over every jagged scar that tears across it.

"These…" I whisper.

His eyes meet mine.

"My mother," he says softly. "The scar on my lip, she hit me with the hilt of a sword when I told her no. I was nine."

My breath hitches.

"These," he says gesturing to the marks on his chest. "When I was a teenager, I tried to leave. She had me chained in the dungeon. The lashes didn't stop until she was done making her point."

I touch them again, softer this time.

"I'm sorry," I whisper. "I wish I could take all of your pain away."

He leans in and kisses my forehead. "I wish I could erase every bit of pain that you carry too."

He slides his hand beneath my chin and our mouths meet, slow and full of ache. We kiss like we are pouring all of our broken pieces into each other hoping that they'll fit better together.

My body shifts in the water, and I move into his lap, straddling him. His hands find my hips instinctively, but he doesn't move, not until I do.

I roll my hips gently, pressing against the hardness of him beneath the water.

A breath hisses from between his teeth.

"You're going to undo me," he rasps.

"Let me," I whisper into his ear.

I keep moving, the rhythm slow and sensual, friction teasing with every grind of my body against his. I want to burn for him, *with* him.

"Are you sure you want this?" he whispers. "We don't have to do this tonight—"

"Please," I whisper. "I *need* you."

Reavian growls, his mouth crashing against mine. He cups my breast, fingers dragging across my skin as he kisses down my throat.

I gasp.

"I want to claim every sound you make," he whispers.

"Take them," I beg. "They're yours."

There's a knock at the door, shortly after the first there is another.

Shit, it's probably the stewards with dinner.

Ugh, not now.

"Go the fuck away!" Reavian shouts, seemingly sensing my

thoughts, and effectively silencing the knocking on the door.

I giggle into his neck.

His hand slips between us, fingers finding me. Circling. Stroking. Driving me to the edge and pulling me back just enough to keep me trembling.

I whimper, clutching his shoulders. "Reav..."

"Not yet," he says, giving me a devilish grin. "I want to *feel* you when you shatter."

Then he lifts me just enough to position himself, and I sink down onto him with a soft, broken cry.

The stretch, the fullness, the depth of him. It's overwhelming and beautiful.

Necessary.

We move.

Slowly at first, deep and intimate. My fingers drag through his wet hair, his hands clutch my waist as our bodies meet again and again in quiet, shuddering ecstasy.

The warm waters laps and sloshes around us, our moans softly rising.

The tension climbs higher.

And so does our rhythm.

I ride him like he's the only thing holding me together, every grind of my hips a cry for *something more*.

I toss my head back, taking him deeper, and deeper, digging my nails into his back. He growls, a guttural moan tearing from him.

His hand grips the back of my neck, guiding me to his lips again.

"Say it," he demands.

I know exactly what he wants to hear.

"I love you."

He groans, shuddering, picking up his pace.

"I love you," he whispers into my neck, before giving it a rough kiss.

The climax hits me—white hot and wild, my body arching into his, trembling through wave after wave of release.

I barely hear his voice when he follows, whispering my name like it's a prayer as he holds me tight, burying his face into my neck.

We stay that way until the water starts to cool. Remaining connected, and breathless.

One.

Then he stands, lifting me gently from the bath. My legs are still wrapped around his waist, my head resting against his chest.

He dries us both off with a nearby thick black towel, never once letting me go. Then he carries me to bed, laying us both into the black silken sheets. He pulls the velvet comforter over us, cocooning us in warmth, in love, and in something deeper than either of us has ever known.

We fall asleep wrapped around each other, with the stars above us, and the echo of each other's names still clinging to our lips.

Chapter Thirty
Three—Auren

I wake to the sensation of warmth. Soft blankets, a weight against my back, and the steady rise and fall of someone breathing beside me. For a moment, I don't move. The world is quiet.

Peaceful.

Reavian shifts behind me, muttering something that sounds suspiciously like 'Put the dress on the horse', his voice gravelly with sleep. I blink once, then again.

And then his stomach growls, *loudly*.

Noctis, curled at the foot of the bed like a dark-furred sentinel, lifts his head with a soft woof, then stares at us with disapproval.

I bite back a laugh. "Maybe you shouldn't have shouted at the steward who knocked last night," I say over my shoulder, smiling. "He probably had food."

Reavian groans and buries his face in his pillow. "He was interrupting."

"You *yelled* at him."

"I was busy," he says, his voice muffled. "*Very* busy."

He presses a kiss into my temple.

I laugh, an actual bubbling sound, and roll onto my back to look at him. His eyes are still closed, but his mouth is curled into that rare soft smirk that I live for.

"You're lucky I was equally busy," I murmur. "Otherwise, I *may* be upset about how hungry I am right now."

"If he had barged in, I would have set him on fire," he says.

"You *don't have* fire magic," I retort.

"I would have figured something out."

I smile, then eventually slide out from beneath the covers. The cold floor is a sharp contrast to the heat of Reavian's body. The air chills every bit of my exposed skin. Noctis lets out a deep sigh, and resettles himself, clearly deciding the foot of the bed is *his* now.

I cross to the large wardrobe along the far wall and open it—then pause. My breath catches.

"Reav, come look at this."

He makes a noise of protest, but curiosity gets the better of him. He walks over, still naked from last night as well, his eyes heavy with sleep.

He stands behind me looking over my shoulder.

The wardrobe is fully stocked. Dozens of garments in varying shades of violet, midnight black, deep blue, and silver hang in elegant order. There are dresses, cloaks, gloves, underthings, and intricately designed shoes. All in my size. Below that, a lower shelf holds neatly folded dark shirts, dark trousers, cloaks, leathers, belts and polished boots. His size.

"It's like they knew we'd be staying here," I whisper, "and that we'd be sharing a room."

Reavian raises a brow. "I'm going to take this as a good omen."

I shake my head, a faint smile playing at my lips.

"This realm is so strange. I never know what time of day it is. Mornings here are still cloaked in night, but it's that almost twilight moment before the stars begin to burn brightly, when the sky is streaked with purple. And then it's just... night. And the sky burns with thousands of bright stars."

"Yeah," Reavian replies, moving to examine one of the cloaks. "But... I don't know. Something about this place feels calming. I feel like I can breathe here."

I look at him, studying the lines of his face as he stares toward the sky above us.

"I feel that way too," I admit. "It's peaceful. Like the land itself is always dreaming, and relaxed."

We both choose outfits from the wardrobe, though Reavian seems to be having more luck than me. He pulls on black leather armor, stitched with silver thread, fitted sleek and sharp against his frame. He looks...unfairly good. Like a perfect painting of some sort of God, readying for battle.

I, on the other hand, narrow my eyes at a selection of dresses.

"Am I meant to fight battles in *gowns*?"

Reavian looks over, a half-smile pulling at his mouth.

"You'd win a battle in anything."

I snort. "Yeah...okay, flatterer."

Eventually I chose a knee-length dress in a deep royal purple. Tiny dark blue flowers are stitched across the hemline and up to the bodice, its sleeves are sheer, the fabric light and flowy.

At the bottom of the wardrobe, I find a pair of silver heels, with delicate ribbon meant to wind around my ankles.

I bring them over to the bed, where Reavian now sits along the edge.

"Can you help me with these?" I ask him.

He kneels before me, lifting one of my shoes with a furrowed brow. "You're really going to wear these?"

"I don't exactly have many options."

He slips the first shoe on my foot, then traces his hands up my calf as he ties the ribbon into a neat bow. His eyes find mine, his gaze feels warm.

"We could stay," he says softly. "Forget the impending doom, the High Lord. Just... stay locked in here. All day. You. Me. That dress."

My breath hitches, and just as I open my mouth to reply, someone knocks.

Reavian groans dramatically, and flops back onto the bed. "I feel like whoever's outside that door is doing this on *purpose*."

I step toward the door just as it opens, revealing three stewards. Two carrying trays of covered dishes and steaming mugs rushing over to the table in our room, and the other hauling in a carved wooden chair.

They enter with practiced grace, carefully setting down the trays. One steward picks up a silver platter from the table and kneels to place it on the floor—a small dish for Noctis. It contains a fresh cut of raw meat, something rich and bloody that looks like a feast for wolves. The other steward follows, placing a pitcher of silver water beside the plate, and then sets down a deep wide bowl. He pours the water in it, leaving the rest in the pitcher beside the bowl. Noctis hops from the bed and pads over, giving the steward a small approving grunt before immediately beginning to eat.

I smile at the steward. "How thoughtful, bringing this for Noctis, thank you."

Before the steward can offer me a reply, a tall figure enters the room.

Vaelisar.

He moves with an effortless grace, draped in twilight dark robes. His presence shifts the air itself. But it's his eyes that catch my attention—sharp, silver flecked, and entirely too knowing.

"Ah, good," he says. "You're both awake. I thought we might enjoy breakfast together before the council convenes."

We eat in silence for a few moments, the clink of silverware, and our chewing the only sounds filling the room. When Vaelisar finally looks up, he doesn't bother with preamble.

"I assume your journey here was not an easy one."

Reavian doesn't answer. I place my fork down carefully.

"No," I say. "It wasn't. I... we came because we wanted to help. I want to heal the land here and push out the corruption. Tharen came back to Solmere Keep after scouting along the border and told Vaedric how bad things are getting here. But Vaedric wasn't going to send aid...because *you* didn't help when he and his people needed it."

Vaelisar stills, blinking slowly. "I... wasn't aware he ever reached out."

His tone isn't defensive. It's shocked.

Reavian frowns. "That's convenient."

I look at Vaelisar, and I somehow just *know* he's being honest.

"No... he's telling the truth," I say.

Vaelisar inclines his head toward me in quiet gratitude.

I take a breath. "I passed through corrupted lands, healing it as I went, until I was attacked by conscripted. That's when Reavian met up with me, the others shortly after. We ended up in a strange hedge maze before reaching your wards. It killed one of our companions. My friend, Kessa."

Vaelisar's expression darkens. "I'm so sorry. The guardians must have activated it—likely as a final line of defense before our wards. They didn't know *who* was approaching and likely did it out of instinct. They were trying to protect us."

I glance over at Noctis, one of those very guardians, and he whimpers softly at me. I can feel that they didn't mean to cause harm.

I look down at my plate, my appetite now gone. It isn't Noctis's fault or any of the other guardians of the land here. If *I* had sent a message first. If *I* had waited and spoken to Reavian and the others, this wouldn't have happened. This is all *my fault*. Kessa paid the price for my stupidity.

Under the table, Reavian places a hand on my knee. His touch calms me a bit.

"She died because of me, and my decisions," I whisper so softly that only Reavian hears me. His grip on my knee tightens a bit, steadying me.

Reavian turns to Vaelisar, his voice harder now. "The conscripted have overtaken the mountain pass, they tried to follow us through the river. Are you aware that their flesh burns when it touches the water?"

Vaelisar's brows lift. "Interesting. I'll have my best look into that immediately. It's connected to the land's natural magic, perhaps we can weaponize it somehow. This also explains why they haven't pushed any farther forward. The corruption can't cross the line either perhaps. The river surrounds the way to Starfall City."

There is a pause. A shift in the air.

"The council," Vaelisar says, "will want to meet with you and your party this morning. They'll want to hear your story. They'll likely not believe that you are the true heir without proof. They'll want to put you through the Dream Trial."

"No," Reavian says flatly, his voice like steel. "You're not putting her through that. I've heard about those trials. People don't always survive."

I swallow hard, and I turn to Vaelisar.

"What is it?" I ask.

"During a Dream Trial you're placed in a sealed chamber, and you're submerged in liquid starlight. It covers you entirely, seeping into you, but you do not drown. Instead, you drift into a deep prophetic sleep. What you experience varies—visions, nightmares, truths. However, if you die in your dream, your physical body dies as well. If the magic of the realm deems you unworthy, you will also not survive. High Lords of this realm, selected by the magic here, have died during dream trials, after being deemed no longer worthy."

Reavian's hand clenches into a fist on the table. "She's not doing it."

Vaelisar looks between us, then smiles—genuine and curious.

"How long have you loved her, boy?" he asks.

Reavian doesn't answer, seemingly feeling like it's none of his business. And it's not. But the tension in his shoulders tells me he's about to go across the table and do something to Vaelisar that we'll both regret.

"I think I've loved *him* most of my life," I say softly.

Reavian's shoulders lose tension, his gaze meeting mine and softening.

Vaelisar's head tilts. "How is that possible? You didn't come to this world until recently. I saw it in my premonitions, you were this age."

"I was about ten, when we first met," I say, "I had dreams of a place cloaked in shadow. We could never see each other. But he would always find his way to me, helping me with my anxiety. Comforting me. I knew the sound of his heartbeat, like it was my own."

"You were always the light in the darkness for me," Reavian says, his voice low, almost reverent. "You brought me peace, when I had none in my waking life."

Valeisar's gaze lingers on Reavian for a moment, something shifting in his expression. "Dreamwalking..."

I blink. "What is that?"

He hesitates for a moment, clearly battling something within, then he turns to me.

"It's an ancient magic from my realm. A rare gift—only I possess it. Somehow... you must have inherited the gift before you ever arrived here."

I nod slowly. "I guess that makes sense. I inherited fire from the Realm of Flame and Forest, like Vaedric. But that didn't appear until I was already here..."

Vaelisar leans back in his chair, thoughtful.

Then Reavian asks, "Who is on this council?"

"It's headed by Bronn Valeaon," Vaelisar replies, the name heavy on his tongue. "You had the displeasure of meeting his son Halrex last night. I'm afraid the apple doesn't fall too far from the tree, so to speak. And then there are the five heads from the noble families here in Starfall City."

My jaw tenses. If Halrex was *that* awful, I shudder to think of what his father will be like.

Reavian's tone drops cold. "If this Bronn threatens her, or anyone else in our party like his son did, I'll tell him the same thing I told Halrex."

Vaelisar raises a brow.

"I'll end him."

I reach for his hand across the table, lacing our fingers. "I'm sure it will be fine."

Vaelisar's expression softens as he looks between us. "I give you my word, no harm will come to her. Or to anyone in your party for that matter. Let them prattle, as High Lord of this realm, I have final say."

We finish our breakfast, the weight of what is to come settling like mist around us. When Vaelisar rises to leave, I stand with him.

"I'd like to see more of the land," I tell him. "To heal it, little by little."

He nods. "We can discuss it with the council today, let them see your heart."

I smile at him. "Also...thank you for the clothes. But if I'm going to fight, I might need some boots. Maybe some leathers."

Vaelisar chuckles. "I'll have someone see to it. Though the dress *does* look lovely on you."

He gives us a final bow of his head and then leaves us.

Chapter Thirty
Four-Auren

The doors to the council chamber groan open like the breath of something ancient.

I step into the cavernous room beside Reavian, my fingers brushing his as we move toward a long, curved wood and obsidian table. Noctis is walking slowly ahead of us, his gaze moving across the room, looking for any sign of a threat. Starfall Keep's council chamber is carved from black stone veined with shimmering silver. A domed ceiling above us displays paintings of constellations in the sky here that didn't exist in the human world.

A cold draft swirls across the floor, making the candles in the sconces on the walls flicker.

It smells faintly of old incense in here.

At the far end of the chamber, seated above the council table on a dais, High Lord Vaelisar Thorneveil waits on a throne of stone intricately carved with celestial patterns. Regal and composed, he sits like he has all the time in the world—and all the weight of it balanced in his palm.

Six council members occupy the curved table, seated in high-backed chairs marked with what I can only assume are their house sigils. The rest of our party is already seated, leaving two spaces for Reavian and I at the center of the table.

Vaelisar's voice carries effortlessly across the space.

"You stand before the ruling council of the Realm of Veiled Stars. Let me introduce them formally, Lady Auren. Please sit," he says, gesturing us to the table.

Reavian and I sit. I bow my head slightly as he gestures toward each noble in polite greeting.

"Lord Bronn Valeaon, Head of the Council."

My gaze settles on the man seated at the center of the other side of the table. He is portly, with dark thinning hair slicked back so tightly it gleams beneath the light. His clothing is extravagant—buttons stretched across his gut, silver rings on every finger—but his eyes are sharp and calculating.

He looks at me like one might assess a stain on an expensive rug.

"Lord Kaeron Mirthal," Vaelisar says, with less warmth.

Kaeron is a tall thin man with birdlike features— a sharp pointed nose that resembles a beak, and cheekbones that are equally as sharp. He wears robes embroidered with what appears to be ancient script. His hands are clasped before him, like he is praying for me to fail. When our eyes meet, I see nothing but contempt.

"Lady Maedra Valoren."

I have to fight not to flinch at her. Her pale blonde hair is twisted into a perfect knot, her lips painted a deep crimson. The way she looks at me makes me feel like I have just tracked ash across a pristine floor, and she is readying my punishment. Her gloved fingers drum slowly against the table, each tap deliberate.

"Lady Theris Naelwyn."

Theris is younger than I would have expected, her honey-gold hair braided loosely over one shoulder. She doesn't speak, but her eyes are gentle and uncertain, like someone still deciding whether to reach or retreat.

"Lord Eryndor Thalos," Valeisar continues, "Veteran of the Rift War."

Eryndor inclines his head. His silver hair is tied back into a warrior's knot, and his weathered face bears lines of grief rather than age. He looks like someone that has seen too much, but hasn't let it turn him cruel.

"And lastly, Lady Celyne Virathis."

Celyne sits with her back straight and her head held high. Her rich brown skin shimmers with faint silver tattoos that wind up her neck, they're intricate constellations. Her expression is unreadable, but not unkind.

Valeisar looks at me, and I introduce everyone in our party, not forgetting Noctis, who dips his head a little when I name him, before returning to guard my back again.

Bronn clears his throat loudly. "Let's begin, shall we?"

His voice is oily with false courtesy.

"You arrive uninvited. You disrupted our defenses. And now you sit before us as if you belong here. So, tell us... what is it exactly that you want?"

I lift my chin, ignoring the ice curling in my stomach.

"To help," I tell them.

Silence follows.

"I came because your land is sick, strangled with corruption," I say, my voice steadier now. "I've seen it, even healed parts of it on my journey here, before the corruption came back and swallowed it up behind me. I feel the land's pain, the moment I stepped into your realm. The corruption is spreading here quickly. I've healed corruption in the Realm of Flame and Forest—"

"That's quite a claim," Lord Kaeron interrupts, his lip curling. "And one we have no proof of."

"She speaks the truth," Tharen says, sitting up straighter. "I saw the land she healed in my realm. There is no longer corruption there. I recently led a scouting party, to check the corruption spreading from your realm toward our borders. I saw how bad it was here, so our party decided to investigate further. We were attacked by conscripted. Those of us who survived, fled your realm and reported it to High Lord Vaedric. Auren left *immediately* upon hearing the state of things here. She came to you without hesitation, to help you and your people."

Lady Maedra scoffs softly. "For us?" she asks, her tone mocking. "Or for *him*?"

Her cold gaze flicks towards Reavian. "Perhaps this is part of his mother's grand plan. You are allied with our enemy's son. You're an outsider, and you do not belong here."

Reavian's jaw flexes, but I gently place my hand on his, calming him.

"I didn't ask to be born with this power," I say. "But I have it. And I'll use it to protect the realms, *all* of them."

"But you were not born here, correct?" Lady Theris asks, her voice soft but laced with curiosity. "You were raised in the human world... you have no ties here, why would you want to help us?"

"I was raised in the human world, yes," I reply nodding. "I want to help because it is the right thing to do, and because this family..." I gesture to everyone seated on my side of the table, "is all I have left in the world. And I would fight for any single one of them until my very last breath."

I turn back to face the rest of the council, scanning all of their faces. "The corruption won't stop with just one realm. Lucien and Liraeth are building an army of horrors, an army of stolen lives. They are taking people from Iska's realm, Tide and Storm, and they are twisting them into mindless, monstrous beasts you call the conscripted. They will do the same to your people. They will not stop until they take everything. If we don't unite—if we don't somehow form an alliance between all the realms—your council won't survive to argue about anything for much longer."

Lady Celyne stirs. "You believe you can stop them?"

"I believe *we* can," I say, glancing briefly at Reavian, then at the rest of my party, before bringing my gaze back to the council members. "But not if we keep tearing each other apart."

Bronn leans back, sneering. "You're saying you're the heir of High King Alarion Veylas. That your blood ties to this realm run deeper than we even know. But bloodlines are not proven with pretty speeches and wide eyes."

Lady Maedra folds her gloved hands atop the table. "Anyone can claim to be the heir. Especially if they figured out how to do a parlor trick with some basic fae light and displayed a few bruises to garner sympathy."

Lord Kaeron nods. "The child of the High King would have been raised among us. Not sent off to the mortal realm. The heir would not be *this*," he says, gesturing to me with disgust.

"She is no more an heir than I am a starlight prophet," Bronn mutters.

I take a breath and let it rise. I look deep within myself just for my flame.

Yes, Little Light.

Show them.

I lift my hand and summon it. A radiant orb of white pulsing flame forms in my palm. Not a parlor trick. This flame is *alive*. The kind I used to burn corruption to ash and remake the space around it.

The council falls silent.

Lord Eryndor stands, his voice catching. "That fire...I've seen it once before. During the Rift War, the High King wielded it when the enemy stormed the gates, before Lucien killed them all. That same fire. It was *his*. This is no trick."

My hand trembles slightly, but the flame holds.

"It's not real," Kaeron hisses. "The Gods wouldn't give that kind of power to her, even if she *is* his child, she's just a bastard outsider."

Reavian's jaw clenches. "She is *no* bastard, and I suggest you apologize to her right now."

Kaeron doesn't blink. "Why? Are you going to start hurling blades next, boy? Like mother, Like son."

Reavian rises, tense and coiled, but my hand slips into his and holds him still.

"Reav," I whisper.

Bronn sneers. "Yes, let's talk about your mother. You threatened my son last night. Now you are baring your teeth in here. The resemblance is... *remarkable*."

"He is *nothing* like her," I snap. "Liraeth tortured Brynn for nearly two years, she tortured me for weeks. Reavian and Kaiel went against her. They risked everything to save us."

Iska sits forward. "They saved *me*, too. I would have been conscripted. I owe them my life."

Bronn's smirk returns. "So, that's all we get? Weepy tales and a light show. That's your proof?"

"She needs to complete the Dream Trial!" Kaeron snaps out.

The council erupts into debate on whether or not I should have to complete the trials. I'm not surprised, Vaelisar *did* warn us about this.

"She's already shown more courage than any of you sitting here," Reavian says, his voice cold. "She's walked through hell and still has come to help you. And there is no point in any of you arguing, because she is not doing any *fucking* Dream Trial."

The look he gives each member of the council sends a shiver down my spine.

Bronn looks at Reavian. "Why are you protecting this discarded mistake? Is it perhaps because it's where you rest your dick every now and then?"

Reavian's chair quickly scrapes across the stone floor, but it's Kaiel who moves faster.

He leaps onto the table in one fluid motion, grabbing Bronn by the front of his robes, and hauling him up into the air. Bronn's feet kick, he's red faced and gasping.

"Say that again," Kaiel growls, tightening his grip on Bronn's robes, choking him with them. "I dare you."

The chamber erupts—council members shouting, guards moving for their weapons.

"Enough!" Vaelisar's voice booms like a thunderclap.

Silence drops like a curtain.

I watch as Kaiel drops Bronn, back into his chair with a thud. The council is shaken, furious, and divided.

"We will vote," Vaelisar says.

One by one the council votes on whether or not I need to complete the Dream Trial. Maedra, Kaeron, Bronn, and after hesitation, Theris vote in favor of me completing the Dream Trial. Celyne votes yes, though states that she is doing so only to confirm my truth. Only Eryndor votes no.

Valeisar rises from his throne.

"As High Lord of the Realm of Veiled stars, I overrule your vote. She will not undergo the trial. She has been chosen by a guardian of this land, he is sitting right behind her. I know in my heart that she is the true heir to the throne. My decision is final."

Bronn stands, outraged. "You cannot—"

"I *can*," Vaelisar says, stepping forward. "And I *have*."

Bronn glares at him, his eyes livid. "You'll regret this."

"I regret many things," Vaelisar replies. "Believing in her is not going to be one of them."

Bronn storms out, Kaeron and Maedra following behind him. The doors slam shut behind them.

Only Celyne, Eryndor, and Theris remain.

I turn to them, my heart still pounding. "Thank you for staying."

Lord Eryndor gives a quiet nod. "You carry your father's fire.

That was no trick."

Lady Celyne meets my gaze. "You said you can heal the land. That is no small promise, nor will it be an easy task."

"I'm not asking you to believe me without proof," I say. "But if you can help me, maybe by gathering a small company of trusted knights. The knights and I can go with Reavian, Tharen, and Kaiel. I can show you that I can do it."

Theris hesitates, then gives me a small nod. "Perhaps... healing is its own kind of truth."

Vaelisar steps down from the dais, his expression unreadable but warm.

"Then let us begin," he says.

Chapter Thirty Five-
Reavian

I want to leave this room, find Bronn Valeaon, and turn him into nothing more than a bloodstain on these walls.

Not with my shadows, not with my blade. With my bare hands.

He looked at her—spoke to her—like she was filth beneath his boots. Like her very presence was an offense to the stone beneath our feet. And what he said about her and I... as if what I feel for her is anything less than soul-deep devotion. As if she's not the one bright thing in all this darkness. My anchor. My fucking reason. That made him number one on my *I'll kill you slowly* list.

I curl my fists, and stare at the floor because if I look at any of the council members still in this room, I may not be able to stop myself, especially after all but one of them voted to put her in danger.

Fucking cowards.

A pulse of something flickers along that thread between us.

Auren.

She doesn't say anything, but I can feel her reaching for me through that thread. That quiet presence, soft and light, brushing up against my fury. Letting me know she's there. To remind me that she's alright.

I breathe through my nose and raise my gaze. Vaelisar is already speaking to the three council members who remain—Celyne, Theris, and Eryndor. They're laying out possible regions for Auren to begin healing. Tharen nods in response to something Kaiel says, but I don't register the words because I am more focused on how Kaiel is just standing there, like nothing happened. Like he didn't just lunge across the council table and nearly choke a man to death.

My eyes narrow on him. Had he killed Bronn, I wouldn't say I'd be upset. But that wasn't just fury I saw in my friend. That was *something else*. Something deeper, barely leashed. I've seen Kaiel angry a hundred times, usually with a joke on his lips and a sword in his hand. But what happened today?

That was *feral*.

Something is wrong.

Brynn's voice cuts through the space, sharp and defiant.

"I'm coming too."

All eyes swing to her. She crosses her arms and lifts her chin. There's still tiredness around her eyes, but her voice holds steel.

"I'm doing much better," she says. "And if things go sideways, I can throw lightning for fuck's sake. You're not leaving me behind."

Auren looks at Brynn, surprised—but there is a faint smile tugging at the corner of her mouth.

"You sure?" she asks her gently.

Brynn nods once. "Just try and stop me."

Iska speaks next, brushing her silver hair behind her shoulder. "You'll need a healer. And I'm not going to just sit around while the rest of you charge into cursed lands without one."

Auren nods. "We'd be lucky to have you both."

The councilors are discussing which members of the Nightguard they will ask to come with us. I stand, and place both my hands on the table.

"Any knights that are assigned to accompany us, must be people that *we* believe we can trust. Bronn's son is *not* welcome in our ranks." I say, my voice low and razor-edged, each word deliberate. I let it hang in the air like the threat that it is, dressed in civility.

Vaelisar lifts a brow, considering me for a moment.

"Agreed," he says.

He then gestures toward a table near another wall in the chamber, where a glowing map of The Realm of Veiled Stars pulses faintly with veins of silver and shadow. The corruption is visible in markings across the map. Thick, dark scars running across what was once sacred ground.

"We have several possible locations where Auren may begin," Vaelisar says, his voice level. "Most are near outlying settlements, where people have fled."

Lady Celyne steps forward, brushing her fingers over the map. "This valley here, Somnarel Hollow. It was once the Dreamkeeper Sanctuary. A place where prophetic dreams were analyzed, and visions were nurtured. There were pools of reflection, it was beautiful. Now the trees are twisted, and the pools choked with ash. But... no conscripted sightings have been reported there."

"Not yet," Eryndor mutters grimly, his arms crossed. "Which makes it ideal. The corruption is thickest there, but the risk of attack would be minimal. If she can heal *that*, the rest of the council will have little ground to stand on."

Tharen leans in, brow furrowed. "It looks like we'll have to travel deep through the woods, then up the mountain. The terrain is difficult. It'll be at least a three day's ride, and then we'll have to continue on foot."

"And if something has moved in since the last scout report?" I ask, hearing the heat building in my voice again. "We would be walking right into a trap."

Vaelisar meets my eyes. His gaze is calm and controlled.

I don't trust it.

"We will take precautions," he says. "You'll have supplies, maps, knights of your choosing."

His gaze flicks to Auren. "It is your choice."

Auren nods slowly, her eyes on the map. "I will start in Somnarel Hollow. It seems it's the only place that the conscripted have not been sighted yet. The corruption is thick there, yes. But it will be a good test of my power, and it puts everyone at the least amount of risk. We'll have to remain vigilant, of course. but I think this is where we should begin."

She sounds steady, but when her hand brushes mine, I feel it—the lingering tremor beneath the surface.

I hate this. I hate that she will be in danger more than anything else. I feel the anger building up in me again, at my mother, at Lucien, at this whole fucking situation.

Without a word, she leans into my side, taking my arm and wrapping it around her. She rests her head against me. I tilt my head down a bit, and breathe her in. The scent of orchids in her hair, and something that is only her. Something wild and bright.

And just like that, the anger subsides, and all I feel is the love between us.

"Then it's settled," Vaelisar says. "You will leave in the morning."

Thesis, who's been quiet through most of the discussion, lifts his head. "After supper, we'll reconvene here," he says gently, looking to Auren. "Each of us will bring forward knights who are willing to volunteer for the journey. You'll have the chance to speak with them and choose who you trust."

Celyne nods. "It's only right. If you are the true heir, and this land is to rise again, it should be done on *your* terms."

Auren straightens beside me, her eyes wide for just a breath, then she nods.

"Thank you," she says, her voice quiet but firm.

As the council begins to file out, Auren slips away from my side. I follow her with my eyes as she crosses to Brynn and Iska. The three of them lean in together, speaking in low voices. Brynn smiles at something Auren says.

There's still a weariness to Brynn, a slight shadow behind her eyes, but... she's doing well.

I didn't know her before that night at the Reach, but I can tell she is reclaiming something. A piece of herself that my mother tried to snuff out.

Kaiel is lingering near the edge of the map table, fidgeting with a carved piece of obsidian. I walk over to him quietly and pull him just out of the others' earshot.

"You good?" I ask, making sure to keep my voice low.

He shrugs, not meeting my eyes. "What, you mean what happened earlier? Bronn's a bastard. He deserved it."

"I'm not arguing either of those things, but it just wasn't like *you*. You nearly crushed his throat."

Kaiel flashes a crooked grin. "I held back."

I raise a brow. He's joking, but it doesn't sit right. The humor doesn't reach his eyes. It's a deflection. A practiced one.

"Seriously, Kaiel—"

He glances past me to where Brynn is standing with Auren, then mutters, "It's fine. Just some... some shit, you know?"

I don't know. Not all of it.

But I nod anyway. "You can tell me when you're ready."

His grin fades into something quieter. "Yeah... maybe."

I clap him on the shoulder and walk back toward Auren. Her laughter floats softly across the chamber, it's a sound I never want to lose.

I slide my arm around her waist, pulling her just a little closer.

"You did well today," I murmur. "Better than any of them deserved."

Her fingers slip into mine. "I'm glad you were here."

I lean down, press a kiss into her temple, then walk with her out of the council chamber.

The weight of what's to come pressing at my back.

Chapter Thirty Six-Auren

T he moment Reavian and I step into our room, I know something is waiting for me.

The silver starlight from the domed ceiling spills across the room in gentle rivulets, casting soft, shifting patterns on the floor and walls. Noctis walks over to his water bowl, gets a drink, and then curls up next to the hearth, already lit with a low fire.

And then I see them.

Laid out across the bed are leathers, unmistakably crafted here in Starfall City. They're midnight-hued, sleek, and soft to the touch. They shimmer as I approach them, catching the starlight in a way that makes them look almost alive. The threads that hold the pieces together glint silver, and the garments seem to pulse faintly with magic. They are ethereal and mysterious.

On the floor at the foot of the bed, several pairs of boots rest in a neat line. One pair in particular draws my eye—tall, elegant, and made of supple black leather that's reinforced with silver-flecked velvet along the inner lining. Built for movement, as well as comfort.

Made specially for me.

But what stops me entirely is the small box resting in the center of the bed, wrapped neatly in midnight-blue cloth, simple and neat.

I sit and slowly unwrap it.

Inside are two thigh sheaths and nestled between them—daggers. Onyx blades, so dark they almost vanish in the low light, but speckled with silver, like someone captured a spray of starlight and embedded it into the dark metal. The handles are smooth and black, perfectly balanced, ending with a single midnight-blue jewel set like a star at the pommel.

They are stunning, and deadly.

Beneath them, on a small rectangular piece of paper, a note.

To protect him.

-Vaelisar

The breath leaves my lungs.

There is no flourish, and no explanation. But I feel the weight behind the words. He's seen something—he's *dreamed* it, maybe even somehow lived it in his mind. This isn't just a gift. It's a warning. A private truth.

"What does it say?" Reavian asks gently from behind me.

I crumple the note slowly in my hand.

"They're from Vaelisar," I answer, soft and nonchalant.

And that's all I say.

I walk over to him and place a kiss to his mouth, then toss the crumpled note and cloth into the waste bin like it means nothing.

But it doesn't mean nothing.

It means everything.

I can still feel Reavian's tension and simmering anger through our bond. He's trying not to show it, but after everything that happened with the council today, he's furious.

I decide to maybe... distract him a bit.

"Would you like to spar?" I ask, stepping back with a teasing glint in my eye.

His gaze darkens instantly.

"Gods, yes," he says, making his way toward me.

"Not that kind of sparring... a real training session. I want to practice my sword skills. And I want to learn how to use these daggers."

He nods.

"Absolutely, I would love to teach you."

I can feel the hint of disappointment in him when I said I wanted a *real* training session, and that is unacceptable. So... I decide to give him the promise of something to look forward to.

I smile and walk toward the bed again. Slowly. Purposefully. I trail my fingers along the leathers, and then... I reach for the back of my dress.

I start to unlace it, deliberate and slow, letting each tie loosen with a gentle tug, until the fabric slips from my shoulders. I let it fall, pooling at my feet.

I step out of it, only wearing my underthings and the silver ribboned heels. I don't turn around, not just yet.

I let him look.

I can feel his gaze burning into me.

Then I lift a leg, and untie the ribbons from my calf, bending over and setting the shoe down on the floor. I do the same with the other, again with calm precision. I stand, slightly stretching, knowing *exactly* what I'm doing to him.

And when I finally turn, his expression is ravenous.

"Well?" I say sweetly. "Can you help me get into these new leathers, or are you going to just stand there looking like you want to devour me?"

"You... you're teasing me," he growls, stepping closer to me.

"I'm motivating you," I reply. "Maybe if you train me hard enough... you'll get a reward *later*."

I step into the leather pants first, sliding them part way up my legs. Reavian drops to his knees without hesitation, guiding them the rest of the way with his hands on my thighs, slowly caressing them with gentle fingers. He smooths them into place, before fastening them at my waist. His touch lingering a bit longer than necessary.

Then he helps me put on the thigh sheaths.

He buckles them carefully, fingertips brushing the sensitive skin of my inner thighs as he adjusts the fit. His hands are strong, but gentle—he knows exactly how to touch me.

I slide the daggers into place.

I turn and grab the corseted armor top, sticking my arms in the sleeves, and then turn to expose my back to him—where the laces that will tie me into the corset are.

"Help?" I ask innocently.

"You're killing me…" he mutters, his voice dripping with lust.

He laces it up, tugging each cord tighter than the last. I can feel him behind me. *All* of him. The heat of his breath on my neck, the strain of his body pressed close.

When he finishes, I turn around, and my hand brushes over the hard line of him beneath his leathers.

"Boots next," I say with a wicked smile, sitting on the bed.

He kneels before me, taking one in hand.

"You are the only person in this world who can have me on my knees," he murmurs, sliding the boot onto my foot and buckling it slowly.

The words hit me, a promise wrapped in desire.

When both boots are on, I rise and strap my sword across my back, then stand on my tiptoes and press my lips to his.

"Come on," I say to him with a wink.

After asking one of the guards for directions, we find the sparring gym. Targets line the walls, and several sparring mats stretch across the room. There are some guards and knights training here themselves. Noctis followed us here and lies curled in the shadows nearby, watching us with drowsy eyes. Starlight drips in from above like a silver rain.

Reavian stands beside me, eyes scanning every line of my form with purpose.

"Ready?" he asks.

"Yep," I answer confidently.

He begins slowly, easing me into the flow of the movement. He teaches me how to find balance in motion, not to just rely on brute force. He corrects my stance, nudges my wrist, and adjusts my grip.

"There," he says. "That's it, now again."

His voice is warm but firm. Encouraging me without coddling. He's focused.

We work through sword strikes, then parries, then evasions.

"You're amazing," he notes. "Kessa trained you well."

I nod.

"She did," I reply, grief crashing into me like a wave, ready to pull me under.

When we switch out my sword for the daggers, something in me just clicks. They're lighter, *faster*. Every move I make feels more instinctive. He teaches me how to dual-wield them with speed and precision. He shows me how to hold them to throw at targets, pinching each one at the tip before releasing them.

He shows me how to slide and dodge and counterstrike from unexpected angles. I hit every target.

Every. Single. One.

Every attack, every strike, it's like someone else has lived in my body, and I already know what to do. It's muscle memory.

"You're a little…. terrifying," he whispers to me, awe creeping into his voice.

"Is that a bad thing?" I ask, panting, but genuinely curious.

"I love it," he replies.

I laugh. "Of course you do."

By the end, we are both breathless and drenched in sweat. My braid clings to my neck. His chest is gleaming in the moonlight, bare now and rising with each ragged breath. We don't say anything as we walk back to our room, but the tension between us is a living thing.

The door closes behind us and Noctis hops onto the foot of the bed, spinning to find the perfect spot to settle in for a nap.

Reavian walks over to the bathing pool and starts the water. Steam curls up from it and I waste no time undressing and getting in—letting the warmth envelop me, soothing my aching muscles. He climbs in and sits on the built-in bench next to me, grabs some soap and begins lathering up my body. He takes the time to rub my sore calves, thighs and arms. Every touch of his is careful.

"That feels so good," I whisper.

He smiles, then washes himself up. We sit enjoying the bath together until the water cools, and I must admit I am surprised at his restraint.

His eyes tell me that the need is still there, the *want*.

He pulls the drain, and steps out of the tub first, drying himself off and then grabbing a pair of clean underwear and trousers from the wardrobe. Pulling them both on quickly.

I walk out of the tub and dry off, wrapping myself in my towel.

I move closer to him.

He turns toward me, and I stop him with a look. I drop the towel to the floor and grab his hand, guiding him to the chair that sits by our bed.

I push him down into it and then begin to slide down his pants. He kicks them off as I slide his underwear down.

"What are you—" he asks, hunger in his eyes.

I drop slowly to my knees in front of him.

His breath hitches.

"You know," I say, voice dripping with honey, "I do believe that *you* are the only person I will ever kneel for as well."

His eyes darken.

"Are you ready for your reward, Reav?" I ask, sweetly.

He nods slowly, his eyes never leaving mine.

His breaths are heavy with anticipation.

The heat between us ignites in a blur of flame and shadow.

***

The dining hall is lit with a soft blue glow from lanterns strung with pale crystal. A long table is set near a hearth, where the warmth of the fire mixes with the scent of roasted vegetables, fresh herbs, and spiced meat. It's simple compared to the overall grandeur of Starfall Keep, but comforting.

The six of us settle in—Reavian beside me, Kaiel and Brynn across the table, Iska between Tharen and Kaiel. Noctis has curled up just behind my chair, a steward brought him a feast of meat, potatoes and carrots, as well as some fresh water. His ears twitch as conversation begins to flow.

Kaiel leans back with a goblet in hand. "So, how many knights do you think are going to try and impress us with dramatic sword flourishes and tragic backstories?" he asks.

Tharen scoffs, slicing into his food. "I've got five gold that says at least *two* of them will start their introductions with something like *I swore a blood oath upon my brother's grave.*"

"Seven gold," Reavian says dryly, "if one of them cries before we even get into skill assessment."

Brynn laughs into her wine, and I catch the subtle movement of her hand reaching over to Kaiel's. She leans in whispering something only for him, then gently presses a kiss to his cheek.

It's soft and simple. But Kaiel freezes for half a second, caught entirely off guard. His cheeks go pink as he stares at her dazed, his usual cocky grin nowhere to be found. Something tender passes between them.

Kaiel clears his throat and lifts his goblet in mock grandeur. "To being casually assaulted with affection in front of my friends."

Everyone laughs.

I laugh with them, the smile on my face lingering a bit longer.

I'm glad.

Truly glad. Seeing the way Brynn looks at him, the way Kaiel lets her in. It softens something inside me.

It's getting easier to separate the man in front of me with the monster who stole me and brought me here. Because he was *never* the monster.

It wasn't him.

I've always known that deep-down, but now I feel it. And I think it's time that I tell him. He deserves to hear it from me, out loud. That I forgive him. That I never truly blamed him. It'll likely be an emotional conversation, one only meant to be had between us.

I'll talk to him soon.

Tharen turns toward Iska, giving her a sideways grin.

"You know," he says, "if you're not too busy patching up wounds tomorrow, you can always come pay me a visit in my tent. If... you're done pretending that you're not at all interested."

Iska lifts a brow. "Alright, if you're sure you can *handle* all of this."

Tharen blinks. Then stammers. "Oh...I... Uh..."

His cheeks flush a deep shade of crimson that reaches the tops of his ears.

Kaiel nearly chokes on his drink. "Gods, she flirted back. Someone write it down. It's a miracle."

Laughter echoes around the table again, warm and full.

As the fire crackles in the hearth, I lean into Reavian's side, and he drapes an arm around my shoulders. Everything feels... right.

Not perfect. Not fully healed. But whole enough to breathe again.

Tomorrow we will venture into danger. But tonight, we are safe. We are together. I glance around the table at everyone here and raise my glass.

"To us...to friendships that have become family," I say with a smile. "Oh... and ten gold says one of the knights recites his entire bloodline to me like I have the slightest idea who any of them are."

Everyone laughs.

"Do you even have ten gold?" Tharen asks mockingly.

"No, but Reavian will lend it to me," I say.

Laughter fills the space again, and in this moment, I feel entirely whole and at peace.

Chapter Thirty
Seven-Auren

The council chamber looks different without the arguing members and veiled threats. Tonight, it's just us gathered to select who will ride with us toward Somnarel Hollow.

I glance around looking for the three councilors that agreed to meet us. They aren't here, but we are not alone.

Vaelisar stands near the table, hands clasped across his back, his expression calm—but I do note something sharpened in his eyes tonight. Like a blade just barely sheathed.

"Where are the councilors?" I ask him.

"I'm afraid they won't be coming. And most of the Nightguard has been poisoned against you," he says without preamble. "I assume Halrex and Bronn have gotten to them first. Bribes. Promises. Some are just loyal to them already, others simply in fear of making enemies."

Reavian's shoulders tighten beside me. I feel it through the thread between us. Rage. Contained, but simmering.

"They are trying to *control* who guards her?" he asks, low and cold.

"They are trying to control *everything*," Vaelisar replies. "But as far as companions, I've found others—volunteers, most not drawn from within their ranks. A few are retired veterans. Others are... unusual. But I trust your judgement."

He hands Reavian a stack of parchment, filled with information on the candidates.

Then he looks at me, and there is something weighty in his gaze.

"Choose with your instincts, Auren. You'll know the right ones."

Then he turns and leaves, the two guards he left stationed at the doors close them softly as he walks past them. The silence left in his wake feels heavy.

Reavian moves to the far wall behind the council table, arms crossed, already sinking into his watchful, brooding stance.

Kaiel slouches into a chair like he's about to judge a traveling circus.

Brynn sits beside him, posture relaxed but her eyes sharp.

Tharen sits, leans back—boots up on the table flipping a coin between his fingers.

Iska sits beside him, her expression saying she's preparing for war.

And me?

I take the center seat, in front of where Reavian is leaning against the wall. Noctis comes under the table, and curls up laying across my feet.

"Let's begin," I say.

The guards open the doors for the first candidate.

He struts in like he owns the room. He has golden tousled hair, armor that is more stylish than practical, and a grin that is far too pleased with itself. He's tall, broad-shouldered, and somehow tan from sunlight, even though there is none of that to be found in this realm.

"Seress Thale," he says brightly. "Twenty-three, very single, devastatingly fast, and possibly allergic to shirts."

Kaiel groans. Brynn snorts. Tharen just mutters something about needing wine.

"Show us what you've got," I say.

And he does. With a grin, he draws his blade and launches into a fast, flashy set of sword maneuvers—smooth footwork, tight spins, and enough flair to make it almost ridiculous.

But under all that show, he *is* undeniably skilled.

At the end he sheaths his sword, rips off his shirt to wipe his brow, and—of course—winks at me.

I giggle.

Not because I'm flustered. But because it's just *so much*.

"Gods," Reavian mutters. "He's clearly not going to fit in."

"I don't know," I say, lips twitching. "I think he has potential. We can work on his flaws."

Seress flexes his pecs in response.

"For Gods' sake," Tharen groans.

"Meet us in the courtyard in the morning. Supplies and horses are being provided by the High Lord."

"Shirt on... or off?" Seress asks.

We are clearly going to have to work hard on these flaws of his.

"On!" Reavian answers coldly.

With that Seress turns and leaves.

"Next candidate please," Iska calls out.

A woman enters like a living shadow. She's short and lean, her armor sleek and dark. Her black braid is looped tightly, and her expression is unreadable.

"Sirah Vex," she says simply.

"Tell us about yourself," Iska says.

"Trained in the north, was part of the Shadowblades, and I don't speak unless it matters."

"Why are you speaking now then?" I ask.

"Because *this* matters."

Without warning she draws two blades. One buries itself in the throat of a straw dummy. The other pins a piece of parchment snatched from Reavian's hand to the wall behind us, dead center.

Impressive.

"Meet us in the courtyard in the morning," I tell her.

She nods once, remaining silent, then slips away.

"You... sure about that one?" Tharen asks. "She's a little...

creepy."

I nod once in confirmation.

"I like that about her," I reply sweetly.

Reavian lets out a soft chuckle behind me.

"Next," Iska calls out.

Another candidate walks in like he's spent too long in battle to ever quite feel at ease again.

A broad-shouldered tall man stands before us, with pale blond hair pulled back. He has eyes so light blue, that they remind me of ice. He wears battered armor with the faded insignia of the Nightguard slashing through the middle.

"Eiryn Vale."

"It says here that you served under Halrex," Reavian says coldly.

"I did. I don't anymore," he replies.

"Why?" I ask.

"Because I followed orders that got good people killed. I won't follow *anyone* blindly again."

He draws twin short swords and moves through a clean, brutal series of strikes—no flair, just precise, brutal efficiency.

"I don't trust his link to Halrex," Reavian says, bending down and whispering into my ear.

I nod. But something about him, makes me want to give him a chance.

"I would like to extend an offer to you for a trial run," I say. "Earn our trust."

He nods once.

"Fair enough," he replies.

"Then meet us in the courtyard tomorrow morning," I say.

He nods and the guards let him out of the chamber.

"Next," Kaiel calls out.

This candidate walks in too polished, too smooth. He has dark slicked back hair, and his armor gleams like it's never seen a scratch. A practiced smile appears on his face, and his posture is perfect, *too* perfect.

"Veyric Halden," he says with mock warmth. "It would be an honor to serve the cause."

Reavian straightens, bringing my attention to him. His expression darkens.

"Something is off," he mutters to me.

Veyric's brow twitches.

"I don't follow," he replies, having heard what Reavian just said to me.

"Your words are right," Reavian replies, stepping forward. "But your *intentions* are not."

Noctis slips out from under the table and growls at Veyric.

The tension in the room is sharp.

I watch as Veyric's mask cracks.

"This *false queen* will doom the realm. Halrex and Bronn will not let her burn it down. *I* won't let her burn it down."

He lunges toward me.

Before I can blink, Reavian flicks his hand forward, and his shadows answer.

A stream of darkness lashes forward, disarming Veyric of the hidden dagger I hadn't seen, then it wraps around his chest and legs in curling tendrils. They lift him off the ground and throw him like he's a ragdoll, slamming him backwards into the doors. Hard.

The wooden panels *burst open* with a bang as he crashes through them and lands flat on his ass in the hallway. For a breathless moment, no one speaks.

Veyric scrambles to his feet, shaking with fury.

"You've made a mistake," he snarls. "All of you."

Then he turns and storms away.

Silence blankets the room.

"Holy *shit*, Reav," Kaiel finally breathes, half in awe and half in shock. "That was badass. Is that the first time you've done that?"

Reavian glances down at his hands, where shadows still curl faintly around his fingertips. He frowns.

"It's nothing," he mutters, like he's ashamed of it.

I feel sadness trickle down our bond.

"He saved me with it, I would have died. My magic had run dry and had he not used his power, the conscripted would have killed me," I say, grabbing his hand. A silent reminder that he is not his mother. That this power is his, not hers.

Kaiel grins, standing up and crossing over to clap him on the shoulder. "That was awesome. Why've you been bottling that up?"

Reavian lets out a soft breath, but a corner of his mouth lifts. Just a little.

Everyone shifts back to their places, except for Reavian and Noctis. Reavian stands right next to me now, and Noctis is fully alert in front of the table. Making sure there is plenty of distance between the rest of the candidates and me.

"Next," Brynn calls out.

A tall statuesque woman enters, silver streaks in her dark braids, her armor is scuffed, she's seen battle.

"Alira Dorne," she says. "Former royal guard for High King Veylas."

I pause at her declaration.

"You served my…" I pause.

What was he? My *father*? He wasn't my father, not in any real way that mattered.

"The High King?" I ask.

She nods.

"Why are you here?" Tharen asks.

"After the Rift war, when the High King fell and the corruption spread, Vaelisar took in those of us who were able to escape Soltharyn. So, I'm here to repay him for his kindness, and to offer myself as a personal guard for the High King's daughter. He was a good man, and it would be my honor to serve you."

My eyes prick with tears at her words, but I can't really pinpoint the reason why.

She steps back and draws a broadsword, then shifts into a calm, solid stance. She's a wall. Her presence is unshakable and commanding, her every move protective and precise.

Brynn speaks up.

"You offer your loyalty, what is the cost?" she asks.

"There is no cost," Alira replies.

"How are you so sure that she is the daughter of the High King? No one else here believes her claim. What makes you different? Why the blind loyalty?" Brynn presses.

"It is not blind loyalty. I came here to see her for myself. And I know in my heart that she is the heir," she says, pausing to look at me. "You have your father's eyes. That is enough for me."

I nod.

"It would be my honor to have you by my side on this journey," I tell her, and I mean it. Something tells me deep down that our futures are tied, and her being by my side is destined. "Report to the courtyard in the morning."

What she does next stuns me.

She takes a *knee*.

"Yes, your majesty," she replies.

"Oh, I am no one's queen," I reply, suddenly overwhelmed by the gravity of her words.

"Yes, you are," she says. And with that, she gets up and leaves the room.

My heart is racing a bit. What she said feels like a truth that isn't mine. I'm growing more confident, but not nearly confident enough to be a *Queen*.

A soothing caress drifts down the bond between Reavian and I. He leans down and kisses me on the cheek, instantly grounding me, calming the rising anxiety that nearly swallowed me whole.

"You have always been *my* Queen, from the moment I met you," he whispers into my ear lovingly.

I look up at him and he smiles. That perfect genuine smile that's only for me. The last of my nerves calm.

We go through ten more candidates, all of them awful or questionable. Before the last candidate walks into the room.

An older man scarred and quiet. His eyes are a soft hazel, they look tired. His presence is steady and strong.

"Mavren Elowyn," he declares.

"You've seen battle?" Reavian asks.

"Enough to hate it. And enough to know when I need to fight," Mavren replies.

He steps back and draws his sword. He moves slowly, every movement clean, exact, and deeply disciplined.

"Why do you need to fight now?" I ask him when he finishes.

"Because I lost someone to conscription. And if you are going to stop it, to end this, then I want to help."

His words crack open something in my chest. So many people here have suffered.

"I'm sorry, that you've lost someone. I've lost people that I loved very much too," I tell him. "We would be honored to have you."

He nods.

"Meet us in the courtyard tomorrow morning," I say.

With that, he turns to leave, and the guards let him out.

"Wait... wait!" someone calls from down the hall.

A short blond man, maybe twenty or so, jogs in. He is decked out in armor bearing what looks like a family crest across his chest.

"There is no one else listed," Reavian says, glancing down at the stack of parchments that Vaelisar left with him.

The man bows so deeply that his hair brushes the floor.

"My lady, I am Sir Hendren of House Ostaril, son of Hendral, grandson of General Sistus the Unyielding, great-grandson of Commander Holden of the Three-Year Siege, descendant of..."

Oh no.

"...Caerwyn the Resolute, nephew of Lord Therondil—"

Kaiel has his head in his hands. Brynn is snickering. Tharen looks like he's going to pass out, from choking down the laugh that's ready to burst from him.

"Enough," Reavian says. "We are looking for skill, not your lineage. You can leave."

Hendren stammers, bows again, and retreats.

Kaiel exhales hard. "Gods, we all owe her ten gold."

"Pay up," I say grinning.

Everyone laughs.

"I stopped listening after Sistus the Unyielding," Brynn says.

"I can't believe that someone just tried to enter themselves into a dangerous situation, not armed with a sword, but with a family tree instead," Iska says.

Everyone laughs again.

We all look at the pieces of parchment laid out in front of us, at the group we've selected.

"It's a strange group," Reavian says. "But a strong one."

"Sounds like us," Kaiel replies.

And he's right.

This will be our circle.

These are *our* knights.

And in the morning—we will ride.

Chapter Thirty
Eight-Auren

The courtyard of Starfall Keep shimmers beneath the hazy purple light of twilight that marks the mornings here. I stand near the gates, my breath curling in the cool air, my heart beating loudly against my ribs.

Everyone is here—my chosen few.

Alira, steady and poised, tightens the braid looped down her back before attaching her pack to her horse. Near her is Sirah, silent as ever, her eyes sharp as flint, glaive strapped across her back. Eiryn adjusts his pack with a smirk, seemingly excited about the adventure to come. Mavren, every inch the noble tactician in weathered leather, secures his saddle with practiced ease. Seress jokes with Iska as they cinch their saddle straps, their laughter cutting briefly through the thick morning air. Tharen stands a little apart though, near the edge of the path. Iska notices him, and steps away from the others, her silver hair catching the light as she moves with feline grace to his side. I watch Tharen's posture shift, he doesn't smile, but something softens in his stance when she nears him. It suddenly strikes me how even those forged by hardship can still lean into someone, if only for a moment. They've both been through so much, and warmth swirls in my heart seeing them together. I'm glad they have found each other.

Beyond them, Brynn adjusts her pack while Kaiel tests the balance of his blade with a twirl. Reavian stands beside me his arms folded, the perfect picture of composed tension, and Noctis waits at his heel—his tail flicking with anticipation.

Vaelisar steps forward, his deep purple cloak trailing like smoke behind him. His voice rises across the courtyard, measured and heavy with intent.

"You stand at the edge of legend," he says. "Somnarel Hollow is not merely a place. It was the sacred home of our Dreamkeepers. Now it is a wound—one that bleeds into the bones of this realm. Healing it will not be easy. It may test your strength, your resolve... and perhaps even your very souls."

His gaze sweeps across all of us, pausing longer on me. There is no fear in his eyes, only a hint of sorrow.

"But I believe in you. All of you have made the choice to walk into the dark with Auren. And that very choice may be what saves us," he continues before turning again to me and finishing with, "Protect each other."

That final line was meant for me alone, I know it.

I exhale slowly, my fingers brushing the hilt of one of my daggers hidden beneath my dark cloak. A gift that came with a warning of what may come.

I glance toward Reavian.

"You ready?" he asks me quietly, once the group begins gathering supplies.

I'm terrified, fearful that I won't measure up. Worried that something may happen to him. But I don't tell him that, I don't want to worry him, instead I give him a half smile.

"Do I look ready?" I ask him.

"You look... like someone who is about to do something that was thought impossible, and make it look effortless."

We mount our horses. Noctis trots beside us, as silent as a shadow in the night. Then the gates creep open, and we ride into the dark.

The morning air is cool, the path north we are taking narrow, and shrouded in mist. We ride in silence for a time, letting the stillness of the realm settle into our bones.

By afternoon, the terrain has changed. The trees lean less like guardians and more like watchers. The moss grows in odd patterns, glowing its familiar faint blue. Brynn calls it glowmoss, and says it was once only found in dream-fed springs.

We cross over a ridge that dips into a winding ravine, where the rocks hum underfoot. It feels like a warning, like we are nearing a place the land can no longer offer us protection. No one speaks, and I note that Reavian's hand stays near his blade the entire time.

I wonder if he can somehow feel it too, maybe through our bond?

When we reach a clearing that evening, we make camp beneath a canopy of silver leafed trees.

Conversation returns with the firelight.

"My worst patrol?" Seress asks, reclining on a log. "There was a banshee on the cliffs. Screamed so loud that it cracked my sword in half."

"That never happened," Mavren mutters.

"It could have," Seress argues. "Eiryn, back me up..."

"I heard, she turned you down," Eiryn grins.

Laughter breaks the tension. Even Alira smirks.

Kaiel leans back. "Tharen? You got a story?"

Tharen doesn't hesitate. "Found a patrol once. Picked clean. No blood, no signs of struggle. Just armor, and strange marks in the soil around them."

Silence follows.

Seress clears his throat. "Right, let's not ask him anything again."

Later, when the fire has burned low, I stand and walk to the edge of camp. Reavian joins me, silently.

"I don't know if I'll ever be ready for what's to come," I tell him.

"That's how you know that what you're doing matters," he replies.

I look up at him.

"You think that I can do this?"

"I know you can," he says. "And I can remind you of that as often as you need."

I reach out my hand and he takes it. For a moment, I'm not afraid.

"Auren, if you have a moment, I would like to show you something," Sirah says, stepping silently out of the shadows.

Reavian and I both startle slightly, she hadn't made a single sound.

"Okay," I reply, giving Reavian a nod to let him know I'll be alright. He walks back to the fire with the others.

"Follow me," Sirah says, heading toward the tree line further from the firelight at camp.

"I want to show you how to expertly use your daggers, and how to use the shadows to your advantage," she tells me. "But let's see what you know first."

I pull my daggers out of their sheaths, and run through the moves Reavian has taught me, before using a tree as a distant target and throwing them at it, hitting the mark I had set in my mind. I walk to the tree and pull the blades out.

"You have good instincts, but you hesitate a little. That will get you killed," Sirah says.

She steps closer and suddenly reaches out as swift as a striking serpent and twists my wrists until the daggers in my hands point downward.

"Ouch..." I say.

Sirah clicks her tongue at me and rolls her eyes.

"Relax. This grip gives you more control in close combat. Reverse the blade. Feel how it sits against your forearm."

She adjusts my stance.

"You're small like me, and that's not a weakness. It allows us more speed. We can hide in the shadows easier and gain the element of surprise."

I glance back toward the campfire. Reavian stands there, watching us.

"But I can't control shadow like you can. I don't have that gift of magic," I tell her.

Sirah's gaze flicks to Reavian, then back to me. "He does."

I blink.

"What?"

Sirah leans in, her voice a whisper like wind through leaves. "He can cloak you in certain situations, I can as well. The shadows listen to our intent."

I look down at the blades in my hand. Something whispers through the space between the trees, not her power...but Reavian's. Has he been listening through the shadows this whole time? A pulse of confirmation comes down our bond.

"You may not be able to summon shadows alone," Sirah tells me, stepping back a bit. "But once he gives them the order, they'll do what he wants."

I nod slowly, understanding. Then with sudden force, Sirah lunges towards me.

I barely have time to react. Instinct flares. I twist, blades up, catching her strike with one, and slicing through the air with another. Then she's gone, seemingly swallowed by darkness.

I spin around to try and spot her, instead finding Reavian, now sitting on a rock at the edge of the camp, his shadows bleeding from his feet like ink across parchment, curling through the grass and creeping toward me. I blink and feel them brush my ankle. A whisper soft caress. And before I know it, I am cloaked in darkness.

I move silently through the woods, searching for any sign of Sirah. To my left a branch cracks, I step out of the shadows and strike. Sirah steps out of darkness and deflects my attack.

"Good... again."

I step back into the shadows.

Without warning, she finds me and lunges. The darkness swallows me just as her blade would have found my side. The shadows around me seem ready now, different, they move with me. Sirah's eyes widen, but only for a heartbeat. Then she too steps into a veil of shadow with practiced ease.

Before long we collide somewhere between the light and the unseen.

Steel rings.

Footfalls whisper.

The shadows cradle my form as I spin behind Sirah, daggers

flashing, my breath shallow but steady. The darkness parts for me like a mist yet still clings to my skin with something more than magic.

Affection.

Reavian isn't just cloaking me with his power. He is letting his shadows choose me.

I strike. Sirah deflects. We twist, and duck. Disappear and reappear like specters dancing through the night.

Finally, I land a strike, my dagger at Sirah's throat, my hand steady.

She grins at me.

"That was *excellent*."

I smile at her.

"Thanks for showing me how to do all this."

"Anytime," Sirah replies, patting me on the back.

She walks beside me in silence, arms crossed, her expression unreadable as always. But there is a weight to the quiet now, a shared respect that hadn't been there before.

"You learn fast," she says at last, glancing over at me.

"I had a great teacher," I tell her.

We step into the heart of camp, the tents now silent around us. The fire is little more than ash, but one figure remains leaned up against a tree near our tent— arms folded, his silhouette unmistakable in the moonlight.

Sirah gives me a low, almost amused grunt. "Good night."

"Good night," I tell her, smiling faintly as she walks away in the dark.

I approach Reavian slowly.

"You didn't stay to watch the ending."

His mouth curves slightly. "Didn't need to, I felt it."

He opens the tent flap for me, and I duck inside and sink into the thick blankets that make up our bed. He follows, sitting beside me.

I study him in the dim light.

"How did you get your shadows to know how I would move?" I ask him.

"I didn't," he murmurs, voice quiet. "I just willed them to protect you, and they did the rest. All I had to do was stop holding back."

He looks at me for a long moment, then reaches out, brushing loose hair from my face.

I search his eyes. "Did it... strain you? To let them go to someone else like that?"

He hesitates for a moment, a flicker of something behind his gaze. "No, they wanted to help you. It felt... right, ike they already knew you."

I reach for his hand. "It didn't hurt you, right?"

"No," he says. "But it scared me."

I look up at him.

"Why?"

"Because I've never shared them like that. I was worried that the darkness from my mother would somehow harm you... that *I* would somehow hurt you."

Silence settles between us for a moment. I move closer to him, resting a hand on his chest, just over his heart.

"They were kind to me," I tell him softly. "Gentle."

Reavian's voice drops to a whisper. "I think they must reflect what I feel."

His shadows move with magic, but his heart moves with something else entirely. And it's that part of him that I trust the most.

I bring my lips to his, to say without words that in all the darkness, *he* is the only thing that makes me feel safe.

***

The next day, we pass under an arch of green vine strangled stone just past noon. Iska said it marked some forgotten boundary. I wonder what it had once separated, what else has been lost?

As the sunless sky darkens into deeper twilight, the silver river shimmers ahead.

We cross in silence. On the far side, everything changes.

The starlight dims.

The trees lean inward.

I can sense the ground pulsing beneath us.

Heal it.

Purge it.

Help us.

The voices swirl within me.

Noctis growls, low and deep. A warning.

I dismount my horse and drop to my knees.

The corruption here is different, changed.... strong and sentient. As I place my palms to the ground, I can feel it writhing beneath them. Twisting and contorting, rot with teeth. It's watching. *Wanting* me. Pain shoots up my arms and I bite back a scream.

It's attacking me.

I reach inward and unleash my purifying flame.

It burns white-hot, flooding the land before us, tearing through the corruption. A scream follows that is not fae or human.

Then silence. The land before us has been healed.

I push myself up, swaying. Reavian catches me.

"It fought back," I whisper to him. "It's different, it's like it... *knew* me."

"Holy hells..." Seress murmurs behind me. "She really did it..."

Our new companions dismount, and one by one they drop to a knee before me.

"The High Queen of Nyvenya," Alira says.

"No," I breathe, "Don't kneel. I don't want that. I just want to help, to heal what has been broken."

None of them move.

"But you *are* the High Queen," Mavren says gently. "The missing heir."

Reavian's slides his palm to my lower back, seemingly sensing my inner turmoil. I don't know if I can be exactly who they want me to be.

"Please rise," I say. And they do just that.

"I never knew the High King. I just know he sent my mother away to protect us from danger he saw coming, perhaps so that this very moment could happen. So that I could help save this world, and your people," I say. "I don't know if I'll measure up to what he was for you. Or if I can be who you expect me to be. But I can promise you that I will fight to my very last breath to protect everyone in Nyvenya. To make things right. To heal this land. I will fight by your side."

In unison, they all take their right hands, fist them and bring them to the left side of their chests. A silent pledge.

"You may not have known him, Your Highness," Alira says. "But your heart is like his. And I believe he would be proud of you right now."

With that they all walk away, and we get back on our horses to continue our journey.

I heal the land as we go, until I feel that I can't possibly do anymore, and we set up camp near a forest of silver-trunked willows that have been freshly purged of corruption. My body aches with strain; the corruption fought back with everything it had. I could feel its anger, its promise to make me pay as I burned it away.

Our fire burns low.

Eiryn speaks quietly. "The other night, you guys were asking about stories."

Kaiel nods.

Eiryn's voice continues, flat. "We raided a northern post once. Halrex claimed it was compromised, the knights within it working with Lireath and Lucien. Our orders were to burn it to the ground. My brother was in that post."

A pause.

"I was a rule-following idiot. I didn't question the order until it was too late. After my own investigation, I found out that one of the knights had dirt on Bronn. That was the real reason Halrex ordered us to eliminate the outpost."

"Did you tell anyone? I can't imagine Vaelisar not holding Bronn and Halrex accountable for that," Iska asks.

Eiryn shakes his head.

"Halrex threatened to kill my sister, my last living relative, if I spoke of it. His family is powerful, and I cannot risk her life."

Silence falls among us.

I reach out gently. "I'm so sorry."

He nods.

"I'll never make a mistake like that again."

We all sit and talk until the fire dies out, and then one by one, we go to our tents to sleep.

Reavian wraps me in his arms, and my eyelids grow heavy, and I surrender to the exhaustion, drifting into a deep sleep.

A scream erupts from one of the tents, blood-curdling and raw. It rips me out of my slumber, and I bolt upright.

Is that Eiryn?

"Stay here," Reavian says before leaving the tent.

Noctis is at my feet, already alert.

I wait for a moment, then decide to ignore what I was told and assess the situation myself.

Kaiel and Reav reach Eiryn's tent first. The latter notices that I ignored his request and shakes his head at me.

"Eiryn!" Reavian calls out. "You alright?"

No response. Kaiel throws open the front of the tent.

"Eiryn, Wake up!" Kaiel shouts.

Eiryn sits upright, drenched in sweat, breathing heavily.

"I'm fine. Just a dream," he snaps out quickly between breaths.

I approach him.

"What did you see?" I ask gently.

Our eyes meet.

Eiryn pauses, then shakes his head. "Nothing, don't worry about it."

He waves us out and disappears back into his tent. But I saw it. His trembling hands. His eyes were hollow when he gave us a rushed 'goodnight' and closed the tent flap behind us.

I feel it.

Whatever he had seen... It wasn't just a dream.

I linger for a moment outside his tent.

"You know, I'd prefer it if you'd let me check for danger before you just go running out into it," Reavian says quietly, only half joking.

I nod, knowing full well if anyone was in danger I would go running toward it, just as I did now—and that surprises me a bit. Just a couple of months ago I would have run away and hid from *any* sign of danger.

Reavian's hand brushes mine as we walk side by side back to our tent. We lie down in the soft blankets, and Noctis curls back up by our feet.

"Must've had a nightmare, from bringing up the things from his past," Reavian says softly.

"Maybe," I murmur, settling in beside him.

But in my heart... I know better.

It wasn't memory that haunted him.

He saw something.

A premonition perhaps. Something that he couldn't bring himself to speak aloud.

And whatever it is... I can't shake the feeling it's already waiting for us in the Hollow.

Chapter Thirty Nine-Auren

We reach the point where we can no longer bring our horses and tie them up to the trees near a small pond. We leave them enough food to last until we get back in a couple of days. I've healed the land here, and it seems to be holding. Like whatever it is that has been fighting against me is losing ground.

We approach the mountain path.

This path isn't a path at all really. It's more like a fractured ledge of loose shale, and jutting rock, narrow enough in places that one misstep would send us tumbling into the misted abyss below. The wind howls, it's sharp and cold, tugging at our cloaks and fraying nerves.

Each step is deliberate. Every breath, a quiet prayer that no one will fall.

The light from the stars barely reaches us here, and what little illumination filters through the cloud-choked air only makes the crags seem sharper. The trees have long since vanished, replaced by gnarled roots and skeletal bramble.

Snaking across the rocks in slow pulses, like veins crawling over the stone, are crimson vines. The same kind I have seen before, on the other mountain pass. Only these... move. Subtly. Like they're watching us.

I feel Reavian shift beside me.

"Those are different," he says, hand on the hilt of his blade.

"I know. Everyone stay away from the vines. They're moving, I think they're aware of our presence," I warn.

Once I get to a more level surface, I can purge it all from the mountain. It's just too risky to do it at this steep of an incline, anything could happen, and the consequences of any misstep would most definitely be fatal.

So far, everything that I've purged has remained healed, unlike when I first entered the realm and tried. Maybe I am closer to the source of it?

We are about halfway up when Iska slips. Her foot twists beneath her, and she goes down hard, barely catching herself on one arm.

"I'm fine," she starts, but the pain in her voice betrays her.

Tharen is beside her instantly. He kneels, and examines her ankle with a healer's care, then meets her eyes.

"It's sprained," he says. "You won't be walking on this."

She tries to argue, saying something about being a healer and knowing her limits, but Tharen doesn't hesitate. With a surprising ease, he lifts her onto his back. She doesn't argue after that.

"We'll rest soon," I say gently, though I am not sure how much farther we actually have to go.

Seress lets out a sharp gasp. "Snake!"

A flicker of red coils across the path.

It isn't just one.

Three crimson scaled snakes slither between the rocks ahead—their bodies glistening, eyes the same oily black as the corruption. One lifts its head, flickering its tongue as it hisses in our direction.

"Don't let them bite you," Iska warns from Tharen's back. "They can give you blood rot, it kills fast."

Kaiel steps forward, drawing his blade. "Allow me."

One of the snakes lunges at Kaiel, but he moves faster. His blade meets its fangs mid-strike, slicing its head clean from its body. The others recoil and slither back into the rocks.

They don't return.

We reach the mountain peak and find a spot where the rocks flatten into a ledge just wide enough for tents and a fire. I kneel on the ground, press my palms into the rock and let my flame roll out in waves. The corruption fights back against it, and I groan out in agony. It feels like it's trying to tear the muscle from my bones. Eventually, it loses the battle, and the corruption is purged from the mountain, becoming just ash in the wind. The stars above are shining more brightly, even the clouds seem to lift.

"Are you alright?" Brynn asks me.

"Yeah, I just... the corruption is very different here," I gasp. "It's fighting back."

"Don't push it, Renna," Brynn says. "You need to rest, you look exhausted."

I smile at my friend.

"I know. As soon as we get these tents up, and a fire going, I'm going to eat and then get some sleep, I promise."

"Good," she says, giving me her signature smirk. "Cuz you've always been super cranky when you don't get enough sleep."

"*Shut up*," I say with a smile.

The wind up here is sharp, and the air thin, but from here we can see the misted basin below. Our destination—Somnarel Hollow—waits there in silence.

I sit next to the fire, my hands outstretched to soak in its warmth. My body aches, I've used more magic today than I ever have purging the corruption from the mountain. The darkness fought against me every step of the way.

I force down dried meat and fruit, chewing without tasting it. Iska, now seated beside the flames, has removed her boot and is wrapping her ankle herself, to Tharen's protests. The swelling is already going down though, no doubt her magic at work.

"You shouldn't walk tomorrow," Tharen tells her.

"I'll manage," she replies, tying off the bandage. "We're close now."

I look back toward Somnarel Hollow and notice large circular pools of dark water glimmering with the faint light of the stars. They're scattered like glass across the ground outside of the sanctuary ruins.

"What are those?" I ask no one in particular.

Mavren joins me at the edge. "The Reflection Pools. They were sacred once. The Dreamkeepers used them to hold and study dreams. Every dream that anyone has ever had ends up in the pools. The magic in dreams is what gives this realm its power."

I stare toward the dark surfaces of the pools again.

"They give power to the land?" I ask. "Perhaps that's why the corrupted can't cross the silver river, are they connected to the reflection pools somehow?"

"No, but maybe the land has empowered the silver river in the way that it used to the Reflection Pools," Mavren says thoughtfully. "Because now, the pools have become something else."

My stomach tightens, and a chill slithers up my spine.

"Everyone needs to be on high alert. Something doesn't feel right," I say, loud enough for everyone to hear.

Noctis pads closer and sits beside me silently. His ears twitch, and his eyes never still. I offer him some dried meat and berries, which he takes with delight.

Later, as everyone sleeps, I lie awake next to Reavian. His arms are wrapped tightly around me, but I can't shake this feeling of dread. I notice that Noctis hasn't moved from the mouth of the tent.

He isn't sleeping either.

He's standing guard.

I yawn. "You feel it too boy, don't you?"

He turns his head toward me and whines softly in response.

"I know. It feels wrong," I whisper, my eyelids getting heavy. "Thanks for watching out for us. Try and get some rest too, okay?"

When I can no longer keep my eyes open I drift to sleep, and dream of whispers in the dark.

****

The next morning, we pack up our things and descend into the Hollow.

The sanctuary waits. It's a broken building, half-swallowed by vines and creeping mist. Its once proud towers sag under the weight of rot. I lead everyone past the pools toward the cracked archway, my magic already flaring beneath my skin in a silent warning.

Without going inside I peek into the sanctuary's great chamber. Giant shattered glass tubes lay in twisted heaps. A couple have remained intact, and a violet liquid pulses within them.

Sirah approaches behind me.

"This is where they held the Dream Trials originally. That

liquid, that's what used to be in these pools before the corruption touched it. A person is placed inside, and they flood it with the water from the pools, it's starlight made liquid. The magic in the water makes a person face their truth, or break beneath it. All of the Shadowblades, myself included, had to complete the Dream Trials."

I turn my back on the arched doorway to face Sirah.

"People die just trying to complete the trials, it doesn't seem right," I say.

Sirah nods.

"I have lost those I cared about, because they were not strong enough to face what the trials brought them."

"It just seems like a waste of life," I whisper, suddenly saddened. The practice seems cruel and unnecessary.

"That's why I left," she replies, before heading back towards the others.

I turn back to the sanctuary. And I can feel something.

A heartbeat.

Not the land's.

Something *beneath* it.

Something alive.

Noctis growls.

I turn and see ripples in the water of the reflection pools.

Just before they explode.

The first scream comes from Seress.

He drops to the ground, writhing, clawing at his arms as if invisible fire clings to his skin.

"It burns!" he screams. "It's melting me... oh Gods, it's melting me!"

But there is nothing on him. No flame. Only his mind fracturing under the weight of an illusion.

I reach for my power—but I can't feel it.

A hollow pang hits my chest.

It's gone.

I try again. Still nothing. My breath hitches, becoming shallow and sharp, as anxiety begins to rise.

Why can't I feel it?

Kaiel turns toward Seress and stops cold. Emerging from the pool in front of him, a towering man. Covered head to toe in armor like blackened bone, jagged and cruel. A long sword is strapped to his back, a horned helmet sculpted with a skull-like face. Dark black hollow eyes look out at him. Blood drips from the blade in his hand.

My father's blood.

I stare in horror as the nightmare version of Kaiel stalks toward him.

The version of him that killed my parents.

Kaiel staggers back. "No...I didn't...I would never..."

The figure raises its sword.

Kaiel roars and charges, the steel of his sword clashing against the steel of the nightmares blade, trying to destroy the twisted version of himself.

I try to summon my magic again—*nothing*.

I reach for Virethyn at my back.

It's gone.

I fumble at my thighs for my daggers.

Gone.

My breath catches. I try to move, but my body won't respond. My limbs are locked, frozen in place, as if something invisible coils tightly around me.

Around my chest.

I can't breathe.

Not far from Kaiel, Alira spins to dodge an attack. She's locked blade to blade with a nightmare version of Lucien, he looks younger, his features more wolfish. Each strike he makes is impossibly strong, forcing her backward.

"You failed my brother, and you'll fail her too," he snickers. "You are nothing. Always needing orders. A *follower*."

"I choose who to follow!" she snaps, as she drives her blade through his heart.

Near the sanctuary wall, Brynn battles with her own personal ghost.

I don't know her, but recognize similar features.

It must be her mother.

Gaunt and pale, lips shredded, and her throat gaping open,

spurting blood, exposing her vocal chords.

"You let them kill me," she rasps out, choking on blood.

My heart pounds so hard it hurts. My hands go numb, fingers tingling, useless at my sides. Panic swells in my chest, sharp and fast. I still can't seem to get enough air.

Brynn trembles, her blade shaking in her grip. "I didn't, I tried to save you. I just...you would have wanted me to do the right thing, and I did."

The nightmare lunges. Brynn screams and throws up her arm, lightning cracks off her skin in wild arcs.

"No more lies!" Brynn shouts. "You are not her!"

One of her strikes hits true, vaporizing the horror. A blast of thunder claps afterwards.

I look left and see Sirah engaged in a brutal dance with a figure cloaked in shadow like her. A male. He is wielding the same curved glaive that she has, moving with the same grace, but somehow his movements are colder.

Unfeeling.

He doesn't speak.

Each time their weapons meet, sparks fly. The clash is a symphony of mirrored power. She bleeds from a cut on her cheek, but she doesn't falter.

"You're not him," she says, finally knocking the figure back. "He had a soul."

She strikes low, sweeping the nightmares legs, and driving her glaive down.

It doesn't scream, it just vanishes like a mist.

Behind her Tharen stands like a wall, shielding Iska as giant spiders close in on them. Their clicking mandibles and twitching legs fill the area with wet chittering sounds.

One leaps toward him, and he bats it aside with his sword, sending it tumbling.

Another comes from the left and Iska turns a dagger in her hand. She stabs it in the abdomen, and it falls away, shrieking.

They fight back-to-back.

I dart my gaze around the area looking for *him*. Looking for Reavian.

But my vision is tunneling. My chest is tight, every breath scrapes like broken glass. I press a limp hand to my ribs, but it does nothing to ease the anxiety.

Movement draws my attention, near the ruins, and my breath hitches.

Mavren.

He's locked in combat with a conscripted. But this one isn't completely twisted. Its head remains fae. A male. White haired with dark eyes. Eyes that look full of betrayal.

"You told me you loved me," the man says to Mavren, his voice like a knife. "But you let them take me."

Mavren stiffens. "No. I tried to reach you—"

"You let me become... *this*."

Mavren lets out a pained roar and lunges. Fury and sorrow crashing through his form as he battles the conscripted male.

My hands are trembling. I can't catch my breath at all now. I'm going to pass out if I don't calm down, but I *can't*. I need to find Reavian. I need him to tell me it'll all be okay.

My eyes finally land on him.

He isn't fighting.

He's kneeling.

In front of *my* lifeless body.

Blood soaks the front of my dress. My eyes are open, glassy and empty.

He doesn't hear the others.

"Reavian!" I shout.

He doesn't hear me.

He only seems to see me, lying dead in front of him.

"No—please, please come back," he sobs into my lifeless body. "I can't...I can't lose you, please..."

I watch in horror as his hands shake, and he reaches for the dagger at his side.

"I can't...I can't go on without you."

I see it all.

I feel it all.

And yet I still can't move.

I can't help anyone.

The fear wraps around me like a coffin, pressing against my skin, my lungs.

My flame still doesn't answer.

Noctis barks at me frantically. He's biting at the edge of my cloak, pulling, begging.

My legs sink into the earth.

I don't see the others now.

I only see *him*.

Reavian is weeping, pressing the blade to his chest.

I open my mouth, and no sound comes out.

Come on. *Come on!*

He pushes the dagger toward his chest.

And in that instant, I realize—

This is my nightmare.

The one I've let consume me for years.

Fear and Anxiety.

I've let the combination paralyze me. Let it make me feel helpless.

But I am no longer helpless.

And finally, I scream.

"No!"

My scream isn't just sound.

It's flame.

It bursts from me—roaring white fire that surges from my body in a tidal wave. The entire area ignites with it. The spiders shriek and crumble to ash. Kaiel's twisted double lets out a warped cry before dissolving into smoke.

This fire burns out the nightmares and purifies the land. The reflection pools shimmer—twisting from black to violet. The vines curl back, smoking. The ground we are standing on stops throbbing.

Reavian snaps out of the illusion he had been seeing and drops his dagger.

I collapse to my knees, gasping.

I hear Reavian's voice.

And then, he's here.

Arms around me. Hands shaking. Heart pounding against me as if it had been shattered and reformed in the same second.

"I thought—I thought I lost you..." he chokes out, his voice raw and splintering.

I cling to him, pressing my forehead to his.

"I'm here. I'm right here," I whisper.

He's crying. Not out of weakness, but out of a relief so deep it trembles through every muscle in his body.

I cup his face. "If something ever were to happen to me, Reavian, you can't do what you almost did. You *have* to go on. I wouldn't want that."

"I..." he can't even speak. He just nods, his face in my hands, my flames still faintly flickering around us.

I suddenly sense a threat. Noctis growls behind me, and I stand and turn.

The central reflection pool inside the sanctuary begins to bubble. I walk toward it, into the ruins of the building. This pool is larger than the others, and it remains dark.

It bubbles again.

And again.

A high shrill wail pierces the air. A scream so sharp it feels like it splits my ears and slices through bone.

It isn't a sound.

It's a weapon.

The others cry out, and clutch their heads as the sound slams into them like a hammer.

The surface erupts.

And a banshee emerges.

A towering creature of shadow, bone, and swirling void. Its limbs are too long. Its chest doesn't rise or fall, it pulses. No real face, just a huge gaping maw filled with dark needle-like teeth.

Before I can react, an invisible force blasts out, knocking the others backward and out of the sanctuary entirely.

Only I remain.

Noctis tries to leap back to my side, but he smacks into an invisible barrier with a sharp yelp. It must be a ward. He tries to use his magic to bring the ward down, but it isn't working.

My body trembles.

Not from fear—but something deeper.

This isn't like the others.

This creature *is* the heart of the corruption here.

The banshee lunges.

I throw out a hand, my flame flaring from my fingertips, but the creature slashes right *through* it, hitting me in the chest. The blow sends me flying backward into a pillar. Stone cracks behind me. My vision blurs.

Get up.

The voices demand.

I stagger to my feet, pain blooming down my spine. I send another bolt of purifying flame forward, but the banshee dodges it. It's fast. *Too* fast.

It lunges again.

Its claws rake my side, and pain explodes through my ribs.

I gasp, dropping to one knee, pressing my fingers into my side, and pulling them away soaked in blood. A gash the length of my hand has been opened beneath my ribs, blood is pouring freely.

The banshee screams again.

"Auren!" Reavian shouts.

But he's not the only one. I hear all of my friends, screaming for me, slamming into the barrier trying to get to me.

It's getting darker.

I glance toward the edge of the barrier and spot Reavian, shadows pouring from his hands as he slams them against the ward. He's trying to breach it. But there's too much magic spilling out of him.

He's using too much.

The banshee strikes again.

Its jaws clamp onto my shoulder, teeth sinking deep into my flesh. I scream as pain rips through me—hot and blinding. It holds me here savoring my blood, a beast tasting its prey.

Kessa's voice echoes in my mind.

If you lose focus, you lose your footing.

I strike the banshee with a blast of my fire, forcing it back, but not far enough away.

I stumble back, clutching my shoulder, blood pouring down my arm.

I'm not going to survive this.

No... not like this.

I can't die like this.

Get up, Auren. Move.

The voices are more urgent now.

But I barely have time to brace before the banshee comes again.

A claw lashes out—slashing my thigh open in a brutal arc. The impact lifts me off my feet and then flings me to the ground. I hit the stone hard. Gasping and trembling, I can feel the warmth of my own blood soaking into the cracked floor beneath me.

Every breath is painful.

The world dims around the edges of my vision.

Is this it?

Is this where it ends?

They all believed in me.

They told me to be the light in the darkness.

That I could save this place.

But maybe... maybe they were wrong.

I lay here, blinking up at the crumbling ceiling. My hand twitches. I reach out, not even knowing why. My vision blurs again, this time from tears that I didn't even realize were falling.

I'm not ready to die.

Not like this. Not before I save them.

Save *him*.

Outside the barrier, I hear Reavian again.

Screaming my name like he could rip down the very sky if it meant he could reach me. I look, and his shadows are still spilling out from his body, trying to claw their way in. But they are flickering now, fading quickly.

I close my eyes.

You are not alone, Little Light.

We are with you.

Let us help you now.

The fire doesn't rise from my hands. It comes from within me. My body lifts from the floor, growing brighter and brighter with every heartbeat.

The banshee screams again—but this time it falters.

Because I am no longer just Auren.

I *am* the flame.

I am the light of every dream that has ever been dreamt.

The echo of hope that refuses to die.

I raise my hands.

The banshee lunges.

And I unleash it.

The chamber explodes into a column of divine fire, a roar of impossibly bright flame that burns everything it touches. The banshee disintegrates mid scream, torn apart by the very power it sought to consume.

Ash falls like snow.

And I collapse to the ground.

My body is trembling, and I am barely breathing. The ward falters and I hear the others start to rush in.

He's coming. He'll help me. I force my eyes to stay open, waiting for Reavian. But he doesn't get here first.

Somehow, Eiryn does.

"Was that thing what you dreamed?" I ask him, my voice weak.

"No, for me it was worse than that."

He helps me up and I hear a snicker.

Halrex.

He steps into the ruined chamber with Reavian in his grip.

"Would've just been easier if you had all just fucking died in our little trap. But now at least, I'll get to participate in the fun," Halrex says with a grin.

Eiryn moves in front of me, the others ready their weapons. I try to rise to my feet, but I can't. I'm losing so much blood.

Six knights step out from the shadows. Weapons readied.

"I told you you would be sorry!" one of them shouts.

I recognize the pompous voice.

Veyric.

"You spineless coward, you hide behind others, there is no strength in that!" Reavian spits out.

"You. Step forward. Say hello to one of our guests, I think you may know each other," Halrex says to another of his companions.

That knight steps forward and pulls off his helmet.

Eiryn freezes.

His swords slip out of his hands.

This knight looks wrong. His face is covered in burns, his eyes hollow sockets. Jaw slack.

"Caelen," Eiryn breathes, his voice breaking. "No...no, it can't be—"

The knight doesn't respond. Instead he just reaches out, grabbing Eiryn by the throat, lifting him effortlessly into the air.

I force myself to my feet, watching it all unfold, my limbs heavy and blood wet on my skin. My body screams that I need to rest, I need to be healed. My magic is silent, dead weight. I search for the voices, and they don't answer.

Eiryn doesn't fight back.

He just stares at the knight, his eyes full of grief.

And I know. That Caelen is his brother.

Was his brother.

I feel it then, a thread tugging inside my chest.

The note from Vaelisar.

Is this who I'm meant to save?

I draw Virethyn, every joint aching, my wounds tearing open further with each movement.

I lunge toward Caelen, crossing the stone floor with everything I have left. The others engage the five other knights, though Kaiel remains by Halrex, looking for a way to save Reavian.

Eiryn's eyes widen as I approach.

"I'm sorry," I whisper, as I bring Virethyn down, and cleave Caelen's head from his body with a clean, swift stroke. What remains of him crumples to the ground, releasing Eiryn from his grasp.

Eiryn hits the ground hard, gasping and sobbing, unable to speak.

I stand over them both, my sword slick with not blood but a black sludge.

My body begins to shake, and I can feel myself slipping away.

That was everything I had, I have nothing left.

I turn to find Reavian, Halrex is holding a dagger to his throat.

"Do you want to watch princess?" he snarls. "Sure, I'll let you watch as the light leaves his eyes."

The blade presses into Reavian's neck and blood starts to trickle. But he doesn't slice it, he's toying with me.

"I love you," Reavian whispers, his voice hoarse.

He's saying goodbye.

No.

My vision narrows.

Something ancient stirs in my chest.

"Let him go!" Kaiel shouts.

My bond with Reavian flares like fire through my blood.

Mine.

He is mine. And I am his.

And I will not let him die.

Not today.

Not ever.

I surge forward grabbing my daggers and leap into the air. The jewels in their hilts pulse with magic. I let one fly, striking Halrex in his right eye. He screams and stumbles backward, dropping the dagger from Reavian's throat.

Kaiel uses the opening to knock Reavian away.

I land quickly, and then I'm surrounded by shadow. Not Reavian's—Sirah's. She darkens the space around Halrex and I.

He startles, grabbing his sword and spinning around trying to find me with the eye he has left. He slashes his sword wildly.

"Where are you?" he calls out.

"Right here," I whisper as I step out my cloak of shadow.

He turns, but I'm already gone.

"I'll kill you!" he yells, stabbing his sword forward.

But I'm not there.

"Missed me." I whisper.

He turns toward my voice and I step out from the shadows.

I take my dagger and slice across his throat with a rage I have never felt before.

It's clean, wet, and final.

He collapses.

And so do I, shadows falling away and returning to Sirah.

Reavian catches me before I hit the ground, wrapping his arms tightly around me, as if to anchor me in place in this world.

My eyes begin to close, the adrenaline that our bond gave me when I saw him in danger, now gone.

"Stay with me, please..." Reavian begs.

I'm dying.

I can feel myself slipping away.

I didn't get to save everyone.

But I saved them.

I saved *him*.

I force my eyes open.

"I..." I choke out. "Love.. you."

I'm coughing up blood.

Something is burning me from within, draining me.

My eyelids feel heavy.

"No!" Reavian cries out. "Iska please, do something!"

And then my eyes close and I am swallowed by darkness.

Chapter Forty-Reavian

Auren's blood is warm and slick on my hands as I press against the jagged wound on her shoulder and neck. A faint pulse flutters under my fingertips. It's weak but there.

"Hold on," I whisper, my voice raw, as if by will alone I can tether her soul to this world.

Around us, Somnarel Hollow is deathly silent now— the creature she destroyed little more than ashes on the ground. The bodies of the traitors litter the space around us.

Iska stops the bleeding but can do little for the corruption that's spreading from the bite wound like webbing, moving up her neck, and toward her chest. She can't get rid of it, she can only slow it. I'll carry her to where we left the horses, we need to get her back to Starfall Keep as soon as possible. I pick up Auren and hurry toward the mountain path.

Someone speaks, but it all sounds muffled to me. Distant. All I can hear is the crunch of my boots over broken ground, and the ragged sound of my own breathing. I cradle her tighter against my chest and force myself along the narrow mountain path out of the

Hollow. Each step is perilous, loose stones skittering away under my feet, and the weight of both of our bodies strains my balance. One slip and we'll tumble down the mountain side. We walk for hours until we reach the top.

The air is cold and thin up here, swirling with mist, but my forehead burns with sweat. From this vantage point I can see the silhouette of the pass that opens to where we had left the horses. We just need to get down there first.

Just a little further.

Behind me, I hear Iska's footsteps and her labored breaths as she keeps pace. Every few moments, a soft glow of healing magic flares in the corner of my vision, it's Iska periodically pressing her hand against the festering wound on Auren's shoulder.

She's doing everything she can to slow the spread of corruption. Even without seeing it, I can feel the dark magic radiating from Auren's injuries, a cold sensation crawling up my arms wherever her blood has soaked through my sleeves.

Iska's healing magic pushes it back a little, keeping it from advancing further up Auren's neck, but it's only a temporary salve.

Auren makes a soft sound—a whimper, barely audible.

Her eyelashes flutter.

"Reavian...?" she rasps, her voice a fragile sliver of sound. My heart leaps and I nearly stop in shock.

She is awake, however briefly. I look down at her face. It's too dark to see much detail, but I can feel her trying to focus on me through our bond.

"I'm here," I choke out, adjusting my grip on her. "I'm here, Auren. You're going to be okay."

She shudders in my arms, her body convulsing as a wave of agony passes through her. I feel a surge of panic.

The black webbing around the wound pulses angrily, creeping further despite Iska's magic. Auren's brief lucidity slips away into a faint groan.

"No, no, stay with me!" I plead, but her head lolls against my chest once more, unconscious.

For a heartbeat, fear threatens to paralyze me. She's become so strong, so fearless. It's strange to see her so vulnerable. It feels wrong in a way that shakes me to my very core.

Iska's hand glows again over Auren's neck, stabilizing her, and I feel the corruption recoil slightly under the healer's magic.

"Go. Keep moving," Iska urges, her voice strained.

The healer is exhausting herself, I know it, but she won't stop until Auren is safe.

Neither will I.

I grit my teeth and push onward down the trail. The smell of smoke and blood clings to us, remnants of everything that we endured. Every time I blink, I see the creature lunge at Auren.

The flash of its fangs.

Hear her cry out.

I couldn't get to her.

I exhausted everything I had trying to.

What was that ward?

It was impenetrable.

And what brought it down?

Maybe Halrex had something to do with it?

Halrex.

That fucking prick got everything he deserved. Auren had leaped through the air so fearlessly. A tremor of rage goes through me at the thought of him, and at the fact that he and his father are working with Lucien and my mother.

Rage at their plan to end her life.

Rage at myself for failing to protect her.

I force that anger down though. There will be a time to unleash it. I swear, there *will* be a time, but not now.

Now, Auren needs me to be levelheaded.

Hours pass and we reach the base of the mountain, and the ground levels out. Before long, through the thinning mist, I spot the shapes of our horses tethered to the trees where we'd left them.

Relief and urgency flood me in equal measure.

My horse tosses its head and lets out an anxious snort as I approach. He can likely smell the blood and the corruption. I quickly soothe him with a touch and carefully lift Auren onto the saddle.

My arms scream in protest as I climb up behind her, cradling her against me to keep her from slumping over. Noctis, never far from our side, lets out an urgent whimper.

The others scramble onto their own horses with far less grace than usual, clearly exhausted. We haven't stopped once for rest. We don't have time.

Brynn shoots me a determined look.

"Let's go," she pants, spurring her horse into a gallop.

I don't bother to reply, I know what we have to do.

With a kick I urge my own horse forward.

We set a careful but urgent pace back to Starfall Keep, guided only by the moonlight, the stars above, and the faint blue glow of the grass.

It really is beautiful here now.

She makes everything beautiful.

Each step the horses take gets us farther from Somnarel Hollow, thank the Gods. But Starfall Keep is still many days away, and Auren doesn't have days to spare.

Time passes in a blur of desperation and exhaustion. We push the horses hard. All of us scarcely speak, our world narrowed to the rhythm of hooves, and the burning hope of reaching Starfall Keep in time.

We ride from the early morning hours, until well into the evening every day. Stopping only when absolutely necessary. At night, we make camp beneath the stars, or huddle under the canopies of the trees.

Sleep becomes an afterthought. I spend the long hours of

darkness sitting beside Auren, wrapping every blanket we have around her to keep her warm, and holding her hand as if the action could anchor her to life.

Sometimes her eyelids flicker and she mumbles incoherently in the throes of fevered dreams. Every such moment makes me bolt upright, hope and dread tangled in my chest. Is she waking? Or slipping further away?

Iska kneels by Auren's side each night without fail, pouring her healing magic into the wound. Pale gold light shimmers between Iska's slim fingers and Auren's clammy skin, pushing back against the tendrils of darkness.

The tendrils hate that light. I can see the inky veins retreat slightly whenever Iska works her spells, only to surge outward again hours later when the magic ebbs. It's like trying to hold back nightfall with a candle.

Iska never complains, even as dark circles form under her eyes and her hands tremble from the effort. I've caught myself snapping at her more than once, driven by panic whenever Auren's condition worsens.

Shame burns through me at every outburst; I have no right to take out my fear on her. She is keeping Auren alive, while all I can do is watch uselessly.

My helplessness gnaws at me relentlessly. My shadows writhe beneath my skin in response to my fear and fury, but they are useless for this kind of fight.

They can't mend her torn flesh or purge the evil seeping through her veins. I can do nothing but hold her and pray.

The realization makes me want to scream into the night.

It takes us three days to reach Starfall Keep. By then I wasn't sure if I was awake or dreaming. I only knew that her heart was still beating, and that I was holding her.

Noctis opens a path in the wards, and the gates open before us like a miracle.

Healers are flooding the courtyard, shouting amongst one another, calling for a board to carry her and various salves.

"My lord, we need to take her now," a healer says softly.

Hands reach for her, but I hold on tighter.

"Reav…" Kaiel says gently, "You've got to let her go, so they can help her."

I look down at Auren's face.

She is so pale

Her lips are cracked.

Her fever has returned with a vengeance.

The black veins curl over her collarbone like vines choking out a rose.

I kiss her forehead, and hand her over. In doing so, I feel like I have been split in two— half of my soul going away with her.

I can't sit still.

Not in the corridor outside the healing chamber.

Not in the dining hall.

Not even outside the barracks where Kaiel stands beside me in silent support.

I keep seeing her.

Held in my arms, gasping for air.

Her wounds. Gods her wounds, the black webbing coming from the one on her shoulder—dark, crawling, and seemingly ancient.

I should have protected her.

Somehow, I ended up back outside the healing chamber, Kaiel by my side. I don't remember taking the steps that brought me here.

I shift back and forth, chest heavy with worry.

Finally, a healer steps out. She's an older woman, her hands stained with some sort of glowing residue.

"She's alive," she says quietly. "But whatever bit her... it wasn't a normal creature. That magic... it's designed to *claim* her."

Lucien.

The name roars in my skull. He orchestrated this, most likely with Halrex, and Bronn—no doubt at my mother's behest.

I turn away before the healer finishes what she is saying. I stalk toward my destination with fury; I am going to make him pay.

The council doors burst open, my shadows nearly ripping them from their hinges, slamming against the walls with a boom loud enough to make several of the councilors jump from their chairs.

"Where is Bronn?" I demand.

Kaeron Mirthal nearly trips over his robes. The thin bastard gawks at me like I'm some sort of beast, charging through his parlor.

Theris gasps. Maedra raises a single pale brow and tilts her head like a bird watching something bleed.

Vaelisar stands still, hands held behind his back.

"Gone," Vaelisar says.

I stare at him.

"What do you mean, *gone*?" I reply, every word dripping with venom.

"It seems he may have fled. He has been missing since early this morning," Vaelisar replies.

Of course he fled. Coward. *Traitor*.

Maedra's voice slithers out like poison.

"Perhaps the girl brought this on herself."

Silence falls throughout the room.

I turn toward her slowly, as if my body needs time to process the depth of what she's just said. My fists clench at my sides, magic trembling just beneath my skin.

"She came here glowing with wild, untamed magic," she continues, brushing off her sleeve. "Power like that may have a cost. Maybe the corruption simply came to collect its due."

The shadows burst from me.

I don't try to stop them.

They rip through the chamber like smoke pulled from the abyss, candlelight shrieking as their flames bend sideways, guttering low.

The table groans under the force of my magic, dark tendrils curling up the legs, crawling toward the place where Maedra sits.

"You think this is her fault?" I ask, my voice hollow, shaking. "You think she *asked* for this?"

"She's a danger," Maedra replies. "To herself, to *all* of us."

My vision tunnels.

I see Auren's blood on my hands.

Her fevered breaths.

The black webbed lines crawling up her throat while I held her.

I had prayed that she wouldn't stop breathing.

And now this bitch—*this walking rot wrapped in silks*—dares to tell me that she deserved it?

"I should end you where you sit," I snarl.

Kaeron cries out. Theris covers her mouth.

Maedra stands, face pale, but haughty. "You wouldn't dare—"

"I would do worse," I whisper and the shadows surge.

I slam my fist into the council table, and it shatters with a roar—wood and glass exploding outward. A shard embeds in Kaeron's sleeve. Maedra shrieks, staggering backward as splinters fly past her face, one of them drawing blood on her cheek. The room falls into chaos.

"Do you want to see what happens to those who betray her?" I growl. "Halrex was one of the first, but he will *not* be the last."

No one dares move.

No one breathes.

"My promise to every traitor still lurking in these halls is this," I snap, stepping into the storm of my own power, "I will find you. I will tear you apart *slowly* with my bare hands. And I will line the streets in all of Nyvenya with your bones."

"You go too far," Maedra hisses, her voice shaking.

"No," I say, shadows curling around my boots like agitated vipers, preparing to strike. "*You* went too far. When you looked at her and chose fear instead of honor."

Vaelisar steps forward, his voice like thunder. "If anyone is found to have been aiding Lucien Thorne or any of his loyalists," he says, "they will be executed immediately. No trial. No delay. No forgiveness. As of this moment, Bronn Valeaon is considered a traitor to the realm. Any of his accomplices will be swiftly dealt with. So, if any of you still sympathize with him. I suggest you break ties or *run*."

The silence in the room shatters, the councilors all talking nervously amongst themselves in hushed tones.

My voice comes out lower than it has been all night, but it strikes harder than any shout.

"You should know, there is nowhere that you could run where I wouldn't find you."

My eyes lock on Kaeron's, then Maedra's.

"No mountain tall enough. No ocean deep enough. You betray *her*, you betray us—and I will hunt you to the ends of this world and beyond. And when I find you, you will *beg* the Gods to take you before I let you die."

With that final promise, I turn and leave, broken table in ruins behind me, councilors frozen like statues in fear, and my shadows dragging behind me like smoke from a battlefield.

Let them remember this night.

Let them fear what I would become.

Because if she dies... regret will be the last thing they ever feel.

Chapter Forty
One-Reavian

It's been two weeks since Auren fell into unconsciousness.

Fourteen days.

Though to me, it feels like time has been suspended in some silent, endless void. It drags like a blade over skin—slow, cruel and deliberate.

They have moved her to the bedroom we share. The domed glass ceiling reflects the stars. I always found it beautiful. Now it feels like a tomb.

She lays silent beneath the blankets and sheets, her golden hair tangled across the pillows, her skin far too pale. Noctis lies curled at the foot of the bed, unmoving except for the slow rise and fall of his massive chest. Whenever someone enters, the wolf's head tilts, his starlit ancient eyes staring at them with suspicion. No one is allowed entry without his silent inspection.

I trust his judgement.

Brynn, Kaiel, Iska, and Tharen are the only visitors that Noctis and I allow to stay, as well as the round the clock team of healers that care for Auren. Auren's knights take shifts personally guarding our door throughout the day.

I haven't left this room. I sit beside her, hour after hour, unmoving in a chair that now holds the imprint of my weight like a grave marker. Sometimes, I speak to her. Sometimes, I simply wipe the sweat from her brow with a damp cloth, whispering words that only the stars themselves can hear.

"I miss you," I murmur. "Please come back to me."

I almost lost her a few nights ago. I close my eyes and the memory of it comes without mercy.

Auren's body—writhing.

Her back arching off the bed in a way that defied nature.

Her fingers clawing the sheets, blood leaking from her nose.

Her mouth open in a soundless scream.

I screamed for her, for help, my voice raw and broken.

Then the world stopped—because she stopped breathing.

I had never known such terror. Not back in Ashwynn Reach. Not even with what we experienced in the Hollow. The healer had barely gotten her back.

Brynn comes often. She sits on the other side of the bed, resting her chin on her arms as she whispers stories from another life, of mischief they caused in the human world. She spoke of a time they dyed all the town square fountains hot pink. I listen silently, grateful for the sound of her voice in a room that has seemingly become a void of silence.

Kaiel just came by, he sets a tray down with an exaggerated grunt, then sits on the chair beside me and folds his arms. "She's gonna need you when she wakes up, Reav. Not just the shell of you. *You*. The one that keeps her steady."

I clench my jaw. "I can't eat."

"You can, and you will." Kaiel nudges the tray closer. "She wouldn't want you doing this to yourself. Do you think she fought as hard as she did, just to have you waste away beside her?"

With shaking hands, I pick up some bread and bite into it.

It tastes like ash.

Like grief.

I force myself to swallow.

When Kaiel leaves, silence returns.

I whisper to her again.

"Fight, Auren. *Please*." My hand trembles where it holds hers. "I can't do this without you."

Her breathing is choppy, air going in and out in an unnatural rhythm.

I begin to pray.

I pray to the Gods I barely remember believing in.

I pray to Serai, the Goddess of Mercy. I pray to Thoryn, the God of Strength, patron of the warriors. Veilen, the God of Memory and Time, who guards the Veil between worlds. And finally, to Lunira, the Goddess of Dreams and Destiny, who's very breath birthed the stars.

I pray to them all.

Begging.

Bargaining.

"I promise, if you help her. If you bring her back to me. I will help her rid this world of the corruption and darkness that spreads. I will help her bring Nyvenya back to what it used to be. I'll do anything really... anything you want. Just help her. Bring her back to me."

As soon as the words leave my lips, her breathing seems to steady. Her chest now gently rises and falls. Maybe I'm imagining things, or *maybe* someone listened.

There's a knock at the door and Iska enters with a vial in her hands.

"We're going to try something new today," she says, holding up the vial. "It's a tonic, it contains silver water, from the sacred river that surrounds the keep."

I nod, and she administers the dose to Auren.

"We're all hoping it neutralizes the corruption. I remembered how the conscripted couldn't cross it and, well I'm hoping that it will bring her back."

Hope swells in my chest. Iska and I both watch for any sign of change. After what seems like an eternity, she pats me on the back.

"Give it time. I'll come back tomorrow to give her some more." Before she leaves the room, she adds, "You need to take care of yourself too. Clean yourself up and eat a hot meal. You need sleep, Reavian. Good Sleep. No more of this, you *only sleep when your body gives out*, crap."

I say nothing and the door softly clicks as she leaves.

Vaelisar arrives later in the evening. This is the first time I have seen him since my meeting with counselors after we first arrived. I'm glad he's here, because I've had nothing but time to think in this silent tomb of a room, and I have questions.

Questions he'd better have answers to.

He crosses the room, his expression unreadable and his eyes shadowed.

"You knew," I say.

Vaelisar's brow creases. "Reavian—"

"The healers were ready when we arrived in the courtyard. You saw it. You had a premonition. *You knew*."

"I didn't see *this*," Vaelisar says, pain in his voice. "Two nights before you left, I had a dream—a premonition. It was only fragments. I saw *you* in danger. That's why I left her the daggers. I told her to protect you."

I close my eyes and think of that day, she had crumpled the note and acted like it was nothing.

"She didn't tell you?" Vaelisar asks.

"No," I mutter, letting my eyes fall back to Auren. "Of course she didn't...she wouldn't want to worry me. That's who she is."

"I would have stopped her, had I known this would have been

the outcome. Gods, Reavian... I would have locked the gates."

For a long moment, neither of us speak.

"How did you know to have the healers ready? You must have seen she was injured," I ask.

"The night before you arrived, I had another prophetic dream. I saw her, like this... and then I saw flashes of a clock showing the time when you all would arrive. I gathered every healer I had and told them to prepare," he replies.

Something about the way he delivers the words tells me he is speaking the truth.

"She's the only thing that matters to me in this world," I tell him, my eyes not leaving her for a second.

"I know," Vaelisar says, putting a hand on my shoulder. "She'll come back to you. The new tonic will help, I'm sure of it."

After Vaelisar leaves, I do something that I haven't allowed myself to do in two weeks.

I bathe.

I wash ash and blood from my skin, scrape the dried sweat and sorrow from my limbs, and let the warmth return to my blood. I dry off quickly and pull on some clean clothes before going back to her.

Noctis blinks up at me and shifts aside just slightly, as if understanding what I need.

I crawl into bed slowly, carefully, lying beside her but not touching her too much. I am afraid of hurting her, afraid of breaking something fragile.

I rest my hand over hers, and watch her chest rise and fall—its steady rhythm is the only thing that matters.

Noctis lifts his head and seems to give a soft, approving huff.

"I used to think that I would be fine on my own. That I didn't need anyone. But then one night I found you in my dreams," I whisper. "I think I have always been waiting for you."

My voice cracks.

"And the first time I saw you smile—the first time I saw you laugh. Gods, I swear... something inside me cracked open. A part of me that I had buried so deep, so no one could use it against me. You helped me remember how to feel again."

I let out a long breath.

"I can't lose you."

I lean in slowly and press a gentle kiss to her lips. A promise.

"I love you," I whisper against her mouth. "And I'm not going anywhere, so you better not either."

Then I lie back down, resting my head beside hers on the pillow.

As my eyes close, her breathing catches my rhythm. For the first time in weeks, the silence doesn't scare me, and I finally allow myself to sleep.

Chapter Forty Two-Auren

My first breath comes out like a whisper—soft, trembling, and nearly lost in the hush of the room.

I feel warmth before I feel anything else. A steady weight against my side, the faint scratch of stubble where his jaw brushes my temple. Reavian. The scent of him—pine, leather, and something darker—wraps around me like a second skin.

My eyes flutter open.

Above me, the stars shimmer through the glass dome. Dozens of constellations weaving silver lines through the dark. They don't seem to sparkle like I remember. They pulse now, like slow heartbeats.

I blink.

No, I'm mistaken.

Those are the same stars. The same light. They sparkle in the sky, instantly calming me.

Reavian stirs beside me, his arm tightening protectively around my waist.

"Auren?" he whispers, voice cracked with disbelief.

I turn to him slowly, my throat raw.

"I'm here," I rasp.

He jolts fully awake, his eyes wide and wet, then brings his hand up, cradling my face like he is afraid I might disappear. He presses a kiss to my forehead, then rests his brow on mine.

"You came back," he breathes.

"I didn't want to leave you," I murmur. The words feel strange as they leave my lips, like I've said them before.

Before I can say anything more, a deep rumbling woof comes from the foot of the bed.

Noctis.

He's been curled up by my feet. He moves toward me, and not gently.

With a joyful bark, he lunges forward, shoving Reavian straight off the edge of the bed with a startled grunt. He plants his massive body across mine.

"Gods...Noctis!" Reavian barks out from the floor.

I don't have time to respond before I am smothered, licked, huffed on, and nuzzled. All with frantic urgency. His snout bumps my jaw, then my nose and forehead, as if he can't decide which part of me needs kissing the most.

"Okay, okay!" I laugh, breathlessly. "I missed you too!"

Noctis lets out a deep, melodic sound, his tail thudding wildly against the bed. His massive body trembles with joy as he finally collapses across my legs with a huff. His eyes never leave mine.

Reavian reappears beside us, muttering as he dusts himself off. "Thanks for that, boy."

Noctis glares at him pointedly, then settles tighter against me.

When I try to sit up, the room tilts.

Reavian catches me instantly.

"Hey, go slow. Don't rush it."

I blink, trying to clear the fog in my head.

"How long was I out?"

"Two weeks," he replies, his voice tight. "We weren't sure if... if you were going to wake up at all."

He doesn't look at me when he says it, just stares at the blankets pooled around my waist, like if he blinks, I'll disappear.

"I'm sorry."

He shakes his head, jaw tightening a bit. "You have nothing to be sorry for. Just... *stay*."

A knock sounds at the door, and before either of us can respond, Iska pushes it open with a tray in her hand. I smell the warmth of something herbal... mint maybe? As well as something bitter. Her eyes widen when she sees me.

"Well," she says stepping inside, "either the tonic worked, or the Gods decided to answer Reavian's prayers."

I give her a faint smile. "Maybe it was both."

She crosses the room with grace and sets the tray beside the bed, then begins examining me.

"Pulse is strong again, that's a great sign," she says, moving to check my shoulder. "The corruption is nearly gone. The tonic is working."

She turns to Reavian, squinting at him. "You however look like someone who has washed up on shore after being tossed around by a tidal wave."

"I'm fine," he mutters.

"No, you're not." Iska sniffs the air pointedly. "Though you *did* finally take a bath. About time... however I would like to recommend another."

I let out a soft laugh. Reavian groans and rubs his face.

"She's been awake five minutes," he grumbles. "Can you not nag me already?"

"Oh no, I enjoy it too much," Iska replies with a grin. She hands me the tonic from the tray.

I drink it slowly, trying not to gag at the taste. Reavian watches me the entire time, like he still can't believe I am really sitting here.

"Bitter?" he asks.

"Like a minty...*ash*?" I say, nearly gagging.

We share a look, the kind that speaks without having to utter a word. His fingers brush mine, just enough to tether me to the moment. Just enough to tell me he's never left my side.

"Iska," he says quietly, holding my hand. "Can you do something for me?"

She arches her brow.

"Depends on what you're going to ask me for."

Reavian sighs.

"There's a guard outside," he says. "Can you just send him in?"

She gives a little nod and turns toward the door. Moments later the soft shuffle of boots echoes down the corridor.

A young member of the Nightguard and Eiryn step inside.

"Thank the Gods," Eiryn says.

Reavian straightens a little.

"Find Brynn, Kaiel, Tharen, and High Lord Vaelisar. Tell them she's awake... but keep it quiet, I don't want anyone else knowing yet."

Eriyn nods, and he and the guard hurry off.

The silence that follows feels heavy with things unsaid.

"Is something wrong?" I ask.

"Not anymore," he says. "But they've been waiting. We all have."

The door bursts open a few moments later, and Brynn all but launches herself into the room. Kaiel is right behind her, his eyes wide with disbelief.

Brynn lets out a breathy, half-sobbed laugh as she crosses the room and throws her arms around me.

"Renna," she whispers, clutching me tight. "You scared the ever-loving *shit* out of me."

I freeze for a second, just soaking in the feel of her hug. The warmth. My best friend.

She pulls back her green eyes brimming with tears. "You were out for so long. Two weeks of nothing. I yelled, I swore, I begged. I even threatened to cut your hair…"

I laugh softly.

"Yelled?"

"Obviously," she sniffs. "Reavian didn't like that so much, so I stopped yelling. However I did feel the threat of scissors that came afterward… was completely necessary, to snap you out of it."

Kaiel steps around the bed, arms crossed loosely, smirking.

"Well, look who finally decided to rejoin the land of the living. I was starting to think you were just ignoring us out of spite."

I raise an eyebrow.

"You thought I was ghosting you? Literally?"

Brynn laughs.

Kaiel grins. "I have no idea what that means, but you can explain your weird human slang to me later."

I laugh.

"How are you feeling?" Kaiel asks me, in a more serious, softer tone.

"Honestly, I feel weak and exhausted," I say, bringing my eyes to his.

He nods, and I catch a hint of guilt behind his eyes. Something in him believes that somehow this is his fault. He masks it quickly.

"Yeah, you look like death warmed over. And no offense but you really could use a bath," he says with his signature grin.

He rubs the back of his neck, glancing away. "Alright, well you're conscious, breathing, and even in this state you look better than the rest of us, so... that's something."

Iska rolls her eyes. "Speak for yourself, I look great."

Laughter fills the space.

At some point Tharen has entered the room. He's posted up near the door with his arms crossed.

"I heard you all, you know..." I say softly. "Not all the time, but sometimes... in the darkness, I could."

Their gazes all snap toward me.

"I couldn't speak. I couldn't make my body move. But I could hear your voices." My throat tightens. "I tried to hold on to them. I fought like hell to find my way back."

Brynn places her hand on my shoulder.

"And Brynn," I add, turning toward her with a smirk, "some of those stories you told? *Definitely* too embarrassing for Reavian to hear."

Kaiel's brows lift. "Oooh, what stories?"

Reavian laughs beside me, his hand gripping mine tightly, he hasn't let go.

"Nothing *you* need to know about," Brynn says quickly, her cheeks flushing.

"Uh-huh," Kaiel drawls. "Is it the one I hear you talk about in your sleep sometimes. You always mention something about a goat."

"I swear to *every* God..." Brynn starts.

But I'm already laughing. And the sound of it is genuine, a little hoarse, but *alive*. It fills the room like sunlight cracking through the night. It's infectious it seems, everyone joins in. When it dies down slowly, warmth settles around the room like a blanket drawn at night.

Tharen steps forward, his voice steady. "I've been patrolling the land you healed. It's holding, there are no signs anywhere of the corruption returning."

I stare at him, relief swirling in my chest.

"The people have started repairing the Dreamkeeper Sanctuary... in the Hollow."

"They are?" I ask, my voice catching a bit.

He nods.

Iska chimes in next, arms folded loosely. "And they've begun clearing the ruins of the temple dedicated to Lunira. Lucien's forces had razed it in the Rift War, but it seems the people aren't content to let it stay that way."

"There are even plans to rebuild the villages that once surrounded it," Tharen adds. "They say the land is calling them to rebuild."

"For the first time in a long time, people here have hope. You gave that to them, Auren," Kaiel says, his voice softened, quieter than I have grown to expect from him.

I can't speak. I just stare at the people around me and let that truth settle over me.

Slowly, one by one, they excuse themselves, offering hugs, gentle smiles, and quiet reassurances. Brynn squeezes my hand once before slipping out behind Kaiel. As he left, he gave Reavian a lingering look that spoke of a hundred things left unsaid. Tharen is the last to leave, giving a simple nod before closing the door behind him.

Not long after they depart, there is a knock and a steward steps inside carrying two silver trays.

"Lady Iska insisted," he says.

Reavian takes the trays from him with a quiet thanks and sets one across my lap. The scent of warm soup and fresh bread nearly make me cry. I hadn't realized how empty I felt—how hollow my body had become after two weeks of stillness.

I dip the spoon in carefully, letting the steam rise against my face before taking a bite. It's savory and smooth and spiced with herbs I don't recognize. The warmth blooms in my chest.

"Are you eating too?" I ask Reavian softly.

"Yeah," he replies, sitting beside me with his tray. "I think Iska would sedate me and force it down if I didn't."

"I would let her," I murmur, smiling faintly.

After we finish, Reavian takes our trays and sets them aside. He strides across the room, and I hear the soft clank of metal, and a low splash of water as he turns on the tap to the bathing pool. The steam rises quickly.

He comes back to me and kneels.

"Let me help you."

I don't resist. He undresses me carefully. Then he lifts me gently, his arms are strong, each of his movements steady. He carries me into the tub, remaining fully clothed. The warmth of the water kisses my skin as he lowers me in and sets me on the bench. I let out a shaky breath as the heat from the water soaks into my bones.

Reavian rolls up his soaked sleeves and sits beside me. He dips a soap-soaked cloth in the water and gently presses it to my shoulders, then my arms, my collarbone. His gaze lingering on my face in between each movement. He washes my hair with such care that I could cry, his fingers massaging my scalp gently, rinsing the strands down my back with slow precision.

Not a word passes between us. We don't need them.

When the water begins to cool, he pulls the plug, draining the tub. He gets out first, swiftly peeling off his wet clothes, dries himself, then quickly changes. Then he attends to me, carefully drying me off, then carrying me over to the bed.

Out of the wardrobe he retrieves a night dress, deep blue satin, as soft as a dream. He slips it carefully over my head, then lifts me gently and tucks me underneath the covers on the bed. He disappears for a moment, coming back with a comb, and sits beside me gently brushing my damp hair.

"I don't want to spend another day apart from you," he says suddenly, his voice raw with emotion. "Not one."

I turn my head toward him.

"I want you by my side, Auren. For the rest of my life. Whatever that looks like... whatever is ahead. I want it with you."

Tears burn in my eyes. My chest aches with how deeply I feel his words. I press my lips to his, tender and gentle. A silent promise between us.

"I want that too," I whisper.

His smile is beautiful.

A quiet knock stirs the moment, and the door opens with a creak.

Vaelisar steps inside, his long silver hair loose down his back, eyes bright with something ancient and unreadable. He closes the door gently behind him.

"I hope I'm not interrupting."

"No, not at all," I say, waving him in.

I sit up a little straighter, though every movement still feels like it takes more effort than it should.

"I owe you an apology," he says softly. "I didn't see it. I had no foresight into what was going to happen in the Hollow. No warnings, just flashes of Reavian in some sort of danger. A danger that I felt the daggers would help with."

His gaze flicks to the nightstand where my daggers rest, their hilts glinting faintly in the starlight.

"That's why I left you the blades. I thought they would protect you if things went wrong. But if I had known—if I had seen what was waiting there for you—I would have never let you leave."

I look at him, and all I see is truth.

Regret is etched into every line on his face.

I lift my hand slowly and shake my head.

"It isn't your fault, I knew there would be risk. We all did."

"Risk, yes. But not *that*. Not a trap," Vaelisar murmurs.

No. Not that.

The air shifts.

The warmth from my earlier bath, and the feeling from our earlier laughter all fades into a hush as something in my mind splinters open.

A scream.

A shriek that split the air, so loud it shook the marrow in my bones.

The banshee.

My heart lurches. I curl my fingers tightly into the blankets.

I remember Halrex, smirking. Laughing at my panic. Taking *pleasure* in it. He wanted to take Reavian from me.

He intended to.

But I took *him* instead.

"Halrex, he's dead," I whisper. "I killed him..."

The statement comes out more like a question.

Reavian turns sharply to look at me.

"Yes," Reavian says.

"He tried to kill you. He said he was hoping that the trap they set up with the nightmares, the banshee, that it would have killed us," I whisper. "What happened to Veyric?"

"Dead," Reavian replies, his voice cool. "They all got what they deserved. Every last one of them."

A shiver runs through me, not from fear but from the weight of it all. Of death. Of the lives we've had to take. I never wanted this to be a part of me.

But it is.

The memory of Halrex's twisted smile. The nightmares they unleashed. They didn't just want power, they reveled in suffering. Their cruelty ran deep, rotten to the core. It stokes something fierce inside me. A fire that won't be snuffed out.

I look up at Vaelisar.

"Where is Bronn?" I demand. I know they planned this together.

He stills. So does Reavian.

"Where is he?" I ask again, my tone much firmer this time.

Reavian's hand closes around mine immediately.

"We believe he fled during the chaos," Reavian says gently. "Most likely when Vaelisar spoke of his premonition and alerted the healers to our impending arrival. But Tharen has sent word to Vaedric, Bronn has been declared a traitor."

I suck in a low breath. The fire within me flaring a bit.

"He ran..." I say.

"Like the coward he is," Reavian says darkly.

Vaelisar takes a step forward, his tone colder than before. "I have Nightguard stationed throughout the realm. Their orders are clear. If Bronn is found, he is to be brought to Starfall Keep for a *very public* execution. One fitting for a traitor."

I blink, a little surprised by the sharpness in his voice.

Vaelisar glances sideways at Reavian, adding dryly, "Reavian has already put the fear of the Gods into the rest of the council."

I glance back at Reavian and he smirks.

"I owe Vaelisar a new table, something more... sturdy."

Both the men chuckle under their breath.

I stare between them.

"What am I missing?"

Vaelisar's expression twitches, and Reavian is looking far too satisfied.

"Let's just say he made quite the impression in your absence," Vaelisar says. "Bronn's allies are squirming. Anyone who has ever so much as whispered support for him, or for Halrex, is being watched. Council members included." His voice lowers, the edge unmistakable. "If any collusion is uncovered, they'll meet the same end we have planned for Bronn."

My gaze drifts down to where Reavian's fingers still grip mine, strong and steady.

"They have to be working with Lucien and your mother," I say quietly.

Reavian nods, seemingly having already drawn the same conclusion. "There is no other explanation, they wanted you gone."

"No, they don't want me dead. Not yet. They need me to give them my power. Perhaps whatever that creature was... their attempt to take what I wouldn't give," I say.

Valeisar straightens.

"Bronn probably ran to them," I murmur.

A tightness winds through my chest again, it feels different this time.

Something is coming.

"What secrets was Bronn privy to, leading the council?" I ask suddenly. "What does he know about this realm? About the defenses of Starfall Keep?"

Reavian and Vaelisar exchange a look.

"He knows all of it," Vaelisar replies.

"Then we need to start changing things. Shift routines, tighten defenses. Something is coming, I can *feel* it. Something big. And we need to be ready before it hits."

Chapter Forty Three-Auren

The warmth of the bed feels strangely deceptive somehow. Outside the starlit sky still glows, silver and soft. But my chest feels tight. Too tight, like the world is bracing for something.

I shift beneath the covers, restlessly. Reavian is already awake, propped on one elbow, watching me with his quiet intensity. Noctis lies curled at the foot of the bed, his glowing eyes already fixed on me.

"You should stay in bed today," Reavian says softly. "You're still healing."

"I can't," I murmur, pressing a hand to my chest. "I keep...*feeling* something. Like the land is holding its breath. Like there is a shadow just out of sight, waiting to fall." I glance at him. "I don't want to wait until it is too late."

His brow furrows. "Auren..."

"I need to get my strength back," I say, pushing the blankets aside. Noctis rises smoothly to his feet, padding to my side like he can feel the same pull. "I can't do that lying in bed all day."

Reavian sits up fully, reaching for me. "I just got you back. I don't want to risk—"

I lean forward and press a soft kiss to his lips. His breath catches, and when I pull back his hand lingers on my waist.

"I need to do this," I say, my voice is low and sure. "Whatever's coming... we don't have much time. I can *feel* it"

There's a long pause, and his jaw works as he wrestles with something internally.

Finally, he nods once. "Alright."

"I was hoping you would say that." I give him a faint smile. "Can you find Iska for me?"

"I'll be right back," he says, then hesitates in the doorway. "Don't move until I get back unless it's absolutely necessary. I mean it."

"Yeah, yeah. I'll try not to fall off the balcony," I call after him. I hear the huff of his laughter as he walks down the corridor.

A few moments later, a soft knock sounds.

"Come in," I call.

Iska enters, balancing a tray, and Noctis gives her a long, unreadable look before stepping back toward the bed. He trusts her, but seems to eye her with suspicion anyway.

"And why aren't you sleeping?" she asks, setting the tray down.

"Because I have been unconscious for a couple weeks, which *is* essentially sleeping. Oh and because I slept *again* last night, so here

I am. All. Rested."

She hands me a steaming cup. "I made it stronger. It should be enough to flush the rest of the corruption out of your system."

I sniff it.

"Ugh...does it still taste like minty ashes?"

"Worse," she replies with a smirk.

I take a sip and gag. "Ugh, Iska—"

"You'll live." She kneels beside me and begins to check my shoulder. "Yes, it's nearly gone. This dose should neutralize it for good."

"I need to start moving again," I say.

She levels a look at me. "Then listen carefully."

I sigh. "Fine."

"No sparring. No magic. No dramatic flourishes with your sword. No daggers. You can walk, and if you're feeling strong enough you can lift *light* weights. That's it."

"I know," I reply, my voice soft. "I'll be careful."

She glances over to Noctis. "I'm trusting you to make sure that she follows my instructions."

He flicks his ears, huffing softly, as if in agreement.

"Alright then, let's get you into some loose-fitting clothes." Iska says, walking to my wardrobe and then returning with some loose-fitting black linen pants, and a long-sleeved purple tunic. She helps me change into them and gives me another quick warning about following her instructions before leaving.

Moments later, the door creaks open again.

"Hope you're not sick of soup yet," Reavian says, balancing a tray.

Brynn follows behind him.

"I brought you some company," he adds.

Brynn strides over and flops into the chair beside the bed.

I smile.

"Are you going somewhere?" I ask him.

"Meeting with Vaelisar and the Nightguard," he replies. "We're going to need to rework the guard schedules. Bronn knew all the rotations."

"Good," I say.

He nods.

"Kaiel and I will also be taking over Nightguard training. We know how Lucien trains his armies, and what Liraeth creates. We know what we will all have to face, and we can prepare them accordingly," he says.

"Do you think they'll send conscripted?" Brynn asks Reavian.

"I'm counting on it," he replies grimly.

I think about the corruption I cleansed in The Realm of Flame and Forest. I was able to purge it so easily. It didn't behave like the corruption here does. It didn't *fight back*.

What makes the corruption here so different?

Why is The Realm of Veiled Stars being hit so hard?

Then it dawns on me. The banshee. She was the heart of the

corruption here. She controlled the pools, and she was able to fight back against me healing the land. She was controlling the corruption.

"They're going to come here, to try and retake the Hollow... they want the reflection pools," I say, my voice low and certain. "They're directly tied to the magic here. They want to use them to create an army of nightmares."

My words settle over the room. A shiver works its way down my spine, and I don't miss the way Reavian's jaw tightens. Brynn's fingers curl slightly, like she's preparing to fight something that isn't here yet.

"I'll tell Vaelisar, we will have to shore up the defenses in the area," Reavian replies.

Once he makes sure I have eaten, and finishes fussing over me, he kisses me on the forehead and leaves.

I turn to Brynn. "Would you walk with me? Maybe start some light training?"

Brynn eyes me for a moment, considering.

"Yeah, sure. I'd love to boss you around."

I smile.

As we walk through the quiet corridors of Starfall Keep, Noctis stays at my side—brushing his shoulder lightly against my hip when I falter. My body feels weak from fighting to survive the corruption that invaded me.

We pass a guard near a corner. He stares at my neck and his

expression shifts.

A look of disgust flashes across his face.

Noctis halts.

A deep warning growl rolls out of him like thunder. The guard flinches and quickly looks away.

My hand flies to the spot he was looking at. I can feel scars there now, webbing out from where the Banshee bit me on my shoulder. The healers must not have been able to get rid of them. I haven't really looked at myself since I have been awake. When Reavian bathed me the other night, all I could bring myself to look at was him.

Brynn loops her arm into mine and squeezes it gently. But she doesn't say anything.

The training room glows under the dome of starlight. Noctis trots ahead and settles on a soft mat near the far wall, watching.

We stretch and then she helps me onto a padded bench. She retrieves two small weights, just enough to test my limits. My muscles complain with every motion, but I breathe through it.

I *need* this.

She starts me on slow curls guiding my form gently, chatting the whole time effectively distracting me through full body trembles.

"So," she says casually, "you and Reavian. When's the wedding?"

I give her a look. "Subtle."

"Shut up, I've seen the way you look at each other. He's one breath away at swearing his undying love for you."

I laugh as my arms are shaking through the motions. "He already has."

"Oooh give me the details," Brynn says eagerly.

I groan and shake my head.

"He's...well...he's *everything*. Strong. Thoughtful. When I look at him, it's like the world steadies. Like I'm complete."

Brynn's face softens. "I'm glad you're happy."

"Thanks," I reply. "I'm glad you're happy too, you and Kaiel."

She shrugs her shoulders, but her cheeks tint. "He's loud. Cocky. Tells terrible jokes. But when I have nightmares—he holds my hand until I fall asleep again. So, I guess he kinda steadies me too."

"I'm glad that you guys found each other," I say sincerely.

She smiles. Then there's a pause.

A long one.

"You know, I think Kaiel really needs to talk to you," Brynn says quietly.

I lower the weights into my lap.

"I know."

"No, I mean *really* talk. After everything that happened with your parents, and your abduction... even everything that happened in the Hollow. He feels like he betrayed you. *Failed* you."

"None of it was his fault. It wasn't him," I reply.

"You and I know that. And maybe somewhere deep down he

knows that too. But I think he *needs* to hear it from *you*."

I nod slowly, my heart twisting in my chest.

I need to talk to him. I have needed to for a while now. I've forgiven him. Truly. None of what has happened is his fault. I'm just now realizing how badly *I* need to have this conversation with Kaiel too.

Brynn watches me quietly for a moment. Then, softer than before, she says. "You know, I'm proud of you."

I blink.

"What?"

"You've changed, Auren. You've grown into someone strong and sharp and brave as hell. You're not the quiet girl I met sneaking books to read behind the register at Carlotta's."

I smile faintly. "I was nervous about *everything* then."

"Yeah, even air," she says grinning. "But you've always been kind and curious, and when we met, I helped you hone a *little bit* of a rebellious streak. And now... now you are still all of those things, but you also have a strength within you. A fire. A confidence."

I look down at my hands. "My anxiety is still there. I wish I could say it disappeared when I found out I was fae, or when my powers started manifesting... but it didn't. I still have to remind myself to breathe more often than not."

Brynn's face shifts with understanding.

"I'm just trying to not let fear consume me anymore. Not like it used to," I say.

She bumps her shoulder lightly against mine. "Well, just in case no one has said it loud enough, you're doing a damn good job."

I swallow the lump in my throat and nod.

There's a quiet pause. Then she says wistfully, "Do you remember that sleepover we had? The one where your dad made pancakes shaped like animals?"

I laugh, the memory bursting through me sending warmth straight to my heart. "Yes. Dad kept telling the *worst* jokes. The bears he made looked more like potatoes and all the giraffes looked like they had broken necks."

"Your dad kept calling it abstract art. And I remember your mom pretending to be horrified and bringing out more syrup, to drown the creations and *put them out of their misery*," Brynn says, a bright smile reaching toward her eyes.

We both laugh as we relive the memory. The smile on my face fades into something gentler.

"That was one of my favorite mornings," I say.

Brynn nods.

"Mine too," she says softly. "I loved your parents Auren... like they were my own."

A lump forms in my throat.

"I know they are proud of you. Of everything that you have become. Of how hard you're fighting," she tells me gently, tears brimming in her eyes.

I don't respond. I just grip her hand and squeeze. My heart is too full to speak.

In a silent confirmation that she knows exactly what I am feeling she squeezes my hand back.

"Alright, now let's go get something to eat, I'm starving," she says.

*****

The scent of spiced stew and warm bread reaches us before we step into the dining hall. It's quiet tonight—most of the Nightguard are absent, likely still running drills under Reavian and Kaiel's command.

Only Tharen and Iska are seated at the long table, deep in quiet conversation.

Noctis enters before us, tail flicking low as he trots to his usual place, right beside the seat I normally sit in. He lays down with a soft sigh, eyes half lidded but alert.

Brynn and I slide into our chairs as steaming bowls are placed in front of us by some stewards. Another comes by to bring Noctis his tray of food and water as well.

"The shrine to Lunira is nearly complete," Tharen says between bites of stew. "The people are excited. And the Dreamkeeper Sanctuary is coming together faster than anyone expected as well."

"I'd like to see it when it's done," I murmur.

"I can take you, when you're ready to make the few days' journey again," he replies with a warm glance.

Iska snorts into her cup. "*If* you don't get yourself skewered on one of those patrols first."

Tharen raises a brow, clearly amused. "You don't approve of my patrol schedule, my Lady?"

She sets her mug down with a little too much force. "I don't approve of you going out into the unstable, corrupted ground without a healer at your side. It's reckless."

He leans back in his chair, lips quirking. "Sounds like someone's worried about me."

Iska doesn't even blink. "So, what if I am?"

There's a flicker of something in Tharen's eyes—surprise maybe? Then something warmer.

Iska continues, her voice softer but still firm. "Now that Auren is healing... I want to come with you. I'm not going to sit around while you walk into danger."

Tharen's amusement fades into something more serious. "You know it isn't safe."

"I don't care," she says. "I've already seen what's out there. I won't let you face it alone."

A long, charged silence stretches between them. A glance. A challenge. A promise.

He dips his head slightly, in defeat. "Then we'll go together."

Iska nods and takes another sip of her drink, the matter now settled.

"I think that Lucien and the others are coming, I think they want the Hollow, that's their target. Reavian was going to talk to Vaelisar about it today. They're coming. I *feel* it. You need to remain vigilant and maybe set some defensive traps while out on your patrols."

Tharen drops his spoon into his bowl.

"How do you know? What exactly are you feeling?" he asks.

I swallow.

"Dread. The stars themselves seem to be holding their breath in anticipation. We need to be ready, all of us," I say a chill running up my spine.

He nods.

A quiet settles over the table.

Brynn sets down her spoon.

Iska sets her cup down and starts nervously tapping her fingers against the table. Tharen's jaw tenses as he looks away, like he can see what's coming in the distance.

They might not feel the threat in the air or the hushed warnings from the stars as I do... but they sense the truth in my words.

Something *is* coming.

And we all know it.

***

Later, I return to my room. Noctis enters first, scanning the corners like always. Reavian isn't back yet, so I decide to take a bath. Noctis waits by the door to the bedroom, standing guard as always. The warm water soothes my aching muscles.

When I feel content, I pull the plug and dry myself off before striding over to the wardrobe. I catch a glimpse of the web-like scarring coming off my shoulder on the full-length mirror next to it. It's reaching up my neck, as well as down to my collarbone. The memory of that guard's reaction replays in my mind. I face the mirror fully and drop my towel.

Thick, raised claw marks wrap around my thigh, more across my ribs on the opposite side of my body. The corruption is gone, but it appears these scars will always remain. If they could've been healed, Iska would have done so by now.

I look like a monster. I know there are way more important things to worry about than vanity. But actually seeing what was done to me...

I almost died.

And the evidence is now preserved across my body.

Reavian walks in and sees me standing bare before the mirror, but he doesn't look disgusted like that guard dig.

I fumble for the towel, bringing it up and covering myself with it.

He walks toward me and takes my hand.

"Are you alright?" he asks.

"I needed to see it for myself. One of the guards today, he stared at these," I say brushing my fingers against the scars on my neck, "and he looked away in disgust. And I had to... see them... for myself." Every word comes out choked.

Reavian's jaw ticks, and I see a quiet rage flicker behind his eyes.

He grabs a black satin sleeping gown from the wardrobe and turns back to me. He tugs at my towel, and I let it fall to the floor. My arms scramble to cover the scars at my ribs.

He doesn't let me hide.

Instead, he kneels before me, and he kisses each of my scars. Starting at my thigh, then going to the ones on my ribs, my shoulder, my neck and finally to my collarbone.

"These are beautiful," he whispers in my ear. "Because they're *you*. I love every part of you."

He grabs a nightgown and dresses me gently, then curls me into his arms and carries me into bed. Tears are steadily spilling from my eyes. He climbs into bed beside me and kisses each of my tears away, until they no longer fall.

"I love you," I whisper, pulling myself as close to him as I possibly can.

"I love you too," he whispers back, wrapping his arms tightly around me. "Vaelisar is holding a council meeting tomorrow, to discuss strategy. He wants all of us to attend, but if you aren't feeling up to it..."

"I'll be there," I whisper. "It's important."

I look up at the stars and notice they're pulsing strangely again.

A warning? I'm too tired to wonder.
I fall asleep with Reavian's arms around me.
Two hearts, beating as one.

Chapter Forty
Four-Auren

The council room glows with candlelight and is thick with tension.

Maps are spread across the new stone table inlaid with obsidian and silver. The council murmurs, and the air in here feels tight, as if the room itself is holding its breath.

Vaelisar stands at the head of the table, tall and composed. He raises a hand, silencing the chamber with a single gesture.

"There is one matter I'd like to begin with," he says. "Something worth remembering before we speak of war."

The room quiets.

"As you know, the Shrine of Lunira has been fully restored."

Soft murmurs ripple across the table.

He continues, "It stands cleansed in Somnarel Hollow, surrounded now by blooming starlight flowers and untainted waters. The people have begun traveling there to pray again. To hope."

My heart swells.

"In four nights time, we will hold a dedication ceremony. A celebration. One night of peace, before the battle we are preparing for."

The tension in the room lifts, for a single flickering moment.

"What if they attack?" Kaiel asks.

Valid freaking question. That's exactly what I was just thinking.

"We received a report from the Nightguard scouts in the southern region," Tharen says. "There were three figures spotted, two nights ago. Moving quickly, heading toward the borders of Flame and Forest. I've sent word to Vaedric."

I blink. "South?"

It doesn't make sense. I glance down at the map, there is nothing there for them, nothing that they would want. I guess they could be trying to take back Flame and Forest, but it doesn't *feel* right. The Hollow, the reflection pools, they're *north*.

"It's a diversion," I say. "They're trying to split our defenses. The Hollow is what they want."

Tharen nods slowly. "Could be. But our people saw the movement. It's not nothing."

From across the table, Kaeron exhales loudly.

"Perhaps," he says, voice dripping with disdain, "you should let those with real experience handle battlefield logic and focus on things that you're good at."

He looks me dead in the eyes.

"Like picking out a pretty dress for the celebration."

The words hit like a slap. Sharp, belittling, and loud enough for everyone to hear.

Before I can respond he turns back to the council, dismissing me entirely.

"Tharen, you and your five chosen knights are to be dispatched immediately to the southern border. We leave nothing undefended."

That's when Seress steps forward. Golden haired and grinning like he's about to perform on a stage.

"No."

Kaeron turns to him slowly. "What did you just say?"

"I said, no." Seress repeats. "You don't command me. Or any of us for that matter. We are not going anywhere."

Kaeron's face begins to flush a deep shade of crimson.

"We were assigned to Auren," Alira says firmly, stepping beside Seress. "And we *stay* with her."

Mavren calmly joins them, Eiryn follows, his eyes stormy. Sirah is last, silent as ever, but her presence is absolute.

One by one they kneel beside me at the table.

"We serve the one the land chose," Mavren says.

"We serve our queen," Alira declares.

Kaeron explodes.

"There is no queen!" he snaps. "There has been no coronation, no crown. There is no throne! This is a delusion!"

Reavian stands and steps towards Kaeron.

"Watch your mouth." His voice is low, precise and deadly. Shadows curl at his heels, thin tendrils slipping into the air like smoke. His eyes promise pain.

"One more insult," he says. "And you and I are going to have a... *conversation*."

Kaeron flinches as the darkness begins to stir behind Reavian, his shadows rising, waiting for permission to strike.

"That's enough," Vaelisar says, his voice smooth and sharp.

Reavian takes his place beside me again, his shadows following then slowly dissipating.

"The land is healing," Vaelisar continues. "She is the one healing it. With it being healed comes its throne. You would do well to remember that the throne does not wait for permission. It *rises* for the one chosen to sit upon it."

He looks calmly at Kaeron.

"She *will* sit upon it. Whether you bend to it or break because of it, is entirely up to you," he says, his threat very thinly veiled. "A small contingent of the Nightguard will be posted at the southern border. The rest will be posted at the Hollow."

Kaeron clenches his jaw, then storms from the chamber, his boots cracking like thunder against the stone floors.

I can feel Maedra's gaze resting upon me. Silent. Cold. Measuring.

I meet it without blinking.

I don't trust her. Or Kaeron. They've made their feelings about me clear. But would they betray Nyvenya itself just to see me gone?

I don't know.

And that terrifies me.

***

A few nights later, wagons roll through the woods beneath a sky dusted with silver.

Lanterns dangle from twisted branches, glowing with a soft flame. Wildflowers bloom underfoot—purple, blue, and gold. The night smells like magic.

My gown swirls around me, the color of midnight. Glimmering constellations sparkle across the fabric, moving like they're alive. I feel like I'm wrapped in the sky itself.

Reavian places a crown he made for me of woven constellation orchids upon my head. The violet and sapphire flowers that adorn it have an ethereal glow. Their petals soft and pulsing faintly with what I can only describe as divine magic.

"Thank you, it's beautiful," I say to him, as he takes a step back to look at me. His outfit is as black as the shadows themselves, threaded with silver that twists like smoke. He smiles, his eyes not leaving mine.

The Shrine of Lunira rises ahead of us, its rebuilt obsidian arches glistening with stardust, the sacred pool reflecting every star above.

A thousand candles line the path.

I step toward the altar.

The moment my hand touches it, the world shifts and a jolt of energy passes through my body.

Thank you.

Heal us all.

Help us.

We are with you, Little Light.

A voice speaks to me.

Lunira's.

The whispers I've heard in every moment of doubt, every moment of danger, it wasn't the voices of fate, or some inner magic. I have been hearing the voices of the Gods themselves.

The realization shocks me to my very core.

My knees give way, but Reavian is there instantly, his arms strong around me.

And just for a moment he goes still.

He exhales loudly, like he's been holding his breath.

"I'm alright," I tell him. "You don't need to worry. I'm feeling better, almost back to my regular self."

He smiles at me, shaking his head and clearing whatever he was thinking about before from his mind. "Yeah, tell me that when you haven't just about fallen over."

"I heard her," I whisper to him. "Reavian... it's Lunira. The Gods. I've been hearing *them* all this time."

He doesn't question it; he just holds me a little closer.

Later, the fires burn low and music curls through the celebration like silk.

Laughter rises and food is passed. People *live*. For the first time in way too long, they *hope*.

Reavian takes my hand, a spark in his eyes. "Dance with me?"

"I'll step on your nice fancy boots," I say looking down at his feet.

"I'll survive."

He spins me into the clearing, and we begin to sway. His hands on my waist. My breath catches with every turn. The stars above feel close enough to touch.

He lowers his voice, bringing his lips near my ear.

"Gods, look over there."

He twirls me, nodding toward the firelight.

Seress is dancing with *Sirah*. She looks vaguely murderous.

Seress looks delighted.

She's stiff, barely moving, but he's clearly narrating every step like a dramatic stage play. Her eyes narrow on him.

"I think she may kill him," I whisper.

Reavian smirks. "Or maybe, she'll kiss him."

I laugh.

The music shifts.

A slower rhythm begins.

A man I don't know approaches; he is young and kind eyed.

He bows. "My Lady, may I—?"

I open my mouth to answer.

"Get away from her!" a voice booms.

I flinch, the sudden bark of the voice cutting through the music like a blade.

It's Kaiel.

He storms over, grabs the man by the collar and throws him back. The music screeches to a halt.

The man stumbles, stunned. "I... I meant no harm."

"It's alright, I'm sorry. You didn't do anything wrong," I say.

Reavian is already at Kaiel's side. "What the hell was that?"

Kaiel's voice is low, dangerous. "It was nothing. I just don't trust anyone to approach her like that. You shouldn't either. I'm fine. It's all of *you* with the problem."

I watch as he storms off into the trees.

Everyone stares.

Brynn moves beside me, her expression grim. Her eyes meet mine.

He's not okay.

Message received, no words necessary.

The musicians slowly resume playing.

I start to head towards where Kaiel went, it's way past time for us to have our talk. Reavian steps in front of me, jaw tight.

"I need to go talk to him," he says. "I need to know what is going on with him."

"Alright," I whisper, and suddenly a bit of dread rises in me.

"Be careful," I say softly, but he's already gone, swallowed by the shadows and flickering torchlight.

I turn back to see Brynn has already gone somewhere else, and I decide to step away from the celebration for a bit.

The stars are bright overhead, scattered like frost on black silk. Lanterns glow behind me, casting golden halos across the clearing. Laughter rises again, but it's becoming more distant now.

I walk the edge of the woods with Noctis at my side, the shrine still gleaming in the distance, when I hear it.

Tick. Tick. Tick.

My breath stills.

The sound is faint—so faint that I think I may have imagined it. But it's there. Mechanical and rhythmic. A clock counting down to something that I can't see.

Then it stops.

I lift my gaze to the sky.

The moon is full and round above me, pink, luminous and low. It bathes the forest of willows in its eerie glow, and every hair on my arms rises in warning.

They're here.

It's Lunira.

She speaks through the marrow of my bones, clear and sharp as knives.

Noctis growls.

BOOM.

An explosion rips through the stillness, echoing like thunder from the ridge beyond the Hollow. The ground shakes.

Screams ring out from the celebration. The music collapses into chaos.

I spin toward the ridge, and my blood goes cold.

A line of figures crests it.

Hundreds of them. Maybe more.

All in black-bone armor that reflects no light. Horned helms with skull-like faces. Gauntlets tipped in clawed steel. Their banners tattered shadows, flapping without wind.

Behind them...

The conscripted. Their faces stretched by pain and hunger. They crawl. Sprint. Shudder. Snarl.

They're coming.

I run.

I gather my skirts in my fists as I tear across the clearing, Nocits running by my side. My heart is pounding, and people are screaming all around me. Smoke begins to rise in the distance.

"High Lord!" I shout, pushing through the scattering crowd. "Vaelisar!"

He sees me and tosses me his second sword without hesitation.

I had left Virethyn behind at the keep, like a fool. I thought we would have more time. How did they get here so quickly?

My daggers are sheathed at my thigh though; I never go

anywhere without them.

"Stay close," he says. "We will defend the shrine. Lunira will help us."

A scream tears through the air and lanterns explode in bursts of flame.

Within moments the battle has begun.

I duck low as a conscripted barrels toward me, its body twisted, mouth agape in an unnatural way. I throw out a hand.

Flame surges from my palm like a river.

It roars across the clearing, slamming into the creature and sending it tumbling, shrieking as it turns to ash. Another rushes me—I spin with my sword, slicing upward into its throat.

"Auren!"

Brynn's voice—fierce and raw—cuts through the chaos. Lightning crackles along her arms as she tears through two conscripted, her feet skidding across blood-slick stone. She reaches me with fire in her eyes.

"I've got your back," she says, sliding in behind me.

"And I've got yours!" I shout.

Together we face the next wave.

Brynn and I move in tandem. Our blades flashing, lightning and flame colliding with bone and steel. A conscripted lunges at Brynn, but I cut it down before it reaches her. She doesn't miss a beat, sending a bolt of her power crackling through a knight's armor.

Our magic hums in the air, wild and bright.

Reavian appears across the clearing, his shadows already writhing, whipping forward like spears. They pierce through the weak points in the black-bone armor, dragging a line of knights to their knees, and holding their heads back exposing their throats. He drags his blade across their necks, and when he releases them, they fall. He continues to move like smoke through the battlefield, his every step a blow, every breath a weapon.

I slam my sword into a charging knight's side, and he staggers. Brynn releases a bolt of lightning that catches two more.

"Where are Tharen and Iska?" I shout over the chaos.

"I haven't seen them all night," Brynn shouts back.

My blood goes cold.

Vaelisar runs towards us. "Where is Reavian?" he asks, panicked.

I point to the last place I saw him.

"Where are the Nightguard that were supposed to be posted here?" I shout to him.

"We've been betrayed, Kaeron sent them south," Vaelisar says, and then he sprints towards Reavian.

Another explosion rocks the hillside. Fires rage across the battlefield.

And then I see him.

I feel my heart stop beating.

Lucien.

He walks calmly through the smoke, flanked by armored knights. His helm is off—his face gleams like polished bone, eyes black with hunger, mouth curled into something like joy.

A guttural scream sounds behind us, it's Mavren. I glance over my shoulder just as one of the black knights drives a blade through his ribs. He drops to his knees, eyes locking with mine for a split second... and then he falls.

A heartbeat later...

"Move! You, Cover me!" Kaiel shouts to a nearby member of the Nightguard.

He sprints past us, blade in hand, charging toward a line of conscripted soldiers breaking through a makeshift barricade.

"Kaiel, wait!" Brynn screams.

He doesn't.

His sword flashes as he dives into them. A whirlwind. A storm. He cuts down two, then three, spinning between blows with the grace of a dancer. Knights rush toward him.

For a moment—he's untouchable.

And then...

A spear catches him low in the side.

Another punches into his chest.

He staggers.

One more, a jagged blade, slashes across his abdomen.

Kaiel falls to his knees, blood pouring from his wounds.

"No!" I scream.

Brynn runs, and I try to follow her, but I'm attacked by another knight. Noctis locks into battle with a conscripted that tried to attack on my left.

I watch between blows, as Brynn tears through the field, lightning exploding from her hands, striking down everything in her path. She doesn't stop until she's at his side, dropping to her knees, grabbing him, holding him.

His lips move.

She leans close.

Whatever he says, it makes her laugh, just once.

Then a dark armored knight appears behind her.

"Brynn!" I scream, desperately.

She turns just as the sword pierces her back.

Her body jerks, and she collapses forward, her forehead touching Kaiel's.

Their hands find each other in the blood-soaked grass.

They don't move again.

"No..." I whisper. "No...no...no..."

I don't have time to cry.

I dodge another attack and slice through a conscripted's abdomen, gutting it. I send out a wave of flame across the battlefield, killing any conscripted in the area, and finishing off those that had just fallen. Noctis leaps at a knight that I didn't see behind me, ripping out his throat viciously before running into the thick of the battle ahead of me.

Beside me, Eiryn falls to a blade in the throat.

Alira is pulled down by three conscripted, while trying to

protect a wounded healer. The healer falls too.

Sirah is screaming—fighting over Seress's body, soaked in blood, surrounded. I send a surge of flame forward, incinerating four of them. By the time I reach her, she's already fallen.

I scream for her anyway.

I turn towards the sounds of another explosion, a magical bomb of some sort has gone off, igniting the field.

And then I find him.

I grab one of my daggers off my thigh with my left hand and wield my sword with my right.

I charge.

"Lucien!" I bellow.

He turns toward me. Smiling.

I strike first—flames roaring across my arms and down my blades as I swing at him. He parries with ease, stepping into the fight like it's a game. Our blades clash, mine burning with golden flame, his glowing an icy blue.

Sparks fly, fire screams.

I drive him back, my flame igniting the grass beneath our feet.

He snarls and slams his palm into my chest. Blue flame burns through my skin and hurls me backward. I drop my dagger, and crash into the earth, coughing, gasping.

He walks toward me unhurried.

"You're weak," he says. "Just like your father was."

I stagger up, sword raised, my flame flickering along the blade.

He circles me.

"All of this devastation..." he says. "It didn't have to happen. If *you'd simply given me what I wanted*, this realm would be safe."

I grip my sword tighter. "You're not worthy of it."

The words break his mask.

I grab my second dagger and hurl it toward his shoulder. It hits its target, embedding itself deep in the joint. He pulls it out like it's nothing, and casts it aside.

Then he lunges, fury twisting his face.

We clash again. My flame versus his, colliding in bursts of light. Each strike sends shockwaves through the field.

He's faster than me.

Stronger.

But I'm *angrier*.

I roar and drive him back, golden fire arcing from my blade. He blocks, counters, and knocks my sword away. I fall to my knees when his boot slams into my stomach.

He stands over me, raising his blade, ready to strike the final blow.

He begins to bring the blade down and I brace myself for the inevitable.

Shadows slam into him.

Lucien is thrown off balance, stumbling backward as darkness coils around his arms.

Reavian stands between us, panting and wounded, but alive.

Lucien straightens, his flame somehow burning the shadows away.

"Stand down, Reavian," he orders.

Reavian doesn't move.

"No."

Lucien's voice hardens. "Get out of the way."

Reavian takes a step closer, shielding me with his body. Then I feel it down our bond. A message from him. Run, he seems to be telling me. He's out of magic, his strength has faltered.

No, no... I will not leave him. I dig deep and find nothing. My magic is depleted as well, and I've been disarmed.

"If you ever cared about me," Reavian says. "If you ever truly loved me like a father... you'll leave."

Lucien's silence is a blade of its own.

"I love her," Reavian says. "I'm not going to let you kill her."

Lucien's face twists into something unreadable.

"Then you'll die for her."

Lucien's blade drives right through Reavian's chest.

I scream.

Vaelisar is running towards us.

"My son! No!" he shouts.

Lucien kicks Reavian off his sword like he's nothing, and I watch in horror as he crumples to the ground, unmoving.

And something in me...

Breaks.

I let out a scream so sharp, the air itself splits, the earth trembles.

The fire inside me erupts.

Golden. Blinding.

It pulses outward in a shockwave, searing through knights and conscripted alike. Armor melts. Screams vanish into nothing.

My fire spreads. The trees catch. The sky cracks.

Everything burns.

I stare at Reavian, lifeless before me, and I grab his hand. Slowly I lift my gaze to Lucien, who's looking at me with terror.

"Now it's your turn to burn," I say to him. And set his body aflame, with a glance.

His screams die out after what doesn't seem like nearly long enough.

Tick. Tick. Tick.

Valeisar drops next to me, and sobs over Reavian's body.

And then there's nothing.

Chapter Forty Five-Auren

My first breath comes out like a whisper—soft, trembling, and nearly lost in the hush of the room.

I feel warmth before I feel anything else. A steady weight against my side, the faint scratch of stubble where his jaw brushes my temple. Reavian. The scent of him—pine, leather, and something darker—wraps around me like a second skin.

My eyes flutter open.

Above me, the stars shimmer through the glass dome. Dozens of constellations weaving their silver lines through the dark. They sparkle, steady and serene.

I blink.

Reavian stirs beside me, his arm tightening protectively around my waist.

"Auren?" he whispers, voice cracked with disbelief.

I turn to him slowly.

"I'm here," I whisper.

He jolts fully awake, his eyes wide and wet, then brings his hand up, cradling my face like he is afraid I might disappear. He presses a kiss to my forehead, then rests his brow on mine.

And that's when it happens.

The room tilts. My breath catches.

It all comes back.

Kaiel falling, Brynn's final moments. The fire everywhere. Reavian dead on the ground before me. Vaelisar's voice, torn in anguish.

A sob escapes me before I can stop it.

Reavian pulls back, alarm flashing across his face. "Auren? What is it? Where does it hurt?"

I press a shaking hand to his chest. Feeling his heartbeat, he's real. He's here, he's *alive*.

"Get everyone we trust. Now. Bring them here. Don't delay. Please," I beg.

His eyes search mine, confusion tightening his brow.

"I've seen what's to come, hurry."

And Reavian—Gods bless him—doesn't argue.

He runs.

The room fills faster than I thought possible. Kaiel is the first to arrive, shoulders tense, eyes flicking over me like he's assessing a wound that he can't see. Brynn steps in beside him, wide-eyed, her hand brushing his without thinking. Tharen and Iska follow, silent and serious. Iska is carrying a silver tray with medicine for me on it. Vaelisar enters last, his expression carved with concern, and worry.

Reavian closes the door behind them. "She asked for all of you."

I sit up, I shouldn't be able to, not this easily.

I shouldn't have the strength, but somehow, I do.

They stand in a loose semicircle around the bed, Noctis still at my feet. The tension in the room stretches thin.

"I need you to listen," I begin. My voice is a little unsteady. "And I need you to believe me."

Kaiel frowns. "Believe what?"

"I've seen it," I say, voice sure. "All of it. What is coming. I attended the council meeting you're set to have in a couple days. And I know what will happen if we don't do something to change it."

They don't speak, so I keep going.

"I was at the celebration. You have just about finished rebuilding the shrine to Lunira, and you are planning for that celebration now Vaelisar, correct?"

He nods.

"I was there. The dedication of the shrine. We danced. There was laughter, and music. I heard the faint sound of a ticking clock." My voice cracks. "The moon was full, and pink. And I heard *her*. Lunira. She spoke to me. She warned me. She said, *they're here*."

I pause for a moment considering that there is no way to ease into the next part.

"Then the explosion hit."

Brynn goes stiff.

"They came over the ridge. Lucien's Knights. Hundreds of them. Behind them conscripted, twisted and screaming. Vaelisar, you told me that Kaeron betrayed us, he sent our troops south against your orders."

I shake my head. "We tried to fight. We tried."

My eyes find Brynn and Kaiel.

"Kaiel," my throat chokes. "You charged in, recklessly. A spear caught you low in the side, and then again through the chest. Brynn lit up a path to you with her lightning, she got to your side but..." my voice splinters.

"She was laughing," I whisper, my eyes stinging with tears. "You said something to her, and she laughed. And then they struck her down. You died together."

Kaiel doesn't move. Doesn't blink. Brynn presses a hand over her mouth.

"Alira died protecting a healer. Eiryn took a blade to the throat. Mavren..." I don't finish the thought. "Seress fell, and Sirah, she was screaming, still fighting over Seress's body before she fell too."

I shudder.

"And Reavian..."

He stiffens beside me.

"You threw yourself in front of me, Lucien was ready to make the death blow. You were wounded, you had spent the last of your magic. I was wounded and spent as well. You tried…" I choke a bit, tears flowing freely down my face at the memory. "You tried to reason with him. You told him to leave. You told him you wouldn't let him kill me. You told him that you loved me. And he…" I choke on the words I need to say for a moment. "He told you to die with me then, and he ran you through like you were nothing."

Something breaks in Reavian's expression, just for a moment. Vaelisar's hands curl to fists at his sides.

"Something inside me broke when I saw you die. And I burned them all, I burned it all. The very sky fractured."

The room is silent. A heavy silence.

"It wasn't a dream," I whisper. "It *wasn't*. I lived it. I felt the weight of every step, every wound. And now I'm here, I'm back. And I shouldn't feel this strong—I shouldn't be this *whole*. But I am. And you're all here."

Vaelisar speaks first, his voice grave. "A gift… from the Gods perhaps, from Lunira herself even."

"I think so," I say. "I lived it…it happened. But I believe I'm being given a chance to stop it. *To change it*."

Brynn steps forward. "What do we do?"

I look at her, thankful. She believes me.

They all do.

Tharen clears his throat. "We let Kaeron think nothing's changed. We play it out. The council meeting. The celebration. But we do it *knowing*. This time, we will be ready."

Reavian nods. "The guests at the celebration can be Nightguard in disguise."

"Perfect. We will train the nightguard, you and I, Reav. They'll need to know how we were trained for battle, how to handle the conscripted," Kaiel says.

"Yes," Reavian agrees.

"I've been patrolling, this time I'll take Sirah and your other knights with me. Make it like we are going on a regular patrol. But instead, we will travel to the Realm of Flame and Forest," Tharen says. "We'll find Vaedric, and we will secure an alliance. We'll need it."

Iska immediately steps beside him. "Then I'm coming too. I won't let you travel through the corruption without a healer."

Vaelisar shakes his head. "I should go with you, to speak with Vaedric. But with Kaeron's treachery, and who knows who else's still festering in these halls, I can't leave my realm unguarded. I'll write a letter, and have you deliver it for me, Tharen."

"Remember, Bronn is already gone. We will have to shore up our defenses everywhere just in case. Guard schedules will have to be altered. His knowledge of the defenses here is a threat," I add.

"Agreed," Vaelisar says.

Everyone looks at me.

"Then let's start getting our plans set into motion," I say.

"Well first things first," Iska says, walking forward with her tray. "You need to take this, I'd tell you that it tastes terrible," she says, handing it to me. "But something tells me you already know."

I sigh. Already cringing. "Yeah. I do."

The others watch silently as I tip the steaming cup back and swallow. The bitterness hits like a slap.

"Ugh." I shudder, blinking through the aftertaste. "Yep, still disgusting."

Iska smirks and then turns toward Tharen. "Come on, let's go loop in Seress and the others. If we're going to be ready for the council meeting in a couple days, we've got some planning to do."

Tharen gives me a short, respectful nod. "We'll make sure your knights are prepared."

"I know you will," I say.

They leave.

The room quiets again.

I glance at Kaiel.

Then at Reavian and Vaelisar.

And for the first time since I woke, the truth sinks in my stomach like a stone. Vaelisar is Reavian's father. I haven't said it aloud.

I remember the way he screamed for him.

My son!

That conversation... *has to happen.*

Soon.

But not yet.

There's another wound that has been festering longer. One I've ignored for too many days, buried in fear.

I look at Kaiel again. *This comes first.*

"Can I have a moment alone with Kaiel?" I ask softly. "There's... something we need to talk about."

Kaiel lifts a brow and gives me a weak smile. "Am I in trouble?"

"No. But this conversation is long overdue," I reply.

His grin falters. "Yeah... alright."

Brynn brushes his arm as she walks past, her expression soft and hopeful. She looks at me for a moment before leaving, her eyes shining with something between gratitude and fear, then she slips through the door.

"We'll talk later then," Valeisar says, lingering for just a moment longer, before he leaves as well.

Reavian hesitates for a moment. His gaze lingering on me, it's protective and understanding. He leans in close, brushing a kiss against the crown of my head.

"I'll be right outside," he murmurs.

I nod.

He closes the door behind him with a soft click.

And then it's just me and Kaiel.

And Noctis of course, still perched like a sentinel at the foot of the bed.

Kaiel hovers by the fireplace, his arms crossed, pacing a little. Like he's not sure whether he wants to face me or bolt out of the room entirely.

I stay quiet for a beat, watching him.

"Kaiel," I say softly.

He looks up. His dark eyes are shadowed, guilt clinging to them.

"I need you to know something," I say.

He doesn't speak.

"I don't blame you. I never did. Not truly." My voice is thick, and sure. "It just... took me time to separate what happened from who you really are."

I look down at my hands.

"Too much time," I say softly.

His head tilts, ever so slightly, but still no words leave his lips.

"I let what happened cloud the truth. And I'm sorry for that, Kaiel. Truly."

He runs a hand through his hair and lets out a bitter laugh. "But it *was* me. These hands struck down your father. My body dragged you from the wreckage that *I* caused. It was me that took you through that portal. Me who attacked you all in the forest. Not some distant shadow. *All of it* was me."

"No," I say, my voice sharp enough to silence him. "It was *her*."

He flinches.

"Liraeth doesn't ask permission, Kaiel. She takes. She steals. She wraps her twisted magic around you until it drowns out your own heartbeat. You weren't walking your path, it was hers beneath your feet. You didn't give her consent. None of what you did was a choice that you made, it was possession."

He looks down, and his throat works around a thousand words

he can't say.

"She's a manipulator," I continue. "She's someone that believes she can control everything, everyone, and maybe even fate itself."

His head lifts slightly, a flicker of something deeper crossing his expression. He doesn't comment. Not yet.

"I know who you are," I say. "And *that*...was not you."

Kaiel's lips press into a thin line, and for a moment, I think he might say something else. I think he may try to argue, to again tell me that I'm wrong.

But instead, his face crumples.

"I should've been stronger," he whispers, his voice breaking with emotion. "I should have fought it somehow. Hells, at the very least, I should have known something was wrong."

I push the blankets off me and stand. My legs are steady and strong.

He tries to take a step back, like he doesn't deserve the closeness, but I don't let him.

My arms circle him, and before he can speak again, he breaks. Deep shuddering, broken sobs begin to escape him.

His arms come around me slowly.

"I'm so sorry," he whispers. "Gods, Auren, I'm so sorry."

I tighten my grip on him. "There is nothing to be sorry for."

He shakes his head against me, still clinging.

"You're my friend," I whisper. "And I love you."

Kaiel stills for a moment, and then I feel his shoulders shake again. Not from grief this time, but something more akin to relief.

Eventually the sobs quiet.

When we finally part, I keep a hand on his arm.

"I need you to promise me something," I say gently.

He gives me a weak, crooked smile. "Not to tell Reav that you held me while I cried like a baby?"

I laugh softly.

"No. Not that," I say. "I need you to promise me that you won't be reckless, no unnecessary risks. Brynn needs you. We all do."

He nods in agreement and is silent for a moment.

"I'll be careful," he says at last. "No unnecessary sacrifices."

"Good," I say, as I squeeze his arm and give him a soft smile.

"I better get going, Reavian is probably pacing in the corridor," he says with a grin, turning toward the door.

He pauses for a moment before opening it.

"Hey Auren," he says.

"Yeah?"

"You're my friend, and I love you too," he tells me with a smile, and with that he leaves.

The space around me feels lighter, a weight from both of us was lifted today.

The door opens again.

Reavian's eyes land on me, on my bare feet, the blankets pushed aside.

I'm not in bed where he left me.

His whole body goes tense.

"Auren, what are you doing?" he asks. "You should be resting."

"I'm okay," I say, stepping toward him. "I mean it. I feel stronger than I know I should. It's like I've already recovered."

He looks at me like he wants to believe it, but fear lingers in his eyes. Just like the fear that lingers in my heart. I lost him. *Gods*, I watched him die. I close the space between us and kiss him, it's soft and tender.

Reassuring.

"I'm okay, you can relax," I tell him, firmer this time.

I feel for that thread between us, I need to feel our bond.

I kiss him again, at first, it's soft, but this time, when he kisses me back and something inside me breaks open.

I lost him.

I deepen the kiss, my hands threading into his hair, anchoring him to me.

"I want you," I whisper.

He pulls back, his eyes searching mine, uncertain.

"Auren... you just came back to me, you nearly died..." he says, voice breaking on the words.

"Please," I say. "I need *you*, please."

There's a moment of hesitation and then something in him unravels.

He lifts me gently and carries me to the bed. We lie together, his eyes not once leaving mine. For a long moment, he just looks at me.

Like he's afraid to touch me, like I may break into a million pieces, right here before him.

"Please," I beg softly.

I send a wave of my strength down the bond. So, he can feel that I'm not weak, I'm not broken.

And then he moves.

His fingers trail across my skin slowly. He peels away the soft nightgown I wear, inch by inch with careful hands. His gaze meets mine, and it's filled with adoration.

When I reach for him, he lets me pull his shirt over his head. My hand immediately goes to his heart; there is no new scar from Lucien. He's here, he's real. *He's okay.* My hands roam freely across his chest, feeling each line of muscle beneath his skin.

He kisses me, it's slow and claiming, and it sets me on fire. He kisses down my throat, then across my collarbone, over to my shoulder. He pauses to kiss each new mark on my body. Every touch of his lips makes my breath catch. My body arches, aching for more, but he's in no hurry.

When he comes back to my lips, I pull him down to me, and our mouths collide with a deeper urgency. I can feel tension in him, like he's still holding back, still trying to be gentle.

When he finally presses into me, my gasp is swallowed by his mouth. We move together slowly, our hips meeting in a rhythm that's unhurried and grounding. My fingers dig into his back, and he groans into my neck.

"Auren..." he rasps. "Gods, I..."

"I know," I whisper, threading my fingers through his hair. "I thought I lost you too."

He moves deeper, maintaining a slow rhythm. Every roll of his hips drives heat into my core, pleasure becoming sharp and overwhelming. My name leaves his lips in breathy whispers. And I give myself to him fully— mind, body and soul.

We fall together.

And when it ends, we are still wrapped in each other, so deeply tangled that I don't know where I end and he begins.

I press a kiss to his chest and rest my head over his heart. The sound of it beating is something I'll never take for granted again as long as I live.

He tightens his arms around me.

"Promise me," I say. "Promise me you'll stay alive. That we'll live a long happy life together."

"I'd like that," he replies.

"Not good enough," I say.

He tilts my chin and looks at me, his expression serious and tender.

"Will you promise me that too?" he asks.

"Yes, I swear it."

He presses his mouth to mine in a slow lingering kiss.

We don't speak after that.

We just lie together, skin to skin. Breathing as one.

Until our lids grow heavy, and we sleep.

Chapter Forty Six—Auren

The courtyard gardens are quiet beneath the eternal twilight, but they are far from still. Starlight spills like mist across the marble paths, dancing over the edges of low walls and winding through vines that shimmer in hues of violet, deep indigo, silver and blue.

Fountains are dotted throughout, their waters not clear but glowing. Liquid silver threaded with pulsing light, it's beautiful. Each one sings softly, the sound like a lullaby.

The air is rich with the scent of things I wouldn't have names for, if not for the descriptive plaques in front of them. Vines of Velora Blossoms curl along ivory trellises, their petals shaped like delicate stars, glowing with a pale violet light. Clusters of Astral Thistle, pulse gently with threads that shimmer between their leaves. And the breeze carries the clean, bittersweet fragrance of Dreamroot, it smells of something like frost, cedar and lavender wrapped together somehow.

I sit on the edge of the largest fountain, shaped like a crescent moon. Noctis sits beside me. My boots are tucked off to the side, my toes pressed into the cool deep blue grass. The water beneath my fingertips glows faintly, each ripple casting a prismatic light across my skin.

I'm not trying to clear my head. I'm not really even thinking all that hard. I just needed somewhere that didn't expect anything of me. Somewhere still.

"Is this where the Queen comes to pretend she's not in charge of saving the world?"

Brynn's voice doesn't startle me. I look over my shoulder to find her strolling along the path, arms crossed, a smirk tugging at her lips.

"I'm not a queen..." I say smiling a little. "I am hiding though...just a bit."

She drops down onto the fountain's edge beside me, with zero regard for grace or silence.

"You better get used to that title. You're going to be our queen, Auren," she says. "But I'm glad you're hiding and taking some time for yourself. I'd be worried if you weren't."

We sit in silence for a while, the bubbling of the fountains and the soft flutter of flower petals the only sounds between us. Brynn leans back, her fingers tapping rhythmically on her knee.

"I heard you talked to Kaiel," she says eventually. "He didn't give me any details. But he looks like someone finally cracked the window to his soul and let some of the smoke out."

I nod, still tracing idle circles in the water. "He needed to hear it. And I needed to say it."

"Your friendship," Brynn says. "It's good for him."

I turn to her.

"Pretty sure *you* are the one who's good for him," I tell her.

Her nose wrinkles. "Gross, don't say it like that."

"You love him," I say, the words come out certain.

Brynn doesn't even blink. "I know."

I raise a brow.

"So, have you told him?" I ask.

She hesitates for a moment. "Well... I'm working on it."

"Brynn..."

She lets out a low groan and flops dramatically back against the stone rim of the fountain.

"Don't *Brynn* me."

I sigh. "You should tell him."

"I know, I just..." She sits up again, brushing her hair back behind her ear. "I've already lost people that I loved. And this, with Kaiel, it's different. That's what makes it terrifying. I've been broken. But if something happens to him, I don't know if I would be able to come back from it."

I study her for a moment. "You've never been broken."

That statement clearly surprises her.

"You have been hurt," I clarify. "But broken people don't keep fighting the way you have. Broken people don't carry others through their pain. You were never broken Brynn. You're someone who has survived something that no one should have to."

Her mouth opens. Then closes again.

"Damn," she mutters. "You're getting good at this whole wise queen thing."

I smile. "It's the gardens. They make me sound *smarter*."

Brynn grins, her green eyes are softer when she looks at me again. "So, you love him... Reavian?"

"I do." The words are steady and certain.

"Was it hard to tell him?" she asks.

I think about it for a moment.

"No, I think I loved him before we even actually met. When I'd see him in my dreams. So, when we told each other, it just felt right. Natural." I look down at my reflection in the glowing water. "We've been through so much, nothing about it scares me anymore. I want to enjoy every moment I have with him. Life is too short to leave things left unsaid."

"Well, I don't know about that, we are fae. There is that whole possibility of immortality you know," Brynn replies sarcastically.

"Yeah, I don't really know too much about what being fae entails, so when we have more time, you'll have to enlighten me," I say. "Besides, you know what I mean, we are going to face real dangers."

She nods.

"So, tell him," I say.

Brynn smirks. "Fine. But if he panics and bolts, I'm fully blaming you."

"Oh please, he'll probably drop to one knee and propose," I say laughing.

"As far as the being fae stuff, I'm always here to answer any questions you may have, Your Majesty," she says, sketching a mock bow.

"Oh, *whatever*," I say, splashing her with water from the fountain.

She squeals with laughter, readying a counterattack.

Before she can fire back, the sounds of footsteps approach. A steward, dressed in silver robes. He bows his head and holds out a sealed scroll.

"My lady," he says. "From High Lord Vaelisar."

I take the scroll, breaking the wax seal without hesitation.

Auren,

Please meet me in my observatory. There is much I would like to discuss with you, in private.

- Vaelisar

As the steward departs, I rise to my feet and slip my boots back on. Noctis rises with me.

"What is it?" Brynn asks.

"Vaelisar wants to meet with me, and I need to find Reavian. I want him to come with me. You... should tell Kaiel how you feel when you see him tonight," I tell her with a smirk.

"Yeah. I will... maybe," she replies.

The halls echo with the steady rhythm of my footfalls. It doesn't take me long to find him. I follow our bond to the training room. The Nightguard spar in circles, blades clashing against shields, the air thick with effort and sweat.

Reavian stands in the center of the room.

He moves with cold precision, his body fluid and measured, sword cutting through the air as if it's an extension of his body. Like he was born with it in his hand. His expression is all focus and calculation.

Kaiel by contrast, is circling a recruit with a half-smile and too much swagger, parrying with just enough effort to humiliate.

Reavian freezes mid maneuver, and turns his head slightly, feeling my presence. His gaze lifts and meets mine.

And just like that, he's moving.

He reaches me quickly, posture tense.

"Are you alright?" he asks.

"I'm fine," I say.

His shoulders instantly relax.

"I just... Vaelisar requested a meeting, and I want you to come with me," I tell him.

"Alright." His answer is immediate.

He glances over his shoulder to Kaiel.

"Oh, I get it, you're ditching me," Kaiel says, catching Reavian's gaze and rolling his eyes.

Reavian doesn't respond.

Kaiel waves lazily. "It's fine. Go be all shadowy and broody with your favorite person."

Then he turns and promptly knocks a knight flat on his ass with a swift twist of his blade. "Yeah, that's not gonna work," he mutters. "Let's go again and try not to lose your balance mid swing this time."

I barely stifle a laugh as Reavian reaches for the door, holding it open for me with a subtle brush of his hand on my lower back.

***

The observatory tower rises high above the rest of Starfall Keep, its spiral stairs lined with smooth stone and ancient etchings that pulse faintly as we pass. I don't know if they are reacting to me or to Reavian.

Maybe both of us.

We don't speak as we climb. His presence is steady beside me. Noctis is behind us, gracefully climbing his way to the top as well. When we reach the doors, they are already open.

The chamber inside is breathtaking.

The walls curve upward into a domed ceiling entirely made

of clear crystal, revealing the sky above in perfect clarity. The constellations wheel slowly overhead, unmoving to the naked eye, but somehow, I *feel* them turning. They're watching. Shelves of open tomes and star maps line the perimeter, and a long, curved desk faces the center of the room, where a shallow reflecting pool shimmers.

Vaelisar stands by a window, arms clasped behind his back, cloaked in midnight blue. His silhouette is haloed by soft starlight.

He turns, and when he sees Reavian beside me, the line of his mouth tightens.

"I asked to see you," he says, eyes settling on me. "Not the both of you."

"He stays," I say, not harsh but definitely leaving no room for argument.

Reavian doesn't flinch. "If she wants me here, I am staying. I won't speak unless asked to. But I'm not leaving."

There is a long silence. But then Vaelisar inclines his head once and gestures toward the semicircle of glass chairs near the reflecting pool.

"Very well," Vaclisar replies.

We sit.

The moment I sink into the cool seat, the room seems to quiet further. Even the turning of the stars above feels slower, as if the world itself is holding its breath.

"I'd like to go over your premonition again. This time using the reflecting pool here. All you must do is touch it, and we will be able to see all that you saw. I want to make sure we have missed nothing," Vaelisar says, his voice as calm and smooth as the pool beside us.

"I'm not sure you want me to do that without discussing something first," I reply.

Vaelisar stiffens slightly.

"Because there was a detail I left out."

My fingers reach for Reavian's beside me, and I thread them with his.

Vaelisar's mouth opens, then closes again. His mask slipping—just for a heartbeat—and I see the weight behind his eyes.

"You need to tell him," I say. "He deserves to hear it from you first, not to get slammed with it in flashes of a memory."

Vaelisar looks between us, and in that moment he changes. He isn't a High Lord. He isn't a ruler. He is a man staring down something he has avoided for far too long.

"I hoped…" he begins, but the words catch. He exhales slowly. "I suspected. For years, I… but I had no proof. Only fragments in dreams. And then you showed up here, with Auren. And I knew."

My grip tightens on Reavian's hand, bracing him for the words that I know are going to come next.

He looks at Reavian fully now.

"You, Reavian. You are my son."

Chapter Forty Seven-Reavian

I don't breathe.

I don't speak.

The words hang in the air between us, sharp and terrible in their finality.

Everything around me disappears. The observatory, the starlight, the weight of Auren's hand in mine. All of it fades, swallowed by the rush of blood in my ears.

My heart isn't racing. It's just... stopped. Like it doesn't quite know what to do anymore.

Son.

His son.

It doesn't fit. It doesn't make any sense.

I stare at Vaelisar, and for the first time since I met him, I don't see a High Lord cloaked in authority. I see a man with regret in his shoulders and a war in his eyes.

"I don't understand," I say. My voice is quiet. Almost hollow.

"You can't just... say something like that and expect it to *fit*."

"I know," he says. "But it is the truth."

I want to laugh. Or scream. Or run.

Instead, I just sit here, my heart cracking open in small uneven lines.

"You knew," I murmur. "All this time, you knew, or you at least suspected. And you said nothing."

"I didn't have any proof," he says. "I didn't know for sure. I got fragments in dreams over time, but they were always shadowed. But when you came here, with Auren. I felt it. I saw it. But I didn't know how to tell you. I wanted to make sure that you were ready for me to tell you."

"Ready for what?" My voice turns sharper. "To learn that my whole life has been a lie?"

Auren squeezes my hand.

That keeps me steady.

She doesn't speak. Doesn't try to fill the space. She just *stays* by my side. Like she always does. Her and Kaiel are the only good I have ever had in my life.

"I spent years wondering who I was," I say slowly, each word weighted like a stone. "Years with a mother who saw me as a pawn. A weapon. And you were *out there*. You could've told me—"

"I would have taken you from her if I had known," Vaelisar says. "If I had known for sure that she bore my child."

"*Stop!*" The word flies out of my mouth and cuts like a blade.

Something in me *already knew*. The dreams that led me to Auren. The starlight quiet between nightmares. I knew I wasn't some random lesser fae's son.

But knowing it and *hearing it* are not the same.

"I am not yours," I say.

He doesn't flinch.

I want him to.

"I'm not asking you to be," he replies. "That would be your decision. But I will not lie to you anymore. Auren is right. You deserve the truth."

I let go of Auren's hand for a moment.

Not to leave.

But just to, Gods I don't know. I need to breathe.

I press my palms into the edges of my glass chair. It's cool, and solid and it keeps me from exploding.

"Then tell me everything,"I say. "No riddles. No more lies. Tell me *everything*."

"Alright," Vaelisar replies.

I reach back for Auren's hand and lace my fingers with hers. I grip it harder than I mean to, but she doesn't pull away. She shifts just enough so her arm presses against mine, her warmth tethering me to her.

"I didn't know who she was," Vaelisar begins. "She came here, claiming to be nobility from a distant isle in The Realm of Tide and Storm. She said her name was Liraeth Nyvaris. She was poised, eloquent, and mysterious. Beautiful in such a way that it made the very stars feel dim in her presence."

He breathes deeply, the memory of her darkening his gaze.

"I fell for her. Hard. And fast."

Of course you did, I want to say. Everyone falls for her. That's the danger. She sets the trap with her beautiful web, before she enjoys the meal.

"But strange things started happening. Citizens started to disappear. And then one day my shadows vanished."

I blink. "What?"

He nods in confirmation, confirming what I'm already thinking. "The shadows Reavian, they were mine. Not hers. I was blessed with the gift of shadow magic—darkness woven from the gaps between the stars. But after she moved in with me... one day they disappeared. I could no longer summon them, couldn't feel them resting beneath my skin. They were just gone."

I feel Auren shift beside me, her thumb gently brushing across the back of my hand. That small movement keeps me from unraveling.

"I went to the healers. They found nothing wrong. So, I turned to the Dreamkeepers. I asked them to search for answers in the reflection pools," he says.

His eyes lift toward the ceiling of starlight, as if he is drawing strength from it.

"The reflection pools can show more than premonitions, or

dreams. They echo fragments of the past too, memories that the stars refuse to let go of. And in one of them... I saw her, standing in our shared room. Performing a ritual over my sleeping body. A siphoning."

His voice turns sharp. "She stole my magic."

My jaw clenches, familiar heat rising in my chest. Of course she did. And now she's perfected this *siphoning ritual,* and she's created an army of abominations while taking every bit of magic from her victims.

"That's how the council came to be here in my realm," he says, his voice tinged with regret. "When I banished her, many thought it wasn't enough. They wanted her executed. Said I had grown soft. They demanded oversight. Structure. So, I gave them a seat at *my* table."

He falls silent for a moment. "I didn't kill her because... something in me said not to. The stars urged me to use restraint. I now know why."

I already know the answer.

"Because she was pregnant with me," I say.

"Yes."

I stare down at the smooth table, trying to breathe through the knot in my chest. "So all of this... everything she did... everything she intends to do, none of this would be happening if *I* didn't exist."

Auren's hand leaves mine, only to press against my back, her fingers drawing soft soothing circles. I feel like I may throw up, until I feel a surge of warmth down our bond. Love.

"I don't regret his decision at all," she says firmly, her voice gentle but unshakable.

Vaelisar looks at her, then at me. "I don't regret it either."

I can't look at either of them. All of this could have been avoided, if he had just ended my mother for her treachery right there. Nyvenya would be safe, Auren would still have her family, she wouldn't have nearly died.

There's a silence I don't know how to fill.

"I don't know what to do with this," I admit. "I've spent my whole life thinking my power came from her darkness. And now, I find out that part of me came from *you*. And the rest of me has come from her."

All this time I've been afraid of it. My power. Thinking it made me just like her. The darkness. Everything about my existence, about who I am, is a lie.

I look up, throat tight. "I don't know what that makes me."

Vaelisar stands, and steps closer to me, slowly. Like he's approaching a wounded creature. "It makes you whoever you choose to be. I can't change what's been done. I can't change the years that I have missed. But if you'll let me... I would very much like to know you. To build something. As much or as little as you allow."

The sincerity in his voice punches a hole through the wall I've spent years building. A wall that only Auren was ever able to truly breach. But I'm not ready to let him step through it yet.

I rise slowly. "Auren and I need to go, I need to think."

He nods. "Of course. I'll respect your space."

I don't say anything else. I just take her hand again and walk out the door to the stairs.

We arrive back at our chambers, and Noctis curls up near the window.

I sit on the edge of the bed, my elbows resting on my knees. Auren moves toward me without a word and sits beside me.

"I feel... torn," I say at last. "Like half of me wants to scream, and the other half... I don't know. I spent years shaped by people who wanted to control me. And now this man appears offering what? Connection? Belonging?"

"You don't have to decide anything tonight," she says gently.

I nod but the ache in my chest doesn't ease. "Do you ever wonder about your father? King Veylas?"

She's quiet for a long moment.

"Yes. All the time actually. I have so many questions. I want to know about him and my mother. She had a whole life here, before he sent her away. One I'll likely never know about fully now. And my power. He had it too. I think I'd ask him about that."

I glance at her. "So, if he were still alive... you would want to meet him? Get to know him?

She doesn't hesitate. "Yes. Because even though he sent us away...

it was to keep me and my mother safe. That was love. Even if it came with sacrifice."

I let those words sink in.

"And Vaelisar," she adds. "He didn't execute her because, even without knowing it, he was trying to protect *you*."

What she says lands hard.

I still feel unsure.

But maybe this is the first step forward.

Auren slides closer to me, her hand slipping around my waist. She rests her head lightly against my chest.

"You're not alone in this," she whispers. "I'll always be here with you. Right by your side."

The words hit something deep within my soul. I don't say anything. I just lean into her, closing my eyes.

Her warmth seeps into the parts of me that feel frozen.

"I just don't know what I'm supposed to do," I admit.

"You don't have to know," she says. "You just have to keep moving forward. Take it day by day. And I'll be right here, every step."

I press a kiss to her temple. It's small. But it means everything.

We sit like that for a long time, wrapped in each other in the hush of the starlight, until the weight of it all becomes something that I can finally carry.

Chapter Forty
Eight-Auren

The council room glows with candlelight and is thick with tension. Just like it was when I experienced it before.

Maps are spread across the new stone table inlaid with obsidian and silver. The council murmurs, and the air in here feels tight, like the room itself is holding its breath.

Vaelisar stands at the head of the table, tall and composed. He raises a hand, silencing the chamber with a gesture.

"There is one matter I'd like to begin with," he says. "Something worth remembering before we speak of war."

The room quiets.

"As you know, The Shrine of Lunira has been fully restored."

Soft murmurs ripple across the table.

He continues, "It stands cleansed in Somnarel Hollow, surrounded now by blooming starlight flowers and untainted waters. The people have begun traveling there to pray again. To hope."

Every word is exactly as I remember.

"In four nights time, we will hold a dedication ceremony. A celebration. One night of peace before the battle we are preparing for."

The tension in the room lifts, for a single flickering moment.

"What if they attack?" Kaiel asks right on cue.

"We received a report from the Nightguard scouts in the southern region," Tharen says. "There were three figures spotted, two nights ago. Moving quickly, heading toward the borders of Flame and Forest. I've sent word to Vaedric."

I blink. Time for my line.

"South?" I ask.

I glance down at the map before me. I know they're not going south. We all know exactly where they'll be. But for this plan to work we need to sell it.

"It's a diversion," I say. "They're trying to split our defenses. The Hollow is what they want."

Tharen nods slowly. "Could be. But our people saw the movement. It's not nothing."

From across the table, Kaeron exhales loudly.

"Perhaps," he says, voice dripping with disdain, "you should let those with real experience handle battlefield logic and focus on things that you're good at."

He looks me dead in the eyes.

"Like picking out a pretty dress for the celebration."

The words hit like a slap even though I knew they were coming. Still sharp, belittling, and loud enough for everyone to hear.

But I don't respond, and he turns back to the council, dismissing me entirely.

"Tharen, you and your five chosen knights are to be dispatched immediately to the southern border. We leave nothing undefended."

That's when Seress steps forward, golden haired and grinning like he's about to perform on a stage.

"No."

Kaeron turns to him slowly. "What did you just say?"

"I said, no," Seress says. "You don't command me. Or any of us for that matter. We are not going anywhere."

Kaeron's face begins to flush a deep shade of crimson.

"We were assigned to Auren," Alira says firmly, stepping beside Seress. "And we *stay* with her."

Mavren calmly joins them, Eiryn follows, his eyes stormy. Sirah is last, silent as ever, but her presence is absolute.

One by one they kneel beside me at the table.

"We serve the one the God's chose," Mavren says.

"We choose to serve our queen," Alira declares.

I smile at them. My queen's guard—pride swelling in my chest. For the first time, I truly feel like I might be able to do this. I could be their queen. They must be exhausted—Tharen and the guard traveled to Flame and Forest and back within two days. I'll have to ask Tharen tonight how exactly they pulled that off.

"We have chosen each other," I tell them.

Kaeron explodes.

"There is no queen!" he snaps. "There has been no coronation, no crown. There is no throne! This is a delusion!"

Reavian stands and steps towards Kaeron.

"Watch your mouth," His voice is low, precise and deadly. Shadows curl at his heels, thin tendrils slipping into the air like smoke. His eyes promise pain.

"One more insult," he says. "And you and I are going to have a... *conversation*."

Kaeron flinches as the darkness begins to stir behind Reavian, his shadows rising, waiting for permission to strike.

"That's enough," Vaelisar says, his voice smooth and sharp.

Reavian takes his place beside me again, his shadows following then slowly dissipating.

"The land is healing," Vaelisar says. "She is the one healing it. With it being healed comes its throne. You would do well to remember that the throne does not wait for permission. It *rises* for the one chosen to sit upon it."

He looks calmly at Kaeron.

"She will sit upon it. Whether you bend to it, or break because of it is entirely up to you," he says, his threat very thinly veiled. "A small contingent of the Nightguard will be posted at the southern border. The rest will be posted at the Hollow."

Kaeron clenches his jaw, then storms from the chamber, his boots cracking like thunder against the stone floors.

I can feel Maedra's gaze resting upon me. Silent. Cold. Measuring.

I meet it, without blinking.

I know Kaeron will betray us. But what is her role in this? Does she have one?

I don't know.

And that no longer terrifies me, because this time. I'll be ready. We all will.

***

The observatory hums with silence, and its starlit chamber feels like a sanctuary. The sky stretches wide above us, stars wheeling slowly across the crystal ceiling, their light dancing across the floor.

We gather in a circle around the reflection pool. Its still surface perfectly mirrors the sky above. Reavian stands beside me, his hand brushing mine. Vaelisar is sitting behind his desk, maps and plans scattered before him. Kaiel is leaning against a pillar, his arms folded, unusually quiet. Brynn is near him, her expression guarded and her eyes sharp. My queen's guard forms a protective arc near the far edge of the room. Tharen and Iska flank the pool. And Nocits is where he always is, right by my side.

Tharen is the first to speak. "Vaedric sends his regards," he says, dropping a huge leather satchel onto the stone floor in front of the pool. "And gifts."

He pulls out several folded bundles of dark, finely crafted leather. It's thinner than any set of leather armor I have seen before. "These can be worn under your normal attire. Light as a whisper but enchanted to be stronger than steel. The Nightguard has already received theirs... quietly."

He looks around the group, then continues. "They know that if any changes in orders come from Kaeron or Maedra, they're to ignore them."

Vaelisar's voice cuts clean across the still air. "I have made it clear that any true command will come directly from me. No one else. And that if anyone disobeys... well, they'll be paying the highest price."

Nods pass between the gathered. No one speaks, but the air shifts a bit.

As Tharen begins handing out the armor, Vaelisar turns to him once more. "Does this mean that Vaedric has agreed to the alliance?"

Tharen nods. "He has. His wardens will be lying in wait in the forests, just outside the perimeter of the battlefield Auren described. All they need is our signal, and they'll strike. A small contingent of Nightguard will receive a group of wardens at Starfall Keep after the festivities have begun. To protect the city and keep it safe."

Vaelisar smiles. "Then we are not alone."

Tharen moves through the group, distributing the armor. Mavren accepts his wordlessly, already inspecting the stitching. Alira flexes the leather between her hands, nodding in approval. Eiryn holds his without a word, his jaw clenched tight.

When Tharen reaches Seress, the knight twirls the folded armor between his fingers and flashes Sirah a grin. "If I fall in battle," he says with a wink, "I hope you are the last thing I see."

Sirah, composed as ever, doesn't even look at him, but a faint blush climbs the curve of her cheek. I catch it and so does Seress. He doesn't press the moment, but I note his grin softens into something more... real.

Tharen finishes passing out the last pieces. We all examine the armor. It's finely crafted. The set he has given me, has twisting flames stitched into the pants, and the corseted top has a golden flame stitched right above my heart.

And that's when I hear them, the voices of the Gods swirl within me.

Show them what was.

Let them see the Blood and Ruin.

Only then will they understand what is to come.

A chill rolls down my spine.

You must be the light in the darkness.

You must be the one to face him.

Alone.

I can feel their words in my bones.

I draw a slow breath, and step forward.

"I think there is something that you all need to see."

Reavian's hand grazes mine, I can feel his tension humming just beneath the surface of his skin.

"I wouldn't ask... but I feel that it's important. You all need to see what I lived. So, we can stop it from happening again." I glance at Reavian, then at Vaelisar. "But I will not do so without your permission, because it reveals a secret that is not mine to tell."

Vaelisar holds Reavian's gaze. "It's your decision."

Reavian nods once, considering.

"Show us. We need to see it. All of it," he says.

Everyone sits in the smooth translucent glass chairs around the pool.

Only I remain standing.

I look to Valeisar. "I just... touch it?" I ask him.

"Yes," he replies. "Tell it what you want to show us and touch the waters. It will do the rest."

I step forward to the edge of the reflection pool. The stars above flicker on its surface.

"Show me what I lived once before, show me the battle at Lunira's shrine."

Then I reach down and touch the water.

Light blooms outward and the air in the room thickens.

The memory begins.

The party. The dancing.

Kaiel storming off. Reavian following.

The explosion.

Screams. Blood.

Each member of my queen's guard falling.

Kaiel charging in recklessly. Brynn chasing after him. Their hands reaching for each other as they take their final breaths. Reavian fighting alongside Vaelisar with his shadows. Me fighting with Lucien, running at him filled with rage. My last stand, being disarmed. Waiting for him to take the final blow. Reavian stopping him, trying to reason with him. The sword piercing his heart, and Lucien kicking him off it. Vaelisar's confession while he runs towards Reavian's body. My scream, raw and feral, tearing through the sky and the destruction I cause after.

In the silence that follows, I hear Brynn's soft gasp. Kaiel reaches for her hand without hesitation. She turns toward him, her voice barely audible.

"I've waited too long, "she whispers. "I should have told you—"

Kaiel interrupts her. "I love you too."

Brynn blinks, her breath catching, and then she squeezes his hand like she'll never let go.

"By the Gods," Mavren whispers.

Reavian steps forward and wraps his arms around me from behind, pulling me close to him. He presses his lips to my temple. "That won't happen again," he murmurs, his voice low.

I step away from the water, my hand in his. Across the reflection pool, I catch Kaiel and Reavian sharing a look. A silent *I'm here if you need to talk.*

No one speaks of the secret that was revealed.

"We're not there," Iska says suddenly, her voice breaking the quiet. She looks at me. "Where were Tharen and I?"

I blink, caught off guard. She's right. I never found her or Tharen.

"I don't know, I couldn't find you," I say.

A shadow passes over her face. "Were we taken? Or killed?"

Tharen's hand finds hers before the thought can root too deeply. "It's alright," he says gently. "We will all be together this time. I won't let anything happen to you."

Iska stares at him, then threads her fingers through his. She says nothing, but the look she gives him is answer enough.

"We can stop it," I say quietly.

I look to each of them in turn, before I settle my gaze on Reavian. "I know what I must do. I have to get to Lucien."

Reavian's body tenses beside me.

"I have to do it alone. It's what the Gods are telling me I'm meant for. I need to be the one to end him."

He steps toward me now, his voice rough. "You don't have to face him alone."

"I do," I tell him, my voice is steady. "I *feel* it. You can't be there. You can't put yourself at risk. You're meant to fight alongside the others."

I meet his eyes with mine. "I'll come back to you. I promise."

He doesn't argue, instead he just presses his forehead to mine.

Vaelisar steps into the circle.

"Let's go over the plans, we have a few nights to prepare. Every moment counts," he says.

We work together the rest of the night; solid plans are formed and are ready to be set in motion.

The battle is coming. But this time we'll be ready.

One by one I watch as they file out. Kaiel and Brynn hand in hand, Iska still holding tightly to Tharen, my queen's guard already discussing formations in low, clipped tones. A glance. A nod. Promises in every step.

Soon, it's just Reavian, Noctis, and I alone in the room with Vaelisar. Reavian leads me toward the door, but he pauses to cast one last look toward the far end of the chamber, toward where Vaelisar stands.

"I think..." Reavian says, his voice rougher than before. "I'd like to get to know you."

Vaelisar doesn't move for a moment. Then he lifts his gaze to meet Reavian's. His eyes glisten with unshed tears. "I would like that very much."

Reavian nods once. Solidifying the beginning of something.

We walk out together. The past behind us, and the future ours to choose.

Chapter Forty Nine-Reavian

Three days have passed since the memory was shared.

Three days since I watched her fall to her knees and scream at the loss of me.

Three days since I heard Vaelisar scream for me, like if he could reach me, he could change the outcome.

Everything *has* changed. Everything *will* change.

We made camp last night in the northwestern hills. The morning air is cool and sharp. Wagons are being prepared for the final leg of our journey, only a half a day remains before we reach the Shrine of Lunira. Before we begin the ceremony.

If that's what we're still pretending it is.

I stand near the lead wagon, tightening a strap across the outer storage, my hands moving with a practiced ease. Each wagon is carrying weapons and healing supplies. My thoughts are far from here though. Everything feels like it's leaning forward, like even the land is bracing itself.

And then I hear them. Quiet footsteps in the dew-damp grass.

I glance up and for a moment forget how to breathe.

Auren approaches with Brynn and Iska at her side, all three are dressed for the occasion. But it's Auren I can't look away from. Her gown is a deep blue, laced with light and shadow that seem to be alive and swirling through the fabric, a train trails behind her like mist. Her golden hair is loose, the starlight catching it and making the strands glow. The hidden strength beneath the beauty makes something primal tighten in my chest.

"You look…" I try and fail to find anything to say that is worthy. "Gods, you look beautiful."

She smiles at me softly. "You're biased."

"Completely," I murmur, stepping closer. My hand brushes her waist, my fingertips grazing the faint outline of armor beneath. I drop my voice to a whisper. "And knowing that you're wrapped in tight leather armor under there… daggers sheathed at your thighs. That's… Gods, that's unfair."

Auren laughs, warm and real, then rises onto her toes and kisses me. It's quick, soft, and *intoxicating*. She pulls away before I can deepen it and moves to climb into the wagon. I follow her in sitting beside her.

Kaiel and Brynn are already inside, seated close together. Brynn is leaning against him, their hands entwined. Iska and Tharen follow, slipping into their usual quiet proximity. Noctis hops up and takes his place in front of Auren by her feet.

The queen's guard rides in the second wagon behind us, along with Vaelisar and his personal guard.

The wheels begin to turn.

Kaiel tugs at the collar of his formal coat, scowling. "Whoever designed this thing clearly had a vendetta against comfort and breathing."

Brynn lifts a brow. "Gods, you're such a warrior."

"Exactly," Kaiel mutters. "Which is why I should be wearing armor and my blade, not whatever the hells this thing is."

Auren laughs and the sound makes something in me ache. I watch as she's talking to Brynn and Iska, teasing them about something that I can't hear because all I can focus on is her.

I just sit here watching her, wanting to memorize this moment.

The way she smiles. The way she tilts her head when she's amused. This beautiful, brave woman *chose me.* I send up a silent thanks to the Gods above for bringing her into my life. For letting us find each other.

I think of everything that we have faced together. Everything we've seen. Everyone we've lost.

How close I came to losing her entirely.

Suddenly fear cuts through me, sharp and cold.

Because I know what's coming.

And I know she has to face it without me.

But every instinct in me—every piece of my soul—is screaming not to let her face it alone.

Several hours pass, and our wagon slows as we reach the outer edge of the Hollow. The Shrine of Lunira, newly restored, is before us. The land here feels like ancient hallowed ground. Lanterns hang amongst the trees, casting a soft glow. The moon casts an ethereal light upon the shrine.

Music drifts through the air, gentle, melodic, and carefully paced. Talented members of the Nightguard now act as the musicians, their hands light on the strings, and holding a steady beat on the drums. I know they are watching for movement along the ridge to the Dreamkeeper sanctuary in the distance, listening for signals.

And for just this moment, I don't care.

Because I only want *one* thing.

Before anyone can distract her, I reach for Auren's hand. "Dance with me."

Her brow lifts, surprised. "Now?"

"I don't want to waste a single second."

She studies my face, searching, maybe sensing what's behind my words. Then she gives me a quiet nod. "Okay."

I lead her into the clearing. The music swells around us, slow and sweet. Auren steps into my arms with no hesitation.

One of her hands finds my shoulder, and she rests the other on my chest, over my heart. Mine rest on her waist. Holding her feels like coming home and saying goodbye all at once.

"I need you to keep your promise," I say quietly.

She lifts her gaze to mine, holding it steady. "I will."

"I mean it," I whisper. "Everything in me... every instinct I have tells me to protect you. To fight beside you. And instead, I have to stand back. I have to *let you go*." My voice shakes. "So, I need to know that you'll come back."

She reaches up, her fingertips brushing the side of my face. "I know. I feel the same way. Every time I look at you, I think about what would happen if I lost you. But I'm not planning on letting that happen. We have been given a second chance for a reason. The Gods are behind us. I can feel it. *Trust me*."

I tighten my grip on her waist slightly. "I love you."

"I love you too," she replies, her voice as soft as a breath.

We dance in silence for a few more heartbeats, wrapped in the soft ache of what is to come.

Others begin to join us in the clearing. Kaiel pulls Brynn into a spin, their laughter cutting through the tension that hangs above us all. Seress dramatically bows to Sirah, who accepts with only a faint roll of her eyes. Eiryn lingers at the edge, still and watchful. Noctis sits by his side, his eyes never leaving Auren. Alira and Mavren lean against a nearby willow, arguing about something under their breath. Iska and Tharen hold each other with quiet intention, dancing like the rest of the world doesn't exist.

For the briefest moment, everything feels light. The future feels possible.

The others begin to drift toward the tables, as Vaelisar prepares to dedicate the shrine.

But I stay with Auren just a little longer, our fingers now interlaced, her head resting lightly on my chest. Leaning into one another, as if our closeness can hold everything together.

I press a kiss to the top of her head, breathing her in.

I don't know what will happen next.

I just know that right now, she's here.

And I'm not letting go.

Not yet.

Chapter Fifty-Auren

The shrine is quiet beneath the moonlight. Not silent, but still in that sacred way, the kind of stillness that settles over a place that is meant to hold prayers and pain. Silver light spills across its stone, softening the carved edges of the script that winds its base. A pool of dark water that shimmers in the starlight rests before it.

We approach together, Reavian and I, side by side. The others walk behind us. No one speaks. The air carries a heaviness, because we all know what's to come.

The shrine stands before me, familiar and impossibly distant all at once. I reach out, fingers brushing the warm stone, and the moment I make contact.

You've done well, Little Light.

You're ready.

It's Lunira. Her voice is clear, and strong. It slides through my entire being.

My knees buckle.

Reavian catches me immediately, an arm snapping around my

waist.

"Auren," he says, and then for a moment he stills.

I steady myself blinking fast. "It's okay."

He doesn't let go. His body tense beside me. He's felt something too, I think. I can see it in the way he's staring at the shrine.

Find your light.

Do not seek to destroy as you did before.

Seek to heal instead.

All will be righted.

You'll know the right time.

A shiver slides through me.

I exhale slowly and turn toward Reavian. "Lunira spoke to me."

His jaw clenches with worry, but he nods.

"Our plan will work. I can do this," I tell him.

I don't know how I say it with so much certainty. Maybe it's because for the first time, I truly believe it.

We walk away from the shrine together. And wait for our friends to join us.

I look up at the stars in the sky and know it's about to begin. I grab Reavian's hand, at least this time I won't see them coming alone. We will all be together. Kaiel and Brynn walk close, her hand tucked into his. Tharen and Iska follow just behind. My guard flanks us, Seress whistling low, Mavren muttering to Eiryn about perimeter lines, Sirah and Alira silently scanning the trees. Noctis walks slowly on my left, scanning for any sign of an impending attack.

We reach the forest's edge, just beyond the clearing. And I look up into the sky, at the luminous pink full moon, then at all of my friends, ingraining this moment in my memory. The calm before the storm. All of us together, and Gods willing, we will all stay together after this.

The wind picks up, in a silent warning that it's about to start. I look toward the ridge in the distance.

And then the world erupts.

A thunderous explosion sounds, sending a blast of heat rushing across the clearing, flames erupt in the distance, orange and jagged, licking upward toward the night sky.

And from the ridgeline, they appear.

Hundreds of bone armored knights surge over the rise like a wave of rot, their weapons gleaming, mouths hidden behind jagged helmets that look as if they've been carved from death.

They charge.

Reavian pulls me back with a sharp curse. "Everyone, run..now!"

We sprint.

The lanterns in the willows swing wildly from their hooks. The Nightguard is already in motion, ripping away formal clothing to reveal their hidden armor. Weapons slide free from the wagons. Shields are lifted. My guard falls into formation on instinct. I see Kaiel hand Brynn a spear, and it begins crackling with electricity as he grabs a blade for himself. I quickly remove my gown revealing my armor beneath and sheath Virethyn at my back.

The bone armored knights are in the center of the clearing now.

Drums start to beat in a primal rhythm, and a magical flare shoots into the sky.

From the eastern and western edges of the forest, they emerge.

Vaedric's wardens, cloaked in fire-touched armor. They storm the battlefield with a thunder of hooves. At their head, Vaedric himself rides astride a black steed, fire glinting from his armor and wreathing his sword. The Nightguard charges into battle with them, their cries joining the drumbeats.

Then, I see him.

Lucien.

He descends the ridge flanked by the twisted forms of the conscripted. Their hollow black eyes glint in the moonlight, their mouths agape, screaming.

Reavian turns to me. "Auren..."

"I know," I grab the collar of his armor, drag him down to me and kiss him desperately.

"I love you," I tell him.

His forehead presses to mine. "I love you so much that my very breaths are tied to yours. I lived in nothing but darkness before you. I felt empty— half alive. You made me want more than survival. You are my guiding light. So remember our promise to each other, you live, Auren. Come back to me, because if you don't… everything else might as well burn."

I nod, my throat tight.

"I will come back to you, I promise."

He kisses me like he's memorizing the very shape of my soul. Then he pulls back, just enough to whisper against my lips, "A long and happy life."

With that he turns and runs into battle, blade drawn and shadows dancing at his fingertips.

Brynn pulls me into a fast, fierce hug. "You can do this Auren, I know you can. I love you, now go kick his ass."

"I love you too," I whisper back to my friend.

Kaiel grabs her hand and pulls her away. They sprint toward the fight.

I kneel beside Noctis, his eyes shimmering like the stars.

"I need you to help them boy, stay with them. I have to do this alone," I say, giving him a hug and roughing up his fur a bit.

He whimpers, licks my face and then turns and bounds after the others.

I draw Virethyn, and it ignites with flame in my hand.

I run.

Past the shrine and onto the battlefield. Screams, metal, and magic clash all around me. Sparks fly, and shadows whip through the trees as Reavian fights beside Kaiel, his blade a blur, his shadows snapping forward and attacking like wolves. Lightning strikes erupt all over the battlefield, taking out multiple targets. Brynn.

I dodge left, flames sparking along my blade, and drive it through the throat of a bone armored knight. He collapses and becomes engulfed in flame.

Eiryn dives into a trio of bone knights, both of his blades flashing in the starlight.

Alira holds the front line with Mavren, shielding the others with coordinated strikes.

One of the conscripted charges me, it's eyes wide with madness. I whisper an apology and hurl fire from my palm. It catches in his chest like sunlight, burning clean through its corruption. I keep running toward my target. I'm nearly there.

Sirah appears and disappears like a ghost, throwing knives into exposed necks.

Seress yells something dramatic and is promptly tackled by a knight twice his size—my breath catches—but he rolls and stabs the knight through the throat.

Valeisar and Vaedric are fighting side by side, rage and burning magic cut through wave after wave of the enemy. I pass Vaedric, and he swings his sword low, decapitating a knight aiming for me.

"Auren, good to see you," he says with a smile. "Thank you for inviting me to the party."

He rides further into the battle.

I run to where I'm meant to be. The scene of our last battle.

And then, there he is.

Lucien is standing in the center of the battlefield. Hundreds of conscripted stand behind him, hunched and waiting.

He smirks as I approach.

"Well," he says. "I'll admit, this little rebellion is surprising. But still... pathetic."

We collide.

Steel against steel, his strength is monstrous. Virethyn sings with each slice, the gold in its blade becoming a bright white light. Each strike of Lucien's jars through my arms. Sparks fly. I duck, twist, and slash—he blocks everything. A group of conscripted charges from the side, I spin and cut through them, my fire blazing from my blade. Lucien strikes again. His unnatural dark flame colliding with mine.

"You should've given me what I wanted," he hisses. "Your power. You could have saved them all. Now you've doomed them."

I roar back. "You're not worthy of it. You'll never be worthy!"

My words hit their mark, and his face contorts with fury.

He knocks my sword away.

I duck low and grab my daggers swiftly.

In a flash, I slice across his thigh and stand and cut through his cheek. He snarls, blood trailing down his face. In a swift movement, he slashes through my arm. His flame cuts right through the enchantments in my armor. I can feel muscle separating from bone. Pain blooms and my grip falters, no longer able to hold onto the dagger—it drops to the ground.

"You're weak," he sneers. "Just like your father was."

I lunge.

He spins and deflects it, knocking my last blade aside. Then he kicks me hard. I hit the ground breathless, blood pouring from my wounds. No. No. No. This isn't supposed to be happening.

I glance behind me. Everyone is still fighting.

Still alive.

I try to reach for the dagger nearest to me, and he backhands me so hard that my lip splits.

The world spins.

He raises his sword.

I'm not going to be able to keep my promise.

I hear Reavian screaming my name behind me. I turn to look at him one last time. A shimmering wall separates us. Like the one at Somnarel Hollow leaving me alone with the banshee. Like the one that caused my parents car to crash.

Reavian beats against it. But he can't reach me.

I look back at Lucien.

"Was it worth it? Trying to stop the inevitable?" he snarls. "You're pathetic."

"You're the one hiding behind a shield," I spit.

He laughs. "Hiding? Auren... my sweet girl. It's not *my* shield. It's *yours*."

I freeze.

"Yes, yes. It really is *all* your fault," he says coldly. "Everything.

It always was."

My breath shudders. The world tips. That same icy pressure rises in my chest.

Panic.

"No," I whisper.

Lucien steps forward, his blade raised.

My shield.

But that would mean...

I caused the accident that night on the mountain road.

I am the reason my father was too injured to run, I caused my mother's death.

It must've reacted to the incoming danger somehow.

I shielded the others from the banshee, protecting them from being attacked.

Just like I'm protecting Reavian now.

I must subconsciously activate it, when I'm trying to keep them safe, keep *him* safe.

"Auren!" Reavian calls out, his voice desperate.

Then the voices come.

Be the Light in the Darkness.

Find your light.

Look within.

They aren't telling me to use my flame, but my light?

I close my eyes, and look within myself, trying to find the light they speak of. Looking past my flame, going deeper, and deeper.

Then finally I see it.

Where the Light Begins.

I reach for it.

Not to destroy, Lunira's voice from earlier echoes in my memory.

Not to destroy, but to heal.

I open my eyes.

Pure blinding light explodes from me like a tidal wave. This time not laced with flame.

The sky doesn't crack open like it did before.

Lucien is thrown back by the blast, his blade knocked from his grip.

The conscripted behind him freeze.

And then, they begin to *change*.

Their twisted limbs snap back into place. Their skin heals, and their howls shift into sobs. One by one they fall to their knees, their faces crumpling in release.

The spell is broken.

They are fae again.

Alive.

And all of them turn to Lucien.

He scrambles backward. Desperately shooting flames toward me. I snuff each wave of them out with my light.

"No... no wait!" he cries out.

I walk slowly toward him, the healed conscripted moving to surround him from behind.

"Who's pathetic now?" I ask him.

He starts to beg.

The healed fae, naked and visibly shaken close in, their eyes fixed on Lucien. Their intent is clear.

I stalk toward him my light at my fingertips.

"Please, this has all been a mistake, a misunderstanding. I'm sure we can work something out," he says.

I raise my chin.

"What you did to them," I say glancing toward the fae, "That was no mistake, but a choice. One made by someone with no soul, no light."

The healed fae stop at his back and watch me.

"Now you suffer the consequences of your actions, and I think this will be very... healing for them," I tell him.

I give the healed fae a nod, and step aside.

"No!" he screams.

They fall upon him like a storm.

His screams echo across the battlefield as they tear him apart with their bare hands. Ripping him limb from limb.

And then—silence.

My shield drops.

Reavian crashes into me within seconds, closing his arms around me. His breaths are ragged. I hold him just as tightly. He presses his forehead down to mine, tears in his eyes.

"I told you I'd come back," I tell him.

We turn back toward the battlefield.

A bone armored knight jolts upright, his body going unnaturally stiff. His head twists too far, and his body convulses.

A scream rips through the battlefield.

Not the knight's voice, but hers.

"You will all pay!" Liraeth screams.

She's twisting her way through what remains of the battlefield, watching through the eyes of her knight.

I freeze for a moment.

"Oh, fuck you..." I hear Seress groan from my right to Liraeth.

She snaps her gaze to him.

You know what? He's right.

"Yeah, fuck you!" I shout, bringing her attention back to me.

Reavian grabs my hand, and we unleash everything.

Our magic merges in a violently beautiful dance, pouring from us in a roaring tide. A storm of burning darkness tears through the field. I will my light to merge with my flame and only burn what is corrupted, to leave the innocent untouched. Every knight of Lucien's that remained, including the one controlled by Liraeth, is quickly turned to ash. Reavian's shadows carrying my fire down their throats and burning them from the inside out.

The battlefield goes still.

The stars above us shine brightly.

People begin to cry and cheer.

I search the field for my friends, I need to get eyes on them. I spot

Kaiel and Brynn first. Then I spot Seress dragging Mavren to his feet. Sirah slaps Eiryn's back near a pile of dead knights. Alira near a tree laughing shakily. I even see Vaedric and Vaelisar.

Noctis finds me, and nearly tackles me jumping up and licking my face.

Everyone comes over to where Reavian and I are standing.

But two faces are missing.

"Where are Iska and Tharen?" I ask.

We all scan the crowd trying to find them. They are nowhere to be seen. My stomach tightens. I saw them fighting bravely, protecting Valeisar.

"Maybe they're injured or…" Kaiel doesn't finish the thought, but his eyes drift to the bodies lying scattered across the field. Immediately Seress, Sirah, and Mavren start to search among the fallen for them.

After what seems like an eternity, Mavren returns with Tharen's sword, and a bloodied blue cloak.

Iska's.

Brynn covers her mouth, tears welling in her eyes. I feel a sob catch in my throat.

"No bodies have been found, Your Highness," Mavren tells me.

Perhaps they were taken, or they had to flee. Whatever it is, Iska and Tharen are gone.

I close my eyes and press my forehead into Reavian's chest as a wave of sorrow sweeps through me. I feel him kiss the top of my hair gently, his own silent worry shared in the gesture.

Vaelisar and Vaedric approach.

"You need to get a healer for that arm," Vaedric says, his voice concerned.

"You fought well today, all of you," Vaelisar says. His gaze lands on all of us, but lingers for a moment on Reavian, pride in his gaze.

"Tharen and Iska are missing," I say.

"We can consult the reflection pool, maybe they have something we can use to find them," Vaelisar tells me reassuringly. "But Vaedric is right, you go get that arm looked at. I'll look into their whereabouts."

The remnants of our combined forces gather the wounded and then begin to lay the dead to rest.

"We'll find them, Auren," Reavian says to me softly.

I nod and slip my hand from his. I look at the devastation around me, stepping through the smoke and ash. But it's not the battlefield I focus on.

It's *them*.

The healed conscripted stand apart, naked and gaunt. Their eyes still hollow from what they've endured. Some tremble, some weep. Other's simply stare, unsure if their freedom is real, or an illusion.

They are not soldiers.

They are not monsters.

They are *survivors*.

My people.

I turn to Vaedric and Vaelisar, my voice steady despite the weight in my chest.

"They need a safe haven. Food. Shelter. A place to remember they are still people, not weapons to be used. Will you help me give them that?" I ask them.

Vaelisar gives me a silent nod, and I note the hint of pride that flickers across his features.

Vaedric bows his head in solemn agreement.

I look back toward the field and feel everyone watching me. Not with doubt, but with hope and expectation.

Reavian moves back to my side and takes my hand in his.

I lift my chin, my light still humming faintly beneath my skin. I may not wear a crown, but I *will* lead them.

The stars above us shimmer, but in the far horizon, I feel her.

Liraeth.

Still watching.

Still waiting.

Let her.

Nyvenya is my home now, and I **will** fight for it.

Acknowledgements

To my family and friends—thank you for believing in me, even when I didn't believe in myself. Your support and encouragement meant more to me than I can even put into words. You definitely kept me going when I wanted to give up, and for that I'll always be grateful.

To *Rebecca Yarros*, and *Sarah J. Maas*—thank you for reigniting my love of reading and inspiring me to start writing again. Your stories reminded me why I fell in love with reading and writing in the first place. I hope it's clear how much your work means to me... and yes, if you noticed some subtle tributes in these pages, you're absolutely right. I couldn't help myself.

To the readers—whether you devoured this book or DNF'd it after a few chapters, thank you. I appreciate you giving my story a chance. And if you found any typos... no you didn't. I swear I stared at these pages until my eyes bled. Let's just agree to keep the magic alive and pretend everything was perfect. Yeah?

And to anyone else who's struggled with anxiety like me—this book is proof that we can be afraid and still do the brave thing.

About the author

H.C. Vale has always carried stories in her head—entire worlds, characters, and plot twists just waiting for a place to land. After years of imagining them, she finally picked up the pen and brought them to life. Now, she writes stories filled with love, heartache, healing, and heroines who refuse to go quietly.

She lives with her husband, two Siberian huskies, and five cats (yes five—certified crazy cat lady status unlocked). When she's not writing, she's usually lacking sleep and over-caffeinating to compensate, hanging out with friends and board gaming, playing video games, or dancing poorly in the crowd at a concert. Music fuels her creativity. Lately it's the haunting sounds of *Sleep Token*, which is almost *always* playing while she writes.

Where the Light Begins is her debut novel, and the first book in the Crown of Nyvenya Series.

Connect with her at **hcvalebooks.com**